About the Author

Born in Bexley, Kent in 1961, Richard found the newly emerging punk rock scene to be the perfect outlet for teenage angst, but after shelving his personal dreams of attaining rock and roll stardom, he put his life on hold to provide for, and raise his son and daughter. Turning his creative focus to photography and writing, Richard found inspiration in the Eastern European countries that he visited frequently on his travels. Following a 32-year absence from live musical performances, Richard made a comeback as a guitarist with punk band The East End Badoes, alongside his son, James, and in April 2017 married his partner, Liane, at Upnor Castle.

Dedication

This book is dedicated to James and Samantha, for without their unerring support who knows where I might be. It is also written in memory of the late, great Charles 'Chuck' Kemsley; a man who inspired me more than he could ever know.

Richard Cruttwell

Room 13

Between Hell & Redemption

AUSTIN MACAULEY PUBLISHERS™

LONDON • CAMBRIDGE • NEW YORK • SHARJAH

A CIP catalogue record for this title is available from the British Library.

ISBN 978-1-78693048-4 (Paperback)
ISBN 978-1-78693049-1 (Hardback)
ISBN 978-1-78693050-7 (eBook)

www.austinmacauley.com

First Published (2017)
Austin Macauley Publishers Ltd.™
25 Canada Square
Canary Wharf
London
E14 5LQ

Acknowledgments

I would like to thank all those who have served to either encourage, support or inspire me to write this book, and any likeness to any persons, either living or dead, or events depicted, are purely coincidental.

Preface

How well do you know your friends, your family or even those closest to you? After all, we are all guilty of only divulging that which we want to divulge. Consider for a moment how far you might go to ensure that some irresponsible act remains forever concealed or, to what lengths you might go to right a personal injustice.

Scratch the surface of any family and I am sure that you will find hidden secrets, usually little more than insignificant nuances or minor indiscretions that would only serve to cause slight embarrassment if ever revealed. Perhaps, on the other hand, consider for a moment the inconsequential man or woman who you walked past in the street, or stood behind at the supermarket checkout. For he or she might harbour a secret so dark that it would be totally abhorrent to even the most liberal minded of human beings. The smiling face of every stranger will undoubtedly hide a tale of grief, loss, pain or suffering but rest assured, it will also hide a secret.

The most powerful weapon in any endeavour to conceal a secret, no matter how large or small, is a lie. Lying is an integral part of human nature. It is instinctive, and rather than being a tool created for deliberately hurting others, it is born out of an innate desire for self preservation.

In this world there is only one certain truth and that truth is that nobody ever really knows anyone.

oooOOOooo

Prologue

The past, what does that word mean to you? A collection of memories, perhaps, maybe for some, the word evokes wistful musings of long hot summer days spent as a child. For others, the word may induce thoughts of some long lost first love, an innocent first kiss or maybe a traditional family gathering at Christmas time with presents around the tree.

We all have a past, and I see it as something akin to a shadow. It is a dark and almost tangible manifestation of all that we have ever done, and the past will follow us around wherever we go. You can turn out the light or you can close your eyes but, no matter what you do, it will always be there. Some people may try and run from their past, while others may choose to hide from it or even deny its existence. The shadow of the past will always know the truth and it will remain there as a constant reminder.

Someday you might wish to bury some sin or indiscretion, but make sure that you bury it deep, fucking deep. For as soon as you turn your back to walk away, your past will already be digging its way out and it will find you, I guarantee it. Surely no depth will ever be deep enough. For some, their past will eat away inside them like a cancer and it will infect every minute of their waking hours, creating fear, paranoia and self-loathing.

Call it Karma, destiny or whatever bullshit label you might want to attach to it, but never forget that everything we will ever do will have a consequence. Consequence has its price, and sometimes that price can be too high.

Please forgive me, for I was not always such a cynic and had laughed and loved in much the same way as everyone else. I lived life by my own set of rules and, despite never being much of a Frank Sinatra fan, when Sid Vicious sang 'My Way', those words rang true. The heart, in my opinion, holds all that is good in a man; love, empathy, trust and compassion. But when a man's heart is torn from his chest by the person he trusts the most and then thrown to the floor before him, bleeding, still beating and rendered worthless, then all that remains is a black hole. That black hole contains suspicion, cynicism, fear, hatred and revenge, and when he is closed off from all that he holds dear, then I guarantee that the very worst elements of the human condition will grow to fill that void.

Fear and respect your past, my friend, for it is the guardian of your darkest secrets. Stand firm and confront the enigma within the shadows, as forgiveness is as powerful and poignant as anything you could ever encounter. Never run from, deny or try to bury your past, for it will follow you, it will consume you and it will destroy you. Hell, it might even kill you.

Chapter 1

The Return

Nervously, I glanced at my wrist watch, took a deep breath and glanced up to double check the hotel name displayed above the plush glass and stainless steel doors; 'Kazimierz Hotel'. It was nearly a quarter to three in the afternoon, and October would soon be giving way to November. The autumnal mist was already beginning to slowly envelop the air as cars and trams rumbled along Starowislna, the main road that runs between the outskirts of the medieval old town and the River Vistula. Distanced from reality, I heard nothing of the traffic behind me and neither did I notice the chill in the air, warning that another harsh Polish winter was just around the corner. My head was filled with the memories of people I had once known and conversations that we had shared. Those memories conspired to torment and haunt me like ghosts from a former life, my life. Standing in front of the Kazimierz Hotel, the scene may only have been a vaguely familiar one, but I could clearly remember standing on that very same spot, some twenty-five years or so earlier.

I had caught the train from Poznan to Krakow Glowny Station and then walked the two kilometres to the hotel.

Collecting my thoughts, I pushed open the hotel door, walked inside and was immediately struck by how changed the reception area now looked with its wooden panelling, polished marble floor and comfortable leather armchairs. My memory had preserved everything just like a photograph, and I had imagined the hotel still looking as if it were some kind of post war Communist museum. I removed my dark glasses and approached the reception desk. "Good afternoon," I said politely, "I have a reservation in the name of Caldwell, Mr Stephen Caldwell."

The smartly dressed, strikingly attractive blonde receptionist looked up and offered me a forced smile which was cooler than the air outside. After checking through her bookings she announced, "yes, Caldwell, room 13". After completing the formalities, she handed me a room key and gave me directions to the second floor.

"Yes, thank you," I cut in, "I remember it well." I doubted if the young blonde receptionist had even been born when I had previously been a guest there, so there was little chance that she would have remembered my name. I was also fairly sure that had she remembered, I would not even have been allowed through the front door.

There may have been no lift when I was there before, but the stairway appeared more or less as I had remembered it. As I emerged onto the second floor landing, the lights came on automatically and my footsteps were silenced by the thickness of the red carpet. I paused outside my room, taking a moment to trace the tips of my fingers over the numbers on the door, Room 13. I should really have known better but had nevertheless felt compelled to request that specific room because that was where, more than twenty-five years earlier, my old life had ended and a new life had begun.

I pondered my next move like I had a choice, then turned the key and pushed the door open with my foot. Finally, I entered the room to discover that it was no longer dark and oppressive but bright, airy and tastefully decorated. Just like the reception area downstairs, it was not at all as I had pictured it for so many years. Gone was the heavy, brown patterned wallpaper, replaced by light yellow pastel colours. Where a large double bed had once stood, there were now two single beds, covered with thick white duvets. My mind had preserved such vivid recollections of this room, because this was where my wife and I had spent our final night together.

I hurried across the room to the single bed by the window, feeling a chill run down my spine. After placing my rucksack by the side of the bed, I pulled the curtains aside, peered out of the window and surveyed the scene beyond, looking, but not actually seeing. Thankfully, I had noticed that the bathroom door was closed. I say 'thankfully' because I was not ready for that, not yet anyway. I turned away from the window and glanced forebodingly towards the bathroom door. Just like a road kill, I did not want to see it, yet there was something which compelled me to look.

Relentlessly, thoughts and recollections spanning two very contrasting lives coursed through my mind. My life had once been idyllic and filled with fun and laughter. Back then, I lived every day with barely a care in the world. I was twenty-four years old and had my house in Kent. OK, so I had a mortgage too, but that did not matter to me as I also had Debbie, my loving wife, confidante and soulmate. What's more, I also played guitar in a punk rock band, L.I.A.R. Those four letters were an abbreviation of 'Lessons in Administering Revenge', a name which the band considered to be too long winded and so we decided to opt for the shortened, punchier alternative instead. In a time before the Iron Curtain had lifted, it had been punk rock that had brought me here to Poland and back then, in my mind's eye, I was a rock star.

Suddenly I became engulfed by a wave of panic and needed to get out of the room, through the door, down the stairs and rushing past the receptionist without even giving her a glance, not stopping until I was back outside on the pavement. A tram rumbled past as the damp, chilled air brought me back to my senses. Needing a drink to calm my nerves, I darted across the road, dodging the oncoming traffic and then headed along Miodowa Street in search of a quiet and hospitable bar, a place where I might lose myself for a couple of hours and drink away my demons.

After walking for a few minutes, I became aware of the faint strains of a song which sounded soothingly familiar to me, and so I tentatively peered inside the bar from where the music seemed to be coming. Entering the dimly lit bar, the raucous sound of 'Bad Man' by The Cockney Rejects, an old favourite of mine became clearly and reassuringly audible. I gazed through the gloom at a multitude of unusual objects hung from the walls and suspended from the ceiling; a pram, a bicycle, guitars in varying states of dilapidation, old television sets, gramophones. The place reminded me of 'Steptoe and Son', the 1960's television sitcom about rag and bone men, which I had loved watching with my father when I was a child. Albert and Harold Steptoe had lived surrounded by junk, but to them their possessions were precious and to them it was home. As I stood in that bar, with the music soothing away my tension, there was nowhere else that I would rather have been.

I approached the bar while my eyes scanned the multitude of beer taps and bottles of spirits with unpronounceable names. The barman was a skinhead, at least he certainly looked like a skinhead, with his close cropped hair, sideburns, Fred Perry shirt and braces. Taking a mental note of the baseball bat propped up behind the bar, I asked, "expecting trouble?" The barman looked up from his mobile phone screen with a half smile that seemed to indicate that he had heard that line a million times before.

"What'll you have?" he responded.

Still mesmerised by the multitude of options on offer I replied, "just a beer, please."

"Vodka?" the barman inquired bluntly, as he passed me a cold beer.

"Hell, why not," I answered. He opened the fridge and selected a bottle from which he began to pour his recommended poison with a reverence and level of care which would not have looked out of place in a scientist's laboratory. I took the glass, necked its contents and placed it back on the bar with a satisfied clunk before collecting my beer and making my way to sit at a table in the corner. I took a long mouthful of the cold, satisfying brew, feeling it cool my insides as it made its way into my stomach. Glancing around, I noted only two other patrons who were seated at a table near the back of the bar. Sitting there in the half light, their features may have been barely visible but I could tell that, every now and then, they glanced back at me quizzically.

Thus, the tone of the evening was set. The music began to blur from one track to another, from punk to ska and back again. I made regular trips to the bar, each time ordering one beer and one vodka, necking the vodka before returning to my seat. Occasionally, I caught sight of my reflection in the smeared mirror behind the bar, appalled to see how life had taken its toll and silently pondering who or what I had become.

I checked the time on my watch, struggling to focus my vision through the alcohol fuelled haze. It was late, certainly past 1am. I raised my glass one last time, draining the remainder like a man stranded in the desert heat, squeezing out the last droplets of water from a hip flask. After returning the empty glass to the bar, I turned and headed for the door, stepping out into the cold night air and began the short walk back to the hotel. It was late and I was tired and desperately needed sleep, knowing that the following day would be a busy one. I had a date with a pharmacist, a forger and a guy named Aleksander or Alex as I had come to know him when we had whiled away our long prison days together.

Chapter 2

The Awakening

I awoke with a jolt and sat bolt upright as my eyes struggled to grow accustomed to the darkness, hindered by my vodka induced confusion. Was I awake or sleeping? Was I drunk or sober? Where, in fact, was I? Relieved to conclude that this was no nightmare after all, I turned to look at the clock on the bedside table; it was 3:47am and I had only been asleep for around two hours. Through the vodka haze, I could see a dim shaft of light. Although I could not remember using the bathroom, at some stage I must have left the light on and the door ajar. I wiped the cold sweat from my brow and turned on the bedside light. After pulling back the duvet, I stood up unsteadily and, with mounting apprehension, I edged my way across the room to the source of the light. I stood motionless, almost panic stricken for what seemed like an eternity, then took a step forward and cautiously pushed the bathroom door open. A wave of relief washed over me as my eyes scanned the polished floor tiles and, feeling reassured that nothing appeared out of place, I turned out the light and returned to bed. Unable to sleep, I lay there in the darkness as vivid memories flooded back, reminding me of the last time that I was rudely awakened in that very same room.

L.I.A.R. had played the final night of our short European tour at a small and sweaty club in Kazimierz, not far from the hotel. Debbie had flown in especially for that last gig and our driver/tour manager Peter, had driven our rented Ford Transit minibus to the airport to collect her. Peter Fankham was an odd fellow to say the least, and someone who we all considered to be a bit of a fool. He had been desperate to become our tour manager and, occasionally, his moderate organisational skills had actually proved quite useful. His desire to be a part of our set up also meant that he was happy to work for nothing, which was a fee that the band could just about afford. Peter Fankham also just happened to be Debbie's brother and thus, rather embarrassingly for me, my brother-in-law. In fairness to him though, it had only been events surrounding the Berlin gig which had seriously threatened to disrupt the tour. Despite our protestations, Peter had insisted on driving us on a senseless detour to see something pointless which none of the band gave a rat's crap about. Already short of time, he had managed to get us hopelessly lost and by the time that we finally arrived at the venue, we had been too late to sound check.

The gig had been a disaster. Gary, or The Spaceman, as we called our dozy roadie, had managed to damage my guitar while unloading the van and the volume level in the stage monitors was way too low. I could barely hear my guitar through the amplifier and Paul's bass was inaudible over the thudding of John's drums and crashing cymbals. Dave, our singer, had drunk far too much in the minibus earlier after becoming infuriated at Peter for getting us lost in the Berlin backstreets. Peter always managed to irritate the hell out of Dave without even trying so, after the gig, it had been no surprise that Dave tore into him, calling him a waste of space amidst wave upon wave of expletives. Even bassist Paul, a usually laid-back guy from Maine in the US, had called Peter a stupid bastard for getting us to the venue barely twenty minutes before we were due to go on stage. Following those tirades however, Peter had got his act together and kept things pretty tight. He had probably been petrified that if he fouled up again, he might be subjected to a swift kicking and left by the side of the road somewhere near Wroclaw.

Debbie had arrived just in time to watch us sound check ahead of our final gig in Krakow, and I waved to her as she walked through the double doors during our second run through of 'Time to Waste'. Once we were all happy with the sound, I switched off my amp, stood my guitar up against the stack and jumped off the stage to greet her. As we had another three hours until show time, I suggested that she and I should take the short stroll around the corner to our hotel and make up for lost time. We had barely got through the hotel room door before our clothes were strewn across the floor.

We pulled back the covers and threw ourselves onto the bed, naked, passionate, our bodies entwined like mating cobras. She wrapped her legs around mine and her body writhed against me as the palms of my hands caressed the curve of her breasts. I could feel the warmth of her breath on my ear as I kissed her neck before my lips almost instinctively worked down to her left nipple. I licked around it, hard and pert, sucking it into my mouth and taking time to tease it between my teeth. My tongue traced across her belly and I positioned myself between her legs and her hips gyrated as I gently kissed her inner thigh. She urged me, compelled me to hasten my advance, then gasped and bucked her hips as I orally penetrated her, hungrily savouring her juices as they mixed with my saliva.

I positioned myself on top of her, feeling Debbie's finger nails digging hard into my buttocks as I slid inside her, warm, wet and enticing. Excited by her own scent on me, she licked her own juice from my lips and chin, her tongue darting into my mouth. Passionately and intuitively, her body responded to each thrust, hard and deep. She groaned and panted for breath as my semen flooded inside her. Semen, love juice and sweat combined, flowing together in an unholy union of lust.

"I've missed you," gasped Debbie as I collapsed on the bed next to her.

"God, I've missed you too," I replied with a self-satisfied smile as she rested her head on my chest. Ahead of the rock and roll mayhem that was to follow, I relished the peace and quiet as the two of us lay side by side in sweat and silence.

While Debbie and I were together, I had not been one to take advantage of the sexual diversions offered by groupies while on the road. After more than a week apart however, I was more than ready for the physical distraction that my wife's arrival provided, and so I took full advantage of the opportunity. I had once joked that I had only bedded one groupie, and then married her. Debbie and I had met following a gig in South London and, although our story contained a few twists and turns, we had eventually become inseparable and saw our romance as not unlike Sid and Nancy's. Debbie had introduced me to a world of drugs, parties and group sex and I got sucked into that murky void willingly. Finally, as far as I was concerned, all the pieces of the rock 'n' roll jigsaw seemed to fit together.

oooOOOooo

We made it back to the venue in plenty of time and, although everyone probably knew exactly how Debbie and I had spent our time together, nobody mentioned it.

oooOOOooo

The gig had gone well, very well in fact. The venue had been packed, the band had been tight, the sound had been good and the crowd had been responsive. Overall, that gig ensured that we had made just about enough money to make the tour worthwhile. We made our way off stage and downstairs to a room where beer and vodka had been laid on for our after show party and we were determined to make the most of the hospitality. Gary had even managed to source some half decent hash and a few grams of speed from somewhere, although no one seemed to care where he had sourced the drugs from. Debbie appeared to have made a new friend too, a rather attractive blonde Polish girl and, although we were introduced at some stage during the party, I was far too drunk to catch her name.

It had been a long day and my stamina waned more so than usual. Perhaps I had drunk my fair share but certainly no more than had been the routine at parties. In a bid to reignite my endurance, I asked Gary for a line of speed but very little remained in the wrap when he opened it. Using the tip of my index finger, I dabbed the remaining powder and rubbed it into my gums, but other than leaving a chemical taste in my mouth and impelling me to chew the inside of my cheek, the drug afforded me no buzz whatsoever. By 3am I was certainly feeling the worse for wear, and so Debbie and I said our farewells and headed back to the hotel. Drunkenly, we peeled off our clothes, dumped them in piles on the floor and collapsed into bed, content in the knowledge that, all in all, it had been a good night. I kissed Debbie on the cheek, told her that I loved her, closed my eyes and went straight to sleep.

oooOOOooo

Suddenly, I was rudely awoken by the sound of shouting in the corridor outside and fists pounding on the hotel room door. Thinking that we must have overslept, I looked at my watch; it was just after 8am. Thinking that Debbie must have been up already, I hastily pulled on my clothes as the shouting and hammering on the door continued. I called back, "alright, alright, hold on, I'm coming," hopping on one leg while pulling on my jeans. The relentless pounding on the door was only matched by the pounding inside my skull. "Just fuck off," I shouted angrily, throwing the door open. Before my eyes were able to focus on whoever had been responsible for the commotion, a hand thrust into my chest with such force that I staggered backwards and fell heavily to the floor.

The room was suddenly filled with military style uniformed policemen and men in heavy black coats, and I had no idea what was happening around me. The drink and drugs cocktail consumed only hours before fuelled a fog which did nothing to offer clarity to the situation. One policeman kicked open the bathroom door just as two of the black coats lifted me harshly from the floor, threw me roughly onto the chair, forcing my hands behind my back before handcuffing me. The bathroom appeared to have become the centre of my visitors' interest, but I could not understand one word that was being spoken. One of the black coats who had just assaulted me was beckoned to look inside the bathroom, and seconds later he flew at me in a rage, a look of horror and disgust etched onto his face. I was confused and unable to understand exactly what it was that the black coat was shouting at me and then without warning, he landed a punch squarely on my jaw which jolted my head back with such force that I thought my neck would snap.

I was grabbed by my arms by two uniformed officials and bundled out of the room, handcuffed and bleeding, and as they dragged me past the bathroom, I saw her, naked and face down on the floor, her blonde hair matted with blood. A crimson pool surrounded her lifeless body, flecks of blood were splattered on the walls while bloody footprints on the white linoleum flooring completed the horrific scene. Two officials crouched over her body as they inspected the butchered remains, looked up at me and glared menacingly but said nothing.

Through my confusion and panic, I wondered who she was and who could have done such a thing. Although I knew, with as much certainty as anyone ever could, that I had not been responsible, I sensed that my visitors had other ideas. In shock and bewilderment, I was manhandled out of the room and onto the landing. My head pounded the like of which I had never known, and my legs seemed unwilling to move fast enough to keep up with the two policemen who escorted me. I fell to the floor and struggled, unable to get back to my feet as punches rained down on me. Along the landing, a man stood by an open door looking alarmed. "Help me," I cried out imploringly. The man stepped back into his room and closed the door just at the moment when a heavy boot smashed into my face, and the lights went out.

Chapter 3

A Guilty Verdict

I vaguely remember being bundled out a black car, cuffed, disorientated and helpless. In the offices of the local constabulary, I had then been stripped of my clothing and given a red boiler suit with which to cover myself. My fingerprints were taken and I was photographed standing against a wall, holding a board that had my name chalked upon it. I had no idea what on earth was going on. I was then bundled along a corridor and thrown in a cell without explanation, where I was left languishing within its confines for what seemed like an eternity. The room contained a bare and filthy mattress along one wall with a bucket in the far corner, and a dim lamp above the heavy steel door struggled to illuminate the recesses of the tiny cell. It soon became evident that pacing in circles was a futile waste of energy, and so I slumped down on the filthy mattress, closed my eyes and drifted off to sleep.

Loud voices, the jangle of keys and the clanking of the heavy door opening, awoke me once more. Two uniformed men, wearing ornate military style peaked caps, grabbed me roughly and hauled me to my feet and escorted me along a series of dimly lit corridors, while holding my arms tightly to prevent my escape. Escape? To where? I wondered. I had no idea where I was or what might happen next. Finally we reached a doorway which was guarded by two more officials, one of whom opened the door and ushered me inside without saying a word.

Once inside the interrogation room, I was greeted by two serious looking men wearing black suits. One stood with his arms folded, while the other was seated behind a desk, and neither looked intent on making this a social occasion. The two guards escorted me to a chair in front of the desk and forced me to sit down and then left the room, closing the door behind them. In broken English, the official behind the desk commenced the formalities by asking for my name. "Steve... Steven Caldwell," I responded obligingly.

"What is your relationship with Annika Radwanski?" he asked.

"Who?" I asked perplexed, incurring the wrath of his partner who obviously considered my response to be a flippant one. He launched at me without warning, grabbed me from behind and rammed my head face down on the table, causing intense pain. He held his full weight on me and I felt the warm flow of blood from my nose. He grabbed my hair and pulled me upright in the chair once more.

"I ask you again, Mr Caldwell. What is your relationship with Annika Radwanski?" repeated the official behind the desk.

"I don't know her" I replied pleadingly, by now assuming that he was referring to the blonde in the bathroom. Once more, my head was slammed down onto the desk, held by the neck so tightly that I thought it might break. This was to become a recurring trend throughout the interrogation. The suited guy behind the desk asked all the questions in broken English, while his colleague repeatedly slammed my face against the desk each time I failed to give them the answers which they were obviously looking for.

I was totally dumbfounded when quizzed about the heroin which detectives had found in my jacket pocket, and a small wrap sealed in a clear plastic evidence bag, was slammed down in front of me. Unable to answer the question, I once again found myself face down on the desk. "Look at it. It is yours," came a stern voice from somewhere above me.

Another evidence bag, this one containing a blood stained knife, was pushed across the desk for my inspection. I had not seen the knife before but I assumed that the blood had probably belonged to the naked blonde. I protested my innocence in vain. "Then explain how your fingerprints are on that knife, Mr Caldwell." By now I realised that I was in trouble, and I was in trouble deep. From the line of questions which were being asked, even I could deduce that it did not look good. My interrogators lack of patience indicated that all the evidence pointed at me being the guilty culprit, and they were expecting a quick confession so that they could wrap the case up, charge me and get home to a relaxing evening with their wives and families.

oooOOOooo

Despite my futile pleas of innocence, I was formally charged with the murder of Annika Radwanski and subsequently put on trial even before my wounded face had a chance to heal. Bemused, I had stood in the dock wearing the same red boiler suit that had been issued to me when my clothing was taken away for analysis. Most of the legal proceedings were conducted in Polish and I had not even been fully able to understand my court appointed defence lawyer. The prosecution definitely had the weight of evidence on their side; the toxicology report on Miss Radwanski's body had found that there was alcohol and heroin in her blood stream, and tests had confirmed that the heroin sample taken from her body matched the heroin which had been found in my jacket pocket. The toxicologist also testified that levels of Librium, a Benzodiazepine, plus alcohol and amphetamine sulphate had been present in my blood, and the prosecution suggested that such a cocktail would cause increased levels of aggression and loss of memory.

As further evidence, the prosecution submitted my white t-shirt, stained with blood, and tests had shown that the blood on the t-shirt matched the blood on the knife. More damning still was the conclusion that the blood had come from Annika Radwanski, a nineteen year old music student. She was described in court as an attractive, outgoing young woman who had her whole life ahead of her. She was intelligent and passionate about music and the arts, and had also been a keen painter with a sharp eye for detail. It had been the city's musical academies which had initially brought her to Krakow to study. As a child, it had been considered that Miss Radwanski had displayed a remarkable and precocious talent in respect of both piano and violin, and she had flourished under the tutelage of her chosen academy. Her parents wept as their daughter's tutor testified how he had expected Annika Radwanski to become one of the finest musicians the country had ever produced.

My defence countered that I had never been a heroin user, and there was no indication that the drug had been in my blood stream. Although I acknowledged drinking heavily and taking amphetamine sulphate on the night that Miss Radwanski died, I assumed that the Benzodiazepine must have somehow been administered by persons unknown and without my knowledge. I sensed that basing my defence on being ignorant of everything, and possibly being unconscious at the time of Miss Radwanski's death, was not cutting much ice with the court. Friends of the dead girl had testified that, to their knowledge, she had never taken heroin before, although the toxicologist could not say for certain whether or not her death could have been attributed to an overdose prior to the mutilation of her body. My lawyer had mentioned before the trial a possible witness, a hotel guest who had seen an unconscious blonde with two men on the hotel landing. Unfortunately for me, the un-named witness could not be traced to give evidence in court.

Amid confusion and commotion, Deborah Fankham, my wife and soulmate, was led into the court room and, visibly shaken, she took to the witness stand. Only once did she glance toward me apprehensively as I waited for her to say something, anything which might help exonerate me of the crime and put an end to my ordeal. There were gasps from the gallery as her evidence was translated for the court and with shock and outrage, I listened to her faint voice quivering as she testified how she had befriended Annika at the party earlier in the evening but, later when returning to the hotel room unexpectedly, she had been shocked to find me in bed with the blonde girl. Feeling hurt and betrayed that her husband could be so disloyal, she had simply turned around and left the room without causing a fuss. Upon further questioning, Debbie told the court how there had been many times in the past when she had been petrified of my violent outbursts which were often intensified by my alcohol and drug use.

I listened to Debbie's fabrications in total astonishment, outraged and mystified by what she was saying until, unable to contain my frustration any longer, I jumped to my feet. "Liar," I shouted, pointing an accusing finger, "I never laid a fucking hand on you in my life." Debbie turned away as two guards wrestled me forcibly from the courtroom, kicking and screaming, "you're a fucking liar, you'll pay for this. You'll fucking pay for this."

I was dragged downstairs, administered another beating and then thrown into a holding cell to calm down. By the time I was returned to the courtroom, Debbie was gone. The prosecution claimed in their summary that I must have taken Miss Radwanski back to the hotel at some point in the evening, plied her with drugs and then, after my wife had caught us in the act, an argument must have ensued in which I had killed her in my drug and alcohol fuelled state. Based on the enormity of the evidence against me, it took the court very little time to convict me of murder. My crime was considered so heinous that only a life sentence could serve to act as sufficient punishment and deter anyone else who might think that being in a rock and roll band made them above the law.

I listened as sentence was passed; life. The judge asked if I understood the sentence but I barely managed to nod my head. Of course, I understood what the sentence meant but did not understand how events had led me to this point. Why would my wife testify that she had caught me with the blonde girl? Had she? I was left questioning my own sanity.

oooOOOooo

I was transferred north to Bialoleka Prison on the outskirts of Warsaw; the largest prison in the Polish penal system awaited me. Although the red inmate uniform made me look like everyone else, clearly I was not. Initially, I was locked in solitary confinement, where guards spoke to me harshly, often with a swift crack from a baton if I did not respond correctly or quickly enough. In time, though, I would find myself being sent out on work details, mingling with others from the prison population. Digging ditches on local farms was back breaking work and, watched over by guards bearing automatic weapons to deter anyone considering escape, there was no respite regardless of the weather. In the summertime it was overbearingly hot and the soil was baked hard like concrete, while during the winter the ground was either sodden or frozen solid. Blisters, sores and calluses developed on my hands, yet I neither protested nor considered an escape attempt. Each day I assumed that someone somewhere was bound to realise that this was all a misunderstanding and that I would then be pardoned and released.

The only one of my former friends who remained in contact with me was Dave, my childhood friend and band mate. His letters would often reach me with sections of text removed due to prison censorship, but despite the frustration that caused, I nevertheless looked forward to reading his communications. He did his best to inform me of things that were going on back at home and always asked how I was bearing up. Writing back to him was a welcome distraction from my daily nightmare and, although I knew that my letters would have to pass through the same censorship method, I hoped that he got the general gist of what I was trying to convey.

A few months into my sentence, I received communication from a solicitor in England, Jacob Reeve, who my parents had instructed to act on my behalf in respect of my impending divorce. Such news was a hammer blow to me at a time when I was still trying to come to terms with my situation but, although we never met in person, Jacob Reeve kept me informed by letter as to how the divorce was progressing. Debbie was suing me on the grounds of my adultery and I was clearly not in any position to contest her claim. Once our solicitors had reached a relatively amicable settlement arrangement, I agreed to let Mr Reeve invest my half, pending the possibility of an eventual release.

The upset surrounding the collapse of my life had also taken its toll on my parents too. They had been out to visit me on one occasion, although my long suffering mother had been unable to contain her distress at seeing me in such harsh surroundings. For my mother, who had been born in Poland, the visit had been the first time that she had returned to the country of her birth since she had left there shortly after WWII. My father, a Londoner by birth, appeared to have aged considerably since I had last seen him, and it was a huge shock when I received word from my mother that he had died suddenly in his sleep. The autopsy had found that the cause of his demise had in all likelihood been a stroke. My mother had found his loss very hard to contend with and, within a few short months, she had gone too.

It was tough on me, losing both parents in such a short space of time, especially as I was not permitted to say my farewells to either of them. As the only beneficiary of their last will and testament, Jacob Reeve was once again kind enough to act on my behalf, overseeing the sale of their assets and investing the proceeds for me. At least, if I were ever to be released, I might have a little put aside with which to rebuild my life. I had to remain positive and cling to whatever hope I could, after all, I had nothing else.

oooOOOooo

Correspondence with Dave continued over the years with fresh letters being exchanged every few months. The fall of Communism had led to major changes within the penal system, and prison life had become a little easier. Work details on the local farms still meant early starts and hard work, but at least we were given appropriate clothing and would no longer be forced to stand knee deep in filth in freezing cold irrigation ditches. I actually began to enjoy the farm labouring and the fresh air in the summer months, although I was more than grateful to find myself working in the warmth of the prison kitchens during the harsh winters.

Out of necessity, I managed to learn a little of the language and picked up various skills, such as motor mechanics and carpentry. With access to computers becoming available, I took IT courses as well as enrolling in Business and Commerce studies, and even studied

Psychology for a time too. Tattooing had been popular within the prison system, with some artistic inmates becoming quite adept at the art. Over the years I had amassed quite a collection of tattoos on my arms, chest and legs, although nothing would ever hide the scars on my face which had been caused by the kicks and beatings that I endured following my arrest. I did whatever I could to fill my time, doing my best to prove that I was a model inmate and then, thirteen years into my sentence, I found myself transferred to Wronki Prison, another huge penal establishment around an hour's drive west of Poznan.

Wronki Prison had been built at the end of the 19th Century, and the facility had been used by the Nazis to detain prisoners of war and political prisoners during the time of their occupation. It was to be during my time in Wronki that I would find myself sharing a cell with Aleksander Kaminski, a man who would ultimately become a most valued friend. Initially sceptical about sharing a cell with an English lifer, Alex also had little time for my pleas of innocence. Eventually we learned that we had much in common and our friendship grew with its roots deeply entrenched in punk rock ideology and a shared love of football.

Once Alex had become intrigued by my trial and conviction, I told him about the disappearing witness who failed to make a court appearance, and how it may have been he who held the key to the proof of my innocence. Knowing how the system worked, Alex considered that there was a possibility that the authorities might have dissuaded the witness from giving evidence, on the grounds that they had not wanted me to be found anything other than guilty. On Alex's release, he promised to do whatever he could using whatever contracts he still had, to find out who the missing witness may have been. I gave him the details of Jacob Reeve to ensure that anything he could find out would be kept from the authorities. Although we were not strictly permitted contact after his release, we vowed that we would meet up when my turn came and that there would be beer, vodka, good food and rock and roll to mark the occasion. Although I was saddened to see him go, I held him at his word and looked forward to the promise of a reunion on the outside.

oooOOOooo

A few months after Alex's release, I had an unexpected visitor. A man, perhaps in his mid twenties, wearing a white shirt, tie and tweed jacket introduced himself as Thurstan Reeve. After qualifying in law he had recently started working with his father, Jacob, and the legal practice representing me had become Reeve & Son. Despite his rather extravagant name, Thurstan Reeve was something of a maverick in his profession and his real passion was not in law, but in music. After reading through the files and notes which his father had amassed after serving as my legal advisor for more than two decades, he had asked his father to allow him to act as my solicitor.

Thurstan had been fascinated by my case; the guitarist in a punk rock band, sentenced to life in a foreign prison for allegedly murdering a groupie. To Thurstan, my story had everything; music, murder, sex, drugs and intrigue. He had grown up with that story, including how I still maintained my innocence regardless of the weight of evidence against me. He had recently been in receipt of some important news that may have been of interest to me and, in delivering this information in person, he had hoped to discover for himself the man behind the myth.

After formally introducing himself, Thurstan Reeve had informed me that he had come up with the name of the witness who had not shown up in court; one Stanislaw Markowicz. Mr Markowicz, a pharmacist, had been a guest at the hotel on the night that Annika Radwanski had died, and during police questioning he had maintained that he had seen two men assisting an unconscious woman. Although it was not much to go on, at least the disappearing witness now had a name.

oooOOOooo

I liked Thurston Reeve, and although he spoke with the air of someone who had received a privileged upbringing, he clearly had a passion for the things that he believed in. Over the next eighteen months or so, he made the round trip from south east London to Wronki Prison several times, and we were often side tracked discussing music and music sub-culture. He even informed me that he had tracked down a copy of L.I.A.R.'s only album through the internet, and had bought it for the princely sum of fifteen pounds. Thurstan was also able to assist me to get dual nationality status granted, on the grounds of my mother's heritage. Perhaps most importantly though, Thurstan was to eventually reveal that under Polish law, after serving twenty-five years of my life sentence, I would shortly be considered for parole. Subsequently, he assisted me to open a bank account and transferred some funds from my investments for future living expenses.

And so, it was that on 14th June 2013, I emerged blinking into the morning sunlight. For the first time in a quarter of a century, I could look up at the blue sky and feel the warm sun on my face as a free man. Thurstan had been kind enough to provide me with a new pair of jeans and a pair of Dr Marten boots, some changes of underwear and a couple of white t-shirts. It felt good to be wearing my old leather jacket once more too, even if I had put on a few pounds in the intervening years and it was now a little tighter. I pulled my dark glasses from my pocket and put them on, taking a moment to breathe in the fresh air. I had a bag in my hand containing my meagre possessions and I had no idea what the future would hold, but at that moment I was just happy to be free.

Chapter 4

Poznan

I will always be eternally grateful to Thurstan Reeve for all that he did to enable my integration back into the outside world. I took the bus from the prison to Wronki train station and then caught the 11:39 to Poznan, arriving in the city around forty minutes later. Thurstan had gone out of his way to rent an apartment for me and, as he had also provided me with a map, it was not too difficult to follow the directions.

The apartment consisted of four rooms on the third floor of a tenement building not far from the train station. Although it was not particularly large nor was it lavishly furnished, in relation to the conditions that I had been accustomed to, I considered my new surroundings to be palatial. With laminate wooden flooring throughout, the living room contained a comfortable grey leather suite and a large flat screen television. Glass doors opened onto a balcony overlooking the courtyard below. The bedroom offered me a double bed that was far more comfortable than any I had previously slept on, and there was more than sufficient storage space for my meagre possessions. The bathroom suite gleamed white, reflected in the stainless steel fittings and the polished black floor tiles. The kitchen and dining area offered me all the facilities that I could possibly need, and on the table I found a mobile phone resting on a piece of paper on which was written a short message. "Welcome home, best wishes, Thurstan." Clumsily, I tried to get to grips with what I considered to be new technology, but eventually found two telephone numbers, one for Thurstan and one for Alex.

Looking in the kitchen cupboards, I discovered that Thurstan had left some tins of food, and he had also stocked the refrigerator with bread, butter, sausages and several bottles of Polish lager. I rifled through the kitchen drawer and found a bottle opener with which to flip the cap from the top of a bottle of Tyskie. Putting the neck of the bottle to my lips, I closed my eyes and took time to savour each gulp of the ice cold beer, unable to remember how long it had been since I had last enjoyed such a delightful flavour. Taking the bottle with me for company, I made my way into the bathroom, feeling compelled to shower before doing anything else. It took a few moments to adjust the controls to a point where the water flowed at a comfortable temperature and then, after peeling off my clothes and dropping them onto the floor, I stepped into the confines of the shower cubicle. Grateful to find shower gel and shampoo, I diligently began the task of lathering and washing away a quarter of a century of prison confinement. It felt liberating, standing motionless, just allowing the warm water to cascade down upon me. Rarely in prison had it been possible to shower alone, so the solitude was a welcome luxury.

Despite the many horrendous tales of sexual assaults taking place in prison showers, away from the prying eyes of the warders, I had neither witnessed nor found myself on the receiving end of such an assault. It was a danger that I had always been cautious of, and had never been off my guard. Only once could I recall an incident when I had been the potential victim of a physical assault in the shower block. I had only been a few weeks into my sentence when a new inmate, Vadim Gusarov, had arrived in our block. Gusarov was a young Russian skinhead who had been convicted of a burglary in which an elderly victim had been beaten and robbed in his own home. Such a crime would never endear any convict to most sections of the prison community, not even the Russian contingent who remained fairly tight knit. Vadim knew that the nature of his crime meant that he would have to assert a reputation for himself as a man not to be trifled with. Therefore, he looked for someone who he considered to be in a weaker position than he, and an Englishman convicted of murdering a young Polish woman, obviously fitted Vadim's criteria adequately.

After keeping myself to myself as best as possible, I had no prior inkling of Vadim's intentions but nevertheless, he had considered his vulnerable position and chosen a moment to make his move. The shower block would not only afford him the perfect opportunity but also a suitable audience, assembled to witness his display of aggression. Vadim positioned himself next to me in the row of showers and I noticed how he kept glancing at me out of the corner of his eye. I grew tense and nervous, unaware of his intentions and fearing the possibility of gang rape. I had been anticipating some form of assault from my fellow inmates and braced myself, half expecting a beating, or worse still.

Vadim clumsily nudged into me and began to shout in his native tongue, and although I had no idea what he way saying, his aggressive stance suggested that he was trying to provoke me. He stood practically nose-to-nose with me and continued to shout, doing his best to alert everyone present that I had nudged into him and committed the cardinal sin of invading his personal space. He stood firm with his fists clenched by his side and his face contorted with rage and hatred. I looked over towards the two prison guards who stood impassively in the doorway, expecting them to intervene, but they did nothing. My mind raced through possible outcomes of any action that I could take. If I chose to be goaded into landing the first blow, then I surely faced the prospect of punishment from the guards for breaking prison rules. I considered the prospect of taking a beating from Vadim, who would undoubtedly claim self-defence. I even pondered the possibility that everyone present may have been itching for me to step out of line, and maybe they were all queuing up to teach me a lesson.

Not wanting to inflame the situation, I turned away as everyone watched on in anticipation. I was fearful that such an action might be perceived as cowardice, but in that instant, my urge towards self-preservation became the overriding factor. Antagonised by my lack of response, Vadim pushed me and I turned to face him and once again, I looked to the impassive guards, imploringly. I guess that in that dog eat dog environment they had seen it all before and, knowing what to expect, they both turned away and closed the door behind them.

I felt like an untrained and uninitiated gladiator, sealed inside a Roman arena with only hungry lions for company and when Vadim pushed me again, causing me to lose my balance, my feet slipped on the wet floor and I fell. Vadim was on top of me in a flash, kneeling astride me as my hands tried desperately to protect my face from the blows that rained down upon me. Onlookers cheered, whistled, shouted and brayed, creating a deafening cacophony which echoed and only served to add to my confusion and desperation.

He fought to constrain my wrists, pinning me down and sinking his teeth into my shoulder. The sudden pain rendered me momentarily paralysed and he continued to rain blows down on my face and body. More out of panic and desperation than any inborn ability to fight back, I found the strength to clench my hand into a tight fist and land one well-placed punch to the side of Vadim's head. My fortune in stunning him for that one moment allowed me the opportunity to finally fight back. In that violent and barbaric arena, I sensed that I had two options; I could either be devoured by the lions or I would have to become one of them.

Gathering all my strength and fortitude, I fought back. It was not like some kind of traditional boxing bout in which punches are considered, thought out and executed with skill and precision. Instead my fists became like clubs, repeatedly thumping him on the side of the head without allowing him time to respond. The cheering and jeering of the onlookers continued as I grasped my chance to turn the tables, and soon it was Vadim's turn to be prostrate on the cold, wet concrete floor and it was my turn to be top dog. I brought my knee down on Vadim's testicles with such force that it was now he who was paralysed through pain.

He threw his head back in agony, his mouth emitting a strange gurgling sound that to me signalled a change in my fortunes. As my fear subsided, my sense of empowerment grew and adrenaline coursed through me like I had been injected with some powerful drug. I sensed that there could only be one victor and that this altercation was not going to end with Vadim and me shaking hands. The assembled onlookers were now baying for blood, sensing that the 'kill' was imminent. To my amazement, the other inmates including Vadim's fellow Russians, appeared to be cheering in support of the Englishman, heightening my sense of power. With neither the refinement nor the ability to fight like a true pugilist, and realising that I might have only one chance of walking away as the victor, I resorted to the only form of primitive attack that I could muster.

The cheering crowd jostled for a ringside position, all wondering what I might have in my repertoire to bring the event to a conclusion. I thought back to the days of rough and ready punk rock gigs in South London, and the retribution which we had affectionately called 'the Deptford handshake'. With Vadim still in severe discomfort and temporarily unable to mount his self-defence strategy, I towered over him, grasping his head firmly between both hands and repeatedly crashed my forehead down on him. It was a brutal, snide and unsporting assault for which Vadim had no defence. Time and again I crashed my forehead down on his face, each time with a sickening crunch as I connected with his cheekbone, his eye socket, his jaw.

Blood flowed from Vadim's wounds, mixing with the water that cascaded down from the shower heads above us and creating a crimson river that coursed to the drain cover nearby. I sensed that Vadim had taken enough punishment and knelt astride him with my hand clenched tight around his throat, pinning him down firmly in a pool of his own blood. "Have you had enough yet, you cunt?" I screamed at him, thumping my forehead down on his once more with a crack, just for good measure.

"No more," Vadim muttered weakly in broken English, barely having the strength to spill the words from his swollen and blooded mouth. One swollen eye could barely open, the other remained closed, his arms lay weak and motionless beside him. Just to be certain that I had made my mark, I clenched my fist one last time and hit him on the side of the jaw with as much strength as I had left. As his head reeled sideways from that final blow, two teeth danced their way through the river of blood to rest side by side, like dice that had been rolled from a cup in a child's board game.

I slowly stood up, panting from my exertions as Vadim lay there. His head turned weakly as he coughed and spat mouthfuls of blood onto the wet concrete floor. The shower block had fallen silent except for the sound of the water raining down from the shower heads, and the other inmates returned to their task of washing themselves. Vadim struggled to his knees, toppling over twice as he tentatively strained to get to his feet. With head slightly bowed, he cautiously peered at me through his half open, swollen eye and he raised his hands in an apologetic and defensive manner as he uneasily edged his way to the other end of the shower block. I watched him stagger away as some of the other inmates mockingly kicked his backside as he walked past.

The door of the shower block opened and the guards announced the end of the shower session, surveying the outcome of the contest which they had chosen to turn a blind eye to. I half expected there to be some form of retribution and I awaited my fate. The water stopped flowing and we were given a moment to collect our towels and dry off before filing out back to our cells. I watched as one of the guards stopped Vadim as he shuffled past, pausing to lift the prisoner's bowed head and inspect his wounds before ushering him on his way without saying a word. As I waited in line to leave, I felt a hand rest heavily on my shoulder. I turned to face the towering figure of Nikolay Barinov, his shaven head still covered in beads of water. Nikolay Barinov was a Russian who had been convicted of a double murder and a figure who commanded the ultimate respect on our block. I froze, fearing Nikolay more so than I did the guards.

"Well done," said Nikolay in his deep baritone voice, patting me on the back as we filed through the open door. The guards looked me up and down, but neither of them said a word, only appearing to grudgingly acknowledge that I had passed a test, earned myself a reputation and elevated my status to carnivore in the prison zoo. Nobody could have been more surprised than I at the outcome of that day's events. I had not offered myself forward as a tough guy before that day and neither did I do so afterwards, but I had clearly done enough to earn my place. Subsequently, I managed to fit into my daily routines without fearing what might lurk around every corner.

Now, safe in the solitude of my new apartment surroundings, it felt good to feel the warm water on my face, cleansing my body without having to share the experience with thirty or so other inmates. I stepped out of the shower with my eyes closed, reaching out blindly for the towel. I wiped the soapy residue from my eyes and rubbed the towel over my shaven head. I had learned that keeping one's hair short while doing prison time had two distinct benefits. It dried quickly which proved beneficial in the cold weather, but also in the event of a fight between inmates, if things got dirty, then there was much less to grab hold of. There had been a large contingent of skinheads confined in the facilities that were to be my home for that quarter of a century, mainly Poles, Germans or Russians, some who had been imprisoned for football violence, crimes against the state or political unrest. In general, the one thing which I shared in common with them was our musical interests. Therefore, with my hair kept cropped short, I was able to merge more comfortably with this group than with other sections of the prison community. As an outsider, this afforded me a vital level of protection. I admit that there were some inmates who had political leanings of a more extreme nationalist nature, with whom I felt less comfortable, but being a thousand miles from home and submerged in a culture a million miles from what I was used to, I was just relieved to find allies wherever I could, no matter how tenuous our links might have been.

I caught sight of myself in the bathroom mirror as I finished towelling myself dry, hardly recognising who I had now become. My face carried the scars of my beatings, and my body had become a canvas for the prison tattooists who were always happy to practice their art as a way of wiling away the time; as any ex-convict will tell you, a prison clock ticks very slowly. In an environment that can be mind-numbingly tedious, where you do your best to block out emotions, thoughts of home, friends or loved ones, a tattooists' needle is a way of feeling something, anything. I use the term 'needle' relatively loosely, as sharpened syringes proved a popular alternative, as did plastic implements fashioned to a point by grinding them on the concrete floor. One elaborate machine was built by a very ingenious German inmate which he constructed from pieces taken from the stolen prison VCR, the telephone cord that had been cut from the prison phone and two batteries which had been smuggled in. Ink was more often than not created by mixing mashed up printed paper with bodily fluids. When you feel nothing, literally nothing at all, except anger, resentment and hatred, then health and safety is not a priority. The pain of the needle piercing the skin is affirmation of life and existence. I feel, therefore I am.

Standing in the bathroom, gazing at my mirrored reflection and surveying the shabby remains of my time ravaged body, I became aware of emotion that I had been devoid of for as long as I could remember. I wept for my loss, for what had been and for what could have been. No, my tattoos are not exactly pretty and may never be considered to be fine art, but each one tells a story of who I am and where I have been. They are a map of my memories, and each one stands to hide the scars inside, the ones that no one sees.

Wrapping the white towel around my waist and reaching for my bottle of beer, I raised it to my lips, took a long refreshing swig and relished its bite as it hit my throat. After browsing through my meagre possessions, I decided that the following day I would need to sort out my banking arrangements and buy myself some new clothes. I was certainly looking forward to an early night and the opportunity of sleeping in a comfortable bed, and relished spending a night without the sound of jangling keys, slamming doors and muffled voices in the darkness. I was also looking forward to waking up naturally the following morning, without the aid of the deafening 6am prison alarm call to which I had grown accustomed. Of course, before any of that, I had two very important phone calls to make.

Tentatively, I clumsily selected Thurstan's number and pressed the call button. After a few seconds, his number started ringing. "Hi, Steve, how the devil are you?" Thurstan's well spoken voice came through loud and clear. Feeling ignorant and puzzled by how he knew that it was me calling him, Thurstan gave me a brief and baffling explanation into how mobile technology works in the 21st Century. I thanked him for all he had done, emphasising my gratitude to him for arranging the apartment, and how overjoyed I was with the creature comforts that my new home offered.

"No problem," said Thurstan, "I was in Berlin on business last week, so I took a detour to check that the apartment would be ready for your arrival. I'm glad you like the place." Then turning to business, he continued, "in the bedside table drawer, you will find an envelope containing your banking details in Poznan. If you ask to speak to Mr. Jan Malinowski, he will give you everything you need so that you can start drawing your funds. Our firm has ensured that the financial assets from your divorce and from your parents' estate have been invested wisely. Therefore, the sum of those investments, combined with interest accrued, should enable you to live relatively comfortably while you find your feet and decide on your future. Needless to say, if there is any financial or legal advice that you might require then my services will be at your disposal, for a small fee, of course," added Thurstan with wry laughter. "You will find that Mr. Malinowski is expecting you and has promised to assist you however he can."

"How can I ever repay your kindness?" I asked, feeling truly humbled by everything he had done.

"Oh, don't worry," Thurstan replied, "I'll think of something." I thanked him once more and asked him to pass on my gratitude to his father too, as he had also proved invaluable to me over the years, and had clearly been working in my best interests, for a small fee, of course.

Before going to bed and enjoying my first night as a free man, there was one more phone call that I needed to make and after selecting Alex's number and pressing the call button, within five rings he answered. I had missed him since his release, much more than I would care to admit, and it was great to hear his voice again. "Alex," I exclaimed, "it's me, Steve. How are you?"

"Steve? Steve? Yeah, I'm good," replied Alex cheerily. Despite his distinct accent, his mastery of the English language was as good as anyone's. "How are you, man? When did you get out?" After telling him that I had only been released that morning, I ran through everything that Thurstan Reeve had done for me. "That's great, man, really great. He's a good lawyer and there are not many of those." Alex laughed. "Do you know that Mr Reeve did talk to me some while ago?" he added. His Polish vernacular sounded more apparent as his tone grew a little more serious.

"No," I replied, "no, I didn't. He didn't mention anything. Why?" I asked, more than a little curious.

"Look," Alex continued, his voice sounding a little excited, "I'm in Prague right now, setting up a new music club, but we must meet soon, really soon."

"Of course," I replied. "Now that we're both free men, we have much catching up to do."

"Yeah, yeah," Alex cut in. "This is important, really important. I have much good news for you." I was intrigued and pushed him for more information. "Look," he said, "Reeve called me with a name. Stanislaw Markowicz. Do you remember this man?"

"Who? Markowicz? The pharmacist?" I asked, somewhat bemused.

"Yes, Markowicz, the pharmacist," Alex confirmed. "I called in some favours for you, my friend, and one of my contacts came through."

"What? What?" Stunned by this news, I was struggling to find the words. "He's still alive?"

Alex had obviously been waiting to tell me this news and he sounded unable to conceal his excitement any longer. "Yes man. Markowicz, your disappearing witness is alive and well. He's living in Nowa Huta and guess what?" Alex paused, teasingly.

"What? Tell me," I insisted. Those few seconds of suspense seemed to hang for an eternity.

"He wants to talk to you, man." Alex dropped it like a bomb and I was dumbstruck. "Well say something, Stevie. Markowicz the pharmacist wants to talk to you, and only you."

"That's... that's amazing. How can I ever thank you?" In the light of all that Alex and Thurstan had done for me, without my knowledge, I felt overwhelmed, speechless and very humbled.

"Sit tight for now, my friend and enjoy your freedom," Alex implored. "I shall make some arrangements for us and I will telephone you and tell you where and when we must meet in Krakow." I promised that I would be patient. "Stay out of trouble," Alex added, jokingly, "and be nice to the beautiful Polish girls there in Poznan. Dobranoc, free man."

I thanked him once more. "Goodnight, Alex. Dobranoc to you also." I placed the phone back on the table, noticing that my hand was shaking. It was just after 9pm when I retired for the night but, despite my exhaustion and the warmth and comfort of my new bed, sleep proved elusive. When might I finally meet Stanislaw Markowicz? What did he have to tell me? I had so many questions to ask, but that was nothing new. There had always been so many questions to ask, but suddenly, when perhaps I least expected it, I was now able to consider the possibility of actually getting some answers.

The following morning would herald my first full day as a free man, but I sensed that the transition might not be an easy one. To even begin to feel normal again I would have to become accustomed to so many things which normal people take for granted. Just the simple act of taking a shower had proven to be an act symbolic of a baptism; my rebirth. The water had cascaded down, cleansing me of my previous incarnation as a prison inmate and I had emerged feeling a sense of regeneration, ready to start my life afresh.

At one time I had a life and a future, a life and a future which I had seen so cruelly stolen away from me. My past had become a fragmented puzzle with many of the pieces lost, hidden or beyond my grasp. I could only hope that Stanislaw Markowicz, the disappearing witness, might prove to be the first piece in rearranging that puzzle.

I wanted my life back.

Chapter 5

A Fresh Start

Over the next few days I found it difficult to concentrate on anything other than the pharmacist, and what he might have to tell me. On the day following my release, I had gone to the bank just as Thurstan had advised and asked to see Mr. Malinowski. After a few minutes he appeared, shook my hand and invited me into his office. Jan Malinowski was a bespectacled man who I found to be both polite and congenial, and who also spoke very good English. After a few minutes of conversation relating to how the bank worked and how I could start drawing on my funds, there was a knock on the office door. After being invited to enter, a smartly dressed lady walked in carrying a tray on which were two cups of coffee, a bowl of sugar and an A4 sized manila envelope. Mr. Malinowski opened the envelope and removed its contents. He passed me a credit and a debit card and a rather elegant looking pen which he had taken from his inside jacket pocket. He instructed me to sign my name on the back of both cards.

I did so and handed him back the pen. "Are you aware of the sum deposited here in our bank, Mr. Caldwell?" Mr.

Malinowski asked. I assured him that I had no idea as all my finances had been handled by Reeve and Son, back in England. I raised my cup to my lips as Mr. Malinowski consulted the paperwork in front of him. Peering over the top of his glasses, he continued. "As of close of business yesterday, your account stands at 2,861,427 Zloty."

"I beg your pardon?" I asked in total amazement, struggling to swallow the mouthful of hot coffee without choking. "How much?"

Consulting the paperwork again, Mr. Malinowski repeated the figure while tapping away on his desk calculator. "At the current rate of international exchange," he continued, "this figure equates to roughly £572,000 Sterling."

I was shocked. Surely there must have been some mistake, I thought. When Thurstan had spoken about the money, he never even hinted about the size of the sum. I had expected maybe a few thousand pounds, but £572,000 was way beyond my comprehension.

After Mr. Malinowski had helped me to withdraw some funds for my immediate expenses, I left the bank that day feeling shell shocked and still convinced that there must have been some mistake. I called Thurstan and asked him. "Yes, that sounds about right," he said. "I did explain that the figure should be enough to tide you over while you get back on your feet. Were you expecting more?" he asked, in his usual wry manner.

I assured him that the sum was way beyond anything that I had anticipated and I thanked him again for all he had done. "Oh, before you go," said Thurstan, "now that you have some funds at your disposal, it may be a good idea to add some credit to that mobile phone." I followed his instructions of where to go in order to enable me to keep in touch, and then spent some time in town buying myself some new clothes and footwear. By the time I had also picked up some vital food and drink supplies, I returned to the apartment heavily laden.

Later that evening, Alex phoned. "We are set," he began. "On Sunday I fly from Prague to Krakow, and we will meet on Monday. I shall let you know exactly where later. One more thing," he added, "you will need to bring 5000 Zloty. Can you do this?" he asked.

"Yes I can, that's not a problem," I replied before enquiring as to why I might need 5000 Zloty.

"I will explain everything when we meet," Alex offered before hanging up. Everything seemed to be happening so fast. I had anticipated that following my release from prison, I would have to undergo a lengthy period of adjustment. Without having so much as a moment to catch my breath, it appeared that my freedom would involve me having to hit the ground running. I spent the next few days killing time and exploring Poznan, a city midway between Berlin to the west and Warsaw to the east. The old town was picturesque with a beautiful old market square enclosed by vividly coloured buildings. I found it hard to believe that it was a city which was rebuilt after being so badly damaged during the Second World War. I remembered the time that the band had played in Poznan a few nights before my arrest, but as I explored the city's narrow streets, making my way to the banks of the River Warta, I saw nothing which appeared even remotely familiar.

The anticipation of what lay ahead in the forthcoming days, weeks and months, was making my mind race. Afternoon autumn afternoon sunlight was beginning to fade as I made my way back to my apartment, cutting through the old market square once more. Noticing the tourist information office, I suddenly decided that I would travel to Krakow the day before I was due to meet Alex. Of course, that meant that I would need a place to stay.

The young lady in the tourist information office was most helpful. I was bemused by how easily and quickly she was able to use modern technology to find the answers to my questions. As she rapidly tapped away at her computer keyboard, it was as if she had the world at her finger tips, she looked up the train times and informed me that to reach Krakow by the Sunday afternoon, I would have to catch an early train and travel via Warsaw. She then searched for a hotel which could accommodate me for the night, but I already had a place in mind, if indeed that place still existed. Although I could not remember the precise location or street name, I asked her if she would kindly check. "Could you find me the Kazimierz Hotel, please?" I enquired.

Looking at me somewhat puzzled, the young lady said that she would check, and within moments she confirmed that the place did indeed still exist. A sudden rush of excitement, anxiety and anticipation struck me as I asked her if she could assist me in making a booking.

"Of course," she said, tapping away at her keyboard once more before asking, "Just for one night?"

"Yes, please," I replied, "and I would like Room 13, if that's possible."

Again the young lady viewed me quizzically before continuing. "Your name?" She enquired, matter-of-factly. I gave her my name and my bank card, and after my details had been entered, it was done. "OK, so you now have a reservation for Sunday night at the Kazimierz Hotel in Krakow in the name of Mr. Stephen Caldwell." She kindly printed me out the details of my reservation and also the directions from the train station to the hotel, before politely smiling and wishing me a pleasant stay in Krakow. I thanked her for her assistance, patience and kindness and then made my way back to the apartment with my mind racing once more, unable to comprehend all that was happening.

In the early hours of Sunday morning, on a cold and dark platform at Poznan Glowny train station, I was waiting patiently for the 05:45 train which would carry me on my journey. I had my phone and I had enough money to cover the amount which Alex had suggested I bring. If all was to go according to plan, I would be in Krakow by one o'clock that afternoon.

Chapter 6

The Reunion

Despite my lack of sleep, I had been awake by 7:30 and had showered and made my way to the hotel dining area for breakfast and coffee. Alex had suggested that I should meet him at Plac Centralny, the main square in Nowa Huta, a suburb on the outskirts of Krakow. I stopped to ask the hotel receptionist which tram I should take and she informed me of where I could catch Tram 4, adding that the journey should take around twenty-five minutes. I thanked her and made my way out to the busy street. It was just after 9am and the early morning autumn mist engulfed the crumbling façades of the ancient buildings, as the residents of the city drifted to their places of work. A queue of commuters waited patiently to get aboard the already crowded trams but I had a short walk ahead of me before I would reach the tram stop I required.

It had been more than two years since I had seen Alex, and I was looking forward to seeing him again. We had become good friends during our time of incarceration in Wronki Prison, after I had been transferred across Poland from Bialoleka. We had spent much of our time discussing either football or music. Alex had been handed a 12 year sentence for the killing of a rival football supporter during an organised fight between the two sides. He was always interested to hear any tales which I had of my younger days on the terraces at Upton Park watching West Ham. I had never personally been involved in any of violence, but I had grown up surrounded by the fierce rivalry with other London clubs, especially Millwall and Chelsea. Alex's team were not perhaps the most fashionable club in Polish football but, despite much smaller crowd numbers, their rivalries seemed far more intense and brutal than anything I had ever witnessed.

Alex was three years younger than me and had been a guitarist in a band too, inspired by many of the same bands who had inspired me. Although his band had been quite popular in Polish punk rock circles, and had played in a few Eastern European countries, they had never really gained any accolades outside of their own country. He explained that, although not exactly right wing, they had a strong sense of pride in their own nationality and so always performed songs in their mother tongue. He was aware it had been commercial suicide to not translate their songs into English, but it was neither about the money nor the fame, instead pride, passion and alcohol.

Initially, Alex had not been convinced by my plea of innocence with regard to my crime. He would joke that everyone in prison says that they are innocent, but over a period of time, I managed to convince him. I told him of my frustration that no matter how many times I would plead my innocence, my words always fell on deaf ears. He had knowledge of how the system worked and how it had worked under the old regime too. The State, he argued, had been faced with investigating the death of a young girl. Drugs had been involved too, and this was not acceptable to the authorities of the day. The prime suspect had also been a musician, a foreigner with a message of subversion, corrupting the youth. He contested that the State would have been more than happy to find me guilty, because a conviction and lengthy sentence would send out a clear message that such crimes would not be tolerated.

Alex's camaraderie certainly played a large part in helping me through the latter stages of my twenty-five year incarceration. Countless nights I had laid awake, plotting my revenge, wondering if I would ever find out who was responsible for my predicament, and wondering if there would ever be justice, not only justice for me but justice for Annika Radwanski too. She had become just a body on a hotel bathroom floor, a series of pieces of evidence. Lost was the fact that she had been a living, breathing person in her own right, full of fun and laughter and with her whole life ahead of her. She deserved the truth, and she deserved justice too.

On his release, Alex had promised me two things. If he could, he would try to help me find out who had really been responsible for Annika's death, and after my release we would form a new band, Skazaniec. Alex felt that this being the Polish word for convict, Skazaniec would be quite appropriate. His second promise had been made in a jocular manner, probably to give me a little future focus, but his initial promise was made with conviction. With the help of my lawyer, Thurstan Reeve, he had been able to use his contacts to trace the witness who had disappeared without testifying at my trial. I had many unanswered questions. Why had Stanislaw Markowicz not shown up to give evidence? Had he been bought off? Had he been threatened? As I sat there on the tram, gazing out of the window as cars, pedestrians and buildings blurred past, the only thing I knew for sure was that Stanislaw Markowicz had agreed to speak to me, but at that point I had no idea what it was that he had to tell me.

The last twenty-seven months had passed slowly since I last saw Alex, and I was looking forward to finding out how he had been getting on since his release. All I knew was that he had been in Prague and that I was due to meet him today. He had not wanted to say too much over the phone, other than where to meet. It was obvious that Stanislaw Markowicz did not want too many people knowing his business, and when Alex and I spoke on the phone the previous day, I had to tease out of him why it was so imperative that I bring 5000 Zloty with me. "Tomorrow we meet, and I will take you to visit a pharmacist and a forger." That was all he would say before he hung up.

It was at little after 10:30am when I stepped off the tram at Plac Centralny in the Kracovian suburb of Nowa Huta, a pleasant and open square with lawned gardens and traversed by pathways that were lined with rose bushes which, despite the misty autumnal air, still bore the remains of their blooms from earlier in the year. I sat on one of the park benches in the centre of the square and lit a cigarette. I felt slightly nervous but full of expectation and anticipation too.

From where I sat, I could see, to the south of me, the wide main roadway on which the tram had rumbled along on its route between the city and goodness knows where. To the north, north-east and north-west, broad straight avenues fanned out disappearing into the morning mist. I took a long last pull on my cigarette, dropped the butt on the concrete and ground it with the toe of my boot. "On your feet, Caldwell," boomed a voice from behind me before trailing off into laughter. The accent was distinct and the voice familiar. I stood and turned to face two men walking towards me. Alex greeted me with a handshake and a warm embrace. "What's happened to you, my friend? You look like shit," he said jokingly, his hands resting on my shoulders as he looked me up and down.

"Well, that's a great way to greet a friend who kept you out of trouble for twelve years," I mocked, before adding, "it's cold, it's early and I have a hangover."

"Ah, too much beer last night?" laughed Alex. "You English will never learn that you cannot drink like a Pole. What you need is medicine, my friend. We must go to the bar up this way." Alex pointed in the direction of the road running directly north, and then holding out his other hand in the direction of the man accompanying him, he said, "this is Daniel. He is the man you must thank for finding your pharmacist." Daniel was a man who appeared to be in his late twenties or early thirties, unshaven, wearing a pair of jeans and a black hoodie zipped at the front. His hood was pulled up partially concealing his face, giving him a certain sinister and menacing air.

I stepped forward and shook Daniel's hand. "Good to meet you Daniel," I said. "Thank you so much for all you have done. I'm very grateful." Daniel's piercing blue eyes peered out from beneath his hood as he nodded without saying a word.

"Daniel does not speak much English," offered Alex, "but he is a good and reliable man. His older brother, Adam, and I have been friends for a long, long time. We would watch the football together and then drink and fight the enemy," he joked, shadow boxing around me, just as I remembered him often doing when we would talk in our cell.

"Dziękuje Daniel, mam przyjemność spotkać się," I said, nodding in Daniel's direction, doing my best to greet him and offer my gratitude in Polish as best I could.

Once more Daniel nodded while offering a mumbled response. "Miło mi cię poznać." Daniel might not have been the most engaging conversationalist but at least he had returned my greeting, and although I was not certain at that point just how he had traced the pharmacist, I was damn pleased that he had.

As we waited to cross the busy thoroughfare, trams rumbled past in both directions. Alex pointed out how the layout of Nowa Huta resembled Paris with many buildings being built in a Renaissance style. He explained how the Communists wanted to build a city to rival Krakow in splendour, and how the back breaking project had been completed in an incredible ten years. "At the top of the hill ahead," Alex proudly informed me, "is the steelworks where the workers belonged to the Solidarity unions. These brave and great men helped to bring independence to our country."

Alex pointed to a spot where a huge statue of Lenin once stood until it was pulled down by local residents in 1989. No sooner had he done so than he ushered me into a lavishly decorated establishment with pillars, a high ceiling, polished mirrors, wooden panelling and padded chairs. "This is Stylowa," announced Alex, with his arms held open, surveying the surroundings. "This was at one time the place to be seen here in Nowa Huta. High ranking officials, doctors and many important people would come here to eat, to drink and to dance."

Daniel and I sat down and I looked around as Alex went up to the bar to order us drinks. The décor was reminiscent of photographs I had seen of places in London, Paris and New York in the 1920's, and the way the light filtered through the heavy drape curtains added to the feeling that this was a place plucked from a bygone age. Daniel sat opposite me, his eyes downcast, consulting his mobile phone, his hood still pulled up obscuring much of his face. Other than Alex, Daniel and I, Stylowa was practically empty; apart from the three of us and the staff, there was only one other customer. A young lady sat at a table in the corner, drinking coffee and reading a newspaper. Alex returned to the table and sat down. "The waitress will bring over our drinks shortly," he said.

Alex explained that a representative of the pharmacist would meet us in Stylowa and that if all appeared to be well, the representative would take me to meet the man. Afterwards I would meet back up with Alex and Daniel in the bar. It all seemed a little bit 'cloak and dagger' to me, but Alex explained that Mr. Markowicz was from a time when the Communist regime had kept a tight rein, and any subversion could well lead to members of the public being whisked away by the secret police, often never to be seen again. "There are many old timers here in Poland who still live with that fear and paranoia," Alex informed me.

"So, Alex, tell me," I began, changing the subject, "what have you been doing in Prague?"

"Yes, I live in Prague these days," Alex answered, "with my wife, Kristina. You will like her, I am sure." Pointing a mock accusing finger at me, he added. "But no touching Steve, or I will kill you." Alex laughed, although

I would not hesitate to believe his intention nor would I deem it likely that I would wish to put his words to the test.

"I would never do such a thing, I promise," I assured him, placing my right hand on my heart, just as an attractive waitress arrived at our table carrying a tray on which were three beers and three glasses of cherry vodka. She proceeded to place our drinks on the table in front of us as Alex continued.

"I know what you convicts are like," he laughed. "You get out of prison and every sniff of pussy makes you mad." I smiled nervously as the waitress gave me a sideways glance as she placed my drinks in front of me, before coolly heading back in the direction of the bar and kitchen. Alex explained how he had met Kristina at a music club in Krakow. A raven haired Czech national, she had been living in the city while she taught music. They had dated for a while and when she had announced that she was returning to Prague, Alex had decided to move there with her. They had rented a flat together and had been married for a little over four months.

"It sounds like things have worked out well for you, Alex," I said. "I'm very happy that you have fallen on your feet. Tell me," I continued, after taking a mouthful of beer, "are you enjoying work? Are you playing music again?"

"This I want to discuss with you, my friend," Alex began, raising his glass of cherry vodka as if in preparation for a toast. "But first, the vodka, this is how we do business here in Poland," he added with a smile. "Na zdrowie. Good health." In unison, Alex and I downed our shots in one. Daniel momentarily looked up from his phone and then drank his shot too, without saying a word. The young lady sitting at the corner table folded up her newspaper, stood up and gracefully glided past us, placing her empty cup and saucer on the bar as Alex continued. "In Prague, I am managing a new music club which we hope will open soon. There are many good bands in the city and so we are hoping to have live music every night."

"That sounds like a great idea," I replied, as my attention was momentarily diverted by the young woman who appeared to be preparing to leave.

"Yes," said Alex. "We have already had much interest. The bar is in a good location and..."

"Mr Caldwell?" I felt a hand on my shoulder and heard a soft voice behind me. "You will come with me, please." I turned in my seat and looked up. It was the young woman who had been sitting quietly in the corner drinking coffee.

"I'm sorry, Alex," I said, a little flustered, "can we continue this conversation a little later?"

"Yes. Yes, of course. Now go," he urged as I stood to my feet. "We will wait for you here. Go." Alex waved towards the door, gesturing me to leave. I raised my hand to gesture goodbye and followed the young woman outside, pausing only momentarily to allow her to collect her three quarter length dark red coat.

"Obviously you know who I am," I said, trying to break the awkward silence as I followed her around the corner and under a large archway which came out into a square flanked by four storey apartment buildings. "So, what's your name?" I asked my companion in the red coat, trying to work her out and studying her appearance with interest. In her red coat, blue jeans, calf length black boots and with shoulder length, mousy blonde hair, she was neither unattractive nor strikingly beautiful. Her apparent reticence towards communication certainly seemed to cross the border into impolite. She struck me as aloof, stand-offish and totally indifferent to my presence. Despite the quickness of her step, she walked with distinguished elegance, her head held high and her vision focused directly ahead. The gracious nature of her poise and deportment belied the ungracious nature of her cool and churlish attitude.

She led me across the square until we abruptly stopped by a park bench in the centre. "You will wait here," she ordered before walking off into the autumnal afternoon mist. I waited, watching her image fade from view, the hem of her red coat flapping and waving in the breeze as she wafted along the leaf strewn pathway as if floating on air. I lit a cigarette and sat down on the damp wooden bench.

Obediently, I waited.

Chapter 7

A Visit to the Pharmacist

I took one last pull on my cigarette and flicked the butt away, watching as it looped up in an arc and landed on the pathway about six feet away. I observed it closely as the dying embers smouldered among the damp, dead leaves. Aimlessly, I looked down at my feet. To my annoyance, I noticed a scuff on one of my new boots. Uncertain as to whether it might be a mark that could be easily wiped off, I bent down and ran my thumb across it. Sure enough, it was a scuff mark. I had been browsing leather jackets in a shop in Poznan when I had noticed these black motorcycle boots. I had always wanted a pair but could never justify spending the money. Although the boots were expensive, I liked the style of them; calf length, heavy set, steel toecaps, two buckles and a zip up the back. On further inspection, I had noted the white fleece lining inside. Just perfect for the cold Polish winters, I thought to myself. I decided that, despite its shabby appearance, my old leather jacket and I had an unbreakable bond. It had character, it had personality and it had patiently hung inside a secure penitentiary for a quarter of a century, waiting for the two of us to be reunited. Despite the extravagance of the price tag I chose the boots, and it was those boots that now had a scuff across one toe.

Feeling tense and killing time, I diverted my attention away from what was in reality only a minor blemish in the leather. I watched the smoke from my discarded cigarette end rise and twist before drifting away on the gentle breeze. Killing time was something that I really should have got used to by now, but my agitation made it clear that I had obviously never mastered the art. Some ten or fifteen minutes had elapsed since the surly young woman in the red coat had ordered me to wait. I reached inside my jacket pocket and pulled out my cigarette packet. It was not that I felt the craving for another, just that it was something to preoccupy my time a little longer. I drew a cigarette from the pack and as I put it to my lips, I heard the sound of footsteps, muffled by the damp leaves. I looked up, replacing the unlit cigarette in the pack, which in turn I slipped back in my pocket.

"This way, follow me," the woman in the red coat ordered succinctly, in a tone that was hushed yet not quite a whisper, but curt nevertheless. Although a 'sorry to have kept you waiting out here in the cold and damp' might have been appreciated, I complied with her instruction obediently. Perhaps those long years in prison, following orders without question, had conditioned me to a point where I functioned as an automaton; obedient, mechanical, unemotional. In compliance with her instructions, I followed. Her step was brisk and she walked slightly ahead of me. Anything to avoid the possibility of conversation, I thought to myself. Once again I noticed how her unbuttoned red coat caught the breeze. It's always the little details I notice. Perhaps my attention to detail was the result of spending years with nothing much to pass the time, I suppose. One gets preoccupied with little details until they manifest themselves into an obsession. I followed the woman in the red coat across the square, and we paused at the side of the road, allowing a silver car to cruise past without its occupant taking any notice of us. I sensed her anxiety at having to wait, even though it was only a matter of seconds.

We crossed the road and she drew a set of keys from her coat pocket to unlock the main door that led into an apartment block. It was an unassuming entrance way, consistent with every entrance doorway in every other block in this identical complex. I followed her up the stairs, watching as she selected another key from the set in her hand. We stopped at a door on the second floor. Turning the key in the lock, she opened it and I followed her inside. "Please take off your shoes," she said, pointing down at my recently scuffed boots. As I bent down to comply with her request, she offered, almost politely, "may I take your jacket for you?"

"Thank you," I replied as I placed my heavy boots neatly side by side in the hallway before removing my jacket and handing it to her. She hung my green combat jacket on the hat stand, next to her red coat. At the foot of the hat stand I noticed a pair of wooden walking sticks.

"This way, please" she said, gesturing me into a room beyond the hallway, and once I was inside the living room, the young lady closed the door behind me. The room was small without giving the appearance of being cramped, and a cream coloured three-piece suite took up most of the floor space, and a coffee table was set in the centre of the room. Light filtered in from the window at the far end, next to which was a large and modern looking television. I looked out through a window which overlooked the tree lined road below, with an identical apartment block beyond that. I sat down on the sofa, taking a moment to admire an ornate and heavy looking oak dresser which housed a number of books. Two vases of flowers stood at each end of the dresser, and there were a number of framed photographs, some of which were clearly taken many years ago.

One sepia toned formal family portrait caught my eye immediately. In another black and white image, a couple on their wedding day; the bride, beautiful in her long white dress, a garland of flowers in her long dark hair, and the groom, handsome and well presented in his dark suit and bow tie. These must have all been photographs depicting the life and times of Stanislaw Markowicz, I thought to myself. In a colour image which looked as if it might have been taken quite recently, an elderly gentleman stood smiling in the sunshine, aided by a walking stick, and pictured beside him was the young woman who had escorted me to the apartment. I stood up and leaned across the coffee table to take a closer look. In the photo, her smile conveyed warmth which belied the image that I had formed of a woman who was colder than the prison exercise yard in the depths of winter.

As I continued to study the photographs, the door opened and a frail and elderly gentleman entered, assisted by the young lady in the photograph. "Please, please, sit down," the elderly gentleman urged, as he was helped into his armchair. Once he was seated, the young lady left, closing the door behind her.

I stood, leaned over and shook his frail and arthritic hand before sitting back down. "Mr. Markowicz?" I asked, before adding apologetically, "I'm sorry, but I was just admiring your photographs."

The old man nodded and smiled, seemingly pleased that I had taken an interest in his collection of personal mementos. Pointing at the sepia portrait with his walking stick, he explained, "this one was taken not long after I moved in here with my mother, father and sister. That was in 1958," he added proudly. "Nowa Huta was still being built then, and we were happy to have the opportunity to live somewhere clean, bright and new. All the apartments were the same, and all apartments were furnished the same too," the old man explained. "Our Communist benefactors wished to ensure that everyone was equal, having the same homes and the same possessions. Of course," he added with a wry chuckle, "some lucky people had bigger homes, with better furniture, because some are more equal than others. In the Avenue of Roses, we even had a statue of Lenin to remind us all of who we were to be thankful to. This picture," he continued, pointing with his stick, "is of my sister. She is two years older than me and she must now live in a rest home near Lublin. And this photo," he continued, pointing to another, "was taken on the day of our wedding in 1963. Sadly, my wife died two years ago."

"She was beautiful," I said, offering my condolences.

Stanislaw then went on to explain how his wife, Irena, had never come to terms with the sudden and tragic death of their daughter and son-in-law, who had died after their car had been in collision with a drunk driver. "My granddaughter was the only one to survive that night," he informed me, pointing out the colour photograph that I had been closely studying a few minutes earlier. "Helena has lived here ever since, and she has been a great help now that I am so old."

Helena, I thought to myself. Finally the abrupt young woman in the red coat had a name. "I don't think your granddaughter likes me very much," I said with a smile.

"I'm sorry if she appears rude," Stanislaw offered, apologetically. "She is very protective towards her old grandfather, and she did not think that meeting you was a good idea."

"I'm very thankful to you for agreeing to meet with me," I replied sincerely, just as the door opened and Helena entered with a tray, upon which she carried a pot of tea in an ornate china teapot with matching cups and saucers, a bowl of sugar and a plate of biscuits. She placed the tray on the coffee table. "Thank you, Helena," I said politely as she poured two cups of tea. The malevolence in her sideways glance was colder than an Arctic blizzard, convincing me that she would be much happier once I was gone.

"At first we were frightened when your friends came to our door," Stanislaw explained. "It was just like when the secret police would knock many years ago." I offered my apologies, telling him that I had not even been aware that attempts had been made to find him on my behalf. "I am sure that we are not here to talk about friends or old photographs, Mr. Caldwell," Stanislaw said, coming straight to the point as Helena left the room once more, pausing only for a moment to place her hand gently on her grandfather's shoulder, a tender gesture of reassurance that she would not be too far away.

Stanislaw sat forward in his chair. "These long years have not been comfortable for me," he began, his voice tinged with sadness and regret, "but I hope that you do not hold too much resentment towards me or my family for the injustice you have suffered." I assured him that I did not hold him in any way responsible for anything that had happened to me, and questioned why he should feel that way. Stanislaw seemed to breathe a sigh of relief and then relaxed back in his chair. "Thank you, Mr. Caldwell," he continued, "but I should have done more. I always knew that you did not kill that poor girl but I said nothing, afraid for myself and my family."

I sat quietly and attentively as Stanislaw told his story. "The police questioned me after the girl was found dead; in fact they questioned everyone who was in the hotel that night" he began. "I remember that one of my colleagues had earned a promotion at the hospital where I was working as a pharmacist. We had been out to celebrate and because it would be too late to get a tram home, I had chosen to spend the night at the hotel." He continued to explain how he had been unable to sleep that night and thought that a late night stroll might settle him. As he had opened his hotel room door, ensuring that he did so quietly so as not to disturb any other guests, he noticed quite clearly at the other end of the hallway, two men carrying a young blonde woman, who he would later consider to be Annika Radwanski.

"What did these two men look like?" I asked, feeling my tension rising as I drew myself forward to the edge of the sofa.

"The hallway light was right above them," explained Stanislaw, "so I could see them clearly, although I could not hear what they were saying because they were whispering to each other. One man was tall, with pale skin and his hair was brown and scruffy, and he was the one who knocked on the door. The other man was shorter and a little fat and he had lighter hair. Once the door opened, they took the girl inside."

Stanislaw's revelation left me feeling cold. After years of being kept in the dark, it was as if someone had just turned the light on and I could see everything more clearly. I urged Stanislaw to please continue. "After the door had closed," he said, "I was curious and so I quietly made my way to the door and tried to listen to what was happening inside. I could hear voices, although I could not understand what they were saying. They spoke in English, but at that time my English was not so good. I could here three voices, two men and one woman, and they sounded like they might be arguing or scared. After a while it sounded like they were preparing to leave. I panicked and hurried back to my room where I watched with my door only open a little. The tall man came out first and as he stepped into the light, it looked like he had blood on his clothing. Then the shorter man came out, followed by a blonde woman who closed the door. It was definitely not the same blonde woman as I had seen go in. This one was not as slim, had shorter hair and wore different clothes."

I sat transfixed, listening to Stanislaw relate his memories of that night. I felt frozen, my mind turning cartwheels, trying to process all the information it was receiving. Everything was finally starting to fall into place. "I can remember clearly that the short man sounded scared," Stanislaw elaborated. "He was only whispering, but he sounded afraid of something. That was when the blonde woman snapped at him and I remember it sounded like she called him Peter."

"Peter?" I questioned, as the final piece of the puzzle fell into place. "Are you certain?"

"Yes, I am," The old man replied, his memories of that night were obviously still clear. "I can also remember giving the police this name when they interrogated me." The old man went on to tell me how he had gone downstairs to the hotel reception desk and that it was he who had called for the police. The receptionist had seen the two men and the woman leave but she had only recognised the shorter man from earlier. "Somehow," said Stanislaw, "the short man must have distracted the hotel receptionist and so she did not see the tall man or the dead girl enter the hotel."

The old pharmacist had done his civic duty just as anyone else would have done. He had asked the hotel receptionist to call the police, and he had given them a full account of what he had witnessed that night. "The police came to our home at night," he explained "and they took me away in a car. It was dark, I was tired and I did not know where they took me. For three days, they deprived me of sleep and kept asking me the same questions."

Although I would not have recognised him, Stanislaw told me that it was he who had stood in the hallway on the morning of my arrest, and had seen me beaten on the floor. He feared the brutality of the police but had been sure that they had arrested the wrong man, and this he tried to explain when they questioned him. "I became scared and confused," he continued. "How could I be sure? They asked. How could I be trusted? They asked.

Why would anyone want a pharmacist who was confused and could not be trusted? They asked."

It soon became apparent to Stanislaw that his testimony would not be a welcome one. In fear for his own safety and future, and for that of his family too, he had eventually been worn down to the point that he no longer felt in a position to act as a witness for the defence. It had been the police who suggested that perhaps he should consider taking a holiday somewhere otherwise they may have to report him to his employers. "They said that I must have been working too hard and needed a rest so that I would no longer be too confused to do my job."

I reassured him that he did not have to feel bad for what had happened to me as it had not been his fault. He explained how the story had been reported in the state run newspaper, highlighting the dangers of foreign musicians with their messages of sex and drugs, attempting to subvert the youth. I had been portrayed as not only a murderer, but also as an enemy of the state, just as Alex had suggested. My trial and conviction was there to serve as a warning and I had been offered forward as a convenient scapegoat. It now appeared clear to me that irrespective of whether or not the police knew the identities of those actually involved, Gary Spackman, Peter Fankham and his sister had conspired to cover their own backs at the expense of my liberty. Despite the fact that Stanislaw Markowicz had spent many a sleepless night, uncomfortable in the knowledge that he had known the truth, I did all I could to reassure him that he had nothing to feel guilty about.

My words of reassurance appeared to comfort him and to finally ease his mind. It was clear that he was an old man who had lived through more than his fair share of pain and heartbreak, and the fact that he had been so troubled by the injustice that I had been served, made me feel truly humbled. As we shook hands and parted company that afternoon, I made sure he was in no doubt that I considered him to be an honourable man for whom I had nothing but respect and admiration. It could not have been easy for him to agree to meet me and relate his story, but nevertheless he had done so with a courage and conviction that was truly admirable. Yes, of course I still had many questions, but at least I now knew that the answers to those questions lay somewhere else, in the hands of Gary, Peter and Debbie.

As I prepared to leave, I asked Helena about her grandfather's sister. "Does he ever get to visit her?"

"It is a long way to Lublin and he is an old man," she replied. "I am sure that he would like to visit her, but he never wishes to speak of it."

"That is such a shame," I said, stepping out onto the landing beyond the front door. "Goodbye, Helena, and thank you."

"Goodbye, Mr. Caldwell, and thank you also," she replied, closing the door behind me.

Chapter 8

Clint Eastwood

As I walked back to the bar to meet Alex and Daniel, I had a feeling that I owed the old man a great debt of gratitude. I would be eternally thankful to Stanislaw for his warmth and his honesty, as his recollection of events had finally put so much into a context which afforded me an element of clarity which I had long been denied. Now that he had spoken to me personally, I believed that he was finally relieved of his personal long standing compunction, and I hoped that he would now be able to enjoy his twilight years free of regret. Regardless, I still felt that I owed him more. True to their word, Alex and Daniel were waiting for me when I returned.

"How was your pharmacist?" Alex asked when I got back to the bar. "Was he helpful to you?"

"Yes, very helpful, thank you," I replied, holding back on the details, not wanting to say too much in a public place. Daniel had walked outside and through the window I could see that he was talking on his mobile phone. "Is he OK?" I asked Alex, nodding in Daniel's direction as I sat down.

"As I told you," Alex explained, "today you will meet two people. You have met one already and I believe that something he has told you today will mean that you will need to meet the other. Have you the money I told you to bring?" he asked.

"Yes, of course." I replied.

"Good," said Alex. "Daniel must make a telephone call to make sure that all is cool for your second visit." The door of the bar opened and Daniel gestured to us, prompting Alex and I to follow him up the road and around the corner to where a black BMW was parked on the street. Daniel unlocked the car with a remote key, climbed in behind the steering wheel and started the engine. Alex rode shotgun on the passenger seat and I got into the back.

"I think that your pharmacist has told you a story that has made you think about going to England to maybe take care of some business," Alex began, cutting through the silence as Daniel drove us through the maze of streets, passing countless uniform apartment blocks. "I'm sure that you will not wish to travel as Mr. Caldwell, and I'm sure that our friend will provide you with everything that you will need to ensure that you can get in and out of England without anyone knowing you were ever there."

"That could be very useful, Alex," I said, looking wistfully through the side window and thankful for his foresight. "I think that I might have some old friends that I would like to visit, although I'm not sure that they will want to see me."

"I thought so," Alex mused, glancing over at Daniel knowingly. Turning his head to face me, he added. "I expect you have much to say to your... friends."

The black car pulled into a parking space adjacent to a large tree lined square which was flanked on all sides by apartment blocks. "I may not actually say that much," I responded, stoically.

Daniel led us from the car to a doorway, and we entered the stairwell before making our way to the second floor. As we reached the landing, he knocked on a door and, a few moments later, we heard the clunk of heavy bolts and the door opened slightly, retained by a security chain. Once the occupant was satisfied as to the identity of his visitors, he removed the chain and opened the door. A short, balding man, with a Lech Walesa moustache and spectacles, ushered us inside after he had checked the landing to ensure that no one saw us enter. I noticed how the layout of the apartment was similar to the one which Stanislaw Markowicz occupied. As there appeared to be no other occupant in the property, I assumed that the little bald man was the forger who I had been brought to see.

We were directed into the living room and I sat down on the outdated brown draylon sofa. "Stand up," the little bald man ordered sharply as he inspected me closely. "Have you the money?" he asked, looking at all three of us in turn.

I took out a roll of notes from my pocket and counted out the 5000 Zloty just as had been requested, and I offered the wad of notes to the forger. "I am pleased to meet you," I said politely, "I'm Steve, Steve Caldw..."

The little bald man cut me off mid sentence. "And I am Clint fucking Eastwood, the man with no name," Clint barked sharply and bluntly as he meticulously counted the notes in his hand. "I am not interested in who you are, only your money. Now sit down please."

Alex, Daniel and I sat down promptly and obediently so as not to incur the wrath of Mr. fucking Eastwood, who by this point had opened the doors of an aged wooden dresser and was kneeling down in front of it while he reached into the back. Eventually his arm re-emerged with his hand gripping a cardboard box which he promptly placed on the coffee table in front of us. We all watched as Clint removed the lid and placed it next to the box. The removal of the lid unveiled what appeared to be a collection of passports and driving licences from various nations, and he flicked through the collection thoughtfully, pausing to check each British one. Lifting one passport out of the box, the forger looked over at me pensively before placing it back. As he continued to peruse the box's contents, he occasionally scanned me carefully. "What is your age?" Clint asked abruptly. Dutifully, I informed him that I was 48 years old.

"Really?" Clint questioned, remarking in a less than complimentary manner "you look older." After examining a British passport in one hand and a driving licence in the other, he finally stood up and announced, "you are John Turner and you are 47 years old. Follow me please Mr. Turner." After pausing to glance quizzically at Alex and Daniel, I followed Mr. Eastwood into another room where a simple wooden chair was positioned in front of a white sheet that hung from the wall. "Please, take off your jacket and sit down," he said, gesturing to the chair, before selecting one of several cameras from a shelf behind him. He attached it to a tripod and adjusted its height, crouching to check through the view finder before taking a couple of shots and checking the results.

"Take off your shirt please," he barked, succinctly. I complied with his request without question, removing my black t-shirt while forger left the room. Moments later he returned carrying a white shirt. "This may not be your style," he said, tossing me the shirt, "but put it on." I did as he asked, fastening all the buttons except the top one, and presented myself sitting upright on the wooden chair. Clint took a few more shots and studied the results before announcing that we were done. "Get dressed, Mr. Turner and follow me."

Back in the living room, I found Mr. Eastwood pouring out three glasses of cherry vodka. 'That's how we do business in Poland,' I remembered Alex saying. After the drinks had been hastily consumed, the forger shook each of our hands in turn, nodding in appreciation. Just prior to shaking mine, he put his hand in his pocket and drew out a key and handed it to me. Clint clasped both his hands around mine and closed my fingers tightly around the key. "Keep this safe," he said, his tone far less terse than it had been. "In two weeks, you will take this key to the main train station in Krakow. This key will open luggage locker number 53. Inside it you will find all that you need." The forger shook my hand tightly. "Good luck, Mr. Turner."

I thanked Mr Eastwood, and then Alex, Daniel and I followed him to the door. Suspiciously, he checked the landing before opening it just enough to allow us to squeeze through. Once the three of us were beyond the threshold of the apartment, I turned to thank Mr.

Eastwood once more, and he nodded silently before slamming the door, and the sound echoed along the landing. As we made our way back down the stairs, we could hear the sound of chains fastening and dead bolts clunking fading into the distance.

It was already getting dark when we got back in the car, and once the three of us were inside, Alex turned to face me. "A good day's business so far?" he asked.

"Yes," I replied, "I can't thank you two enough."

"Tonight we celebrate your release," announced Alex cheerily. "We will drink, we will sing and you and I still have business to discuss." Alex smiled and turned to look at Daniel. "C'mon, what are we waiting for? Let's go."

Chapter 9

Purgatorio

After all that Alex had done for me, I felt guilty that I had been far too distracted to show my thanks to the extent that he deserved. Both he and Daniel had been very good to me, not only on that particular day, but in all they had done to find Stanislaw, arrange meetings and bring it all together. In the evening, Alex had organised a party to celebrate my release, and not only had it been an opportunity for him to be back among his own, but it was a chance for me to meet his friends too. We all got drunk on strong beer and vodka while exchanging stories of youthful stupidity, our time spent in prison and general tales of bravado. However hard I tried to enjoy the evening, my mind was preoccupied by all that the old pharmacist had told me. The more often his words went round in my head, the more my blood boiled. I may have been unable to fathom how or why Annika Radwanski had so unfortunately become embroiled in those events, but from what I could gather from Stanislaw's descriptions, it could only have been Gary, Peter and Debbie who were involved.

It angered me each time, when the thought of the three of them plotting against me came to the forefront of my thoughts, and I still could not shake off the fact that Debbie, my wife, had lied to cover for the guilty parties during my trial. Even when Alex sat me down to excitedly explain how the club project in Prague was progressing, it was the pharmacist's words which I concentrated on. I found myself constantly saying, "I'm sorry Alex, what did you say, again?" Stanislaw had spent twenty-five years regretting that he had vital information which he had held back, even though he never really had the option of doing otherwise. The others, however, had buried the truth, colluded together, covered their own backs and done so at my expense. Not once in all that time had any feelings of guilt or remorse ever compelled any of them to breathe a word. Mental images flashed into my mind of the three conspirators, bound and gagged, wide-eyed and awaiting their fate, as back in Stanislaw Markowicz's apartment, my mind had already found all three of them guilty of crimes against me. Even though I tried hard to convince myself that any thoughts of wreaking revenge would only be to serve justice for Annika's sake, I could feel that my resentment toward my transgressors was fuelling an appetite for revenge, and I sensed that the growing appetite would only be satisfied by murder.

Anger clouded my judgement and I wanted revenge to be swift and painful, but I also reasoned that I could do nothing that would risk the possibility of me going back inside. I tried hard to calm myself with the assurance that I would act, and all three would eventually see their judgement day. I would have to placate my anger with the knowledge that retribution would have to be measured, considered, composed and, most importantly, I would have to remain clear of any implication. I tried hard to focus my attention on what Alex was telling me. "When the club is up and running," he said, "we will have a place where we can put our band together, just like we always said we would." I smiled. It was a nice idea. "Here's to Skazaniec," shouted Alex, raising his glass.

"To Skazaniec," I had responded, raising my glass too. Alex proposed that I should move to Prague and work in the club too as, after all, I would need to work and there were not going to be too many opportunities for someone like me. With a rising level of alcohol fuelled excitement, he had told me that he knew of musicians who could join us. He could teach me some of his old songs, I could teach him some of mine and with a few cover versions thrown into the mix, we could be the first band to play on opening night. Although such a venture would require practice, I had to admit that his idea sounded good.

oooOOOooo

The following day I left Krakow and returned to Poznan by train, reaching my apartment quite late in the evening. Alex had understood that although I appreciated his suggestions about relocating to Prague, there were certain things that were standing in my way, things that would need to be brought to a conclusion before I would be able to move on. He realised that my answer had not been 'no', it was a 'not just yet'. Of course, as I sat on the train for that seven hour journey, I did begin to consider how easy it might be to relocate to Prague. The city was a little more than 350 km away, and Alex had painted a wonderful picture, offering limitless opportunities, and there was nothing to actually keep me in Poznan. Most of the journey however, I had been preoccupied by the words of the old pharmacist. Strangely enough, it was not only the words which he had spoken that troubled me, but it was also something about the man himself.

I thought of his collection of photographs and felt saddened that, other than the loyalty of his granddaughter, life had robbed him of so much. The image of Stanislaw and his wife on their wedding day concealed the heartache which they must have endured when they lost their only child and their son-in-law so cruelly. Undoubtedly, he must have worked hard throughout his life, only to lose his lifelong partner and be deprived of the two of them living into old age together. I was humbled that despite his losses, heartache and hardship, he still found time to consider the injustice served to someone he had only witnessed for a few seconds, taking a pounding in a hotel hallway. I felt guilty for considering Helena to be nothing but a cold hearted, ball breaking bitch, as she was a woman who had witnessed the lives of her parents being torn from them by a drunk driver. Despite her suffering and anguish, she had the compassion to care for her elderly grandfather with a loyalty that was truly admirable. As they say, never judge someone unless you have walked a mile in their shoes.

oooOOOooo

On the day following my return to Poznan, I telephoned Thurstan. I wanted to let him know how my meeting with Stanislaw had gone, and also, I was intrigued to discover how he had managed to learn the identity of the old pharmacist in the first place. Thurstan had quickly cut me short, insisting that there were certain conversations that would be best conducted in person and in private too. He preferred to wonder what my future plans might be, if indeed I had any, and when we discussed the proposition which Alex had put to me, Thurstan sounded genuinely interested.

"I'm sure you'd love Prague," he said, informing me how often he was required to go there on business trips. "Much of my work involves corporate law," Thurstan confessed, "and we have clients who are based in the Czech Republic. It would be a good opportunity for you to start afresh and become involved in something which I'm sure would interest you." Thurstan informed me that he was due some time off in the New Year, and suggested that he could come over and visit for a few days. He felt sure that we could find a concert or two to attend, and it would also give us an opportunity to discuss the pharmacist.

"It really would be great to see you," I replied, before adding, "you're welcome to crash here, as long as you don't mind slumming it on the couch." And so we agreed that nearer the time we would make some firm arrangements.

oooOOOooo

Over the next few days, I did my best to occupy my mind with things that were constructive, and commenced by purchasing a laptop computer. I had been afforded the opportunity of learning a little about computer technology while I was still in prison and, within no time, I was able to keep in touch with the few friends I had, via email. Dave, my former band's vocalist, had actually been the only one of my old friends to keep in touch while I was in prison. His letters, although often heavily censored by the prison staff before reaching my hand, were greatly anticipated and appreciated, and his communications had done much to keep my spirits buoyant. I had of course written to him to inform him of my release, and let him know that I now had an email address. I had been excited to receive a reply from him a week or so later and, from then on, we were able to keep in touch more often. Our companionship would later prove to be an invaluable asset to me.

My arduous return train journey from Krakow had made me realise that, if I were to gain full independence, I would need a car. A neighbour was selling a red Volkswagen Polo and, although I considered it to be a little on the small side, he assured me that I would find it comfortable, reliable and cheap to run. And so a deal was struck and I became the proud owner of a car, just in time to return to Krakow and collect the documents which the forger had promised to deposit in the train station locker. However, my first road trip coincided with the first early snowfall of winter, ensuring that it would have probably been quicker to have travelled by train.

Clint Eastwood had been true to his word, and inside luggage locker 53 was an envelope which, on closer inspection, contained a passport and drivers licence, both in the name of John Turner. "A white shirt? What was he thinking?" I smiled to myself as I looked at my photograph on the documents before tucking them safely back into the envelope. The elderly pharmacist and his granddaughter had played heavily on my mind since we had met, and I felt compelled to pay them a visit that day. Helena had been shocked and a little disgruntled to find me on their doorstep but, despite her initial mistrust, I had a proposition to put to her and her grandfather.

Despite Helena's initial reticence, I had managed to convince her that my offer held no ulterior motive, and the following morning I returned to collect her and Stanislaw. The three of us braved the wintry conditions and I drove them the 330 km to Lublin to enable Stanislaw to see his ailing sister. Apparently, the old man had been too unwell to visit his daughter's grave on All Saints Day and so, after stopping at a roadside florist, we had taken a short detour to the cemetery. I waited in the car while Stanislaw and his granddaughter paid their respects and they had returned dewy eyed, with Helena resting a comforting arm around her grandfather's shoulder. When we arrived at our destination in Lublin, I once again waited patiently in the car but, despite the cold, I felt that it was something which I had to do. My kindness that day was rewarded by an invite to Stanislaw and Helena's Wigilia, the traditional feast on Christmas Eve. I felt honoured to be invited into their home on such an important festive occasion and share in the feast that Helena had painstakingly prepared. Not wishing to outstay my welcome, I left their apartment just before midnight and made the long, lonely drive back to Poznan, arriving back at just before 5am on Christmas Day.

Although we were never destined to become firm friends, Helena was added to my email list and I was saddened when, in March, I received word from her that Stanislaw's sister had passed away peacefully in her sleep. Once again, she thanked me for the day I had taken them to Lublin, informing me that her grandfather often spoke of his gratitude. He was happy to have been afforded one final chance to see his sister before she passed away.

I too was thankful for an opportunity to divert my thoughts from the one thing that was never far from my mind - revenge.

I had not yet planned quite how I would track down Debbie, Peter and Gary, if indeed they were still alive, but while the rest of the world celebrated the Christmas and New Year festivities, I pondered how I could ensure that the three of them would not see another one.

oooOOOooo

At the end of January I had another timely diversion, when Thurstan Reeve flew over and stayed for a few days. I got to show him the delights of Poznan and spend some time getting to know him as a friend, rather than a legal advisor. Although he was some twenty years younger than I and his appearance suggested that he could never be mistaken as an old school punk rocker, his knowledge of the music both past and present, far exceeded my own. He asked many questions about my days in the band, what I remembered about the music in the late seventies and early eighties, and whether I had any plans to play again. We also discussed my pharmacist friend too.

I related the story of my meeting with Stanislaw, giving him a little insight into the information which the old man had for me, and I also told him of our road trip to Lublin. What still intrigued me was how Thurstan had uncovered the identity of the disappearing pharmacist in the first place. Although he was not comfortable in revealing the full extent of his professional network, a few beers encouraged him to explain in simple terms how he knew someone, who knew some, who, in turn, knew someone else. "Let us consider for a moment," he slurred, perhaps a little unaccustomed to the strength of Polish beer, "that someone might have access to certain historical records. And perhaps, if the right person were to search hard enough, then they might find a name."

And there it was; the facts as to exactly how Thurstan Reeve had uncovered Stanislaw Markowicz's identity were now as clear as mud.

oooOOOooo

It had taken me until March before I had finally got around to making the five hour drive to Prague to visit Alex. I had promised him that as soon as winter had given way to spring, I would take him up on his invitation to spend some time with him and Kristina. Upon my arrival, I discovered that Alex had been right, and Kristina was as lovely as he had described her. She worked during the day as a music teacher in a local school and, with her striking looks and long black hair, her appearance suggested that she was much younger than forty-two years old. The couple rented an apartment close to Vitkov Hill, which was only a thirty minute walk from the centre of Prague, and the week that I spent with them just flew by.

In the evenings, when Kristina was at home, she was a generous and congenial host with a wonderful sense of humour and a passion for cooking. Alex and I spent our days at the club and, although I was not much of a craftsman, I was still able to chip in with some of the much needed work. Alex explained that the lack of money to invest in the project had become an issue, and so work had been sporadic, especially over the winter months. As he showed me around the large cellar space which was eventually to become the Heaven and Hell Club and Music Venue, I could not help but find Alex's enthusiasm to be infectious. He pointed out where the bar would be and where the stage would be constructed. He explained how there would be plenty of space for storage and also pointed out where the backstage area and changing rooms would eventually be.

For those few days, it felt good when we returned to his apartment each evening, tired but fulfilled, covered in dust and grime, following a days' honest labour. After a well needed shower, a change of clothes and a good meal, we relaxed with a few beers before plugging in a couple of Alex's guitars and jamming together. He was a far more accomplished musician than I, and it dawned on me just how much I had forgotten and I was embarrassed by how rusty my playing was. Alex didn't seem to care though, and he was still keen on the idea of forming a band together. By the end of my first week in Prague, my playing had progressed sufficiently to keep alive his hopes of Skazaniec becoming a feasible proposition.

I had returned from Prague feeling positive and enthusiastic, and visited a music shop in Poznan where I spent nearly two hours browsing guitars and amplifiers and marvelling at the modern effects pedals. Without breaking the bank, I came away with a 30 watt Marshall amplifier, an overdrive pedal and an ESP EC-200QM guitar. No, it had meant nothing to me either, but, with its reasonable price tag and blue pearlescent quilt finish, I had decided that it was the guitar for me.

By the time I returned to visit Alex and Kristina again in July, my hours of practising had paid dividends. I took the guitar with me and proudly presented it to Alex on my arrival, but after initially dismissing it as 'a little pretty', its sound had soon won him over. My playing had encouraged Alex to the point where he felt that it was time to look for a bassist and drummer. Developments at Heaven and Hell however, were still being hampered by financial constraints, and it was then that Alex put forward a suggestion. He felt that if I were looking for a financial investment, then the club could be well worth my consideration. I told him that I would certainly give some serious thought to it, even though Alex seemed reluctant to tell me who the other investors in the project were. "At this moment, I can't say. But you will learn, I promise." That was all he would tell me.

oooOOOooo

During those months following my release, another diversion had been the email conversations which I had shared with Dave. He had left his heady rock and roll days long behind him, and now questioned the validity of my idea of possibly attempting to rekindle mine. He sent me internet links to listen to many different kinds of new music. "Punk is dead," he would often write. "It was a genre that was in the moment, and that moment has long gone."

Although he still lived in the same area as he always had done and, thanks to the internet, was still in contact with a few of our old friends, it seemed that the old social scene that I had once known had fragmented long ago. It sounded like everyone I had known had been dispersed by the four winds, although I was interested to learn what had become of our old band mates. I was shocked and saddened to learn that Rob, our original bass player, had died of stomach cancer a few years before and John, our drummer, had suffered two heart attacks. He survived the first one but, sadly, not the second. John had always been a lad who was, as the expression goes, big boned, and had never taken life or his health too seriously. Rob had been complaining of health problems for around two years before he had finally sought medical help, but by then it had been too late. Rob died within two months of his diagnosis.

Rob and John had never seen eye to eye, and it was because of the animosity between them that Rob had decided to quit the band. It was ironic that these two formidable figures had passed away at such relatively young ages. Paul, who had replaced Rob on bass, had given up on music too, and gone on to study computer technology. After moving back to America at the end of the nineties, he had set up a company which had ridden high on the 'dot-com bubble'. When the value of his stocks had risen to exceed fifty million dollars, he bailed, sold up and retired to the Bahamas as a multi-millionaire before he was forty years old. If I said that I was not made a little envious by this news of Paul's good fortune, I would of course be lying, and I got the impression that Dave, despite his philosophical rhetoric, was as jealous as fuck too.

Peter, Dave informed me, had confounded everyone by marrying a woman. We had always thought that, despite his denials, Peter was actually gay, and so when he had announced that he was getting married, the news had caught some by surprise. Dave had heard that Peter and his wife had moved away, somewhere near Wales as far as Dave knew. Dave had always detested Peter and I was not surprised to hear how thrilled he had been to learn that Peter's wife Pam, had seen the light and left him.

"Did you know that Debbie and Gary had become an item?" Dave had tentatively asked me in one email, and I replied that I had only recently been led to that conclusion. In a later email he mentioned that it was his understanding that they were no longer together either, although he was a little sketchy on the details. Our email conversations were usually in depth, but in relation to discussing Gary and my ex, he was often a little guarded, almost as if there was something that he was not telling me.

Toward the end of August, I received another email from Dave in which he explained how his sister-in-law, who lived in Lancashire, was due to go into hospital for a relatively routine operation. Sarah, his wife, had kindly offered to travel up and stay with her sister for a few weeks to help out while she recuperated. This news got me thinking, as I had often mused over the possibility of seeing Dave once again. We had kept in touch over the years and I hoped that I could trust his loyalty. So, while his wife Sarah made plans to play Florence Nightingale in Lancashire, John Turner made plans to fly home to England.

Chapter 10

Passport Control

David Bradshaw and I had been friends longer than either of us dared to remember, and to many who had not known him as long as I, Dave had been known as Brad. I first met Dave on our very first day at school when we were just five years old. Already a pair of social misfits in those formative years, fate and classroom seating arrangements had cast us together. Initially, Dave's lack of imagination had annoyed me. On our first day, the teacher, Miss Pennyworth, had handed every pupil a sheet of sugar paper and a pencil, and instructed us to draw our favourite animal. I set about drawing a horse and then noticed that Dave appeared to be copying my masterpiece. However, when he discretely pointed out that my spelling of the word 'horse' was a little wide of the mark, that was the moment when our friendship was forged.

Dave and I also soon learned that we both lived close to each other, too. This proximity of residence, which would prove to be continuous for the next fifteen years until his parents bought a bigger property in nearby Welling, helped to cement our friendship, as would our joint passion for football and cycling a few years later. Of course we had our fallouts in those early years, which friendships don't? I can clearly remember a disagreement over a game of conkers and then, when we both started to collect matchbox labels, we had a huge row over a discarded matchbox which I had been the first to spot. Dave had wrestled me out of the way to claim it, and further inspection of the box had revealed that it had been the one in the 'Cornish Wrecks' series which I had needed to complete the set. This incident had led to the two of us not speaking to each other for about forty-five minutes. As we grew into adolescence, our sense of camaraderie reached a level where we shared everything. Well, almost everything.

Janet Silcott was two years older than us, and also lived on the same suburban housing estate as we did. Janet was a young lady with a dubious entrepreneurial skill which cornered a very niche market. After school, young lads of all ages could often be found lurking around on the playing field behind the local shops. If she was around, Janet would lead them along the alley that led to the local bus shelter where, if they all paid her ten pence, she would lift her skirt, pull down her knickers and let them see her vagina. Janet placed no age restriction on these events and it was all done on a 'no money, no show' basis. For the lads who had a paper round, a decent pocket money allowance or the gall to steal from their mother's purse, the princely sum of fifty pence would buy them the privilege of actually touching her bush.

In the winter months when it was already dark by the time that most young boys were expected to be home for supper, Janet had devised a way of ensuring that the darkness would not impact on her bank balance. She would arrive, armed with a box of Swan Vestas, and would proceed to carefully position a struck match so as to ensure that her viewing public could still be guaranteed an illuminated view of her nether regions. Humorously, this ingenious practice had earned Janet the nickname Fanny by Matchlight. Any lad who dared to push his luck however, and attempted to venture any further than Janet's furry exterior, would find her to be an aggressive and formidable adversary. After all, Janet Silcott was a young lady with moral standards and as such, it was only her boyfriends who were allowed to finger her.

On one particular day, Dave and I had both bunked off school. We had got as far as the bus stop but decided to spend the day hanging out instead. We waited until our parents would be safely away at work and had then gone back to our respective homes to change. A short while later, Dave and I met up again. I had borrowed a screwdriver from my father's toolbox and Dave had procured a bottle of Blue Label Smirnoff from his father's drinks cabinet. We decided to hide out in the local bus shelter for a while and work out what course our mischief should take. We sat on the bench in the shelter, passing the bottle of vodka between us and laughed at some of the graffiti that embellished the walls. I even used my screwdriver to carve an anarchy symbol in the wooden seat.

It was around that time that Janet Silcott arrived. Always a chatty and outgoing girl, she seemed particularly intrigued to know why two sixteen year olds were not in school on that particular day. According to Janet she was waiting for a bus to take her into Dartford, where she planned to do some shopping. Politely, Dave offered her the bottle of vodka. She took a long gulp and, as the feisty spirit hit her throat, she gagged slightly

102

before wiping her mouth on the back of her hand and then handed the bottle back. "Thanks," she said.

Janet was also intrigued to learn why I needed to be in possession of a screwdriver, while we hung out in the bus shelter rather than attending school. "We're gonna rob some garages," I replied, trying hard to sound more like a villain and less like an immature school boy. Suddenly, as far as Janet was concerned, a bus ride to Dartford seemed far less exciting than a vodka fuelled garage heist with a pair of sixteen year olds. She grabbed the bottle from Dave, took a mouthful and then enthusiastically started to help plan the crime, or maybe I should say, she planned the crime.

Janet scanned the properties which were visible from the bus shelter, noting which ones had cars on the driveway and which ones did not. "That one," she exclaimed, pointing out our target residence and calling my bluff. "There's no car on the drive and the garage is set back from the house. You can see that there's a door on the side that you can use your screwdriver to break open." It seemed apparent that Janet knew exactly what she was talking about. "Go over and check it out," she instructed Dave. He looked at me and I just awkwardly shrugged my shoulders, before Janet and I watched intently as Dave diligently set about his reconnaissance mission. Obviously he had learned much from watching American cop shows on TV, and I was suitably impressed.

A few minutes later, Dave ran back across the main road and informed us that there appeared to be nobody home. Together, the three of us made the return trip, trying hard not to look suspicious. At eleven o'clock in the morning the road was relatively quiet and there appeared to be no one around to witness the crime. Janet, being worldly wise, suggested that she would act as lookout while Dave and I gained access to the garage. After a minute or two of making a complete mess of the woodwork in my unsuccessful attempts to jemmy the lock, Dave pulled on the handle and the already unlocked door opened. We were in.

Inside the garage we found the usual assortment of tools, a full set of golf clubs and a motorbike, stood on its centre stand, parked in the middle. "Oh wow," exclaimed Janet, climbing onto the machine, "I just love motorbikes." She checked her make-up in the mirrors, pulled on the brake levers and twisted on the throttle as if imagining that she were racing along a country lane somewhere idyllic. I think that Dave and I were both feeling a little uncomfortable with the situation, but Janet was in her element and had pretty soon turned our chance meeting into an illicit party in someone else's garage. The bottle of strong vodka had been practically glued to Janet's hand and the alcohol was clearly taking its toll. Her speech slurred a little and grew alarmingly louder. She turned around on the bike seat, hitched up her skirt for comfort, and laid back across the fuel tank, resting her head on the clocks. Dave and I stared at her white thighs and the visible crotch of her blue cotton knickers, and then looked at each other, trying hard not to giggle. Janet may have been talking, but our preoccupation with her underwear seemed to render us deaf.

"Didn't you hear what I said?" Janet questioned, suddenly sitting bolt upright, as she pulled her skirt back over her knees and restored our ability to hear.

"Pardon?" Dave and I said in unison, slightly embarrassed to be caught out.

"I was just saying," Janet slurred, in rather a matter of a fact way, as she returned to her previous prone position on the motorbike, "I was saying that the doctor told me that the rash on my fanny would clear up if I kept applying the cream and taking the antibiotics." Janet hitched up her skirt deliberately and pulled her blue cotton knickers to one side. "There's no discharge now, so it really should be OK," she announced before brazenly offering, "if you want to, you can both fuck me."

So, there it was, Janet had a price list. Ten pence for a look, fifty pence for a feel, and for half a bottle of vodka, she'd re-enact the Kama Sutra, astride a Honda Superdream. Up until that point, my only experiences of seeing ladies' private parts were found in the pages of the top shelf magazines that we occasionally managed to steal from the local newsagents. Gazing upon Janet's holiest of holies, I must confess that it did not look as inviting as any lady garden that I had ever seen before. I thought long and hard about my father's uncomfortable sex education chats and certainly did not relish the prospect of announcing to my family that I had contracted venereal disease. Therefore, I politely made my excuses and left with the bag of golf clubs.

Dave, however, elected to stay a little longer, and although he also graciously turned down the offer of playing Russian Roulette, Janet dutifully rewarded his resolve with a blow job. He and I had met up later in the afternoon, and although I had to contend with his smug sexual self-satisfaction, at least I got first pick of the golf clubs. At an age when male hormones run riot and friendships contain a certain element of one upmanship, I had missed a sure fire open goal and Dave had gone one nil up. However, during the forthcoming school summer holidays, when Dave's fears of contracting some kind of tropical disease of the penis had subsided, and we began playing pitch and putt on the course at Northumberland Heath, the fact that I had a seven iron and a putter certainly gave me the edge.

oooOOOooo

I smiled to myself as I shuffled my way to the front of the queue at Gatwick Airport's passport control, following my 8am flight from Warsaw. Nervously, I thumbed through my forged passport, trying hard to mask my fear of being caught out. I could feel beads of sweat forming on my forehead the closer I got to the head of the line. "My name is John Turner," I kept repeating in my head. Finally, I was at the head of the line, feeling the tension as I waited for my turn to approach the passport control booth. Momentarily I froze as the uniformed official in the booth beckoned me forward. For a second I felt like I should turn and run, but to where? I approached the booth and slid my passport under the security window. For what seemed like an eternity, the official studied my photo and then looked back at me. Eventually, without saying a word, he handed me back my passport. I was clear. I picked up my bag and strolled through 'Nothing to Declare' without a hitch, before making my way to the exit.

I stood outside, squinting in the September morning sunshine before putting on my sunglasses and lighting up a much needed cigarette. Following nearly twenty-six years of enforced absence, I was finally back in England. I

106

was really looking forward to seeing Dave after all these years and I hoped that, despite the nature of my impromptu arrival, he would be pleased to see me too.

Chapter 11 Reminiscence

The front door of the terraced property opened and Dave stood in the hallway, looking perplexed. It had taken me the best part of three hours to find my way from Gatwick Airport to Dave's house in the back streets of Bexleyheath. "Fucking hell, what happened to the cinema and the bowling alley?" I asked. I could almost hear the cogs turning in his head before the penny finally dropped.

"Steve?" Dave asked in disbelief. "Steven Caldwell? Is that you, you old fucker?"

"It's John Turner these days, mate," I whispered, giving him a wink in a conspiratorial way. "Aren't you going to invite me in then?"

"Yes, yes, of course. Come in. What the fuck are you doing here? Why all the cloak and dagger bollocks?" he asked in amazement and suspicion as I stepped across the threshold, pausing for a moment to wipe my feet on the doormat.

"I've come for my royalties cheque," I answered with a smile. A warm handshake was followed by an awkward hug which had been twenty-six years in the waiting.

"Royalties?" Dave scoffed. "You're having a fucking laugh, aren't you? Of course I'll write you a cheque for the sum total of... let's see..." He paused for a moment while he did the sums in his head. "Fuck all split four ways means your cut is roughly... erm... fuck all." He laughed as he ushered me into the living room.

Dave had put on a few pounds in the intervening years and had lost a little hair too but, most strikingly, I could not help but notice his rather pronounced limp as he walked uncomfortably. Despite the changes in his appearance and physicality, Dave Bradshaw had clearly not lost any of his cutting wit or charm. For years he had led his rock and roll lifestyle to excess and as a result of the heavy drinking, the cocaine and his excessive amphetamine use, he had suffered a stroke at the age of thirty-three. Following many months of rehabilitation, most of his mobility had returned, although he had still been left with a slightly stooped shoulder and a disability which explained the limp. After almost a year away from work, he had eventually been able to return to his job as a sound engineer for a local radio station. Unfortunately, due to an amalgamation of positions and job titles, as part of a restructure and money saving exercise, Dave had finally been made redundant and had since turned his hand to freelance writing. "What are you working on?" I asked nonchalantly as I sat down, after noting the word document on his laptop.

"It's a piece about the rise of the right wing in music, back in the early Eighties," he informed me. "I'm basing the article on peoples' personal experiences from that era; you might even be able to help me out with one or two memories of your own," he suggested. "I'm calling it 'A Head Full of Hate, and a Pocket Full of Memories'." I certainly remembered those days well. Crayford Town Hall had at one time been a good place for bands to play, but once the right wing elements had begun to infiltrate such events, they had almost always brought violence and mayhem with them.

"So when are you gonna fly over to Prague and make your comeback?" I flippantly asked.

"What?" Dave laughed mockingly. "With your new mob?" Then, as if he were flicking through the pages of an imaginary diary, he paused. "How does, erm, never sound?" We both laughed. Although in reality I knew that dragging Dave out of retirement was never a possibility, there was just something inside me which hankered for one last shot at the good old days. Our conversation turned to how things had deteriorated in L.I.A.R. once I had been imprisoned and Gary had stepped in to take my place.

"I was never comfortable with it," Dave began, "but when that fucking hippy started to take over and turn us into some sort of Hawkwind cover band, that's when I decided that I was out. I'd been rehearsing with another band for a while, Passed Tense, and so I just jacked it in. I never made an official announcement or anything, I just stopped turning up to L.I.A.R. Rehearsals and let them figure it out. After that, Gary took over on vocals too and changed the name to The Cosmic Knob Scoffers or something equally puerile." Dave shook his head in mock disbelief and I could not help but smile at the cynical way he related the story. "We'd all noticed how The Spaceman and Debbie had started to cosy up together," Dave continued. "He was always going round to see her to make sure she was doing alright, and then the next we heard was that they were living together and having a kid." After a moment's awkward silence, I asked him about Peter.

"I always hated that prick," Dave confessed. "I couldn't stand the way he would never listen to anyone else's opinion." This, I had to agree, was something about Peter which I had also found to be an annoying trait. He would insist on butting into a conversation with his own opinion, even if that opinion had been formed instantaneously, just so that he would not be left out of the conversation. Often, it was Peter's whim to be deliberately obtuse for no other reason than to be an attention seeking annoyance. Dave explained how these traits had led to many fall outs between the two of them over the years. "If someone disagreed with him, he would either sulk or start calling them wankers behind their backs," Dave surmised.

I thought back to the first night that I had spent with Debbie; well, the morning after, to be completely honest. We had both been awake by about 8am and I had gone downstairs to telephone work and let them know that I was feeling 'unwell'. Having made sure to put on my best 'at death's door' voice, I hung up the phone, went back upstairs to Debbie's room, climbed back into bed and then Debbie and I had sex. Afterwards, I retrieved my underwear from the dishevelled heap on her bedroom floor and pulled them on, before taking myself off to the bathroom for my morning piss. When I had opened the bathroom door, I was stunned to be confronted by a chubby young man whose face had an unusual freckled and rubbery appearance. The chubby faced young man stood on the landing, appearing shocked, confused and looking at me like I was a being from another planet.

"Who the fuck are you?" the rubber face chubster had asked rather brusquely.

"I'm Steve," I replied, cheerily. "Who the fuck are you?"

With that, the young man flew downstairs and out of the front door, slamming it behind him with a force so hard that I was surprised that it stayed in the door frame. "Who the fuck was that?" I asked Debbie as she pulled back the quilt, revealing her naked body and enticing me back into bed.

"Oh, that's just my brother, don't take any notice of him," she replied, dismissively, "he's a complete wanker." And that had been my introduction to Peter Fankham; 'take no notice of him, he's a complete wanker'. At the time, I remember thinking that Debbie's description of her sibling was rather harsh, after all, it must have been a shock for him to be confronted on the landing by a stranger wearing nothing but a pair of boxer shorts. But, in time, I would come to the realisation that her description was probably quite accurate. As Dave and I continued to reminisce about the good old days, he mentioned his dislike for Peter's unusual sense of humour too. "He once started a rumour that I was a drug dealer," said Dave. "I couldn't go for a beer without some idiot asking me if I could sort them out with a score. I got sick of telling people to fuck off."

That was also typical of Peter Fankham, a man who had a sense of humour which only he found funny. Often he would say the most inappropriate things at the most inappropriate times, just because he loved getting a reaction. I remembered meeting Dave in a pub one evening and Peter just happened to be there too. I had actually felt quite sorry for Peter on that occasion, as he appeared to be the butt of everyone's jokes and his discomfort at their jibes was clearly apparent. It appeared that the regulars treated him like the village idiot, and he sat quietly on a bar stool nursing the same half pint of lager for two hours. I watched him taking cigarette ends out of the ashtrays on the bar, breaking them open to collect enough tobacco to roll himself a smoke. In a strange way, eventually it would be his sheer stupidity which gained him a level of acceptance and tolerance. Purchasing drugs had always been a risky business and, despite the pleasures which the highs provided, few people were willing to risk getting caught. Peter had such a need and a desire to fit in that he would offer to go and buy drugs for anyone. No one ever gave him the money up front, preferring to wait until he was able to come up with the goods. His payment for the risks he undertook might be in the form of a pint of beer, or perhaps enough hash or weed for him to skin up with on the way home. Although he would consider the people he would gopher for to be his friends, everyone took the piss out of him behind his back, if not to his face. As a gopher, Peter was used more often than a train station urinal, and probably treated with less respect too.

It had been this overwhelming urge to be seen as a man who could organise and get things sorted which had actually made Peter a half decent manager for our band. Yes, there were occasions when he fucked up, but he organised some decent gigs too, and was also happy to drive us around, despite the fact that he had an unusual weaving driving style. His driving style resulted in him never being quite able to keep a vehicle in a straight line and rarely could he drive us anywhere without mounting a pavement or clipping a kerb at least once. Having Peter Fankham around was a bit like having a dog; he had an innate desire to please, but you could never be surprised if he bit your hand, tried to shag the leg of a passing stranger, or licked his balls in public.

"Do you remember the time that Rob and John had the fight?" asked Dave with a smirk. How could I forget! John, our drummer, and Rob, our bassist at the time, had never seen eye to eye and there was always a palpable level of tension between them. If anything went wrong during a gig, they would always blame each other and often, even if all had gone well, one or the other would manage to find some fault. Tensions came to a head one evening at band practice and John had launched himself at the bassist after Rob had criticised his timing. John, being the bigger of the two, was soon on top with Rob pinned down beneath him and Peter, as the man who got things sorted, jumped on John's back to try and break up the scuffle. This intervention had meant nothing to a man of John's physical frame who, by this point, was so pumped up that he was not even aware that he had Peter clinging to him like he was riding a rodeo bull.

Each time that John punched Rob, the action caused Peter's head to bash against Rob's bass amp, and it was only when Peter rolled unconscious onto the floor that John was brought to his senses and stopped. In effect, Peter had stopped the fight but not quite in the heroic fashion that he had anticipated. Rob stood up, a little beaten and bruised, packed away his gear and his pride, before announcing that he was leaving the band. "So, you mentioned that Pete's wife had left him," I said, after we had enjoyed a good laugh retelling the story. "What was that all about?"

114

Dave explained how he had heard that Peter and his wife, Pam, had moved away after money had gone missing following a charity event which Peter had organised. Despite Peter's denials of any wrong doing, there were many who still pointed an accusing finger. "Next thing I heard was that Pam was back in Chatham or somewhere. My wife bumped into her working in a clothes shop in the high street," Dave explained. "Apparently he got nicked for kiddy stuff or something. The bloke was always a wrong 'un."

I was shocked and astounded by such a revelation. Surely Dave must have been exaggerating or somehow got the story wrong. From what I remembered of him, Peter had always had an overzealous interest in sex, but I had always attributed that to the fact that he and his right hand spent too much alone with only a porno book for company. On one occasion, he had sought medical attention over an affliction to his penis, and the doctor had advised him to leave it alone for a few weeks, suggesting that Peter had 'over-stressed his member'. His overzealous interest in matters of a sexual nature had never endeared him to the females of the species either, as he had a habit of always managing to steer a conversation around to something he had seen in a hardcore porn film. He never seemed to be able to comprehend why a woman would not be enthralled by a chat-up line which began, "I was watching this porno and..."

"I can't remember the exact details," Dave continued, back tracking a little. "Do you remember Mike?" he asked. I looked at him blankly. "Oh, come on," he said, "Mike from the pub?" Dave tried to prompt my memory. "He used to ride a Norton."

"Yeah, vaguely," I said, trying in vain to picture a Mike on a Norton.

"Well, Mike and Pete had stayed friends for years, and Pete was always doing him little favours; you know, getting him weed and stuff. Anyway, after Peter moved, Mike's daughter started telling stories about Pete, you know..." Dave paused, clearly feeling uncomfortable. "She reckoned that Pete used to try and to touch her up, and that once, after he'd stayed over after a party, she'd come out of the shower and Pete was on the landing, asking if he could see her, you know, naked like. Anyway, whatever happened, she told her mum, she called the old bill and they turned up at his new house and nicked him. That's all I know. Like I said, he was always a fuckin' wrong 'un. I hope he got the shit kicked out of him inside."

"Do you remember when he took singing lessons?" I asked, trying to lighten the conversation after noting Dave's rising anger and discomfort. Because Peter had been around bands for so long, he eventually decided that he wanted to form his own. Peter was often dissuaded from pursuing anything which required time, diligence and practice, and after convincing himself that his fingers were too short and fat, he had given up trying to learn the guitar. He had then embarked on a course of singing lessons until his tutor broke the news that Peter was probably tone deaf. "The prick couldn't carry a fucking tune in a bucket," Dave laughed hysterically. "The last time I saw him, he was emptying dog shit bins for the council," he added. "At least he finally found a job that suited him."

Dave stood up, asked if I was hungry and offered to rustle us up some food, suggesting that after we could take the short walk to his local pub and have a few drinks. I asked him how he was coping on his own with his wife away for a few weeks. "I do most of the cooking anyway, these days," Dave replied. He confessed to having developed a liking for cookery and that he had been a vegan for some time. "I only eat healthy stuff these days," he explained. How things had changed while I was away, I thought to myself.

Dave and I sat down to eat the vegetarian chilli which he had quickly prepared and I must confess that I had been impressed by Dave's culinary skills, and it was also good to hear that he was finally taking care of his health too. "Do you still get up to see the Hammers play?" I asked.

"Nah, not often, mate," Dave replied. "Tickets can cost up to eighty-five quid nowadays and I can't afford those prices; I often go down to watch Erith and Belvedere instead. The standard isn't great but it's a game of football at the end of the day, and at least that way I'm putting my money into something local and not some greedy bastard's pocket. I tell you, the fucking Premier League and television rights are killing football. When was the last time you went to see West Ham then?" Dave asked.

"1989, mate." I replied coyly, scooping the last of the vegetarian chilli onto my spoon and clearing my plate. "It was 22nd April to be precise." I certainly remembered that day well. West Ham had beaten arch local rivals Millwall at home by three goals to nil, and after Paul Ince had grabbed the only goal of the game in the away fixture earlier in the season, it was the first time that either team had completed a league double over each other. Although it had been a glorious and historic victory, ultimately the season would end with Millwall finishing tenth, their highest ever league finish, and West Ham finished the season in nineteenth place and were subsequently relegated.

"Yeah, I remember," said Dave, "that was a good day out, wasn't it? We all went fucking mental when Julian Dicks scored. How did we ever get relegated that year, eh? I mean, apart from Dicks at the back, we had Frank McAvennie up front, Phil Parkes in goal and Paul Ince in midfield. We had a good team that year."

"That we did, mate, but we just lost too many games," I pointed out as I cleaned our empty plates in the sink. "Out of nineteen home games that season, we lost ten and only won three. You'll never stay up on that home form." Dave appeared taken aback by my memory of that fateful season, but on many sleepless nights in my cell, I had torturously relived all of those fixtures and results in my mind. "C'mon, get your coat on. Let's go," I said.

In no time, we were strolling to his local pub with Dave leading the way, assisted by his walking stick. "I can't get used to your accent," he mused, before adding in a jocular manner. "When you turned up on my doorstep, I thought you were a Russian, or something."

I had never stopped to consider my own accent to be honest, but I suppose that after being away for so long, it was feasible that I could have picked up certain aspects of the accents which had been around me. "I'll get these," I said, as Dave pulled his wallet from his pocket at the bar. "I think you've waited a long time for it to be my round."

Clearly my offer amused Dave. "Yeah, you tight bastard," he said. "You either used to disappear to the toilets or suddenly had to leave whenever it was your round." We took our drinks, sat down and continued to reminisce, swapping stories about our childhood, football, the band, music and whatever else came up. I tentatively asked him a little more about Pete's wife, Pam. Although I had said nothing to Dave, I had been trying to formulate a plan in my head ever since he had told me about her leaving Peter. If I could get to her then I was sure that I would be able to discover where I could find that piece of crap, Peter Fankham. Dave pulled his phone from his shirt pocket. "My wife is a friend of hers on Facefuck," he said, as he tapped and scrolled away on the little screen. "I don't really like that social media shit," he said, "but it's a way of finding out what people are getting up to these days, I suppose." Finally he found her. "Here she is. Pamela Carter she calls herself these days. I reckon she doesn't want to be associated with that scumbag, Fankham, anymore." He handed me his phone, enabling me to scroll through some of her photos.

"Not bad," I remarked before handing Dave his phone back after noting Pamela Carter's long hair, laughing eyes and pretty smile. "Looks like Fankham was punching above his weight there. I may have to look her up," I quipped before taking a mouthful of beer and changing the subject. "Look mate, I know it's a huge ask, but I'm only over here for a few days, a week or so at the most, just to tie up a few loose ends. Any chance I could crash on your sofa?" I asked, adding, "I'd be happy to pay you for your trouble."

"No problem," replied Dave. "It will give us a chance to catch up. Fuck knows it's been way too long, mate. If there's places you need to get around to, you can borrow my car as long as you put petrol in it, of course." I thanked Dave for his magnanimity and was certain that the use of his car would indeed come in very handy. As the evening wore on and the drinks flowed one after another, Dave eventually turned the conversation to how the last twenty-six years had been for me, although, to be honest, my time in prison was not something I wanted to dwell on. Once I had finally turned the pages of that chapter, I had little interest in reliving any of it. I gave him a little insight into work details, the boredom and described a few of the colourful characters who I had come into contact with during that time. I could feel my anger rise, explaining how isolated I had felt when my parents had died, and how frustrated I had been knowing that I was stuck in there for something I had not done. "But you did shag that blonde Polish bird though, didn't you," Dave interjected in his usual inimitable style.

"No I did not," I replied tersely, almost snapping back at him, adding, "I never touched her and I certainly never killed her. Those police bastards did me over good and proper when they arrested me." I pointed to the long scar on my right cheek. "How's that for a souvenir," I asked bitterly, as Dave moved in his seat to get a better angle. "That was a size 9 that did that," I added for effect, before asking, "did you all have a pleasant journey back to England without me?" Dave explained how they had all been questioned by the police that morning, and once he, Paul, John and Gary had satisfied the police that they knew nothing, they had been unceremoniously hurried out of the country. They had travelled back to England without Peter and Debbie, assuming that Debbie must have been held as a witness, and Peter must have been permitted to wait for his sister, and he also had the responsibility of the van too.

I wondered how The Spaceman had managed to convince the police that he had known nothing, but I bit my lip and chose not to mention it. "No one knew what the fuck was going on," exclaimed Dave. "Gary just said that the police needed to ask Debbie more questions, and that her brother had hung around to wait for her. They flew back two days later."

"How was Gary on the way back?" I enquired.

"He was quiet, man; he hardly said a word," replied Dave. "I suppose we all were. Like I said, no one knew what the fuck was going on. He told us that you'd been arrested and that Debbie had caught you shagging that blonde bird from the party, and we all just assumed that you and your wife had had some sort of bust up. We didn't find out any more until a few days later."

"Never trust a hippy," I said coldly, taking another mouthful of beer, remaining stony faced while the alcohol started to make my head swim a little. We had always regarded Gary Spackman as a bit of a hippy, with his unkempt hair and denim jacket. The Spaceman, we used to call him, because more often than not he would be high on drugs. He was a pretty good musician too, probably better than the rest of us. Occasionally he would jam with us during practice sessions but he would always have to contend with being a roadie. He may have had the ability and he may have known his stuff, but we dismissed him as a 'fret wanker' who lacked our style and panache.

So, how did we meet Gary in the first place? I don't know really, it had been as if Gary had just materialised in our local pub one evening and within a few weeks, he had become part of our circle. No one knew much about him and no one really seemed to care. We learned that he played guitar and smoked weed, and that seemed good enough to the rest of us. We had all been quite partial to popping a few pills too and, on many evenings, our circle of friends would be sharing 'mandies', 'barbs', weed or hash, but it had been Gary who had introduced us to amphetamine sulphate and, within no time at all, speed had become part of our 'five a day'.

Both Dave and I had been relative latecomers to that drug scene. Admittedly, we had previously been quite partial to smoking a little weed on the rare occasions that we could get hold of it, but the treasure trove of narcotics had really been opened to us through Peter and Debbie. Dave excused himself for a moment and then returned from the pub toilet and wriggled somewhat uncomfortably in his seat. "I saw Debbie a few times after she left The Spaceman," he confessed.

"Really?" I questioned, a little accusingly.

"No, no, it wasn't like that," said Dave, defensively. "I hadn't seen her for years and then all of a sudden, she just turned up on my doorstep out of the blue. She started to get weird and clingy though and kept turning up at the house. Eventually, I had to ask her not to come round because my wife was starting to get suspicious that something was going on between us. It started to make my life complicated, and life's complicated enough without throwing someone else's problems into the mix. Anyway, it wasn't even as if I was getting my leg over; she would just come round, talk about weird shit and then burst into tears." Dave looked at me apologetically.

"Sorry," he offered, "I didn't mean to talk about your ex-wife like that." I assured him that it had been an awfully long time since Debbie had been my problem, despite the fact that I had returned to England with her very much at the top of my shit list.

Dave told me how he had asked her about what had really happened with Annika Radwanski, but his line of questioning had made Debbie very uncomfortable. "She just dodged the question, making out she couldn't remember the details," he said, "and then she told me a few things about her dad, and started crying her eyes out. I thought she was upset about her old man dying, but she started saying some really fucked up stuff. Did she ever say anything to you about him?" Dave asked. I had to confess that during our time together, she had dropped a few hints regarding the relationship she had with her close family members, and it had seemed that perhaps her family had been a little on the dysfunctional side, to say the very least.

"Dysfunctional?" Dave scoffed. "They were a fucking freak show. She told me that when she was a little kid, her old man used to ask her if she had any pubes, and her brother had once wanted her to watch him while he tossed himself off." I had to admit that both of these had been stories which she had mentioned to me many years before. She had been angry after arguing with her father over something which I had long forgotten, and I remembered her words had been tinged with spite when she had accusingly related those same stories which she were to later tell Dave. I had sensitively tried to ask her if she had been in some way sexually mistreated, but she had not wanted to elaborate. On another occasion, she had mentioned that her father had a friend, Henry, who she and her brother had been taught to refer to as 'Uncle Henry'. Although she had not wished to be pressed into divulging any intimate details, Debbie told me that she had once tried to confide in her parents that Uncle Henry had been acting inappropriately. When I had asked her what she had accused him of, all she would say was, "I can't respect my father because he told me never to say anything bad about Uncle Henry again, and I can never respect my mother because she should have protected me."

"She told me all that too," confessed Dave, awkwardly. "Apparently that Henry geezer was a school teacher who used to hang out at that pervy club with her old man, and he was always round at their house. He got banged up a few years back; it was in the local paper and everything, mate. Once one girl had made a complaint, then loads of others came forward too. Seems like that dirty fucker had been at it for years. You can draw your own fucking conclusions from that, I guess." Dave slumped back into his seat, breathless. He had always been a man who had a strong sense of injustice, and our conversation had clearly angered and agitated him. "Say what you want," he said, sounding a little more relaxed, "it ain't fucking normal to be in a club where people walk round starkers in front of kids, is it? Nudists? They're fucking perverts, if you ask me." Dave was becoming animated once more. He leaned across the table and hissed, "those cunts fucked their kids up good and proper. I mean, what sort of parent teaches their kids to lie to their friends about where they've been?"

I had to admit that Dave had a point. "I really need a fucking cigarette," he announced as he got to his feet. "You coming?" he asked. We stood outside the pub, savouring the nicotine laced smoke as it hit our throats and burned down into our lungs. It was dark and there was a chill in the air as the occasional car rumbled past, using the back street as a rat run. "So," said Dave with a smirk, changing the subject. "Have you got any prison shower stories?" he quizzed, as his sniggers grew into raucous laughter.

"No I fucking don't," I replied, shaking my head in disbelief at the absurdity of his implied suggestion. I took one final draw on my cigarette and dropped the butt on the pavement, grinding the sole of my boot into it, and once again I noticed that unsightly scuff across the toe.

Chapter 12

Customer Service

I watched her from a safe distance, keeping one eye on the rows of men's' t-shirts, not yet wanting to catch her attention until I was sure of my next move. Dressed in her rather unflattering store uniform, she looked more inconspicuous than she had appeared in the photographs which Dave had found of her while searching through social media websites. As I watched her putting out new stock in the ladies' section of the store with her long auburn hair tied back in a simple ponytail, I became convinced that this definitely was the same woman whose pictures Dave had shown me. In my mind, I pictured the photographic image I had seen of a smiling woman, flanked by two friends, clearly enjoying a night out. I was convinced that the woman who I now saw arranging ladies' tops was indeed one and the same. It had to be Pamela Fankham, estranged wife of Peter, the man who I was searching for. I made my way towards her, nonchalantly browsing the merchandise along the way until I reached the aisle where she was working. As I looked at the items which she had neatly displayed, she turned and gave me a cursory smile before continuing with her task. "I wonder if you could help me," I said, attempting to get her attention.

She stopped what she was doing and turned towards me. "Yes, of course I can." Her response was polite and her tone surprisingly chirpy. "How can I help?"

Pam was certainly not an unattractive woman by any stretch of the imagination, and, regardless of that rather unflattering store uniform, I could ascertain that her build was slender. Her smile was warm, and her eyes carried a glint which I found to be quite captivating. I could not help but wonder how a woman like this would ever want to get mixed up with someone like Peter. "I'm looking for a gift for my sister," I lied, "but I'm not sure what style would be most suitable."

"Well," replied Pam, smiling, "what size is she? That would be a good start."

"I'm not really sure," I mused, trying to summon up a mental image of an imaginary sister. I bit the corner of my bottom lip thoughtfully for a moment and then said, "I guess she's a similar height and build to you, I suppose." Once again I paused for a moment, before adding, "but obviously, she's not quite as attractive as you." That line just came out of nowhere, and I could feel my face glowing red with embarrassment following the clumsy, stumbling nature of my pass.

Pam smiled, perhaps a little nervously, and given the awkward nature of my flirtatious attempts, her response was understandable. Fortunately for me, however, Pam's professionalism meant that she appeared unfazed. We discussed styles and colours which my imaginary sister might approve of, and Pam remained bubbly and friendly throughout as we conversed. I noticed that as she spoke, she had a tendency to pull her ponytail over her shoulder and stroke her hair. I eventually chose two jumpers for my fictitious sibling, one powder blue and one white. Having made my decision, I thanked Pam for her help before commenting on her chirpy demeanour. "How come you're so happy today, anyway?"

Pam laughed and looked at her watch. "That's because I've only got twenty minutes until I finish work, and it's my day off tomorrow."

"And I've kept you from your work," I joked, trying to avoid making my fishing sound too obvious, although by that point I felt that I had no other option if I were to engineer a way of eliciting the information which I required. "So, have you any plans for this evening?" I enquired nonchalantly. Again Pam smiled before telling me that she was just planning to spend another boring evening watching television. "Look," I said, "I don't make a habit of this, but would you let me buy you a quick drink when you finish." I paused briefly before adding, "just as a thank you... for your help."

Pam seemed to consider my ungainly advance for an inordinate length of time before announcing her decision. "Look," she replied, "I don't make a habit of this either but if you give me half an hour or so, I will meet you in The Prince." She added "you know where it is, don't you? Just go down to the end of the High Street and turn left towards the railway station."

"I'll find it, I'm sure," I replied, heading towards the store checkout. I felt somewhat uneasy at the prospect of the murky water which I was endeavouring to get myself into, and I doubted that Pam would be too enamoured at the prospect either if she knew that my intentions were less than honourable.

oooOOOooo

I stood awkwardly at the bar in the Prince of Wales public house and checked my watch wondering if Pam would actually show up. She had suggested meeting in half an hour but, despite my anxiety, less than twenty-five minutes had elapsed. I looked around noting how most of the other patrons appeared to be enjoying a pint, whereas I stood, leaning on the bar, holding a glass of sparkling mineral water. I was certainly not going to run the risk of drinking over the alcohol limit, considering that Dave had so kindly entrusted me with his car. I stared wistfully into my glass, watching the bubbles as they rose to the surface. "Shall we have that drink then?" A cheery voice to the left of me disturbed my train of thought which up until that point, had not actually been travelling in any particular direction.

"And what would you like to drink?" I asked Pam in a manner as gentlemanly as I could muster, genuinely pleased to see her. As she could not decide whether to have a gin and tonic or a glass of red wine, I asked the barman for one of each.

"Are you trying to get me drunk?" Pam asked playfully. I replied that it was merely a ploy to ensure that she would at least stay for a second drink. Pam smiled, which at that point I took to be a good sign.

"I'm John," I offered, holding out my hand in a gesture of friendship which belied the perfidious nature of my deceit, "John Turner."

Pam delicately took my hand and shook it gently. "I'm Pamela. Pamela Carter. But you can call me Pam," she offered in return, smiling a shy smile while still retaining that sparkle in her eyes. Pamela Carter, I thought to myself as a paid for the drinks before handing her the glass of wine. I suppose that I had expected her to introduce herself as Fankham, but I could understand if she were doing her utmost to distance herself from her estranged husband. Bearing in mind Peter's recent stint at Her Majesty's pleasure, I considered that using an alternative surname was understandable, suspecting that Carter had been her maiden name. Pam took off her jacket and draped it over her arm and I suggested that we could sit down, gesturing towards a table in the corner by the window. As I followed her, I could not help but notice that for a woman in her forties, Pam's buttocks looked very pert in the blue denim jeans which she was wearing. She was also wearing a white, short-sleeved t-shirt which accentuated her slender body, and which also partially revealed a colourful tattoo at the top of her right arm.

"Do you need a licence to wear those jeans?" I quipped, sitting down opposite her and passing over the accompanying gin and tonic. "They certainly look better on you than your work uniform," I added teasingly.

"Don't you like a girl in uniform?" Pam teased in return, wriggling in her seat to make herself comfortable.

I took a mouthful of the cool sparkling mineral water. "Under the right circumstances, I guess I could be corrupted," I replied flirtatiously.

Pam laughed. "You look like a man who's been corrupted already, as long as you don't have any ideas of corrupting me too." The phone which she had placed on the table in front of her started to ring, prompting her to look down at it and momentarily changing her expression to one of concern. Pam appeared to reject the incoming call and placed her phone back on the table without shedding any light on the identity of her mystery caller.

Placing my hand on my heart in mock sincerity, I said, "I wouldn't dream of trying to corrupt you, Miss Carter."

Pam looked up coyly before replying "that's a shame," and then quickly changed the subject to avoid embarrassment. "It's not actually Miss Carter," she added. "It's Ms Carter... or it will be soon, anyway."

"Really?" I replied in feigned surprise. "Who would be foolish enough to let a woman like you slip through their fingers?" Pam blushed, nervously running the fingers of her right hand through her long hair, without venturing to reveal any further details as to the status of her present relationship with Peter.

"Anyway," she said, regaining her composure, "what about you? I noticed that you're not wearing a ring, so either you're single or you're hiding the fact that you're married."

I bought the two of us more drinks and then endeavoured to answer her questions as best I could. She was bright, bubbly and inquisitive, and I did my utmost to not weave too complex web of lies which I might be unable to remember. I told her that I had been divorced for a long time and that I was a musician, and had been living abroad for a good few years. I also mentioned that I had returned to England to look up a few old friends, while considering the prospect of returning to live in England permanently. "In fact," I added, "I used to live near here, just across the river, as it goes." I confess that I found Pam to be enjoyable and quite compelling company, and at times it was difficult to conceal my duplicity. Noting that her glass was nearly empty, I offered her another drink, afraid to let the opportunity slip as we had yet to venture any closer to the root subject of my deception. Pam glanced at her watch, as if there might be somewhere else she should be.

"Look," I said, in a desperate effort to convince her to remain at least a little longer, "I can drive you home, or wherever you need to be. I haven't been drinking, I'm not married and my car is only two minutes' walk from here." I pointed in the direction of the car park. Maybe reality had kicked in and she appeared not unsurprisingly, a little sceptical. I was a stranger, it was getting late and she was probably already a little tipsy. Pam explained that she was currently staying with her daughter, who may have been growing concerned that her mother had not returned home from work at the expected time.

"That's simple," I offered, trying to put her at ease. "Call her, tell her where you are and who you're with." I took a pen from my pocket and wrote my mobile phone number on a beer mat, suggesting that she could let her daughter know my number just in case Pam mysteriously disappeared. As I stood at the bar ordering us both another round of drinks, I glanced back towards Pam who appeared to be talking to someone on the phone. I paid for the drinks and heard a text alert tone from my pocket. Wondering who could be trying to contact me, I checked. There was a message from an unknown number which simply read, 'now you have my number too'. As I returned to our table, Pam smiled and thanked me as I passed her the half of lager topped with lime which she had requested. I smiled back as I sat down, just as her phone rang again. We both watched it vibrate on the table.

"Aren't you going to answer that?" I asked. "It could be your daughter checking that you're alright."

"No, it's not important," replied Pam, looking a little more irritated than she had previously. Once again she rejected the call and we returned to our conversation. We talked about travel and music for a while, and although she admitted that it had been some years since she had travelled abroad, she seemed genuinely interested in my musical involvement and the places where I alleged that I had lived. I did my best to improvise and feed her a feasible story. Pam appeared to have a diverse musical knowledge and I hoped that the diversity of her knowledge would not stretch as far as the clubs and bars of Poland and the Czech Republic.

It was a little after 10:30pm when I went up to the bar to buy one final glass of red wine and another mineral water. As I paid the barman, I could hear Pam's phone ringing again and noticed that, just as before, she rejected the call. When I returned to our table, I flippantly mentioned that someone seemed hell bent on getting in touch with her. It appeared that her caller's attempts to intrude on our conversation were causing her a degree of annoyance. "It's my ex," offered Pam by way of explanation. "He often tries to call me, especially if he's had a few drinks." For the first time that evening, Pam sounded bitter and a little angry. "You would not believe what that man put me through. I spent years always doing everything he told me, too scared to leave him. It's taken a long time for me to rebuild my life and I won't let him bully me again." Pam drew a long breath through gritted teeth and, battling to regain her composure, she smiled her textbook smile before concluding, "but that's enough about him. Maybe I'll tell you the full story another time."

Before I knew it, closing time was called and it was time to be true to my word, call it a night and drive Pam home before heading back to Dave's place. As we walked the short distance to the car, Pam thanked me for an unexpected but enjoyable evening. I could not help but ponder as to how different the evening might have been had we met under different circumstances, as I had honestly found her company to be quite enthralling. She was fun, we had laughed, shared interesting conversations and, although I did not want to admit it to myself, I also found Ms Pamela Carter to be rather attractive.

oooOOOooo

With the volume almost inaudible, the car radio burbled away on its own as I followed Pam's directions. Although it was dark, I found much of the route to be a vaguely familiar one. It had been many years since I had seen this neighbourhood, but despite the quarter of a century which had elapsed, very little appeared to have changed. I battled to quell my growing sense of unease when it became apparent that our route was to take us past a place that I remembered all too well. A row of houses on the right loomed into view, illuminated by the orange glow of the sodium street lights. Driving past one house in particular would prove to create the pinnacle of my mounting anxiety. It was a house which I had not laid eyes on since the night before we had embarked on that fateful tour of Eastern Europe. It was the house that I once shared with Debbie.

I tried in vain to not even glance at the house as we passed it. I looked over at Pam and smiled. She smiled back. "It's not far," she said. "Just down the hill and turn right and we're almost there." I followed her directions and soon enough, Pam pointed to a convenient parking space, exclaiming "there's my house. That's the one, the one with the blue door." Following Pam's instructions, I parked the car, turned off the engine and turned to face her. Pam leaned across and kissed me on the cheek. "Thanks for a lovely evening and kindly giving me a lift home too," she said, before adding with a wry smile, "I'd like to see you again, if you're interested." She looked into my eyes deeply in apparent anticipation of my response, placing her left hand on my thigh in a suggestive manner. She smiled flirtatiously, her palm stroking my thigh before sliding suggestively towards my crotch, her fingers tucking themselves around my balls. "Mmm," she sighed with a glint in her eye as she became aware that my cock had responded instantly to the sensitivity of her touch.

I unzipped my jeans, relieving the building pressure of my erection and allowing her hand to stroke along the length of my bare flesh, her fingers enfolding me in her grasp. She leaned forward and lowered her face to my crotch. I pushed myself back in the seat, allowing her more room beneath the steering wheel as her tongue ran salaciously along the length of my hard cock, gently flicking across its tip. Pam's risqué advances invoked a distant memory of an encounter with a young lady named Beth, many years before. Just as had been the case way back then, I found myself in a situation in which, although it had not been my expressed intention, the weakness of my gender and nature of my disposition rendered me powerless to resist.

My mind was unable to distinguish between the woman who was now pleasuring me and the woman who, for so long, had turned a blind eye to her husband's wrongdoings and in that moment, she both aroused and disgusted me in equal measure. Her mouth felt soft, warm and moist as she drew me inside. Her lips repeatedly slid effortlessly up and down my shaft, moistened by her saliva as her tongue lasciviously encircled the head of my penis before she engulfed me with each mouthful. Pam's capacity to arouse through fellatio was clearly skilled, but I sensed that she performed more out of an urge to feel the close contact of another human being, rather than through desire or passion. In the darkness of the car, I tightly gripped her auburn hair, forcing her down on me and fucked her mouth more out of spite than lust. Dutifully, she responded to each thrust until without warning, I jerked and thrust into her, ejaculating deep into her mouth, holding her head, encouraging her not to waste one drop of my semen. Finally my muscles relaxed and I loosened my grip on her hair, allowing her to sit upright in the passenger seat. She wiped the corner of her mouth and instinctively pulled down the sun visor, and I watched her as she adjusted her hair in the vanity mirror.

"So, have I convinced you to call me tomorrow?" Pam asked, without turning to look at me, as she untangled her hair in the mirror. At that moment I lamented my actions as she clearly deserved better, but there was much that I still needed her to tell me.

"Of course I will," I replied. With that, she leaned towards me, kissed me on the cheek and then turned, opened the car door and stepped out onto the pavement.

"Maybe I'll cook you dinner then," she said with a smile before closing the car door. I watched her as she walked through the darkness to her front door, illuminated only slightly by a nearby street lamp. She unlocked the door and stepped inside, pausing momentarily to turn around and wave before closing the door behind her. I fastened my jeans, started the car and, deciding that I was not in the mood for late night radio, I leaned forward to see what CDs Dave might have concealed in the glove box of his car. It was then that I noticed a purse laying in the passenger foot well. I picked it up and turned on the courtesy light to check the contents. Inside the purse I found three ten pound notes, two bankcards bearing the name Pamela Fankham and a few receipts. Interestingly, I also found Pam's driving licence, bearing a different address to the one which I was currently sitting outside. Rushworth Farm, Beech Lane, Painswick, Gloucester. "That's it," I thought to myself. "Got ya, you bastard."

I looked in the direction of the terraced house which I had watched Pam enter just a few minutes beforehand. Noting that the hallway light had now been turned off, I glanced at the digital clock in the car; it was 23:56. Therefore I decided that I did not want to cause a disturbance at such a late hour, and would call her in the morning and offer to return her purse. I put the car into gear, checked the mirrors and pulled away. As I drove along the dark, narrow back street, lined with parked cars on both sides, I was already thinking ahead to the following day.

Chapter 13

Ghosts of Our Past

I checked my watch as the train pulled into Bexleyheath station, it was 13:36 on the dot. Although it had been a struggle for him, Dave had accompanied me part way on the walk between his house and the station. Some days, he had explained, were good days and others not so good, and as we walked, he was clearly in discomfort. We had made it as far as his local pub and I had suggested that we could have a lunchtime pint and he could take the weight off his leg.

Dave had still been awake when I had returned in the early hours, and he was intrigued to know whether or not I had tracked down Pam. As he automatically assumed that I had, his inquisitive nature dictated that he would not pass up on the opportunity of bombarding me with questions. I explained how I had managed to talk her into agreeing to a drink after work and that I had offered her a lift home, and that was all I was willing to divulge. However, never a man to leave any stone unturned in his quest for the full facts, Dave had been relentless in his questioning that morning. Had I been in her house? Had I had sex with her? Even when I explained that Pam was staying at her daughter's house, Dave had indignantly asked whether she and I had behaved inappropriately in his car. Of course, being a gentleman, I denied that any such exploits were undertaken during the course of the evening.

I climbed aboard the train and a few disinterested faces had looked up at me as I took a seat for the first leg of my journey to Rochester, remaining mindful to change at Dartford. I had phoned Pam at around ten o'clock in the morning to inform her that she must have dropped her purse in the car the previous evening. She, in turn, informed me that her daughter would be staying overnight with a friend and that she had been entrusted with looking after her daughter's two cats. An invite to dinner had followed, giving me the opportunity to do the gallant thing and return Pam's purse. I also hoped that maybe I could glean a little more information regarding her estranged husband.

The route which Pam had advised me to take the previous evening had led me to consider that if I afforded myself enough time, I would be able to spend a while getting myself reacquainted with a neighbourhood which I had once considered to be home. I disembarked when the train pulled into Rochester Station just before two thirty in the afternoon, and strolled along the old high street. Although it still looked familiar, so much had changed in the intervening years. I walked past bars that had not been there previously, and it appeared that some of the restaurants which I had at one time frequented had been lost to the mists of time. I recalled that there had been a host of interesting second hand bookshops, all worthy of a browse on a quiet afternoon, but all bar one had been erased from history only to be replaced by a multitude of coffee shops. Clearly, in these fast moving modern times, the act of relaxing with the written word had been replaced by a need for caffeine to be ingested almost intravenously, fuel for the modern day consumer in their race to reach the end of their days as quickly as possible.

I crossed Rochester Bridge with the River Medway flowing timelessly and agelessly beneath, and paused momentarily at the halfway point to look over the parapet at the water flowing below. I watched as eddies swirled around the bridge supports, an indication of the dangers that lie in the murky depths of the river. I took a moment to look back at the historic castle and cathedral, towering over buildings which did their best to mask the view, and then I continued to make my way into Strood on the opposite side of the river.

Reaching Angel Corner, I recalled that there had been a pub on that spot, one that had defined the road junction as something of a local landmark for centuries. I questioned how an estate agent could ever have been permitted to swallow up such a historical and well-known landmark. As I walked up the hill towards Wainscott, I could not help but notice how all the public houses that I had at one time frequented, had all disappeared, only to be replaced by mini supermarkets and takeaway restaurants. Within little more than thirty minutes of stepping off the train, I found myself standing opposite the house in which I had once lived. The old place, which nestled inconspicuously in a row of Victorian terraced houses, looked unremarkable and appeared to have changed very little since the days when I had called it home. At the time, I had considered it a happy place to live, somewhere that Debbie and I could relax in the evenings, shut ourselves away from the world and just get stoned together. I could recall weekends where we would only leave the house if we deemed it necessary to stagger to the local shop to pick up the snacks which we required to pacify our 'munchies'. We would laugh until our sides ached.

In my naivety, I guess I thought that the laughter meant that we were happy, but now I know better; after all, stoners will laugh at anything. In retrospect, the relationship which Debbie and I shared was probably built with drugs as the cornerstone. Admittedly, we had both been casual users when we had initially met, but maybe the cynic in me could suggest that as I was the one with the regular income and she was the one with the regular dealer, we were a match made in the gutter.

I stood on the pavement opposite my former home reminiscing about a bygone era with a degree of warmth, regretting that life had not worked out quite as I planned. I realised in that moment that I had not always been a man consumed by hatred and revenge. During my years of incarceration, I had often pondered how and why I had allowed myself to become embroiled with the woman who would ultimately betray me. As those ponderings had gone around and around inside my head in ever decreasing or increasing circles, I often came to the conclusion that there may well be those who, despite my personal sense of injustice, might consider that I got everything I asked for.

Lisa for instance, had she knowledge of my predicament, might have closed her eyes at night with a warm glow, sensing that justice had been served. After all, I had broken Lisa Wright's heart when I left her for Debbie only a few months before she and I had planned to marry. Lisa and I had been together for some two and a half years despite never actually having had anything remotely in common. She hated just about everything that I loved; my music, my friends, and I guess that I was equally unenthusiastic about her friends and interests too. Lisa had never been interested in coming to watch the band when we played; she did not like our music, the scene or the people involved, and was probably sick to the back teeth of hearing me churning over the same old tunes on my electric guitar in the confines of the flat we shared.

Lisa usually decided to have an evening out with her friends on the nights when I would have a gig, and that decision would occasionally leave me open to distractions. Whether those distractions were drink, drugs, women or a combination of the three, mattered not to me. In my own mind, I defended my actions and infidelities by basing my defence on one fact. After she had once returned from a week away with her friends, she confessed that she had been unfaithful. As shocking as I initially found her confession to be, I learned that her desire to confess may have been less about her yearning to be honest, and more to do with damage limitation. This became abundantly clear when one evening I answered the door to a man who looked to be in his late twenties or early thirties, and who appeared the complete antithesis of me. This man, with his straggly long hair, flared jeans, baggy shirt and brown velvet jacket, had jauntily introduced himself as Des who had met Lisa on holiday. I doubted very much that he had any idea who I was, because he had smiled and politely held out his hand to shake mine. Needless to say, although we did not shake hands, Des did descend our steps somewhat quicker than he had made his ascent. Lisa and I did not discuss the matter further.

Shortly after that event, Lisa had awkwardly announced that she had missed her period, and a trip to the doctor confirmed that she was indeed pregnant. Although she did her level best to convince me that the dates concluded that without doubt, I was the father, the chances of her possibly conceiving as the result of a drunken shag in a Butlins chalet troubled me deeply. Despite doing my best to console her when she suffered a miscarriage around a month later, deep down, and I am ashamed to admit it, I did have a slight sense of relief that our child would not grow up with a question mark forever hanging over the possibilities of its parentage. I had actually grown accustomed to the prospect of becoming a father, sensing that the responsibilities of parenthood could be the making of me as a man. I would console Lisa with a recital of our doctor's platitudes, relating to how these things unfortunately happen sometimes. Although I made her promises of how we would try again in the near future, we probably both knew that this was never destined to happen. In reality, from the moment that Lisa made her confessions of holiday infidelity, our relationship was akin to a downhill ride on a bicycle with no brakes, and ultimately Debbie's arrival in my life was destined to be the junction at the bottom of that hill.

The relationship transition which led to Lisa's heartbreak was not exactly a straightforward affair either. I had met Debbie one Thursday night at a gig in South London, along with her friend Beth. Both girls lived not far from the area where the band and I were heading that evening, and they were flirtatious and clearly angling for a lift home. Needless to say, no one objected to the prospect of two slightly drunken and attractive girls sharing our rather dilapidated Ford Transit minibus for the fifteen or so mile journey back from Deptford. During the journey, the girls proudly informed us that they had been to a few of our gigs, and mentioned that they also frequented some of the pubs which were on our regular drinking circuit too. Maybe they had or maybe they were just trying to impress for a free ride, no-one knew, and I doubt that anyone really cared either.

Those had still been early days for the band, probably somewhere around early summertime in 1983 if my memory serves correctly, and we were still mainly playing local gigs at that time, around North Kent and South London. Once all the gear had been loaded into the back of the minibus, Dave, our front man, ushered Debbie into a seat and sat down next to her and I took the window seat behind them. Rob, who was our bass player at the time, sat opposite and John, our drummer, once again had been entrusted with the task of remaining nearly sober and driving us back. We usually took turns with the driving duties, but it was always a nightmare for whoever's turn it was. While everyone else in the back were able to drunkenly laugh and joke around, the driver had to concentrate on getting the vehicle, its occupants and the equipment safely back, whilst avoiding the risk of getting stopped and breathalysed by the late night police patrols. The paranoia which accompanied this task was never a pleasant experience, and I can clearly remember that I was a very happy man that it was not my turn that night.

Beth was the last passenger aboard the minibus and she took the vacant seat next to me. "You don't mind, do you?" Beth enquired cheerily as she made herself as comfortable as possible in our old wreck of a vehicle. I

144

told her that it was fine by me and then noticed how Debbie turned around and gave Beth a disdainful glare. She muttered something which was not clearly audible over John's tirade of expletives, as his frustration grew that the tired old Transit was clearly not in the mood to start. Whatever Debbie had said to Beth, it did not faze her in the slightest and neither had the scornful glare which followed. Debbie sat back down and wriggled uncomfortably in her seat. Beth turned to me and cheerily exclaimed, "I think you live quite close to me." The minibus eventually spluttered into life with John urging the tired engine to run at least one more time, cheering as he finally won the battle of wills between man and machine. It was just after midnight when we began our journey back, and Beth and I chatted amiably about where we lived and people we knew locally, making small talk to fill in the gaps between meaningful conversation. Of course, I neglected to mention anything about my relationship with Lisa.

Perhaps, if I'm honest, Debbie with her long blonde hair and pouting lips was the more attractive of the two girls. She was taller and certainly the more feminine of the pair. Beth with her short brown hair, jeans, denim jacket and Doctor Marten boots, struck me as being something of a tomboy. Perhaps this was due in part to the fact that she grew up with two older brothers. One thing which was most noticeable about Beth however, was that it was impossible to not note that her white t-shirt did nothing to conceal her breasts which were disproportionately large for a girl of such petite stature. Lisa ran through my mind, momentarily reminding me of my commitments and loyalties, and in the haze of the evening's excesses, I felt guilty for mentally undressing

145

Beth and Debbie and comparing the two of them. Life with Lisa had been complicated and I reasoned that I was in no position to complicate things further, but my mind conceded that surely there was nothing wrong with a little harmless window shopping.

It was not as if I felt a spark between Beth and I either. Yes, she was cute and attractive in a tomboyish way, but we had probably both consumed our fair share of alcohol that evening and I could smell the cider on her breath as we talked. I sensed that she was more than a little flirtatious, and taking into account that I was supposed to be in a long term relationship with Lisa, it was therefore rather foolish of me to reciprocate. After a momentary lull in our conversation, I turned to look out of the window as the minibus trundled across Blackheath. I remembered childhood car journeys with my mother and father, returning from visiting the grandparents in East London, and I had always been fascinated by such a huge open expanse of green, seemingly out of place and surrounded by so much urban development. Each time I had travelled across Blackheath Common, the historical stories which my father had related about the possible burial of Black Death victims and ruthless highwaymen, including the infamous Dick Turpin, were never far from my imagination.

As I gazed through the darkness, I caught sight of a man walking his dog past the gateway to Greenwich Park and I felt Beth's hand rest gently on my thigh. I said nothing; my gaze firmly fixed on the man and the dog. My erection grew involuntarily as Beth's hand gently massaged my penis through my jeans, and lost in the moment, I felt compelled to slide down in my seat, unfasten the button and ease down the zip. I continued to stare out of the window into the vague darkness beyond, feeling the warmth of Beth's warm lips around my cock, sucking me slowly, silently and unashamedly. I closed my eyes. Any thoughts of the evening, work the following day, the band or Lisa, were replaced by images in my mind of dangerous highwaymen mounted astride magnificent black steeds, taking what they desired without fear or consequence and in that moment, I was one of them.

"Fucking hell," exclaimed Rob in shock and disgust as he glanced across from his seat, realising the nature of the act being brazenly performed just a few feet from where he was sitting. "Do you two have to?"

Dave and Debbie turned around to see what all the sudden commotion was about. "You dirty bastard," Dave chimed in scornfully. "You just can't fucking help yourself, can you." Debbie said nothing and just turned back around before proceeding to look uncomfortably out of the window.

"What's happening back there?" John enquired from the driver's seat. "Am I missing out on something again?" he laughed.

"You really don't want to know, mate," added Dave, sitting back down in his seat and giving Debbie a sideways look which conveyed his apparent revulsion. Not for a moment did Beth falter in her actions and despite the derision of our fellow passengers, she blatantly continued, undaunted and unashamed. I said nothing in my defence as there was nothing really which I could say, and the atmosphere in the minibus descended into uncomfortable silence. I relaxed with my distant alcohol buzz, stroked Beth's hair gently and encouragingly, and

147

continued to gaze vacantly through the window as we passed parked cars, houses, traffic lights and the occasional figure illuminated by the faint orange glow of the sodium street lights. As Beth's soft lips continued to silently sooth me, in my mind I became the highwayman once again.

Beth sat bolt upright as John eased the van to a stop, bumping two wheels up onto the pavement. Rob leaned into the back, retrieved his bass guitar and pulled open the side door of the minibus. "Goodnight all," he said, stepping into the road. "I'll see you all at band practice on Tuesday." We bade him farewell and watched him light a cigarette on the pavement as the van pulled away into the night. At the next stop it was my turn to alight, and Beth climbed out of the van ahead of me.

"Aren't you staying at mine tonight, Beth?" Debbie enquired somewhat icily as I leaned into the back to collect my guitar case. Beth declined with a cheery smile, saying that she would telephone Debbie in the morning. We wished the remaining occupants of the tired Transit a safe journey and a good night, and I slid the side door closed as weary mutterings were offered in return. I lit a cigarette and offered one to Beth as the minibus disappeared around the junction at the end of the road. She accepted and I offered to walk her the short journey back to her house as the hour was late. Once again we made small talk as we walked, but as we neared Beth's road, I began to sense that if I did not make a move soon then an opportunity could be lost forever. Of course I thought of Lisa, but at that point I was a little drunk, a little tired and all I could think about was the softness of Beth's mouth and the fullness of her breasts.

Passing the end of the alleyway that ran along behind Beth's house, I took hold of her hand and pulled her into the darkness, dropping my guitar case before leaning my hands on the fence behind her on either side of her head. I lowered my lips to hers as she stood on tiptoes to reach mine, her arms reaching around my neck. As we kissed passionately, I pulled up her t-shirt and reached around to unfasten the clasp on her bra as our tongues entwined. My hands trembled in anticipation of her soft warm skin and the knowledge that what I was doing was wrong. Eventually and unskilfully the clasp was undone, and my hands caressed her warm back and I momentarily felt the chill of the night air as my hands cupped Beth's ample breasts for the first time. Strangely, I could not help but notice how small her nipples were in relation to her breasts, and I teased one gently between my thumb and forefinger.

Nervously, I unbuttoned her jeans, slid down the zip and eased my right hand inside her knickers. Her pubic hair was soft and wispy to the touch and Beth eased her legs apart slightly as my fingers worked their way toward her moist pussy. Her arms loosened their grip around my neck and in a hurried, awkward and fidgety manner, she managed to ease her tight jeans down to her knees while I endeavoured to do likewise with mine. With Beth being that much shorter than myself, I bent my knees while she draped her arms around my neck once more, and I slowly worked my erect penis inside her as she shuffled her feet awkwardly to allow deeper access. I pulled up her t-shirt and bent down to suck her right nipple but found myself unable to maintain rhythm, growing frustrated each time that I accidentally slipped out of her. Finally I elected to concentrate my efforts on simply fucking her right there in the dark alleyway while she leaned against her neighbours' fence. That was the story of our first clandestine encounter, and although it may not have been particularly classy, it was fuelled by alcohol and driven by passion and lust.

I walked Beth the rest of the way home and promised to call her and, just to ensure that I would not forget, she wrote her telephone number on my white t-shirt in pink lipstick. Soon enough Beth would learn about Lisa, and our sexual relationship would continue in relative secrecy for the next six weeks. Lisa would eventually learn about Beth on the afternoon she came back unexpectedly and caught the two of us in bed together. There were no rows, no cat fights, no screams of anger, she just turned around and walked back out. Maybe I expected Lisa to call time on our relationship as a result and I suppose that Beth harboured hopes of such an outcome too, but in true British tradition, Lisa showed resolve, a stiff upper lip, avoided the subject and just tried to keep me on a tighter leash. After that, on the few occasions when Beth and I found time for our trysts, I suppose that I just did not feel the same intensity any more. Either I had disliked the feelings of guilt or I had merely craved the danger, but once the truth was out, I began to make excuses for not showing up when Beth and I had arranged to meet, blaming Lisa when in truth, I no longer had the same appetite.

The complicated triangle that developed between Lisa, Beth and I became something of an open secret amongst my circle of friends. Although it was slightly less complicated by the fact that it was a social circle in which Lisa had no interest, there were a few embarrassing times when she would phone the Station Hotel public house which my friends and I would frequent, to check up on my whereabouts or who I was with. Fortunately, Harry the landlord always covered for me, even though he voiced his displeasure at having to do so. However, there was one evening when Lisa made an appearance and on finding Beth sitting on my knee, she picked up a beer and threw it at us before storming out. After a few moments of stunned silence, Beth and I were soon the focus of ensuing banter. Perhaps not unsurprisingly, there was hell to pay when I got back to the flat that night. Lisa was waiting; she was angry, she felt humiliated, she shouted, she swore and she slammed doors. My response was largely pathetic and I meekly spent the next few nights on the couch. Very little in the way of conversation passed between us over the next few days, with little more than polite and civil exchanges over the next few weeks. Perhaps both of us were expecting the other to call time on our relationship and certainly Beth grew agitated by my indecision. I felt between a rock and a hard place and so I did what I did best; I got drunk with my friends, I got stoned and I buried my head firmly in the sand.

It was on one such occasion when I had escaped to the pub on my own, thus avoiding an evening with either Lisa or Beth, when I bumped into Debbie. It was soon blatantly obvious that Beth had been confiding in her close friend regarding her escalating frustration that I had not left Lisa, and that she was quite understandably beginning to wonder where she stood. Debbie certainly gave me both barrels without holding back. I was a selfish, two timing bastard who cared about no-one but myself. I was being unfair to Lisa for seeing Beth behind her back and moreover, I was being unfair to Beth for, what she considered to be, stringing her along. Once again my defence was pathetic; after all, Debbie was right. That chance meeting with Debbie on that particular evening, that strange quirk of fate, was to ultimately lead me to finally make a decision on my future, a future which would involve neither Lisa nor Beth, because the following morning I woke up in Debbie's bed.

When I announced my intention to leave her and temporarily move back in with my parents, neglecting to mention anything about Debbie entering the equation, Lisa was distraught and tried hard to convince me to stay, with assurances that we could work out our differences. I felt bad but I had made my decision. On a few occasions over the next few weeks, I returned from work to find Lisa at my parents' house, eyes damp and swollen from crying and casually sipping tea with my mother. My mother, needless to say, always liked Lisa, and finally convinced me to tell her the truth. Of course, it was not quite as simple as that either, as things of that nature seldom are. On the evening which was to prove to be Lisa's final visit, I was in a rush to wash, change and meet up with Debbie. Unbeknown to me, Lisa had followed me upstairs and caught me putting on a clean t-shirt and had noticed scratches on my back. These were wounds which any detective worth his salt would conclude could only have been inflicted by another woman's fingernails. To say that Lisa was upset would be an understatement, and I had no option but to finally tell her the truth. In one final, desperate attempt to convince me to change my mind, Lisa resorted to plan B; the offer of sex. I was shocked, saddened and deep down I knew that Lisa was worth more, much more. The moment I graciously declined her offer, she knew we were finally over. And what about Beth? Well, it goes without saying that when she found out that Debbie and I were seeing each other, the news had more than a detrimental effect on their friendship.

Lisa walked away, quite rightly feeling that I had wasted two and a half years of her life and Beth, as a result of her sexual act that night in the minibus, had perhaps cruelly earned the moniker BJ. As I stood there opposite my old home in the early evening sunshine, I could not help but feel that if Lisa and Beth had known how my life had turned out, I dare say that they would have considered it to have been justice served.

My indulgent reminiscing was brought to a sudden halt as I recognised the elderly gentleman who had emerged from the house next door. Regardless of his advancing years, I recognised Victor in an instant. He was struggling to deposit a bag of rubbish into the wheelie bin by his front door, something which he always had done to ensure that the urban foxes did not make a mess by ripping them open. Victor had been my neighbour when I lived there, and I confess that I was a little surprised to see that he still lived in the same house. A Welshman by birth, Victor, with his broad accent, had been an interesting neighbour. More often than not, he was an affable fellow who enjoyed a chat over the garden fence, but he was also a man who enjoyed an occasional beer and the tranquillity of silence and solitude. If the noise inside our house ever reached a level that were to have an adverse effect on Victor's tranquillity, then it would not be unusual for him to come knocking on our door. If he had been drinking, however, his visits could well be an interesting and occasionally feisty encounter. There was never any bad blood between Victor and me though, and within a day or two we would be happily chatting over the garden fence once again as if nothing had happened.

Debbie began to dissuade me from speaking to Victor, claiming that his outbursts were a sure sign that he was mentally unstable, and she had personally begun to avoid him. On one occasion after Victor and I had been talking across the gardens about football, a television programme or something equally insignificant, Debbie had appeared edgy and questioned me regarding our conversation. She claimed that Victor had spoken to her a few days before and had told her that he knew what was going on in our house. She claimed that either I had been up to something or that Victor was going mad and therefore best avoided. I had ignored that surreal conversation, merely attributing it to Debbie's cannabis induced paranoia, and my cross garden conversations with Victor had continued as usual.

The reason why I was so surprised to discover Victor still residing in the same house was that I could remember that he would so often tell me of his plans to emigrate to Spain. Year after year he would holiday in Spain, often looking for potential properties while he was there. Now, nearly twenty-six years later, he was still living in the same house and putting out his rubbish just as he always had done. I crossed the busy road, carefully dodging the oncoming traffic. "Alright mate, do you want a hand with that?" I asked, as Victor struggled to lift a second rubbish bag into the wheelie bin. He looked at me blankly, perhaps a little surprised. "John," I said, offering my hand for him to shake. "John Turner. Many years ago I had a friend who lived in that house next door. Steve his name was, Steve Caldwell."

"I remember him," said Victor, sounding a little astonished. His voice may have been a little more frail than I remembered, but the strength of his Welsh accent was still well marked. "Decent sort was Steve. I was sorry

154

when he died." The nature of Victor's response made it clear that Debbie had probably been rather economical with the truth surrounding my disappearance from the neighbourhood. "His wife sold up a few years later," continued Victor, "but she only moved around the corner. A rented place, I think. I didn't see her so much after that, but she always sent me a Christmas card every year."

"I suppose she felt that the house held too many memories after Steve had gone," I said, in an attempt to prolong our conversation and fish for more information.

"Who, Deborah?" Victor asked. "I doubt it, lad. She was a sort, that woman. Led him a merry dance when he was alive, she did." The old man's response was cutting and tinged with cynicism. "I warned her once about having her other men in behind his back, but she didn't listen."

"Really?" I asked, sounding genuinely surprised. Even all those years after the fact, Victor's words still shocked me. "I never knew that."

"She moved her new man in before your friend was cold in the ground," Victor continued. "They'd been carrying on for ages before and I'd seen him skulking around while Steve was at work. That was why I warned her that I knew what was going on. These houses have thin walls you know, and I'm not deaf or stupid."

"A noisy neighbour, was she?" I quipped.

"Never satisfied, that one," added Victor. "I mean, I never understood what she saw in Gary, as he was a right long streak of piss; painter and decorator, or something. Anyway, she was soon cheating on him too, just the same as she'd done with Steve. She used to come across really sweet and nice, but she really loved herself. Like I said, she really was a piece of work, that woman."

"Sounds like it," I said, considering that Victor appeared to have had a better insight into my past than I did. I began to wonder if this chance encounter with my former neighbour might lead me to learning either Debbie's or Gary's current whereabouts. "Is she still local?" I asked.

"No, they moved some years back. She knocked on my door and told me that they were buying a boat. Up north somewhere, if I remember correctly," Victor added with a bit of a sneer.

"Oh, that's a shame," I said. "I lost touch years ago and it might've been nice to catch up."

"She did give me her address before she moved," Victor cut in helpfully. "I could let you have it if you'd like. You could always send her a letter, I suppose."

"Yes, thank you," I replied, "that would be very kind of you." Victor disappeared inside his house as I waited outside, and he returned a few minutes later with an address written on a scrap of paper.

"Here you go, son," the old man said, handing me the address. "She did send Christmas cards for a few years, but I never replied. I heard after she moved that she'd been messing around with a neighbour's husband, nasty business, apparently. The woman turned up on the doorstep, shouting and screaming, and then after she'd kicked her husband out, her five kids started hanging around outside Deborah's place. They'd throw things at the windows and make a nuisance of themselves, banging on the front door at night and stuff. People said that was why she moved out, to get away from all the trouble, like."

I glanced at the handwritten address, making a mental note of it and thanked Victor as I slipped it into my back pocket. "I suppose I better let you go. It was a pleasure to see you..." I cut myself short, realising that I had nearly slipped up.

"Victor," the old man offered without noticing anything amiss.

"It was a pleasure to meet you, Victor," I continued, patting my back pocket. "Thanks for that address, I dare say that I shall write to her or something." The old boy went back into his house and closed the door behind him, and I started to head off in the direction of Pam's, reminding myself that I should buy a bottle of wine on the way. I paused one more time and looked up at what was once my front door. I remembered the times when I would return home and there would be my dog, Honey, faithfully waiting at the front room window. She knew the sound of the car engine and she could recognise the sound of my footsteps as I walked along the pavement. I smiled to myself as I reminisced about how that dog was always so obedient for me, yet she would never take a blind bit of notice of anything that Debbie ever said. Debbie always resented that dog. On one occasion her frustration had reached boiling point and she announced in no uncertain terms that either the dog went, or she would. I had simply replied, "OK, pack your bags and I'll give you a lift." How much simpler our lives might have been had she'd called my bluff that day.

I sensed that there would be nothing which would ever take me back to that house again, although I had to concede that my chance meeting with Victor had been interesting and most informative to say the least. I smiled wistfully as I remembered once leaving the house as my elderly dog sat and watched me, longing to accompany me as she so often had in her younger days. She closed one eye as if she had winked at me and instinctively, as if in some sort of secret canine-human code, I winked back. While still watching me attentively, Honey had yawned and I found myself yawning back. It was as if she and I shared some deep and primal level of communication which transcended the boundaries of species. As I continued on my journey, it was with a heavy heart that I remembered that by the time that I returned home that particular evening, Honey was gone. A sudden stroke in an arthritic old hound and the vet could do nothing. "It's for the best," Debbie had exclaimed philosophically, appearing sympathetic to my loss. She offered me a consoling hug, masking her glee that in the power struggle between woman and beast, time had proven to be the deciding factor. I, on the other hand, hid my tears behind a bottle of Jack Daniels and a locked bathroom door.

And that memory reminded me that time was getting on and I really did need to buy a bottle of wine.

Chapter 14

The Return Match

I knew very little about wine other than it was polite to turn up with a bottle when invited to someone's home for dinner. I had spent an inordinate amount of time in the supermarket trying to choose, before finally asking a fellow shopper for guidance. A well dressed lady standing next to me in the aisle had appeared to know exactly what wine she was looking for, and so I made my choice based on her advice. I arrived at the house to which I had driven Pam the previous evening and checked my watch. Noting that it was a few minutes before seven thirty, I knocked on the door holding the bottle Merlot which I had just purchased, and within a few moments I could see a figure approaching through the frosted glass pane in the door. Although the panels in the front door made it impossible to see exactly who was approaching, I assumed that it would be Pam and sure enough, as the door opened, I was greeted by her cheery smile. "Right on time," she exclaimed with a grin. "Dinner is just about ready. Come on in." I stepped inside, closed the door behind me and kissed her on the cheek. Handing her the bottle of wine, I informed her that I had not wanted to turn up empty handed after she had so kindly invited me to dinner.

"You're not trying to get me drunk again, are you?" Pam asked suggestively as she accepted my offering, looking at the label in a way that suggested she knew her wines much better than I did. "Thank you," she said, "that will go very well with dinner. I've prepared parmesan polenta topped with lemon and sage steaks, followed by panna cotta. I hope that's all right with you."

"That sounds great," I responded, despite not having a clue what she was talking about. As I followed Pam though to the dining room, the inviting aroma of her cooking wafted from the kitchen, reminding me that I had not eaten anything since the morning. I suddenly felt rather hungry, and although I had never heard of the dish which Pam had described, I was sure that it would taste better than Dave's toast and cereal. Pam had certainly made an effort to be a congenial hostess, and wore a tight fitting black dress which emphasised her slender body. The hemline of her dress came down to a little above her knee, enabling me to get a good look at her shapely legs. She had obviously taken time over her hair and make-up too, and the pout of her lips was accentuated by red lipstick. After making a point of complimenting Pam on her stunning appearance, I remembered the nature of my return visit. "Oh yes, you nearly made me forget," I said, reaching into my jacket pocket. "Here is your purse."

"Thank you," Pam replied. "I was really lost without it this morning." I followed Pam into the kitchen as she explained that she had been trying to remember where she last had her purse, and how she had phoned the bank to cancel her cards and order replacements. We continued to make small talk in the kitchen as Pam served our evening meal. Two cats, one black and white and one tabby, brushed themselves impatiently against our legs, looking up at us expectantly. For some reason, I had not previously noticed that Pam was probably only around five foot two or three, but as she stood beside me, barefoot, in close proximity within the cramped confines of her kitchen, I realised just how petite she was. Neither could I fail to notice that the subtle fragrance of her perfume was an aroma far removed from the sweat and stench of the prison environment to which I had grown accustomed.

I carried the plates of food to the dining room where our places at the table had already been set in preparation. We sat down opposite each other and I opened the wine before pouring us both a glass. As I raised my glass and toasted Pam's good health, the duplicitous nature of my deception did not sit comfortably with me. She appeared to have gone to great lengths for my benefit, yet here was I, laughing and chatting with her, eating the food which she had prepared, and all the while I was attempting to underhandedly solicit information from her with regard to her estranged husband's whereabouts. "Have you had any more nuisance calls today, then?" I asked casually, taking a sip of wine and hoping that Pam might reveal some information which I might find pertinent in my quest for Peter Fankham.

"He's tried to call me twice this evening already," began Pam. "I just wish he'd leave me alone." The subject of Peter was obviously one which agitated her immensely. "You wouldn't believe what life with that man was like," she continued. I did not let on that there had been a few revelations which Dave had made to me, nor that I had been an acquaintance of Peter, albeit many years before. However, Pam's account would prove to be most enlightening and a clear indication that Peter seemed to have made a transition from harmless village idiot to dangerous sociopath.

She explained that when she had first met him, through mutual friends, he had been kind, polite and charming. He had been extremely generous and had taken her to visit many interesting places. Pam had been recently divorced following a tempestuous previous marriage, and the early days with Peter had been fun. Within a year, Peter and Pam were married and that was when things began to change. She had previously noted that he often would say or do things that were inappropriate when they were out socialising with friends. She sensed that although she often found this trait to be embarrassing, he appeared to enjoy saying inappropriate things merely for the shock value. I did not push her to divulge any greater details on this subject, but I found myself thinking back to the days when I knew him, and this penchant for the inappropriate was certainly something I remembered well. I could recall instances when it would be only Peter who laughed at something he had said, while the rest of us cringed in discomfort, and that appeared to be a response in which he revelled.

Pam disclosed how, shortly after they were married, Peter's behaviour had become increasingly volatile. He would often drink heavily in the evenings and he smoked copious amounts of dope too. He grew paranoid and began to often question her as to where she had been that day and with whom. She grew increasingly uncomfortable with his constant questioning and wary of his temper, and always found herself trying to appease him just for a quiet life. She noticed how Peter was prone to having fallouts with friends too, sometimes over the most trivial of things, and he did not take kindly to anyone who had an opinion which differed to his. It seemed that if there was one thing which had never changed about Peter over the years, it was his that he was still by far the most opinionated of individuals. Pam complained that he would find reasons to criticise her friends and her acquaintances, and took great pleasure in belittling her with little comments which slowly eroded her self-confidence. Little by little, Peter had managed to discourage her from maintaining friendships and she had eventually become isolated from just about everyone she knew.

She further revealed that on occasion he would go out and upon his return, he would be evasive about his whereabouts. Pam began to have suspicions that maybe her husband was having an affair, but he would either be angered by her questions or ridicule her for her apparent 'madness'. Apparently, Peter had developed an interest in classic cars and motorcycles and had painstakingly organised a local charity event centring around a car show, with local bands giving up their time to perform for free one Sunday afternoon. The event had been a success with a great deal of money being raised, but problems later arose when Peter decided to secretly repatriate some of the money in order to help fund his new business venture. He subsequently invested two thousand pounds in converting their loft and installing hydroponics equipment, and then began to cultivate his own cannabis. This had worried Pam as they only lived one hundred metres or so from a primary school, and suddenly they had all manner of unsavoury characters turning up at their home to do business.

Pam admitted that there had been an occasion when a friend had turned up unannounced at Peter's place of work and an incident had ensued. In front of another work colleague, the friend had openly accused Peter of attempting to molest his daughter. Although he protested his innocence, dismissing the young girl's accusations as a simple case of unfortunate misunderstanding, the family concerned rapidly became distanced from Pam and Peter. Despite her growing concerns though, Pam had decided to give him the benefit of the doubt. One evening, her own daughter, Ruth, complained that her stepfather had walked in on her while she had been in the shower, and further claimed that he made lewd comments about her breasts. When Pam later quizzed him about it, Peter grew angry and once again suggested that it was a simple misunderstanding. Ruth had eventually left home at sixteen after telling friends that she could no longer tolerate living in the same house as her 'pervy' stepfather.

Peter, it seemed, had even managed to fall out with his own sister after making further lewd comments about his own niece. When Debbie had recoiled in horror at her brother's disgusting behaviour, he claimed that he was only joking before storming out of the house and slamming the door behind him. I found Pam's revelations regarding Peter's behaviour to be truly abhorrent and disgusting, and yet another example of just how far down the human food chain he had spiralled. I could not understand why neither woman informed the police but Pam informed me that she had begun to live in fear of Peter's angry outbursts. He had always told her to keep quiet about the drugs in the house too, claiming that if the police ever found out then she too would be arrested as an accomplice. Besides, when she had reached a point where she found herself isolated from her friends, who was there left to tell?

After digressing from the charity event story, Pam proceeded to explain how the allegations regarding the misappropriation of charity funds had continued, and Peter began to distance himself from those he had previously been associated with. Once veiled threats towards him had started, his paranoia reached fever pitch and he had grown almost too afraid to leave the house for fear of reprisal. So, as a result, Peter and Pam discussed the issue of their future and Peter decided that they would sell up and move. Within months they had relocated to a village close to Stroud, in Gloucester. The topic of conversation during our evening meal had really been an eye opener, and I got the impression that there was much that Pam had needed to get off her chest. Pam's version of events certainly seemed to corroborate Dave's story.

With dinner and dessert eaten, I helped Pam by clearing the table, and between us we washed up and tidied the kitchen while Pam continued to relate her hellish account of life with Peter. I suspect that there might be some truth in the old adage that the innocent do not run away, but will fight allegations tooth and nail. Former friends appeared to have been talking amongst themselves and comparing notes, and finally someone had decided that enough was enough and had informed the local constabulary. Therefore, it was probably no surprise when officers from Gloucestershire Police turned up on the doorstep of their new home to question Peter in relation to the missing funds. In addition, there had been questions for him to answer about the allegation made by his former friend's daughter.

The police had questioned him at the house and later at the police station in Stroud, and had also taken away his computer and his mobile phone for analysis. They also took paperwork relating to both their bank accounts, and a few days later the police returned following their investigations, and formally arrested him. Peter's computer had been analysed by forensics experts and they had found over two thousand indecent images of minors. Pam, through her fear of Peter's volatile outbursts, had been conditioned to always give him the benefit of the doubt, but now her worst fears had been realised. To compound her disgust, the police revealed that Peter's cache of images also contained images he had secretly taken of his own niece. The police had informed Debbie and Gary of the discovery, and they had been questioned under caution as to whether or not they had prior knowledge. Once the police had unearthed Peter Fankham's dark sexual secrets, they had no further interest in the missing charity money.

During the resulting court case, which had culminated in Peter being sentenced to two years in prison, Debbie had been called as a key prosecution witness. As Pam related the details of the court proceedings, I said nothing but could not help but hope that Debbie had been a more honest and reliable witness on that occasion than she had during my trial. Peter had not expected his own sister to give evidence against him, but after a life of constantly having to make allowances for her brother's depraved behaviour, not even she could forgive such a crime against his own niece. Finally she made the decision to wash her hands of him once and for all. Peter served eight months of his sentence before being released on licence with the provision that he would remain on the Sex Offenders Register for ten years.

Pam poured us both another glass of red wine and we retired to the sofa, sitting at opposite ends, facing each other while we relaxed and talked. Pam seemed so self-assured that I simply could not comprehend how she had allowed herself to become so manipulated and downtrodden. She explained how she looked back and believed that Peter had chipped away at her over a period of time, and little by little she had lost sight of her own identity without even realising. Once she had been given the opportunity of distancing herself from him, she had slowly been able to rebuild her life, concentrating on her inner strength and dexterity. She knew that his attempts to contact her were merely a ploy to try and exercise his powers of control but as far as Pam was concerned, the psychological ties that once bound her to him were now well and truly severed.

"I spent months seeing a counsellor," revealed Pam, "and that really helped me. He taught me that it was Peter who was the weak one and not me. His bullying and manipulation was done because of low self-esteem and a fragile ego; according to my counsellor anyway. He explained that Peter's anger probably came from what he called narcissistic rage, and it was most likely a reaction to his low self-esteem being challenged. Anyway, we discussed coping mechanisms and such, and I learned a lot which helped me to grow stronger. I've been able to rebuild friendships with some of my old friends, and I've also made some new ones." Pam smiled, leaned forward and patted my hand.

Much of what Pam said sounded like psycho-babble to me, but who was I to cast aspersions? To be honest, what she said did seem to make sense, and the important thing was that her counselling sessions had obviously made a difference to her. Not once during the course of the evening had either of us even remotely touched upon our unexpected sexual encounter of the previous evening. Listening to Pam recount those horrific revelations of her relationship with Peter, I began to feel that she was far too vulnerable to take advantage of, and my discomfort compounded as a struggled to come to terms with the situation which I had engineered. Noting that our glasses were nearly empty, Pam leaned forward and picked up the wine bottle from the coffee table and asked "would you care for another glass, Steve?"

Instinctively, I answered her. "Thank you, that's very kind of you." No sooner had those words leapt out of my mouth than I realised my error. I tried hard to mask my sudden sense of unease and I awkwardly readjusted my position on the sofa, unable to look Pam in the eye. "But my name is John, remember? Who's Steve then?" I stuttered flippantly, while smiling in an attempt to regain my composure and hoping that Pam had simply let the wrong name slip out. After topping up our glasses, Pam placed the empty wine bottle back on the coffee table and sat back at the opposite end of the sofa. She took a sip of her wine, smiled back, but said nothing. It was the kind of smile that someone smiles when they know that someone else is trying to be evasive. I sensed that Pam was watching me closely, trying to gauge my reaction. I nervously feigned laughter. "What?" I questioned defensively and sat waiting for her answer. Still smiling while taking another mouthful of wine, Pam continued to observe me. The inordinate length of time she took to reply did nothing to quell my rising discomfort.

"Oh yes, of course. It's John, isn't it," Pam eventually replied. She casually placed her glass on the coffee table before adding, "I'm so sorry. For a moment I got you confused with Steve." She paused once more to gauge my reaction before asking, "Steve Caldwell. Do you know him?" Once again she observed me closely, but now her expression appeared impassive. In vain I tried to plead ignorance after all, I had been so cautious in concealing my deceit. Surely there was no way that Pam could have seen through my veil of duplicity. Pam sat facing me, with one foot on the sofa, her knee drawn up and her arms folded, guardedly. "Come on Steve, you can drop the 'John' thing now, I'm not stupid. I worked out who you were in the pub yesterday evening." Pam was certainly intuitive and clearly more perceptive than I had had given her credit for. She had noted how often I had glanced away when she asked certain questions. It was obvious that Pam was not bluffing and I wondered how she had worked out who I really was, and more to the point, what she would do if I openly admitted to my pretence.

Pam commenced her evaluation by informing me of a conversation which she had once overheard between Peter and Debbie. "Debbie stayed with us for a few days after she left Gary," Pam began. "One evening I left Pete and Deb sharing a joint in the living room while I made coffee, but when I came back, the door had been pushed closed a little although I could hear them talking quietly. I heard Deb saying that she was worried that 'Steve' might try looking for them. Peter told her that he doubted if they would ever see 'Steve' again. When I opened the door, they suddenly stopped talking." Although Pam had considered the conversation which she had overheard to be strangely secretive, it was not until a few weeks after Debbie had left that she tentatively questioned Peter about who 'Steve' was. Peter, in his usual dismissive fashion, had simply waved away any significance, dismissing it as 'just Debbie getting paranoid about an ex'. Peter had never been one to be able to conceal other people's secrets for too long though, and he loved being in a position where he had knowledge of a confidentiality. The sense of power created by such knowledge would positively inflate his ego to the point where he would find it necessary to drop little hints, just to maintain his sense of supremacy and further bloat his self importance.

And so, over the weeks which followed, Peter's loose tongue had given away enough threads of information for Pam to stitch together the outline of the story. She was aware that Debbie had a former husband; someone who had never really been spoken of in the past. It seemed that this mysterious ex could eventually be released from a prison in Poland, and during one evening when Peter's weakness for cannabis had rendered him less restrained in secrecy than usual, he had told her that Debbie's paranoia had been building up and she was growing fearful that 'Steve' would come looking for them. "I asked him if you were dangerous," said Pam. "He just giggled like a child and said no, you had actually been a musician. When I asked him why you were in prison, I was really shocked when he told me that it was for murder. He was really stoned and laughed when he told me that not only were you not guilty, but they could have got you off. He seemed to think it was funny. After that," added Pam, "he wouldn't talk about it again."

It was clear that there was no point in continuing my charade any longer. "So, tell me," I asked, "when exactly did you realise that I wasn't John Turner?"

Pam explained that while Debbie had been staying with them, Debbie had shown her some photos in an album which had been taken when she was much younger. In one photo, Debbie was standing next to a man who was wearing a black leather jacket, and both of them were holding horses by the reins. Pam had asked Debbie who the man was, and she replied that it was her ex-husband who she never spoke about. "You had more hair then," Pam quipped. She had thought it strange that Debbie had kept a photo of someone she did not want to be reminded of.

"Christ," I exclaimed, unable to hide my surprise, "I remember that photo. It was taken after we'd been horse riding on Dartmoor."

Pam proclaimed how that memory had enabled her to see through my deception. "I started to wonder when you said last night that you were a musician, and you also mentioned Poland. For someone who didn't even know Peter, you seemed very interested in him. And then," she added, "I remembered seeing that photograph, put two and two together, and just knew it had to be you."

I was trying to comprehend this sudden change in circumstance. "But that means when we were in the car last night, you already had your suspicions," I contested.

Pam had a wicked glint in her eye. "Yes, I know," she said. "Pete would have hated it if he knew what I was doing with you, and the thought of that really turned me on." I sat perplexed and wanted to know why she had

171

allowed the charade to continue unchallenged. "I suppose that I just wanted to be sure, and maybe hear your side of the story," she replied.

Pam listened in shock and disbelief as I put forward my self-defence. I told her about that fateful night in Krakow, how Annika Radwanski had found her way into my hotel room and, more pointedly, how her naked and lifeless body had been found in a pool of blood on the bathroom floor. I told her about the elusive Polish pharmacist witness, and how Debbie's testimony had ultimately left me languishing in a foreign prison for a murder which I had not committed. I could feel my anger smouldering as I stupidly asked Pam if she had any idea what it felt like being made a scapegoat, abandoned and left to rot. Of course she didn't, but she too had her own story of her years of virtual imprisonment with a perverted bully. I had suddenly felt backed into a corner and had not expected to be telling her my story. "I'm sure that it was Peter, Gary and Debbie who the pharmacist had seen that night," I said, taking a sharp intake of breath to calm myself, "but I just need to find out the truth."

With a sense that a great weight had been lifted off my chest, I began to regain control over my raw emotions. Despite the passing of more than a quarter of a century, my inclination towards indignation and confusion had not abated one iota since the moment when I had been arrested and beaten. "Oh my God," exclaimed Pam, unable to hide her shock, "that's absolutely dreadful." She leaned forward and stroked my arm soothingly before remarking, "God, you're tense."

I said nothing but felt calmed by the sensation of human contact. Pam edged her way off of the sofa and knelt in front of me, resting her hands on my knees. "So, you thought you could work on me to find out where Peter is, did you?" she asked as she rubbed her hands along my thighs. Feeling a little embarrassed to say the least, I nevertheless felt compelled to confess that it had been my intention. "Well personally speaking, I think that Peter owes you an explanation," Pam declared as her right hand began to gently massage my crotch. Despite my anxiety, I could feel my cock starting to grow as Pam rubbed her hand along its length.

"You only had to ask and I'd have told you exactly where that bastard is," she proclaimed as she began to unfasten the button on my jeans before provocatively unzipping them. I relaxed back onto the sofa as Pam licked the tip of my penis, seductively looking up at me, her eyes transfixed, relishing her power over me. I watched intently as her red lips effortlessly worked their way up and down the length of my shaft, and I saw how her eyes sparkled with the same wicked glint that I had noticed the previous evening. Pam stood upright with her slender legs parted slightly and whispered, "well, in my book, you owe me." Powerless, and devoid of any will to resist, I watched her lift up her dress to reveal a pair of black lace knickers.

"Anything, you say," I replied, held captive by the rising tide of sexual tension, "just name it." Shamelessly, Pam slid her hand inside her knickers, slipping her fingers into her pussy as I watched. She leaned forward and traced her fingers across my lips, enticing me to savour the juice which glistened upon her red painted nails. Salaciously, I took her fingers into my mouth, feeling highly aroused by the taste of her love juice. Pam pulled her knickers to one side and straddled me, grasping my

173

cock before guiding it inside her. She closed her eyes and gasped as she slowly lowered herself onto me. With my hands on her thighs, I lustfully pushed the hem of her dress out of the way to enable a clearer view, and almost instinctively she pulled her knickers aside a little further to expose her shaven mound. I became transfixed as I watched her pussy lips stretch and slide around my erection as we moved rhythmically in our union. Excited by the vision of Pam's love juice glistening along the length of my cock, I began to repeatedly thrust hard into her, causing her to lean forward and place her hands on the back of the sofa on either side of my head. I could feel her juices trickle down my inner thigh, soaking my balls as I placed my hands on her small breasts, squeezing them gently.

"Anything I say?" whispered Pam provocatively, "what a wonderful philosophy you have." Reaching around her, I unzipped her dress and unclasped her bra to reveal her breasts. Passionately, I pulled her towards me and sucked both of her hard nipples in turn, taking time to tease each one between my teeth, flicking my tongue across them. I cupped her breasts in my hands and pinched her nipples between thumb and forefinger before Pam sat upright and tossed her discarded bra onto the sofa beside us. "Kill him!" she gasped as I continued to thrust inside her. "I want you to kill him."

In a single movement, I lifted her up and flipped her onto her back without my cock slipping out of her. I leaned over her, kissed her neck and whispered, "are you sure?"

"Oh fuck, yes," she commanded, her eyes wide and her voice carrying more venom than an angry cobra. "I want you to make him suffer, just like he made me suffer."

Pam both shocked and excited me at the same time and I could feel myself close to my moment of ejaculation. I slipped out of her to avoid cumming too soon, too caught up in the passion to allow it to end too quickly. I kissed my way down her body and knelt in front of her, placing my hands on her thighs and gently pushing her legs apart. "Do you really hate him that much?" I asked, as Pam slipped two fingers into her moist vagina,

Seductively, she licked her fingers before spreading her pussy lips wide to exhibit her well fucked hole. "You'll never know how much I hate that evil bastard," she said, staring me straight in the eye. "Now lick me," she ordered. I followed her instructions, sucking her clitoris before slipping my tongue into her wet pussy, savouring her taste while she spread her lips, encouraging me to work my tongue inside her as far as it would go. She held my head tight against her crotch, grinding herself against me, gasping and moaning as her juice moistened my face and ran down my chin. I slipped two fingers inside her vagina while my other hand sought the warmth of her breast. Hungrily, I lapped the juices that almost seemed to flow unabated from her wet cunt, soaking my fingers as they repeatedly worked their way in and out. My other hand continued to caress Pam's breast, squeezing her nipple until the desire to feel my cock inside her once again had become a need, a hunger that only fucking her could satisfy.

"How shall I kill him?" I whispered as I plunged my cock deep inside her once more.

Pam gasped as I entered her. "You'll need to make it look like an accident," she answered with a wicked smile as her hips gyrated rhythmically and perfectly synchronised with each thrust. I may have sought this woman with the expressed intention of deceiving her, but I was playing a game which clearly Pam played better. "He usually goes out for a drink on a Friday evening," she said, her words punctuated by gasps as I fucked her harder and faster. "You could be there waiting, ready to surprise him." Moaning in pleasure, she bit the corner of her bottom lip, awaiting my reaction. She slid her right hand between her legs and closed her fingers around my shaft, feeling me sliding in and out of her. Frantically, she rubbed her clitoris, her fingers pressing hard into the soft flesh.

I felt her warm juices pumping from her pussy as her muscles twitched and tightened around me. With her head tilted backward, her hips bucked as she reached orgasm, unable to suppress her screams. Pam must have known that after many years of being isolated from the warmth of a woman's naked flesh, I would have at least one weakness; sex. It felt totally immoral to be planning her husband's murder during intercourse, but Pam appeared to derive a distinct sexual pleasure from it, arousing her to the point of orgasm. Caught up in that intense moment of passion, Pam's obvious level of arousal was without doubt intrinsically linked to mine. My breathing quickened and I gasped as I edged towards my own orgasm. "Cum inside me," Pam urged as she locked her legs around me. My thrusts accelerated until I finally drove hard into her, my cum spurting deep inside as she groaned, "oh fuck, yes." Her arms collapsed by her side and she lay back exhausted. I sank back onto my knees, my cock slipping out of her, sticky and glistening with a mixture of love juice and semen.

Pam lay there for a moment, gasping for breath, her legs still spread and her body glistening with sweat. She gently ran her hands over her body, teasing her nipples and pulling them as far as her small breasts would allow. Her dishevelled dress was crumpled around her midriff and my semen oozed into her knickers. Pam slipped her hand inside her lace panties and sat upright to survey the sticky mess. "Where's your phone?" she asked. "I want you to take a photo." Without question, I did as she asked and then showed her the resulting image. "Oh, that's good," she smirked. "I want you to show that to Peter, and I want it to be the last thing he ever sees," she hissed, her voice spiteful and filled of hate.

The scenario which I had planned for the evening was certainly not the one that had actually played out. Pam skilfully played her hand better than I, and had somehow managed to turn the tables in her favour. Either Pamela Carter would prove to be a powerful ally or a very dangerous enemy. Only time could answer that question.

Chapter 15

Human Garbage

I had caught the train to Stroud and then walked the three miles into the village of Painswick. By the time I had finally reached Rushworth Farm, the light on that warm September evening was starting to fade and the place appeared deserted. One of the downstairs windows had been broken, making the house look almost derelict, and I stood on the driveway for a few moments, pondering my next move. It was serene and peaceful except for the twittering of a few birds in the nearby trees. As swallows darted silently back and forth in pursuit of the evening's insects, I walked cautiously along the driveway at the side of the house. Around the back I noticed a small barn, beside which was a pen housing a few scraggy looking chickens who were pecking away at the bare earth.

I tried the handle on the back door, slowly and gingerly, trying hard not to make a sound which might alert any occupants inside. The handle turned with an audible groan, and I paused once again before gritting my teeth as the door creaked open a fraction. "How careless," I thought to myself, "leaving the door unlocked." I waited for a moment, listening for any sounds from within, but there was nothing. I slowly and quietly entered the house and tiptoed through the kitchen. The sink was full of unwashed dishes and pans, dead flies lined the window sill and a partially eaten sandwich sat on a plate which had been left on the worktop next to rows of empty beer cans and wine bottles.

I made my way down the hall, pausing to check the downstairs dining room and front room. The house was small, a little run down and more than in need of a lick of paint. The dining room contained a table, a few wooden chairs and a dresser, on which was piled a stack of letters and a pile of newspapers. The curtains were only open a crack in the front room, allowing a limited amount of light to filter in, creating a rather dingy atmosphere. As my eyes struggled to grow accustomed to the darkness, I knocked my shin on the corner of what appeared to be a rather decrepit brown cloth sofa. Through the half-light, I could see two book cases, an armchair and an aged television set. There was a small coffee table in the middle of the room which was stacked with more newspapers, and an ashtray which was full to the point of overflowing. The contents of the ashtray appeared to indicate that Peter still maintained his liking for weed, and the smell of stale cannabis smoke hung heavily in the air.

The stairs creaked as I slowly made my ascent, dust and grime sticking to my hands as I gripped the bannister rail. The pungent aroma of fresh cannabis grew stronger as I climbed the stairs. I pushed open the bathroom door to reveal a level of unspeakable squalor which surpassed anything I had yet seen in the house. There were two more rooms upstairs, one of which was full of boxes and appeared to be used solely for storage, and the other was the bedroom. I kicked open the bedroom door and immediately noticed a stack of porno books beside the bed, another sign that Peter's habits had changed little in the intervening years. The sheets on the unmade bed appeared as if they had not been washed since the dawn of time, indicating that domestically speaking, Peter Fankham was clearly not fairing too well on his own. In the corner of the bedroom stood a wardrobe in which there were no signs of any female items of clothing, only garments which I would associate with some sort of farmer or country type. Obviously, Pam had been right when she told me that Peter had been living a solitary life since his release from prison, and it was also abundantly clear that Peter the Pervert was not at home.

Stepping upon the wooden chair on the landing, I opened the loft hatch and pulled down the ladder. The sweet smell of herb was almost overpowering as I climbed into the brightly lit loft space. There must have been thirty plants at varying stages of growth, all heated by large overhead lamps. Clearly this was not just for personal use, I thought to myself. Peter always liked to think of himself as something of a dealer, but it appeared that he had expanded his operation these days. A pack of cable ties lay conveniently by the opening, and so I slipped a handful into my pocket before climbing back down the ladder and closing the hatch.

I made my way back outside to investigate the barn, and once inside it I found a vintage 1968 BSA 650 Lightning motorcycle. I took a moment to admire the classic machine and its gleaming chrome work before continuing my search. I noticed a work bench and a collection of tools, a sack of chicken feed and a couple of wooden crates. One of the crates was empty while the other contained potatoes. Beside the crates, coiled up on the floor, I found a length of rope. "Perfect," I thought to myself. Over the years I had played out so many revenge scenarios in my mind, but now I would have to rely on current circumstances and my imagination. I emptied the contents of the potato crate onto the floor, picked up the rope and fashioned it into a make shift noose, placing it in a neat coil on the work bench. I stood back to admire my handiwork with a sense of satisfaction and then returned to the house. I made my way into the living room and sat in the armchair, lit a cigarette and waited for my prey to return. Although I had no idea where he was, I was prepared to wait as long as it took. This moment had been a long time coming and right now, I had nowhere else that I needed to be.

It was dark and I had just lit another cigarette when I heard footsteps outside. I braced myself as keys jangled in the lock, and then I could hear the front door opening. I listened intently as he took off his coat in the hallway, and then followed the sound of his footsteps as they came closer. Gauging by the uneasy footsteps, I could assume that Peter was drunk and had probably returned from the local village pub, just as Pam had suggested. Through the darkness I could now see his silhouette in the doorway as he fumbled for the light switch.

"Good evening. Peter Fankham, I presume." From the comfort of his armchair, I greeted his return as he finally managed to flick on the light switch. He stood there perplexed, unsure of whom or what was relaxing in the gloom. Despite the fact that he was now sporting a beard, and I had not seen him in nearly three decades, I still recognised him immediately. He was also currently sporting a very swollen and very painful looking black eye. Perhaps he was now a little more rotund than I had remembered but other than that, time, and his stint in prison, appeared to have been relatively kind to him. Without word or warning, Peter turned and clumsily made a run for it. I jumped up and raced after him, reaching him just as he was opening the front door. I pushed him hard in the back, causing the door to slam shut with such force that I thought the frosted glass panels would shatter. I grabbed his neck with one hand and his shoulder with the other, spinning him around and pushing him face down on the stairs. I twisted his arm behind his back and lay my full weight on him to prevent his escape.

"Does this remind you of prison?" I whispered in his ear.

"Fuck off," Peter groaned in discomfort, "who are you? What do you want?"

"That's a lovely way to welcome an old friend, I must say" came my reply through gritted teeth as I struggled with my free hand to get a cable tie around his wrists.

"Who the fuck are you?" Peter repeated. "Do you want the weed? Is that what you've come for? Go ahead, take it." He pleaded, clearly having no idea as to who I was or the reason for my visit. I dragged him to his feet and escorted him forcibly into the living room, throwing him onto the sofa. I took out a cigarette, lit it and inhaled the smoke as the pumping adrenaline subsided. I watched Peter struggle to sit upright with his hands cable tied behind his back.

"So who gave you the black eye?" I enquired, devoid of any genuine concern for his welfare.

"Some wanker down the pub," he replied tersely. Peter obviously still had the ability to rub people up the wrong way and then consider their response to be a result of their own character flaw. We sat in silence for what seemed like an eternity and I watched him as his drunken, puffy eyelids grew heavy. Jumping up, I slapped him hard across the face just to keep him awake. "Ahh fuck," he cried, struggling to sit upright, unable and unwilling to fight back. "What the fuck do you want anyway?" He muttered the words as if he were close to tears.

"Can't I come and visit an old friend?" I calmly replied, leaning forward to stub out my cigarette. "So, how have you been? What have you been up to lately?"

"I... I... I don't know what you're talking about," Peter protested.

"Oh Peter," I replied, "you're really disappointing me, you know. I've heard that you've been a rather naughty boy recently."

Not only was Peter Fankham monumentally stupid, but his list of sins was probably lengthy. So stupid, in fact, that there appeared no way that he was ever going to work out why he was in this current situation. Was it drug dealing, cannabis production, child abuse, child pornography or a prison debt? Not for a single moment did he think of his former brother in law, who he had fitted up for murder nearly thirty years earlier. His eyelids grew heavy again, and once more I jumped up and slapped him hard across the cheek. "What happened to your window?" I enquired, with an air of disinterest.

"Fucking kids" came his sneering reply. "I fucking hate 'em."

"That's not what I heard," I responded, unable to resist the chance to be both poignant and sarcastic in the same sentence.

"Fuck off," barked Peter, clearly not in the mood for witticisms.

"Alright, alright, calm down," I said, barely able to contain my delight at winding him up. "You better get that fixed before winter comes or you'll freeze to death in here," I added.

"What do you care?" Peter muttered, with a hint of sarcasm of his own.

"I don't," I responded bluntly. "It's your funeral, I guess".

"So, what do you want?" Peter asked once more after a long silence, and I sensed an element of desperation in his voice. The hour was late and Peter appeared drunk, tired and less than comfortable. From the look of the bruising and graze around his eye, it could be concluded that an evening which had already ended on a sour note in the pub, was now clearly getting worse. "I, I, I've got no money lying around, if that's what you're after," Peter stuttered, pleadingly. I did not respond, choosing instead to just stare blankly at him while I lit another cigarette. "Is it the weed you're after?" Peter continued to try and fathom out the purpose of my late night visit. "It's just a little personal gear. You know, just for my own use, like…"

"Personal?" I cut in. "You're growing weed on an industrial scale upstairs. If that's just for personal use, then you've got yourself quite a habit, my ol' son." Peter looked embarrassed and slightly shocked at the same time. "It's fucking obvious, mate." I added. "You can get stoned on the smell when you walk in through the front door. I'm surprised you haven't been nicked already. Anyway," I continued, "no I don't want your fucking drugs and I don't want your fucking money. I just want you to think long and hard for a while, and if there are any brain cells which you haven't burned out yet, then maybe you'll be able to answer a few questions for me. Deal?" Peter looked up at me, although I would not say that he appeared overly enthusiastic. I glanced at my watch; it was 3:05. "Come on mate," I said in a hushed tone, "you're tired. Let's go for a little walk and see if we can wake you up a bit."

"Where to?" Peter enquired with a sudden overwhelming sound of panic in his voice. I pulled him up from the couch and escorted him into the kitchen. He may have been drunk, tired and confused but just before we reached the kitchen door he began to struggle. He turned suddenly and made an attempt to head butt me but I stepped back and dodged the blow. With his hands fastened behind his back, he began frantically kicking at me. I grabbed for the kitchen drawer and pulled the handle so hard that the entire draw came out in my hand, sending forks, knives and spoons jangling and clattering to the floor. As Peter's frantic kicks continued, I swung the empty draw hard at the side of his head, connecting firmly and sending him staggering sideways. His knees buckled and he collapsed, breathless, onto the kitchen floor. I bent down to pick up a sharp kitchen knife and crouching over him, I held the knife with the tip of the blade pressed against his neck. With the adrenaline pumping within me once more, and the blade pressing into his skin, I could have slit his filthy child molesting throat there and then. However, that was not how the night needed to end.

"Pull a stunt like that again, you paedo fuckstick and I'll tear you a new one." I growled, with a growing menace. I pulled him up, wrenching his arms behind him. I opened the door and still holding the knife to his throat, we ventured outside into the darkness. A blast of cold night air tensed my every fibre further, making me feel like a tightly coiled spring. I bundled Peter into the barn and grabbed the rope from the work bench. I slipped the noose which I'd fashioned earlier in the evening around his neck, before he even had time to notice. I yanked the rope hard, pulling it taut around his throat and causing him to stagger backwards. Peter lost his balance and fell awkwardly to the floor, emitting a stifled yelp which was not dissimilar to the sound made by an unruly dog which had been pinched by the sudden jerking of its choke chain. "Get up," I hissed, pulling the rope upward. Peter struggled to his feet with little co-ordination. I threw the end of the rope over the wooden rafter above the crates and caught it as it fell back down, with a sense of self-satisfaction that I had successfully completed this task in one attempt. Once again I pulled the rope taut, ensuring that the evil fucker had no way of escape.

I had an overwhelming feeling of empowerment as I gazed upon this cowering wretch, this human garbage with his hands bound, trussed up like a Christmas turkey. It was a feeling for which I had yearned, ever since I had first been given a hint about the role which Peter Fankham had played in the theft of my life. It began to alarm and anger me that not only did it seem that Peter had not recognised me, but he appeared to not make any attempt to fathom out who I was either. He seemed to be unable to grasp the gravity of his current situation, or how it may have consequences for his long term future. I wanted him to grovel, to plead for his life but instead his eyes were cast downward, unable to look me in the eye. It was as if Peter was resigned to his fate, ready to accept the inevitability of death and perhaps even longing for it. I began to wonder if I could have been wrong. What if he had not been involved in the act of leaving Annika Radwanski's naked and lifeless body in my hotel room? "How much do you value your life?" I asked.

"Pardon?" he answered, his eyes looking directly at me for once.

"Well Peter," I continued, "do you honestly believe that you have made a valuable contribution to society as a whole? I mean, you seem to have made yourself quite an unpopular fellow."

"I, I, don't know what you mean," he stammered.

"Let me put it this way," I began to elaborate further. "Do you feel that history will judge you kindly? How many people do you think would turn up at your funeral, if it were, say... tomorrow?" I pulled the rope a little tighter, causing Peter to choke.

"I, I, don't know what you mean," Peter pleaded, gasping for breath.

I pulled the rope even tighter, lifting his chin upwards and causing him to struggle agitatedly. "Perhaps I'm not making myself clear," I said pointedly, releasing the tension on the rope just enough to allow Peter to breathe. "Allow me to elaborate. It seems that you have a remarkable ability to piss people off and infect every person you come into contact with, just like some sort of cancer. Everyone you've ever known has grown to either dislike or despise you and now, here you are, on your own, living in this filthy shit hole. Fucking hell, Peter, even your fucking chickens are digging an escape route, just to get away from you." As Peter looked at me quizzically and embarrassed, as if he were some scolded schoolboy, I began to lose patience. Pulling the rope tight once more, I growled and motioned towards the crates behind him. "Get up on those fucking boxes, you cunt." Peter struggled for breath, choking as I pulled on the rope harder, his feet performing some kind of bizarre dance as he tried to maintain control of his footing. "Get up on those fucking boxes before I choke the fucking life out of you," I barked, feeling myself on the verge of losing self-control completely.

Peter turned awkwardly and did as he was told. Without the use of his hands, it took him a few attempts to make the ascent. Just like a dog on a choke chain, it only took a little gentle encouragement with a few timely jerks on the rope, and he managed to perform the task which I had requested. Keeping the rope taut enough to ensure that Peter would not attempt to disembark from his pedestal, I edged over to the motorbike and sat astride it, all the while keeping tight hold of my end of the rope. "Nice bike," I said. "Is it yours?" Peter nodded. "Is it fucking yours?" I barked louder, punctuating my words. "Where are your fucking manners, you bastard? I expect you to answer me, not nod like a fucking idiot."

"Yes it is," replied Peter. "I bought it after my father died".

In mentioning the passing of his father, I sensed that he may have been trying to evoke some feeling of compassion inside me. What a cynical attempt to defuse his current situation, I thought to myself. After all, as I remembered their relationship, Peter had spent much of his time either trying to impress his father or gain acceptance from him and either way, he had failed miserably. Needless to say, as far as Alan Fankham was concerned, he considered that his son, Peter, was something of a great disappointment to him. "Oh yeah," I said, without warmth or condolence, "I heard about that. A heart attack on holiday, wasn't it?"

"Yes, that's right," answered Peter, sounding more than a little surprised. "How do you know that? Should I know you?"

"Damn right, you should, you fucking waste of spunk," I hissed, pulling the rope tighter. "Room 13, 1986, does that ring any bells?" I added with a hint of sarcasm in my voice as I looped the rope around the motorbike's fuel tank, before securing it firmly. I took a moment to admire my handiwork before turning my attention back to Peter Fankham as he balanced on top of the two crates. I then allowed my vision to follow the line of the rope, upward from his neck and over the beam. It was unable to slip sideways as it was lodged against an upright roof support. The rope then angled down to the point where it was secured around the motorbike.

"Room 13?" Peter appeared somewhat perplexed for a moment.

"Yes, that's right. Room 13, you fucking cretin," I snapped back, staring him straight in the face. "Krakow, Poland, 1986," I reminded him. "That was where I woke up to find a dead, naked blonde in my bathroom and police kicking my door down. Even a fucking idiot like you must be able to remember that."

"I, I, I don't know anything about it." Peter protested his innocence, although I noted that he was no longer able to look me in the eye. I also sensed from his agitation that it had now finally dawned on him exactly who I was. I had to concede that the long years which I had spent in a foreign prison had obviously taken their toll on my appearance, and to such an extent that I was now unrecognisable to anyone who had once known me. Since my release, I had continued to shave my head close, just as I had grown accustomed to during the time of my incarceration. Had I changed so much that Peter could not recognise me now? Had his life been so full of wrongdoing that he could not remember this one minor transgression against me? How many people must there be queuing up to hang this bastard in the early hours of the morning, or was he just monumentally stupid? I was beginning to think that the latter could well have been the case.

"So, Peter," I continued after a moment of silence, "what can you remember about that night? I mean, I clearly remember the gig, I clearly remember the after show party, and I clearly remember going to bed with my wife, but I don't remember your sister checking out, and I'd certainly have remembered if I'd left a fucking dead blonde on the bathroom floor the night before." Peter seemed unable to find the words to formulate any sort of coherent sentence. Perhaps he was trying to think of anything which might enable him to wriggle out of this situation.

I continued to enlighten him. "You see, Peter, it troubled me for so long; did I do it, didn't I do it? I had even begun to wonder if I'd ever know. And then I received news that someone had actually come forward, someone who was watching from the landing that night. A pharmacist who had watched two men carry an unconscious blonde into my room; one was tall and skinny, and the other was short and fat. Now, I'm no Sherlock Holmes, but even I can work out that it was you and Gary who dragged that woman into my room, either unconscious or dead already, and you left her there in my fucking bathroom. All I need you to do now, Peter, is to tell me why."

"And then you let me go?" Peter enquired, his voice quivering with desperation.

"I'll think about it," I replied, reassuringly. "After all, I'm only here for a few answers, mate."

"You've gotta believe me, I didn't want any part of it." Peter whimpered, pleading his innocence. "Debbie and Gary had been seeing each other behind your back for a while, and..."

"How long for?" I cut in, with interest.

"Err, I dunno, maybe about six months, I suppose," Peter answered. "Gary had been sorting Deb out with gear for a while before that, and you weren't supposed to know. She didn't want you to know that she was doing drugs heavier than you realised and she knew you wanted her to stop. I think she started sleeping with Gary just for the gear, man, and it all got out of hand..."

"What?" I cut in again. "And you never thought to tell me any of this at the time?"

"She was my sister, man, and she didn't want you to know. What the fuck was I supposed to do?" Peter pleaded.

"OK, fair point, I suppose," I offered, shrugging my shoulders before reaching into my jacket pocket for a cigarette. "Carry on," I urged as I lit one and took a long draw, blowing out a large plume of smoke which drifted upwards in the cool night air. "This is getting interesting."

"Anyway," Peter continued, "Deb was pregnant and she'd worked out that it must've happened while you were on tour and so it must've been Gary's. Gary told her that all would be fine and he promised her the earth. The only problem was that you were in the way. Then, that night of the after show, Gary gave that Polish bird some smack after you'd gone. We had shared a joint with her, and Gary was trying to impress her with his stash, like he was some sort of drug lord. She said she'd like to try the speed, but Gary didn't have any left so he offered her some heroin. She wasn't sure about it, but Gary convinced her that it was the best drug and she'd love it."

I had not even been aware that Gary was using heroin, and it had been a drug that I had always steered clear of, and the people who took it. Heroin users will lie, cheat and steal and drag down everyone around them. "Of course he took smack at the time," said Peter, "even my sister was taking it." That announcement from Peter stunned me. How could I not have noticed that my own wife was taking heroin? I asked Peter to explain further what had happened to Annika Radwanski.

"Gary took her into the toilet and a few minutes later he came rushing back out, saying that the girl was struggling to breathe. When I went in there with him, she was doubled up in pain and then collapsed on the floor, like she'd OD'd or something. He was shitting himself that he'd get done, so when we got the chance to get her out of the place, we carried her back to the hotel. Gary thought that Debbie might know what to do but when we got there, the girl had no pulse and no heartbeat. That's when he got me to help him set you up."

"So, why didn't you just tell him to fuck off?" I quizzed.

"Because he... he... because he had something on me," Peter answered, looking ashamed.

"So what exactly did he have on you?" I asked, now even more interested. After all, what leverage could one man have on another which would make him willing enough to murder a woman, and set up someone who was supposed to be a friend? Well, alright, so 'friend' was pushing it a bit, I guess. Peter was by now looking visibly embarrassed and ashamed in equal measure and so I encouraged him to continue. "Go on, Peter, you may as well tell me. You've got nothing to lose." Peter then proceeded to tell me a story of how Gary had caught him with a rent boy in his room one night and had threatened to expose him for his liking of sex with young lads and, his willingness to pay for it.

"Jeez, you really are an arsehole. Everyone had already sussed you out," I said, almost laughing out loud. "There was nothing that you would have ever considered too depraved, was there. Anyway, so what happened once you got the comatose blonde into my room?"

"We knocked on the door and Debbie opened it. She had been expecting Gary to come to the room once you'd fallen asleep," Peter elaborated. "Gary had slipped a Librium into your drink earlier in the evening, so that you wouldn't be woken up by her leaving the room. Deb was shocked and a bit panicky when we carried the girl in. Honestly, we'd only taken her there because we didn't know what else to do with her."

I must say that listening to Peter's story about the Librium explained how all this could have happened without me noticing a thing. "So, whose fucking idea was it to slash her up, leave her in my bathroom and let me take the blame for it?" I asked him, with an element of understandable anger in my voice.

"It was Gary's idea." Peter was now singing like a bird. "You were out for the count and he suggested that as we all needed a way out of the situation then it was a perfect opportunity."

"So, what was Debbie's reaction?" I interjected.

"She was panicking... we all were," answered Peter, "but Gary said that it would all work out perfectly for everyone."

"Everyone except me," I reminded him, angrily.

"Oh, c'mon," Peter continued, "Gary didn't give a shit about you. All he was interested in was Debbie. Things couldn't have worked out better for him. He just dragged the girl into the bathroom and took off all her clothes, and then just started to stab her all over. I mean, you gotta believe me, man, I didn't even know he had a knife. He just pulled it out of his pocket and started stabbing her."

"So what did you and Debbie do while all this was going on?" I wanted to know.

"Nothin' man. We didn't know what to do. It was all just so fucked up, I guess," offered Peter. "Gary just took over and told us not to freak out. He wiped the handle of the knife on your t-shirt, and then used it to place the knife handle in your hand while you was asleep. He left the blade in the bathroom right next to the body, and then the three of us left and went back to his hotel room. In the morning, we met up with the others and told them that Debbie had caught you with a woman who you'd picked up at the party, and that she'd left you after a row." Continuing the story, Peter added "everyone was shocked when they heard that the police arrested you, but the three of us just agreed to keep it quiet. Honestly, you gotta believe me, none of us thought you'd get life."

Well, I guess they had all been wrong, because life had been just what I had been sentenced to. Life, for something I had not even done, a crime so heinous that I would be labelled for the rest of my days. The murder of a talented and innocent young woman would hang around my neck like an albatross.

"I've told you everything, man," Peter begged, "so will you let me down now?" I gazed up at him, thoughtfully. After all those years of not knowing, it had only taken a little gentle encouragement to entice Peter to finally tell me the truth about what had happened. Granted, I had only heard Peter's version of the truth, but it was a confession nevertheless. Gazing at Peter while considering my next move, I could not decide who I detested more; this vile, fat turd on the end of the rope, or The Spaceman who, according to Peter, had manipulated the whole thing in a callous and calculating manner.

For all I knew, Peter may well have put his own slant on the story just to try and save his own skin. "Thank you for your honesty, Peter," I said eventually, "but just one thing before I let you down, what's heavier, you or this motorbike?

"What?" Peter asked, confused and agitated by my question.

"Oh, don't worry. I was just wondering," I mused wistfully before asking "don't you want to know how I found you?"

"How?" asked Peter, sounding as if he was beginning to find this all a little tedious.

"Well," I began, reaching into my pocket and pulling out my mobile phone, "I just happened to have a chance meeting a few days ago with a very lovely lady. Now what was her name again?" I teased, feigning a momentary lapse of memory. Peter looked at me somewhat perplexed, probably wondering who could have done something so treacherous as to give away his whereabouts. "That was it," I continued after a few moments of silence, just to build up the tension, "it was Pamela, Pamela Carter. Do you know her?" I enquired, sarcastically.

"What? Pam, my wife Pam?" Peter seemed unable to comprehend what I was telling him.

"Yes, that's right, Peter." I responded, prosaically. "She asked me if maybe I could discourage you from trying to phone her again in future. Apparently, she finds your repeated attempts to contact her to be rather tedious."

Puzzled by this revelation, Peter questioned the truth and validity of my statement. "No, you're lying. Pam wouldn't say that. She loves me. You don't even know her." I sensed that Peter was perhaps a little deluded as to the current status of his marital relationship, and maybe he was under the assumption that he still exercised enough control over Pam to convince her to return to him.

I accessed the photo of Pam on my phone and glanced at it with a degree of self satisfaction, pondering how he might react when he saw the image. "Your wife did wonder how I might be able to convince you," I said, "so she's sent you a little message." I took a little time to pay closer attention to Pam's compromising photograph, portraying her sitting on the edge of the sofa, semi-naked, her bare breasts looking pert and her legs spread. Finally I showed Peter the photo, stepping forward to enable him to get a good look at the image. Baiting him, I teased, "she looks good, doesn't she."

"That's Pam," remarked Peter in astonishment. "How did you get that? Who sent it to you?" He was still unable to comprehend exactly what was going on.

"I'm afraid it's Pam's farewell message to you, Peter," I informed him, adopting a sullen tone.

Still totally dumbfounded, Peter's inability to grasp precisely what I was telling him was monumental. "So, did Pam send it to you, then?"

Peter's stupidity was beginning to irritate me and I felt that it was time to put him out of his misery. "No, I'm afraid not, Peter," I pronounced, placing the phone back into my pocket, "I took that photo of your wife myself... after I'd fucked her."

"You bastard," screamed Peter, suddenly kicking out at me without making contact and the word 'bastard' would ultimately be the last word he would ever utter, and a photograph of his semi-naked, unfaithful wife would be the last thing he would ever see. He lost his balance, sending one crate toppling off the other as the heavy motorcycle collapsed sideways, leaving him dancing and cavorting in mid air like some demented marionette. The sudden stench of faeces filled the barn as Peter choked and wriggled on the end of the rope like a fish on the end of a line, clinging to his worthless life for as long as possible. Finally there was nothing except for the gentle creaking of the rope as his lifeless body swung and gyrated slowly, illuminated by the moonlight which seemed, at that moment, to envelop and welcome his demise. My calculations had been correct and my question had been answered. The BSA had indeed supported Peter's weight.

I used the knife which I had taken from the kitchen, to cut the cable ties from Peter's wrists and then put them in my pocket. His arms now hung heavily by his side, his body still slowly gyrating, first one way and then the other, reminding me of a clock which my grandmother had owned when I was a child. I picked up the bag of chicken feed and closed the barn door, pausing only for a moment for one last glimpse of Peter Fankham, his now lifeless body suspended from the rafter above, illuminated by the moonlight. The only sound was the gentle creaking of the rope as it continued to slowly twist and turn perpetually. I carried the chicken feed over to the run and listened to the muted clucks of appreciation from inside the coop as I poured in the contents of the sack.

Returning to the kitchen, I wiped my finger prints from the knife on a tea towel and carefully tidied as best I could. I retraced my steps around the house, taking care to wipe any surface with which I had come in contact, ensuring that I left no fingerprints which might implicate me in assisting Peter's untimely expiration. I lit another cigarette as I finally left the house and checked my watch; it was nearly 4:30am. As I made my way back toward Stroud, the sun was just starting to rise over the fields and the early morning dew rose to a mist above the dips and hollows. Adrenaline was still pumping as thoughts and flashbacks of the night's events flicked through my mind. I had expected the Peter I had known to put up more of a fight but in the end, the tired and weary man I found seemed resigned to his fate, like an old dog that knew it was time to say goodbye. All I could now hope was that no one had seen me either enter or leave the house, and that I had made sure that all traces of my presence were eradicated.

Admittedly, I wrestled with my conscience in order to justify what I had done. Yes, I had put the rope around Peter's neck and yes, I had forced him to stand precariously on the crates. But no, I had not pushed him. My mind argued that it was his final act of anger and violence which, by his own volition, had brought about his own demise. And what about the chickens? Although I cannot say that I had ever been the greatest chicken fan, they had never done me any wrong and I had honestly been concerned about their welfare. Therefore, I continued along the road back to Stroud safe in the knowledge that regardless of my involvement, I was still a good person.

I pulled the phone from my pocket and called Pam. Despite the early hour she answered within a few seconds. "It's done," I said, and then hung up.

Chapter 16

Paying My Respects

For my poor mother Irena, the prison sentence which had been handed to me had ultimately proved too much to bear. After the Nazi invasion in 1939 had annexed their home town of Leszno and integrated it into the Third Reich, my mother and her family were forced to relocate to the east of Poland. After surviving the bitter war that would wage for the next six years, the onset of Communism encouraged my mother to seek a new life in America. Irena would only get as far as England though, where she would meet and marry my father Tommy, and subsequently became known as Irene.

Thomas Caldwell, the son of a market trader, grew up in London's tough East End. While Irene's childhood had been fraught with the fear of her country's brutal Nazi invaders, Tommy had only the vaguest memories of Britain's fight against the rising tide of Fascism in the 1930's. His father, George, had always felt proud to tell the story of how, on October 4th 1936, he had stood alongside countless other demonstrators against Oswald Mosley's Black shirts in what became known as The Battle of Cable Street. During the Blitz, little Tommy had been evacuated to Devon, but the bullying he was forced to endure at the hands of the local children, convinced him that he would sooner face Hitler's bombs than another moment in the school yard. As Tommy grew older, he developed an interest in photography and slowly built up a regular pitch in Brick Lane Market, selling any camera that he was able to acquire.

When my mother fell pregnant, my parents decided to leave the city and move to the newly developing suburbs, finally deciding to buy a home on a new estate close to Bexley. Thanks to a business loan, my father opened a shop in Dartford selling new and second hand cameras, while offering an affordable repair service too. Over the years, he built up a reputation for his knowledge and reliability, and the income from his business ensured that, whilst we were not rich, we were comfortable. When not working, my father would spend hours tending our garden and my mother loved seeing the red roses come into bloom, and she would always cut a few to display them in a vase set on the mantelpiece.

I can remember times when my father could be a strict disciplinarian, but I can also remember times when he covered for me when the police came knocking on our door. "Like I told you, he was here all night, I promise you", were words I overheard him say to visiting police officers on more than one occasion. He never understood my passion for football or for the music he would always describe as 'noise', and I tired of him continually asking me to turn my music down, as much as he tired of having to ask. My long suffering mother was a proud and upstanding woman who was so often pained by the embarrassment of having a son who had grown up to become one of the local tearaways. Nevertheless, I was never in doubt that I had a mother and a father who both loved me.

On many Sunday afternoons when I was a child, my father would drive us to Greenwich where we would stroll through the park and follow the pathway up the hill to the observatory at the top, where the vantage point offered an unrivalled view of London, the River Thames and my personal favourite landmark, The Cutty Sark. Our journey to Greenwich would take us past Eltham Crematorium and, on one occasion, when I could only have been five or six years old, I remember my father pointing out a funeral procession. At that moment I became aware of my own mortality and that of my parents too, and I grew fearful of their eventual passing.

On the morning that I stood in front of the simple memorial plaque inscribed with the names Thomas and Irena Caldwell, I was saddened that I had missed those passings which I had feared the most. I was also saddened that I had been deprived of the opportunity of apologising to them for being such a shit son, who should have done more to live up to their expectations. I was grateful to Jacob Reeve for, as our family solicitor, he had gone to great lengths to arrange both funerals in my absence, so that now I finally had the opportunity to mourn my parents passing and pay them the respects they deserved. I neatly positioned two red roses on the ledge below their memorial plaque, wiped away a tear and took a deep breath. I had a long journey ahead and another funeral to arrange, although there was little chance that it would be a funeral which I would attend.

Chapter 17

Ashes to Ashes

Gary Spackman, the Spaceman. I was sure that I could still recognise that fucker anywhere. According to the address which Victor had given me, to find Gary I would first have to make my way north to a boatyard not far from Nantwich in Cheshire. The address offered no name for the boat I was looking for, but if he still collected his mail from the same box number at the boatyard, then I could assume that his boat would be moored somewhere nearby. Following my visit to see Peter, my levels of paranoia were still running high, and therefore I reasoned that I should try to remain anonymous on my travels and thus avoid the suspicion of the locals. It would be easy to simply ask around the local community when I got there, but then I risked raising suspicions if anything sinister happened to Gary if I actually managed to find him. What I would require was stealth, cunning and a gun with a silencer. In the absence of a gun with a silencer however, I would have to rely on stealth and cunning.

Despite not knowing exactly where to go, Dave had kindly lent me his car and I drove north-west on the off chance that the trail would not go cold when I got there.

Dave had shown me how to use his satellite navigation system, and I followed the directions as instructed by the computerised female voice who was to be my travelling companion. After booking into a bed and breakfast in Nantwich, I had spent some time checking out likely places where I thought that I might find The Spaceman. I had planned to stay in the vicinity for a week and then head back to London if I had no luck, and by day three of my search, I had begun to fear that I was wasting my time. It was a quiet rural area with not many places to check out, but it still felt like I was searching for a needle in a haystack. I had spent some time walking along a stretch of the Shropshire Union Canal, as I figured that where else would you find a canal boat in this neck of the woods? I had watched the boatyard and had also sat in the car watching the comings and goings at the local village store on the main Wrexham Road. I had also been in and out of the local drinking establishments, all on the off chance of finding Gary.

I had previously visited the Plough Inn in the nearby village of Acton but decided to give the place another go, and at 7pm on that Thursday evening it was relatively quiet. I stood at the bar in the beautiful Georgian country public house and ordered a pint of lager, regardless of the choices of traditional and local ales on offer. I surveyed my surroundings, pondering the richness of history within the walls of the old building. Its large open fireplaces, oak beams, assorted brass objects and articles of farming paraphernalia, certainly complimented the décor and gave the place an aura which could surely not be found elsewhere but in the country. It had been a long time since I had visited a pub like this and I realised how much I had missed such places. I found myself reminiscing about some of the good times spent drinking and laughing with friends at similar pubs in rural Kent many years before, and long summer evenings spent without a care in the world. Those memories were so vivid that I could practically feel them, and The Plough Inn was certainly evocative of my erstwhile, misspent youth.

The notice written on the chalk board outside the front door had announced that on this particular evening, The Plough Inn was to host a live band playing rock covers. If Gary were still in the area then maybe the promise of some live music on a Thursday evening might be an event which he would consider quite appealing. I watched with interest as four musicians filed in through the door carrying their musical equipment, and began setting up in the corner of the pub between the door marked 'toilets' and one of the large open fireplaces. All probably in their late thirties or early forties, they looked as if they had done this sort of thing many times before. Each one knew their role and set about it without exchanging much in the way of conversation. I watched the guitarist with the closest interest, perhaps with a hint of jealousy that it was he and not I, who would be playing that evening. I sipped my pint as I watched him setting up his pedal board, noting how carefully and precisely he adjusted the levels on his Vox AC30 amplifier. He flicked the catches on his guitar flight case, opened the lid and lifted out a gleaming white Fender Stratocaster, proudly holding it up to the light to check for any signs of damage. Satisfied that his pristine weapon of choice was indeed good to go, he plugged it in to tune it and checked that all his effects pedals were functioning correctly.

If nothing else happened that evening then I hoped to enjoy some live music regardless, as I had been away from that scene for a long time and I had missed it. I had missed the atmosphere and the appreciation of musicians coming together to create something tangible. Even if it were perhaps not exactly to my personal musical taste, then I would still appreciate it for what it was. I had never been a fan of the Fender guitar sound myself, but I could not help but wonder what my old Gibson Les Paul might have sounded like in a place like this.

I checked the door each time it opened just to see who was coming in. Each time the door opened I felt a surge of anticipation and adrenaline, only for it to subside with disappointment at the realisation that each person to enter was someone other than who I was looking for. By 9pm I had just ordered my third pint when the band opened their set with a rendition of 'Mustang Sally'. I watched them until the song concluded and placed my beer on the bar, enabling me to applaud along with the other fifty or so people who had turned up. As the band continued with The Rolling Stones classic 'Under My Thumb', I considered that perhaps they could have done with a better singer. He seemed to think he was pretty damn cool though, fronting a group of musicians who were quite proficient and musically tight, and the local audience certainly appeared appreciative of their efforts to entertain.

I turned my gaze from the band, picked up my glass and took a sip as I glanced along the bar at the people who were drinking, trying to hold conversations over the volume of the music or just waiting to be served. A sudden rush of adrenaline hit me like a speeding Cadillac the moment at which I noticed one particular gentleman, leaning on the bar waiting to be served. I watched him intently trying to make himself heard over the sound of the band, eventually leaning forward to shout his order in the barman's ear. The barman pulled a pint of dark coloured ale and the customer handed over a five pound note. He took a sip of his syrupy looking liquid and strained to see the band from his current position. After another mouthful of beer, the gentleman held out his hand to accept his change. I noted that he had only ordered and paid for one drink, indicating that he was there on his own. Maybe he was waiting for friends to arrive but for now, he was on his own.

Gary Spackman, the Spaceman. Yes, I'd definitely recognise that fucker anywhere. He looked like he had just returned from working somewhere, dressed in army surplus overalls and chequered lumberjack shirt. He still had all his hair though, even if it was now pure white, blending perfectly with the pallor of his skin. His face looked even more gaunt than I remembered it, giving him an almost ghoulish appearance in the half light. As he watched the band, I watched him intently while trying hard to not make my level of interest too obvious. I did not want to catch his attention just yet, but felt compelled to stare nonetheless. I felt a jolt inside as he spotted me staring, and he looked back at me directly. Could he recognise me as easily as I recognised him? I raised my glass in a friendly gesture and he raised his in return before he continued to watch the band.

The band played on, covering one song after another; some good, some not so good. At times I was hardly listening, but instead I concentrated on Gary's every move even though he seldom moved far from the bar. The band were working their way through David Bowie's 'Ashes to Ashes' when I saw Gary heading towards the door. I quickly finished my pint and cautiously followed him, concerned that he may be leaving for home. I noticed him lighting a rolled up cigarette outside the pub and so, without acknowledging him, I took my pack from my jacket pocket and lit a cigarette too, blowing smoke into the cool night air.

"What do you think of 'em, then?" Gary enquired right out of the blue, negating my need to engage him in conversation myself.

"They're not bad, I suppose," I answered, "although I'm not convinced about the vocals though".

Gary laughed. "That's just what I was thinking."

"Have you seen them before?" I asked, hoping that by continuing our conversation, I might gain his trust.

"Yeah, a few times. They play here about once a month," he replied before adding, "there's not a lot else happens around here, musically speaking." As Gary re-lit his roll up and took a long draw, I noticed the brown nicotine stains on his fingers. "You're not local, are you?" he asked.

"No, mate," I said, "I've come up from London, am just up here visiting friends," adding "and you don't sound like a local either."

Gary dropped the remainder of his cigarette and began to roll another as we chatted. He explained how he had moved up from Kent with his lady, and they had bought a canal boat together. "She'd bought her house before the boom in the eighties and then the value of it shot up and she made a mint," Gary informed me. Initially, their move had seemed like it would offer an idyllic lifestyle, but things had not really worked out as planned. Gary loved the sense of freedom that life on the canal offered, and he survived by picking up a few odd jobs just to make ends meet. As long as he had enough money for a crust of bread, a few beers, cigarettes and a little weed, he was a happy man.

"Have we met before?" Gary asked, as he looked at me quizzically, in a rather intense and perhaps uneasy manner.

"No, mate" I lied, adding with as much conviction as I could muster, "I doubt that very much. I've never been up here before. Fancy another beer?" I asked, rapidly changing the subject while stubbing out my second cigarette.

"Thanks mate, that's very kind," he answered gratefully, if not sounding a little surprised. "What's your name, by the way?"

"John," I replied, remembering the alias on my forged passport. "John Turner. And yours?" I enquired, offering a handshake as a gesture of warmth and apparent honesty.

"Gary" came the gaunt gentleman's reply, as his pallid hand loosely gripped my mine. "Gary Spackman".

"Well, it's a pleasure to meet you, Gary Spackman," I said. "Let's have that beer then, shall we?"

We made our way back to the bar, edging our way through the crowd, and after ordering our respective poisons, we continued to watch the band, exchanging small talk between songs. The band played their last number and Gary and I finished our drinks as the pub slowly emptied of customers, leaving the band to pack away their equipment. Gary and I were soon standing outside and just as I pondered my next move, to my surprise Gary suddenly suggested that as his boat was moored on the canal just a ten minute walk away, we could go back there, have a few more beers and smoke a bit of weed.

"Haven't you got to get up for work in the morning?" I enquired with interest.

"Nah, mate," he answered with a smile. "Nothing I can't put off until the afternoon." As we walked, Gary explained how he scratched a meagre living by doing odd jobs around the local villages. A bit of decorating here, a bit of gardening there and occasionally he would help out with some renovation work down at the boatyard. Gary was convivial and chatty, if not a little drunk, and in no time we were standing on the canal towpath and he was introducing me to his boat and showing me aboard. "She's 47 feet," he cooed. "All mod cons".

I guess that it was just what a narrow boat should be; narrow. There's not enough space to swing a kitten let alone a cat, I thought to myself as Gary continued to swoon over his floating palace as if I were a perspective buyer. "She's got a Beta 38 water cooled diesel engine," he swooned as if that was meant to mean something to me. "There's a double bedroom through there," he said, drunkenly pointing a vague finger, "toilet and shower through there and this is the galley," he added, patting his hands on the laminate worktop. Gary opened the fridge door, pulled out two cans of John Smiths and passed one to me. "I just fitted this yesterday," chirped Gary as I pulled the ring on my can, sipping the bitter froth that spurted from the opening. "It's a Spinflo Triplex LPG oven," he exclaimed proudly, stroking a hand across the hob and grinning in an inane manner. "I got it for four hundred quid, but I hope that I fitted it right," The Spaceman quipped.

"Nice," I replied, looking around and feigning interest.

"And this is the lounge." Gary gestured in an absurdly flamboyant manner. "Take a seat, my friend, and make yourself comfortable." I sat down, took another sip from the can and watched in silence as Gary pulled out an ashtray, a pack of cigarettes and a bag of cannabis from an overhead cupboard. He sat down and then proceeded to lick and stick cigarette papers together. "So, tell me, what do you do? For a living, like," Gary enquired while rolling the joint.

"Nothing really," I replied. "I've been living abroad for a few years, and although I've recently been staying with a mate in London, I'm only really back in England to look up a few old friends."

"Ahh, nice," he said, concentrating more on lighting up the fat joint he had rolled then what I had just told him. The Spaceman took a long pull before handing the joint to me. I thanked him and took a few short draws myself, before handing it back. Despite being aware of the need to make Gary feel like we had things in common, to nurture his trust for the time being, I certainly had no plans of being drawn back into that seedy drug world; remembering the way that cannabis distorts reality while secretly working to create nothing but paranoia, his weed held no interest for me.

Feeling the need to change the subject, I asked him whether he lived there alone. Gary nodded, blowing out a huge plume of acrid smoke. "So what made you want to spend your life up here on a boat?" I asked, hoping to keep the conversation flowing without the idiot passing out.

"Because it's organic, man," gibbered Gary. He was always something of a conspiracy theorist, and as I listened to him smugly preaching his 'Gospel according to Gary Spackman', I recalled the reason why we had nicknamed him The Spaceman in the first place. "The Government can look into our homes, man," he informed me. "You gotta line your walls with tin-foil to keep out their harmful rays."

"Really?" I answered sceptically, with more than an air of disbelief.

"Yeah, man, really." Gary continued his rhetoric. "You gotta be aware of what goes on out there, man, it's all on the internet, you know. Do you know why they put chemicals in the tap water?" he enquired, pointing an accusing finger.

"Erm, to purify the water?" I responded.

"No, man, you gotta wise up," came his stoned and brash retort. "The Government puts chemicals into the tap water so that they can control us. Living here on this vessel, I can live a utopian existence. It's organic, it's pure and it's hidden from all the satellites and cameras which track your every move." Gary accentuated his words by lifting his hands skyward and looking toward the heavens, drifting off into silence to allow what he had said to sink in. The sight of this ageing, stoned hippy gazing up at an overhead panel light as if it held the answers to all life's mysteries was both bizarre and ridiculous. If Gary Spackman had been rightfully convicted of the crime for which he had set me up, I can assure you that his fellow inmates would have happily kicked the hippy fucker to death for spouting that shit.

Gary spoke with an arrogance that suggested that it was only he who knew the truth, and only he who held the answers. The internet was the new bible and he was the modern day Jesus fucking Christ, sent to save us all from the devils who rule the world. Gary claimed that he knew exactly how the multi-national corporations were in league with Governmental agencies to control the books that we read, the food that we eat, the water that we drink and even the air that we breathe. "It's all a huge fucking conspiracy," he informed me, sitting bolt upright with his arms held wide open, just like Jesus Christ himself. For a moment I thought that he might actually produce loaves and fishes and perform a miracle of his own. Gary Spackman had clearly become a man with a God complex, and at that moment I could have gleaned so much pleasure from killing him, right there, right then, but there was still more that I wanted to know. As the night wore on, we smoked a little more weed and we drank a little more beer.

"So tell me," I began, hoping that I wasn't pushing my luck, "what went wrong with the lady who you moved up here with? Didn't she subscribe to your utopian dream?" I then sat back as Gary opened his soul and related his relationship history. He related his story of how he and his woman had met, although it could be contested that the mists of time had conspired with various narcotic substances to create a viable alternative which suited him better. Apparently she had been married to a bit of a loser but he had been able to offer her a more positive future. They had a daughter, and although his woman had acted a little strangely from time to time, life had seemed pretty good.

"Strangely?" I asked with interest as Gary made his way uneasily to the galley for more beer. "In what way?"

"Oh, I dunno," he replied, reaching into the fridge. "Drugs and shit, I guess. Things just got kinda fucked up." Gary stood up with a can in each hand and kicked the fridge door closed. Drunkenly making his way back, he lost his balance, staggered sideways and collapsed in a giggling heap on the floor, sending one of the beer cans rolling towards me. As he laughed hysterically, I trapped the rolling can under my foot, bent down, picked it up and pulled the ring, dodging the froth as it spurted out.

"So, is that why you two split up, the drugs and shit?" I continued to quiz him as he got back to his feet, regaining a modicum of composure. Gary went on to explain how she had studied hard, qualified as a nurse and had landed herself a job working in the community through a doctor's surgery in nearby Nantwich. He felt that maybe the stress was getting to her a little, and had noticed that she had started to smoke weed in alarmingly industrial quantities.

"She was around death and negative vibes too much, I guess," offered Gary, by way of explanation. "Being around death just kinda freaked her out. She'd just wanna get home, kick back and mong out."

"That doesn't sound like very responsible health promotion," I quipped. "A stoned nurse could be a bit of a liability, I reckon."

"Yeah, I know, mate," Gary replied. "She would often go to work stoned and was starting to make bad mistakes.

She fucked up someone's injection and got herself suspended for a drug error, or some shit. Poor cunt could've died, by all accounts."

"Shit, mate, that sounds a bit heavy," I responded.

"Nah, mate, it gets worse. She was getting really weird, I mean really weird. No sooner was she back at work when a woman made another serious complaint about her and she ended up suspended again." Gary grew animated and more than a little edgy.

"Christ sake," I exclaimed. "What the fuck had she done this time?"

"She fucking denied the allegation," began Gary, tentatively, "but this woman's husband was dying of cancer and she accused Debbie of, erm..."

I could tell that Gary was not comfortable with this element of the story, but I felt compelled to hear the rest nonetheless. "So Debbie?" I asked, "That was the name of your woman, was it?" Gary nodded. "Anyway, please go on." I said, imploring him to tell the whole story.

"Debbie was supposed to be giving the guy a morphine jab," continued Gary, "for the pain, like. Anyway, the guy had been upstairs in bed, so Debbie went upstairs while his wife was downstairs making a cup of tea or something. After she'd gone, the shocked guy told his wife that Debbie had put her hand under the duvet and touched his cock. So the wife complained about it, and said that Debbie had flown out of the house without even saying goodbye or drinking her tea."

"Jesus Christ," I exclaimed in total shock. "You reckon that was true?"

"I dunno, mate," Gary replied, downcast. "She denied it, saying the woman and her husband were nuts, but she'd been acting so strange that I just don't know what to believe. Anyway, she said she wasn't gonna hang about for the enquiry and so she quit her job." I began to get the impression that Gary did not exactly care a great deal for Debbie's chosen profession anyway. "I don't believe in all that medical crap," he announced. "I think that nature holds the key to curing all ills. Homoeopathy, that's the answer." Gary continued to explain how he had been concerned about her growing drug habit, but she had maintained that it was the only way she could relax. He added that she had gone through phases where she would act a bit like a child, and had become prone to tantrums. "She was becoming paranoid that her past was going to catch up with her."

"Fucking hell," I exclaimed. "Her past, sounds like she should've been more worried about her present and maybe her future too."

"Yeah, I know," continued Gary. "Her ex-husband had been put away for murder and although he'd got life, she was worried that he might be released and come looking for her."

"Fuck me!" I said. "You two didn't do things by halves did you? So that's why she left, was it? She ran off for her own safety, leaving you to clean up the mess?"

"Nah, worse," said Gary quietly, looking down into his beer as if a half empty can might contain the answers.

"Worse?" I countered, hardly able to suppress my laughter. "How could that get any worse?"

"Because," he said looking up, "it turned out that the girl I had raised as my own daughter wasn't even my daughter after all. Debbie had known the truth all along and just fucking lied to me. We'd been arguing about her quitting her job and the prospect of us having fuck all money, and the bitch just came straight out with it. She was right in my face about it. You know, all matter of fact, like." Suddenly Gary sounded rather bitter.

"Wow, what a headfuck," was all I could offer in response to Gary's revelation. "What did you do?"

"What would anyone do in that situation?" he paused and pondered, perhaps looking a little ashamed. "I slapped her and kicked her out." Continuing to protest his defence, he added, "I'd put up with so much shit for so long; the drugs, the nagging and she was damn lazy too. When I think of the times that I'd forgave her for stuff she'd done, or given her the benefit of the doubt. I mean, she was even fucking my brother at one point," Gary added bitterly.

"No," I exclaimed, trying hard to conceal my delight as I listened to this sad sack's tale of misery, "not your brother?"

"It fucking killed me when I found out, man," whimpered Gary. "She knew that I hated that bastard. What sort of woman does that to a man, eh?" I felt compelled to listen to that drunken idiot spilling out his guts, and the more I learned of Gary's miserable existence, the happier I felt. After The Spaceman's mother had thrown her alcoholic husband out of the family home, his older brother John, had taken on the role of man of the house. Their mother never hid the fact that John was her favourite son, while never holding back in her admonishment of Gary. "I wish you had never been born," she would often say, or "you're just like your damn father."

Bitterly, Gary told the woeful tale of his childhood, living in the shadow of a brother who basked in the sunshine of their mother's love. While Gary was destined to spend his life pecking around in the dirt, John had built up a successful business in the construction industry, and lived a very comfortable lifestyle with a wife and children who wanted for nothing. The two brothers were like chalk and cheese; one a success and the other a failure, and each year when the family got together to celebrate Christmas, John never failed to rub his brother's nose in it. It was on one such occasion when Gary had proudly introduced Debbie, the love of his life, to the family.

"She'd tell me that she was going to visit her father," explained Gary bitterly, "but she was really going to meet John. I only found out when I started to get suspicious about all the text messages she was sending. She said they were messages to work, but I checked her fucking phone," he announced spitefully, pounding his clenched fist against the table.

If ever I thought I'd had a rough deal as a child, my mother would always say 'just remember, son, there's always someone worse off than you'. Those words had meant nothing to me back then, but listening to Gary whining on as if the world owed him, I realised that she had been right. There was someone worse off than me, and I was drinking his beer and revelling in his misery. "Sounds like you're well rid, mate," I said, offering scant consolation, before repeating the same platitude which had once been a favourite of my mother.

"Yeah, I suppose so," he solemnly conceded, inspecting the back of his pale and weathered hand before flexing his fingers, as if in pounding the table he might have caused himself a painful injury. "She headed back down south and stayed with her father for a while," he continued. "Apparently he croaked while on holiday somewhere and then she had a huge fall out with her brother. She was constantly on my case to leave my home here, saying it was her money that bought it and she wanted to sell. Then the last I heard, she'd had some sort of mental breakdown and ended up in a nut house or somewhere, down near Dartford, I think. She'd gone total fucking psycho. Anyway," concluded Gary, "enough of that shit; I need a piss."

"What a complete dickhead," I thought to myself as I watched him drunkenly zig-zagging his way to the bathroom. How on earth had this idiot conspired with Peter and Debbie Fankham to rob me of the best part of three decades, and actually got away with it for so long? I heard the toilet flush and I watched as Gary staggered into the bedroom. I could hear the opening of a cupboard door, followed by a few heavy clunking sounds and then finally the beaming clown re-emerged, clutching a guitar in his right hand. He bashed it twice as he made his way uneasily through the narrow galley, before holding it aloft like he was holding the FA trophy after a cup final victory.

"Here," he said, swelling with pride, "you'll like this. It's my Gibson Les Paul Custom." He turned the instrument around, gazing at it in awe, running his hand along its neck and caressing its wooden curves. "My ex gave it to me years ago." Gary handed over his prized possession for my perusal and sat down. "What do you think of it then?" he enquired with a grin, as I took my time examining his guitar in detail.

Turning it over, I noted the instrument's serial number on the back of the headstock. "Hmm, a 1978 model," I exclaimed with more than a degree of interest.

"Yeah," replied Gary. "A real classic piece. Do you play?" he asked.

"I used to" I replied, while still looking over the guitar, checking out the wear on the neck, the little dinks and scrapes on the body and noting the letters L, I, A and R, etched deep into the mahogany back. "Mind you," I said, "that was many years ago."

"Believe it or not," Gary mused, "I used to play in a Punk Rock band back in the day." The Spaceman had momentarily disturbed my train of thought. "We were originally called LIAR," he babbled on, pointing to the rudimentary carvings on the instrument, "but we kinda morphed into something more psychedelic and changed our name to The Sons of Ra."

"Really?" I responded, trying hard to quell my sarcasm. I could hardly believe it; not only had this prick framed me and stolen the best years of my life, but he had fucked up my band too. What's more, that conniving bitch, Debbie, had given him my guitar to do it with too. I stood up, holding the heavy instrument by the neck. "That's funny," I said, following a few moments of thoughtful silence, "I used to play in a band called LIAR too. But that was before I found a dead girl on my bathroom floor."

Gary looked at me from his seat in total bewilderment, and said nothing. Just like some colourless, primitive fish that scavenges along the deepest ocean floor, Gary's mouth opened and closed without ever uttering a word. To be fair, he did not have time to say much. "Miss Radwanski sends her regards," I spat with venom. Taking the guitar by the neck in both hands, I swung it with full force. The instrument's mahogany and maple body connected firmly with Gary's head, nearly splitting it in two. The blow had taken him by surprise and he had no time to even raise his hands in self-defence, or take any evasive action whatsoever. The force of the blow hit him so hard that his head lunged sideways, crashing against the wooden panelling by the window with a sickening crack, before rebounding. I stood motionless, clutching my guitar by the neck, watching as the momentum of my assault caused Gary to slide off his seat and on to the floor, seemingly in slow motion, his chin thumping against the table top as he fell.

The Spaceman did not move. Blood spilled from a hole in his temple that looked large enough to drive a truck through. I stood the guitar on the seat and walked into the galley. Suddenly I felt as sober as anyone who had ever just caved a man's head in with a guitar, could have done. I opened the oven door, turned on the liquid propane gas and after placing the ashtray on the worktop I lit a cigarette, took a long slow pull and left it to burn. I stepped over Gary's prostate body to pick up my guitar. "Adiós muthafucker," I said with spite as I looked down at his vampiresque features, now drenched in blood. "Looks like you've finally got a bit of colour, mate."

I left the boat and walked across the field with my guitar slung over my shoulder, making my way towards the trees, not wanting to be seen taking the route back to the main road along the towpath. I had not walked far when I heard the explosion, and turned to see the remains of Gary's boat engulfed in flames. The towpath was illuminated by the orange glow of the fire, and smoke rose into the night sky as debris rained down. Even at a distance of one hundred metres or so, I could feel the heat from the inferno on my face. I turned back and continued to make my way to the trees.

oooOOOooo

I don't know what it was, but something compelled me to return to the canal in the morning, and it was a little after 9:30 am when I found myself walking along the towpath once more. Even from a distance I could smell the smoke in the air and I could see that the path had been cordoned off with police tape. Beyond the imposed boundary, I could see what I assumed to be police and fire investigators, working hard to ascertain the root cause of the explosion.

A bearded man, wearing Wellington boots, a green wax jacket and a flat cap, walked towards me with a black and white Collie dog scampering along by his side. Excitedly, the dog bounded towards me with an expression of happiness, almost as if it were about to impart some wonderful news. As I bent down to welcome the animal, it circled my legs before rolling onto its back. The dog looked up at me with wild eyes and its tongue lolled heavily to one side as I stroked the long hair on its chest.

"What's happened here then?" I enquired, as the bearded man drew closer.

"Ah, a nasty business," responded the bearded man. "Someone at the boatyard told me that a chap who worked down there got himself killed in the blast. Gas leak or something, they reckon."

"Oh, that's awful," I said, in a manner quite befitting of someone who has just received some rather shocking news.

"Nice fella, they said," added the bearded man.

"I'm sure he was," I replied, looking up at him while still stroking his dog. "I'm sure he was."

Chapter 18

From Addiction to Affliction

I really should have known better, but no matter how many times I berated myself, it was never going to change a thing. Even on that very first evening the red lights had been flashing and the alarm bells ringing, yet I ignored every warning sign. All it took was a pretty face, the offer of a shag and I had literally sold my soul. There was I, thinking that I had won her over with my charm and wit, while all along she played me like a pinball machine, knowing exactly what buttons to press.

Deborah Fankham was a girl who always wanted the things she couldn't have, and she was not averse to using her charms to claim the personal victories which she required to feed her fragile ego. To most children, home is the safe haven where they can grow up safe and secure, guarded and protected from danger by loving parents. Sadly, to the unlucky ones like Deborah Fankham, home would prove to be the place where the greatest dangers lurked. At the tender age of thirteen, she had been introduced to the wonders of drugs by her older brother, Peter, and that narcotic epiphany had offered an easy route of escape from her grim reality, and escape was something for which she desperately yearned. In that chaotic home environment, Peter's soporific supplies would unfortunately come at a price that would merely serve to widen the viciousness of her circle.

Following the chaotic nature of her upbringing, Debbie became a young woman who relished chaos. She would create it and then revel in its effects. From a relatively early age, she learned that she could use her body for the one thing that so often eluded her; control. So why did I not stand safely aside when this human train wreck came hurtling toward me? Well, I guess there were a few reasons, if I'm brutally honest. Primarily, I was a slave to my gender; shallow and not immune to a warm smile, big brown eyes and the attributes of a naked female body. But, before you judge me on my stupidity, there were other reasons too.

Almost immediately I had sensed that masked by her smile, bravado and sensuality, there was fragility and a hunger to be loved and cared for. During a simple walk together in the park or a visit to a petting zoo, she might appear to display certain almost childlike qualities which would manifest through behaviours that could be sweet and endearing. It was only later, on the occasions when she would begin to open up and offer hints of her upbringing, that I came to realise that those behavioural manifestations ran much deeper. Her candid intimations suggested a desire to regress into the innocence of the kind of childhood that her school friends may have enjoyed, but one which she herself had been robbed of.

Debbie had seemed so very different to all of my previous girlfriends, all of whom had been stereotypical girl next door types from good, safe, middle-class families. They had all been nice girls who seemed to have a liking for someone with a bit of a rough edge. Alright, so Beth had been a little different in that respect, but there had been something about her which smacked of desperation, and her demeanour often created a wall between us which I was either unable or unwilling to climb. On the occasions when she and I would meet, Beth always seemed to have some issue or another which she would need to discuss in depth. It may have been financial, emotional, social or personal, but whatever her issue might have been at any given time, her neediness and intensity discouraged me from getting too close. She was a girl who seemed to cling to me in the hope that I might have all the answers, at a time when I was the last person on earth who was qualified to offer any meaningful advice.

Beth had a big heart which she wore on her sleeve, but in a superficial manner befitting my relative inexperience, I chose to keep her at arms' length. Debbie, on the other hand, exuded a hypnotic and alluring element of danger from the dust cloud of chaos which she created around her, but the more I got to know her, the more I sensed that she wore a shroud to mask the fragility of her personality. She would display a brash and outgoing public persona, while in private she could be soft and sensitive. If I am honest, it was the private persona which I preferred.

There was just something that drew me to her like a moth gets drawn to a candle, I guess, even though the warning signs were indicating that I should leave well alone. Within a few weeks it became apparent just how chaotic her life could be, when she announced that she had lost her job in a local bakery. Although she had kept it quiet, Debbie admitted that she had until recently been having an affair with her boss, Steven Easthill, and just to further complicate matters, Mr Easthill's wife had been heavily pregnant. If the situation was not complex enough already, Steven had missed the birth of his first child because he and Debbie had been in bed together at the time his wife was in labour. Obviously the wife had not been happy about the lateness of her husband's arrival at the hospital hours after the birth, and during the first few weeks that the newborn was at home, she noticed that her spouse appeared distracted. At a time when most new families would be bonding together and taking snap shots for posterity, Steven Easthill was preoccupied and troubled by something which he had overheard in the bakery.

According to a regular customer, Mrs Patricia Fankham, her daughter, Deborah, had recently been seen keeping company with a punk rocker type and she and her husband were not keen, fearing that their neighbourhood was fast becoming overrun by undesirables. Pushed into a corner by his wife's questioning and desperate to make a huge gesture of his eternal love for Debbie, Mr Easthill confessed his sins and duly announced that he was leaving his wife and newborn child for one of his employees. When he had informed Debbie however, of the dramatic steps which he had taken to ensure that they could be together forever, she was less than impressed. To Debbie, their affair had only been a game; a game in which she revelled in her powers of seduction and the boost it gave her ego. After she revealed that their trysts were merely a bit of fun to her, and suggested that he should have never taken things so seriously, the foolish baker took the only course of action he had left available, and he sacked her.

Debbie assured me that it had all been a huge mistake on her part, and it was all in the past. She had learned her lesson, felt bad for the distress she had caused and vowed that she would never do anything like that ever again. Of course I believed her, why wouldn't I? Sex with Debbie was great; it was highly adventurous, exciting and often performed spontaneously in risqué outdoor places and, to be honest, I did not see anything beyond than those simple pleasures of the flesh. Through her brother, she was able to procure a seemingly endless supply of drugs which, needless to say, I paid for. For the first few months it seemed like every evening and weekend was spent in bed together, fucking and getting stoned, only occasionally getting up for something to eat or to take a piss.

Then there was her brother, Peter. Following the morning of our initial introduction on the landing, we had developed a grudging acceptance of each other, although I sensed that he considered me a wedge between his sister and himself. Debbie was never slow to express her dislike for Peter and his tendency to rely on her for his social life. Peter had tried to integrate himself with just about every social circle; punks, skinheads, soul boys, rock 'n' roll, hippies, you name it, Pete had worn the uniforms and tried to fit in, but despite his best efforts, he was always a square peg in a round hole. As I would later learn, he even tried to ingratiate himself into the biker fraternity, but they had shunned his request for membership. Peter had fantasised about the kudos and respect which a motorcycle fraternity membership would bring him, and so he devised a scheme to convince them to change their minds. His plan had been to convince his sister that in order to maintain the regularity of her narcotic supply, she would need to sleep with the gang members. Only in Peter

Fankham's twisted mind would this scheme work; prostituting his own sister on the off chance that he might get into a gang. His plan had been scuppered only by the protection afforded by my arrival on the scene, and partially explained why he resented my presence so much.

Where Peter did come in useful, however, was when our drugs supply began to run low. All it took was one quick phone call and Peter would turn into a cross between a puppy, desperate to please, and a carrier pigeon, all flap and no brains. He would hurry off, purchase our requirements and then bring it to our flat, appearing on the doorstep with a big grin, his tail wagging, awaiting a pat on the head for being a good boy. By 'a pat on the head' I mean that he would want to come in and share some of it with us. He would then hang around like a bad smell, getting stoned and occasionally passing out, but never taking the hint to simply fuck off.

Ultimately our excessive narcotic intake would lead to the point where I would seldom go to work, and one morning when I had finally made the effort, I got as far as the office door and then turned around and went back home. With both Debbie and I on the dole, money became an issue or rather, the lack of money became an issue. Debbie became adept at helping herself to items of clothing from shops and markets, and then she would sell them on to friends and friends of friends. Often she would steal to order, but either way she was finally making a financial contribution to the household.

The band did not make a fortune from the gigs we played, but for a while I enjoyed not having to get up for work early the following morning. Debbie liked the fact that I played in a band, even if our music was not wholly to her taste. She would invariably come to our gigs and occasionally to practice sessions too, but it was becoming far too often that my personal level of performance would come under scrutiny from the other band members. I never considered my playing to be shoddy, but perhaps on reflection that might be because drugs have a tendency to give you a false impression of your abilities. You become witty, charming, infallible and awesome, although to the untrained and sober eye, one could be mistaken for being a complete arsehole. However, to me, if I could earn a few quid, sink a few beers and still have enough strength in my legs to shag Debbie in the car park at the end of the evening, I considered it to have been a good night.

Have I mentioned the sex? Our sex life could only be described as adventurous, experimental and fun. We even kept a diary for a few months, making notes of how many times we had performed each day. These daily entries would also include coded details of unusual places where we had fucked. 'Car bonnet' referred to a night when Debbie had a desire to be taken on the bonnet of my car. We had parked up in a country lane and both stripped naked, neither of us giving a damn about the headlights of occasional passing cars illuminating our copulating forms in the darkness. 'Driveway' had been in reference to a night that we had drunkenly staggered home from a party. Feeling adventurous, Debbie began trying the door handles of parked cars, and eventually she found one carelessly left unlocked by its owner. That car just happened to be parked on the driveway in front of a house which presumably belonged to the vehicle's owner. Despite my initial hesitancy, Debbie was soon able to goad me into it. "You're not scared, are you?" she mocked, with one hand holding onto the open car door for balance while she lifted up her skirt and removed her knickers with the other. Despite my initial restraint, I later had to confess that the encounter had been great fun, and I had felt the danger of possibly being caught to be extremely exhilarating.

One evening as the two of us lay side by side, sweaty and breathless and enjoying a post coital cigarette, Debbie suggested that she could arrange a special treat, just for me. The prospect intrigued and excited me, and so a few days later we had a visitor. Linda turned out to be a chubby girl with short dark hair and a huge smile, and I will admit that my first impression of her was that she was rather cute. To accompany her beaming smile, she had also arrived with a carrier bag containing a bottle of vodka, a carton of orange juice and a vibrator. I had never envisaged that an evening of such unbridled pleasure was possible, and by midnight, I honestly thought that I had died and gone to heaven.

A few weeks later, Debbie excitedly informed me that we had been invited over to Linda's place, and if I am to be completely honest, I was not averse to the prospect of a repeat performance. However, when we arrived and I was introduced to Linda's boyfriend, whose name I cannot even remember, I felt a little stupid to think that I had jumped to the wrong conclusion. We all spent much of the evening drinking wine and vodka, smoking dope and sniffing amyl nitrate, but it was only later when things began to get a little too weird for my liking. Despite my discomfort, the alcohol, the dope and the amyl nitrate combined to lower my barriers of constraint while heightening my arousal. It was like some kind of out of body experience which I both hated and enjoyed in equal measure. I certainly did not want to be seen as some kind of prude or killjoy, especially when the others appeared so enthusiastic. The combination of drugs and drink made my head pound, and paranoia and confusion built up to the point of panic. I found it impossible to reconcile the enjoyment of Linda's enthusiasm while sucking my cock, with the anguish of catching glimpses of Debbie having sex with someone else. Although I did not want to see her and tried hard to keep my eyes closed and just block it out, it was like driving past the scene of a terrible car accident.

It had come as something of a relief that Debbie and Linda's boyfriend had finished first and the two of them sat back naked, voyeuristically anticipating the finale which Linda and I might provide. I put on a good performance, trying my best to make it look like I was having the time of my life. I fucked Linda not out of personal enjoyment, but as a way of punishing Debbie for encouraging my involvement, hoping that it might dissuade her from suggesting a four way encounter again. However, when Debbie began to caress my buttocks while kissing Linda's breasts, I sensed that the enforced voyeurism merely served to excite her.

The following day, Debbie had been back to her usual monogamous self, convincing me that it was all just a little bit of fun which would serve to enhance our relationship and make us stronger. In her words, it was nothing more than a 'glorified wank'. Although these liaisons did not become regular events, it had seemed to make us closer in some kind of drug fuelled, confused and fucked up way. It was as if the two of us had become bonded together by our joint secrets, the knowledge of which gave us a sense of empowerment.

When Debbie introduced me to a couple who were probably in their late thirties or early forties, I sensed that Debbie had been into this kind of lifestyle long before she met me. Angie and Mike lived in a large mock Georgian house, and clearly lived very comfortably. Following my initial introduction, it appeared that they and Debbie were not complete strangers, and neither were they averse to the drug and alcohol combination. The couple's level of affluence was further highlighted by the size of their cocaine supply, a drug which was certainly beyond our realms of affordability. While Mike snorted the white powder like there was no tomorrow, Angie seemed to prefer having it sprinkled on her clitoris. I had never even taken cocaine before, and certainly never anticipated that my first experience would involve snorting it from a stranger's snatch. Following our second visit to their lavish home, Debbie had felt the compulsion to leave with a pair of Angie's earrings and an expensive looking necklace. Although nobody deemed it appropriate to mention the missing jewellery, we were not invited to their home again.

For a time at least, Debbie and I revelled in the apprehension that we had become Bonnie and Clyde, Sid and Nancy, all rolled into one. All rolled into one big fucking drug fuelled mess. In a rare moment of lucidity, I decided that we had several pressing needs. We needed more money, I needed to work, we needed to limit our drug intake and I needed to take the music more seriously and, before long, we seemed to be on track for a bright new future together. I landed another warehouse job, Debbie secured herself employment in a shoe shop and with a little financial assistance from my long suffering parents, we were eventually able to obtain a mortgage and bought ourselves a modest home.

We took our new found responsibilities seriously, worked hard and our narcotic habits became confined to weekends and the occasional evening. We were on the ladder and living the dream, and after deciding that marriage was the next logical step, we took the plunge. It had been a small affair with guests limited to family and a few close friends and, in time honoured tradition, Debbie and I were stoned during the ceremony. Although neither Debbie's mother nor father had been in attendance, her brother, Peter, had been present, and Dave had agreed to be my best man on the understanding that he would not have to make a speech. Overall, it was not the most traditional of weddings and the music at the reception was limited to punk classics, with a bit of Alice Cooper thrown in for good measure. Although Debbie and I did take to the floor for a slow dance to 'Germ Free Adolescents', the day was mostly memorable for one thing; for reasons which could only be apparent to himself, Peter had deemed it necessary to announce out loud, and subsequently display the evidence, that beneath his suit he was sporting a pair of black silk ladies' knickers, which he confessed to having stolen from a washing line.

Chapter 19

A Bitch Called Karma

"Good afternoon. I'm looking for Deborah Fankham," I announced in a hushed tone to the rather stern looking nurse who was manning the ward's reception desk.

Looking up from her paperwork and peering over the top of her spectacles, she asked "and you are?"

"John Turner," I lied in a friendly manner. "I'm an old friend of hers. Could you tell me where I might find her, please?" I expected security to be quite tight on an 'acute impatient ward', and so I was rather surprised when the nurse, without further questioning, simply directed me to the third room down on the left and then went back to her paperwork. The break in silence on the ward, caused by my arrival, had alerted the attention of an attractive brunette woman who had been looking out of the window when I arrived. I guessed that she might have been early to mid-twenties, wearing blue jeans and a black jumper. Standing by the window and holding a cup of tea or maybe coffee clasped in both hands, she watched me as I strolled past on the opposite side of the communal lounge area. I looked over, noting that only two of the large red, padded chairs were occupied.

Both occupants appeared to be middle aged women, sat in silence, wearing dressing gowns and slippers. Both looked downcast as if they had the weight of the world on their shoulders. Alongside them, the brunette by the window looked a little out of place. She sipped from her cup as her eyes followed the direction of my movement, causing me to feel slightly uneasy, as being watched made me feel very self-conscious. Gary Spackman, shortly before his unfortunate boating accident, had mentioned that Debbie might have been in a hospital near Dartford, and after making enquiries at other hospitals in the area without success, I thought that I may have finally found her this time. When the nurse pointed me in the direction of the third room on the left, I had felt that same adrenaline rush as I had when finding both Peter and Gary, but this time I knew it would be very different. I had been alone with both of them, and on both occasions their demise had been hastened beyond the sight of prying eyes.

There was no way of planning how this reunion might go, even if the patient to whom I had been directed did in fact turn out to be the Deborah Fankham that I had been searching for. I might have to evaluate the situation for now, calculate my moves and bide my time; after all, this was a hospital. On the other hand, I had never been able to lose sight of the fact that it was her testimony which had ultimately seen me convicted for the murder of Annika Radwanski. When she lied to the court that she had discovered me in bed with the blonde girl, it was Debbie's act of betrayal which sealed my fate. Deborah Fankham was my nemesis. I momentarily looked over my shoulder, somehow sensing that the young brunette was still watching me. Once more, we made eye contact and my sense of unease increased. The door to the third room on the left was open when I reached it and, as I entered, a young nurse cheerily greeted me. "Hello, are you here to visit Deborah?" she asked as she was adjusting the blinds.

The room was bright, the white walls reflecting the light that streamed in through the large windows. The minimal furnishings gave the room a sense that it was larger than it actually was. There was a bed with its screening curtains pulled back to the walls, a bedside table and two armchairs by the window. "Yes, I am," I answered before venturing any further into the room. "I hope I haven't come at a bad time."

"No, of course not," the nurse replied. Then, in her chirpy tone, she spoke to a seated figure shielded from my view by the high back of the armchair. "Look Deborah, you have another visitor. You are having a busy day today, aren't you," the nurse added before stepping back and beckoning me forward. As I approached the obscured patient, the nurse, practically speaking in a whisper, informed me, "I'm afraid that Deborah has a condition that we call Catatonic Psychosis, so please don't expect too much from her."

"Oh, I'm very sorry," I said, somewhat surprised, not quite knowing what to expect and not sure what else to say. "I didn't realise."

"I'm sure she will appreciate your visit, and speaking to her will be very therapeutic," replied the nurse. "I will leave you to your privacy," she added as she left the room, closing the door behind her. Personally, I doubted that Debbie would find the ghosts of her past descending upon her like the Grim Reaper to be at all therapeutic, by any stretch of the imagination. However, I was rather hoping that finally catching up with her after all this time might well be beneficial to me.

I pulled the spare armchair around so that it faced Debbie's, and I sat down in front of the woman I had not laid eyes on since she had testified against me in court. Somehow, throughout my years of incarceration, planning for this very moment, my mind had envisaged her as looking exactly the same as she had done back in 1986. Don't ask me why I had not expected her to have altered, but any illusions which I had harboured of her with long blonde hair, pouting lips and immaculate make-up, were dashed in a moment. Instead, she just sat there, motionless, expressionless and gaunt. Her shoulder length hair was now brown and unkempt and her face was pale and thin, almost emaciated. It was only her now sunken, partially closed brown eyes that bore even the slightest resemblance to the beautiful woman who I had once known.

As I stared into her empty sunken eyes, I found it hard to comprehend just how much she had changed. At one time, this woman was so vain that she would never have dreamed of showing herself in public without her hair being just right. Her lipstick always needed to be the perfect shade to compliment whatever she was wearing, and her make-up was always applied in the most immaculate fashion. Now, each line etched into her face either told a story or held a secret. I looked at her mouth, her cracked and swollen lips, remembering how I would have once held her face affectionately in my hands, gently tracing my thumb across her bottom lip before kissing her softly on the cheek. I had not heard her voice since she

238

had damned and condemned me in court and now, as I gazed upon her dry and shrivelled lips, remembering how they were once painted red, dripping the venom which poisoned my life, and I wondered how many lies had spilled from that mouth over the years.

"I'm back," I whispered, leaning forward in my seat. "I think you've been expecting me." I watched closely but could not even detect the faintest flicker. Her almost deathly stare remained firmly transfixed on something outside, beyond the window, beyond this room, perhaps even beyond life itself. I sat with her in silence for what seemed like an eternity, although in reality it was only around twenty minutes or so. For so long I had waited for the opportunity to confront her and listen to her version of events. Moreover, I wanted to understand why she had lied so easily in her testimony. I felt the need to hear her explain what I had done to her that was so bad that it should warrant a life sentence, and why Annika Radwanski had to die to make it all possible.

During the intervening years, there had been no contact between us, no letter of explanation and no word of regret. My frustration had grown into anger, and my anger had grown into hatred. Often was the time when I had pictured her mouthing the word 'sorry' as my grip tightened around her neck, watching her struggle for her last breath. Often was the time when I had envisaged stabbing her through the heart; poetic justice for the way she tore out mine, leaving me with a black hole of loathing and anger. Her prison seemed little different to mine, and perhaps had I held a pillow firmly over her face and stolen her final breath then, who knows, she may even have thanked me.

I would like to have been able to say that she had looked into my eyes and said 'I'm sorry', or that she had shed a tear of guilt or regret, but although I watched and I waited, there was not even a flicker. The once beautiful and self-assured woman just sat there, devoid of expression, a sad, dishevelled creature now not even a shadow of who she had once been. As she sat there with the afternoon sun shining on her face through the window, there was nothing in her appearance which gave the even slightest hint of who she had been or what she had done; or perhaps it did. Maybe being reduced to an empty shell, her life practically extinguished, perhaps said it all.

I cocked my head to one side and stared into the vacant eyes of a hopeless, helpless, pathetic shadow of the woman I once knew. Her lifeless eyes prompted me to recall a vivid memory from a time when life had seemed much less complicated, a time when I foolishly thought that we were truly happy. Although I was never keen on DIY or gardening, one spring morning I had felt compelled to tidy our garden following the ravages of winter. I removed the sealed lid on the water butt and had been greeted by an awful stench. Closer examination revealed a dark mass, literally crawling with maggots. After opening the tap at the base of the water butt, a fetid liquid gushed forth, surrounding my feet. A noxious smell prompted me to cover my nose and I jumped back in disgust. I waited until the blackened water had finished trickling from the tap and then lifted the empty water butt, carried it to the lawn and turned it upside down, allowing its macabre contents to slide out onto the grass.

I recoiled in abject horror upon the realisation that what had been sealed inside the water butt was a cat, and now it's soaked, decaying remains lay there on the turf.

The maggots had feasted well and had eaten away nearly half of the poor creature's face, revealing its teeth, jawbone and part of its skull. Strangely enough, despite the flesh being stripped from its eye socket, the eye remained in place and it stared up at me, accusingly. This had not been just any cat though and I could tell from its little pink collar and bell that it had once belonged to a neighbour. It was the cat that had a liking for ripping open our dustbin bags at night, leaving the rubbish strewn around by the back door. Debbie hated that cat and would often open the back door and encourage our dog to chase it away.

I went to the shed, took out the spade and dug the poor animal a makeshift grave as fast as I could before shovelling the grotesque feline aberration into the hole. As I piled earth on top of it, that one eye, devoid of surrounding flesh, continued to stare up at me until it was finally completely covered. I took off my trainers and threw them into a bin bag. Still shaken, I then went back into the house to wash. Throughout this ordeal, Debbie had been laying on the couch in the living room, watching television. I sat down in the armchair, regained my composure and then related the story. Although she said that she was sorry the cat had met such a grisly demise, trapped and downed in a water butt, I remembered that she had appeared neither shocked nor horrified, but had merely offered insincere condolences without ceasing to stare at the television.

For months afterwards, the image of that cat seemed to be transposed onto the inside of my eyelids, haunting me each time I closed my eyes and I could not sleep without the aid of prescribed tablets. How had it become trapped inside its water filled coffin? It could not have removed the lid itself and climbed in. Our garden fences were high enough to keep the dog from escaping and so who could have climbed over and sealed the poor animal inside? What manner of sick individual would even consider such cruelty? I would sometimes get out of bed, go downstairs in the darkness, roll a joint and sit smoking in silence, forcing the smoke to the bottom of my lungs. I would return to bed and lay there in the darkness with the room spinning and thinking of that cat's final panic stricken moments as it fought for its life, unable to escape, the air in its little lungs rapidly replaced by the water as it struggled for breath, finally succumbing to the inevitability of drowning.

Looking deep into Debbie's vacant, expressionless eyes, the image and that memory had suddenly returned like a spectre. I leaned forward and whispered. "It was you, wasn't it, you drowned that cat, didn't you, you evil fucking bitch." Once again there was no sign of a response, not even the faintest flicker of emotion. So many times I had heard the term 'Karma is a bitch', yet never gave it much thought. Maybe there might be something in that adage after all, I wondered. Perhaps it could be argued that all we do, either good or bad, will eventually come back to us in some form or another.

I would like to be able to say that my twenty minute reunion with Deborah Fankham had been an epiphany, but I would be lying. After years of murderous thoughts, I simply realised that her hold over me never really existed. Maybe you might like to think that despite the length of time and distance between us, there was a chance that I still loved her. Maybe you would like to believe that I had pitied her plight and subsequently forgiven her. If I were ever to attest to such feelings, then once again, I confess now that I would be lying. Time and distance paints a very distorted image. Perhaps there was an element of pity involved, but there was certainly nothing that I could do which would cause Debbie any more pain than she was suffering already, and it was all a consequence of her own life and actions. I realised that in my quest for revenge, maybe it was Debbie who had unwittingly been my greatest ally.

"Goodbye," I said, standing up to leave, "I'll see you in Hell." I smiled and held her limp, cold hand in mine for just a moment before heading for the door. I turned around for one last look, unable to believe that the living corpse sitting and staring blankly through the window was someone I had considered to be my nemesis for so long. I closed the door behind me, somehow feeling that a chapter in my life had finally closed with it.

"Are you a friend of my mother?" asked a voice which suddenly shook me from the depths of my thoughts and confusion. "Sorry, but should I know you?" The gentle voice sounded slightly perplexed and I turned around to find myself confronted by the young brunette woman who I had previously noticed standing by the window.

"We were friends many years ago," I offered by way of explanation, unsure of what else to say "so I doubt that you would know me. I'm John, John Turner," I informed her uneasily, taking care not to reveal my true identity.

"No, my mother has never mentioned you," said the young brunette, quizzically. She had an intensity which I found most unsettling, and I sensed that my explanation had not fully satisfied her curiosity.

"Oh, it was a very long time ago, I'm afraid," I began to elaborate. "So long ago, in fact, that I was not even aware that Debbie had a daughter, so please forgive me."

"No, please forgive me, I didn't mean to appear rude," she cut in, "I'm Elise." Suddenly the brunette had a name. Elise held out a hand by way of formal introduction. "I was so surprised when I heard you asking after my mother at the reception desk. She doesn't exactly get many visitors," Elise added in an almost sullen tone.

Despite my understandable urge to get as far away from that place as was humanly possible, I grasped her hand and shook it in a warm and friendly manner. I could not help but notice that there was an element in the way Elise spoke, and perhaps in her movement too, which made her appear something of a lost soul. Maybe she felt that the very nature of my visit could be the key to unlocking a great mystery. "Has your mother been in here long?" I enquired, hopefully sounding less alarmed and defensive than I may have done a few moments earlier.

"Mum has been in here for nearly six months now," replied Elise in a softly spoken voice, looking somewhat downcast. "I think she's actually got worse since she's been here. They're treating her with anti-psychotic drugs and benzodiazepines, but she has had electro-convulsive therapy too, but nothing seems to help. She's just withdrawn into herself."

The irony was not lost on me for a moment, as it was Librium, a benzodiazepine, which Gary had used to drug me back in Krakow. That drug led to my incarceration and now here was Debbie, locked away and being given the same drug. I sensed that Elise needed to someone to talk to, even a stranger like me, so I asked her if she would

244

like a coffee and a chat in the relative com[...] lounge area. "Yes please," she answered with a half [...] "that's very kind of you." I got us both coffees from the nearby vending machine, hoping that 'white with sugar' would be to her taste. Handing her a plastic cup of what appeared to be brown hot water, I sat down in the chair opposite Elise.

"So, how come no one else visits your mother?" I enquired, taking a sip from my cup, screwing my face up in mock disgust at the unpleasant taste.

Elise half-heartedly laughed. "Yes, the coffee from that machine is horrible, isn't it? I'll get us a proper coffee next time." Then, with eyes downcast, she continued. "I suppose mum just hasn't got anyone else who cares enough to come and see her." Elise had no idea what her mother had put me through yet even so, her comment seemed like a damning indictment. "So," she proceeded after a moment gathering her thoughts, "you said that it has been a long time since you last saw my mother; was it a shock seeing her today?"

"Yes, it was," I replied in all honesty. "The nurse I spoke to in her room told me that she has catatonic psychosis, or something. How on earth did she get herself in that state? When I knew her, she was beautiful, vibrant and full of life." Elise smiled through the tears that were welling up in her big brown eyes. I guess that the picture I painted of years gone by were in stark contrast to her mother's present state of mind and body. "I'm so sorry," I said, "I didn't mean to upset you."

"Don't worry, you haven't," replied Elise, sniffing and wiping away tears with the back of her hand. It seemed surreal talking about Debbie like this while she was only a

y, locked away in her private world,
ven knowing that we were there. "I
not used to hearing anyone say nice
r," she added poignantly. Elise talked
erely, maybe she was a little too open for
, I had thought to myself, especially as I was
er but a stranger. I really got the impression
tha. .st needed to talk to someone, anyone in fact.
Over the next fifteen minutes or so I just sat and listened
as Elise unburdened her soul. Even for someone as
hardened as myself, I found her revelations to be shocking
and I could say little that would be of any consolation to
her.

She told me all about her little girl, Gracie, and
opened her purse while once again wiping away her tears,
and took out a couple of dog-eared and clearly treasured
photographs. I smiled as I looked at the innocence
depicted in those images. I handed them back, remarking
how beautiful her tiny daughter was, while Elise
explained how her mother had been angry and extremely
disappointed to learn of her daughter's pregnancy, and had
urged her to seek a termination before it was too late. I did
not understand how she could have been so unsupportive
of her own daughter's situation. Elise further explained
how her mother had always striven to maintain influence
over her, even as she grew older; where she went, who she
went with, her boyfriends. "I suppose that mum could
never accept that I had grown up and as she lost control
over her life, I guess she just tried to control mine," she
said, trying to fathom the complexity of their
mother/daughter relationship.

Elise confided in me that when she had initially told
her mother that she was pregnant, she had expected her to

be supportive, caring and happy that her daughter was bringing a life of her own into the world. She had been shocked that her mother, without hesitation, without care, without compassion, had coldly demanded that she get rid of it. There had been no consideration for the tiny, fragile life which was growing in her daughter's belly; her granddaughter to be was merely an 'it'. Elise had protested for the future of her unborn child and her mother had responded by slapping her hard around the face. Faced with the prospect of losing her ability to manipulate the last person over whom she still maintained control, Debbie had resorted to becoming a bully.

"Your mother always liked to be the centre of attention when I knew her," I offered. "Maybe as she grew older, she became a little jealous?"

"Maybe," replied Elise. "It wasn't really until I'd left her and dad and moved back down South, that I realised just how much my mum had always tried to control me. When I look back now I can remember lots of little details, but it was after Gracie was born that things really worsened between us."

"How do you mean?" I asked.

"Well, she was always quick tempered with me, I suppose," Elise elaborated. "I could never do anything right and when Gracie cried, mum was always impatient with her, and when mum got angry it would just make Gracie cry more. Mum said that she was disappointed in me for getting pregnant. She had taken me to the doctor and put me on the pill when I was fourteen but I hated taking them, so she would force them into my mouth and hold it shut until I swallowed." Seeing my shock and horror at hearing her tale of such parental cruelty, Elise defensively added, "I know mum was having some problems at work, and she complained that she couldn't sleep. I also overheard mum and dad arguing and I heard her saying that she was depressed. Maybe that was where her illness started."

Hearing Elise referring to Gary as 'dad' and thinking back to Gary's revelation that Debbie had duped him into being a father to a child who was not actually his, I was not sure how much she knew. However, genuinely intrigued, I asked, "Did they argue often?"

"They didn't argue that often," answered Elise, "but mum was stressed out all the time and she really nagged him. It was like no one could ever do anything right. Mum never saw anything from anyone else's point of view and always wanted her own way. She hated living on a canal boat, miles from anywhere and really wanted a house, especially in the winter, but as dad didn't earn much we couldn't afford to move."

"But didn't he ever stand up to her or stand up for you?" I enquired, looking to delve deeper. After being so resentful of Gary for taking everything that was once mine, I was beginning to think that his life with Debbie could have been far from idyllic.

"Occasionally he would argue back," she said, "but usually he would just go off to the pub and come back hours later, usually drunk. Sometimes when he returned, mum would still be angry and I would hear them fight. When things got really bad and I couldn't take the arguing and the bad atmosphere any more, that was when Gracie and I moved out. A friend offered to put us up until I was able to get a little place sorted out, but it hasn't been easy for me or my daughter."

I was saddened to hear this young woman's sorry tale but, despite my desire to at least say or do something which might make her life even the slightest bit better, my words sounded hollow and meaningless. "Haven't you got any other family who could help you out?" I asked. Elise informed me that her grandfather had recently died, and although she had an uncle and an aunt in the West Country somewhere, she had no intention of looking for them.

"Mum and Granddad fell out a long time ago, and she was really angry that he left her hardly anything in his will," Elise exclaimed, cynically. "Most of his money is locked away in a trust fund for Gracie and I. Mum hated that and said that I should give the money to her because it was rightfully hers. She said that my grandfather owed her." Apparently, Gary had also been disappointed that the long awaited inheritance was not forthcoming, but he had done his best to placate Debbie's anger.

"I've waited years for that money and that old bastard owed me," Debbie had said, "and now I've been robbed by my own daughter too," she shrieked bitterly, pointing an accusing finger in Elise's direction. Despite her daughter's attempts to calm the situation by explaining that not even she could draw on the funds for the foreseeable future, and that it was earmarked for Gracie's future, Debbie would hear none of it and in her mind, she had been betrayed by her own flesh and blood. The altercation had frightened Elise and only served to hasten her departure into a life of independence.

Elise assumed that her Uncle's meagre share of her grandfather's estate would also have been a bitter pill for him to swallow. "Mum and Uncle Peter would often have disagreements over who should get the biggest share of the money, and even when I was young I used to think that it was cruel to talk about my grandfather like that, when he wasn't even dead. My uncle Peter is a real sleaze, though," she added. "He would sometimes say really disgusting things which made me feel very uncomfortable when I was small, and I hated being alone in a room with him. My Auntie Pam is quite nice, though, and I do feel sorry for her. Mum even fell out with them for some reason, but she never explained why. I know he went to prison, but I don't know exactly what for, but I do think it had something to do with that."

I thought of Uncle Peter swinging in his barn on the end of a rope, and sensed that my actions had probably done Elise a favour too. I kept my mouth shut on the subject though and chose to change the direction of our conversation. "It's got to be really tough for you, bringing up a daughter on your own." I knew that my words offered scant consolation. "It's such a shame that you can't even turn to your mum when you could do with the support."

"Mum? Support?" exclaimed Elise. "She turned up at my door when she left dad and stayed a while, but it was always all about her. I tried to encourage her to go back to him but she wouldn't. When I tried to defend him, she told me that he wasn't even my real dad. She just dropped it into the conversation like it wasn't important. I was really shocked. When I asked her who my real father was, she just casually told me that he was a musician who had died of a drug overdose before I was even born."

"Wow," I said, trying to make it sound like I knew nothing of it, but remembering how Gary had already told me a similar story. "That must really have been a bombshell," I added, feeling that suddenly my train of thought was distracting and disconnecting me from our conversation. My mind was putting two and two together and coming up with many numbers, none of which were four. I thought back to the conversation which I had with Victor, remembering how Debbie had told him that I was dead. My head was suddenly filled with possibilities and questions. Her mother had also told Elise that her biological father was dead. Could there be a link? Surely not, I reasoned. I stared at Elise, dumbfounded and lost for words as my brain tried to process the thunderbolt that she had unwittingly hit me with.

Should I say something to her? What would I say? How would she take it? "Hi, I could be your father," or "oh yes, I came here today because I was considering killing your mother." After Elise's emotional outpouring and soul-baring, there was no way that I could casually slip any of that into the conversation. "Oh, and by the way, I'm not really John Turner, but I was once married to your mother and now I'm back from the dead." No, there was no way that I could mention any of that. Another lying, cheating, conniving loser in their lives would be the last thing that this young woman and her daughter would need right now. Besides, surely I must be wrong. Surely my confusion was leading me to jump to the wrong conclusions. I needed time to consider everything that Elise had told me. As far as she was concerned, I was John Turner, former family friend and that was all she should know. I felt a sudden wave of panic, ashamed of my urge to get away. I needed a drink and a chance to think through my options. Nervously, I glanced at my watch. "I'm so sorry, Elise," I began to make my lame excuses, "it has been lovely to meet you, but I really must go."

"Of course," she replied, momentarily flustered. "I'm so sorry that I've kept you talking for so long," the young lady added apologetically.

"Hold on, just a moment," I said, leaping out of my seat and rushing over to the reception desk to ask the stern looking nurse if she could spare two sheets of paper and a pen. Indignantly, she pulled two sheets of paper from a pad and placed them on the counter with a pen. I thanked her, promised to return the pen in a few moments and avoided the urge to suggest that she could benefit from a personality transplant. I went back to where Elise was seated, sat back down opposite her and proceeded to write down my telephone number, before handing it to her along with the spare sheet of paper and the pen.

"Look," I said, hurriedly, "here is my number, if you let me have your number and address it would be good if we could keep in touch." As Elise began to write, I explained my current position as best I could. "I'm due to fly back home in a few days' time and there's also a chance that I might relocate soon too. So I guess you could say that I'm between addresses at the moment, but if you want I could let you know my details when I'm more settled."

"Thank you," replied Elise, as she wrote down her details and handed me back the paper and pen. "I would like that," she added.

"Any time you need to talk, just call me or message me." I assured her, trying my best to sound sincere, supportive and comforting. As I stood to leave, Elise hugged me and thanked me for taking the time to talk.

"It's funny," she said, "but although we've never met before, I feel like I know you." I smiled, said my farewells and walked towards the door with the sheet of paper and the pen still in my hand. After returning the pen to the reception desk, I paused to glance at the sheet of paper before folding it and putting it in my pocket. Pensively I turned to look back. Just as when I arrived, the attractive brunette wearing blue jeans and a black jumper was gazing out of the window, only now I knew who she was. "Goodbye Elise Fankham, of Knights Manor Way, Dartford," I thought to myself as the ward door closed behind me.

Chapter 20

Raising a Glass to the Future

I ordered myself a pint of lager, sat down at a table in the corner and looked around. The pub was inordinately quiet. The sign outside, hanging above the door, had called this place The Ship, but I think The Shit might have been a little more accurate. I took a mouthful of beer as I continued to survey my surroundings. The taste was harsh to my palate; perhaps I should have been more specific when placing my order with the landlord, I thought. What he had given me was flat and tasted like either the pipes needed cleaning or he had given me the slops from under the bar. I glanced over at the landlord who stared back at me disdainfully as he wiped around the inside of a pint glass with a dishcloth. As he reached for another glass to dry, he appeared to be more interested in me than the task in hand. He continued to stare, seemingly suspicious of my presence. For a publican who should have been grateful for any trade that came through the door of this shithole, he did not strike me as the most genial of hosts.

Other than me, the only other patrons of this rather dour drinking establishment were two lads who were playing pool. The pool table was situated at the rear of the pub and was flanked by the ladies and gents' lavatories in the corners, signs acknowledging 'Gents' to the left and 'Ladies' to the right were strategically placed to avoid any confusion. I guess the lads were in their late teens or maybe early twenties, and the repetitive 'chink' as one ball struck another and the occasional 'clunk' and rattle that signified that a ball had been sunk into a pocket were sounds which were occasionally interspersed by their laughter as they mocked each other's efforts. Each sentence they spoke appeared to require a mandatory expletive. "Fuck me, you're shit today," the lad wearing a baseball cap exclaimed to the other as he leant across the table to play his shot. The other, sporting a rather unmasculine ponytail, returned with, "fuck you, wanker," as he took a sip from a bottle of beer, before placing it back on the edge of the table and lining up his next effort.

I relaxed back in my seat, took another mouthful of the foul ale and returned the landlord's unfriendly stare. After the events of the day so far, all I wanted was a quiet drink and a chance to take stock. Nothing had gone quite the way that I had anticipated. The scene which had played out in my mind prior to visiting the hospital, had been much different to the one which played out in reality. Seeing Debbie in her catatonic state, reduced to something little more than a vegetable, had been a shock which I was not prepared for. I had envisaged her pleading for forgiveness, struggling for her last breath as I choked the life out of her, but in the relative solitude of the pub lounge, I questioned my lack of action. I reasoned that her condition could possibly leave her permanently in some state of eternal damnation, leaving her to ponder her wrongdoings for the rest of her days. I hoped that even in her catatonic, locked in condition, she would have been aware of my presence. Regardless of my reasoning, something nagged away inside, making me feel tense. After all, I had orchestrated the demise of both Peter and Gary with almost reptilian intuitive cold calculation. Had I acted out of compassion? Was it that I no longer had the stomach for revenge? Surely I could not have been blinded by some misplaced sentimentality that subdued my anger and resentment. I tried hard to put such thoughts out of my mind.

My chance meeting with Elise had caught me off guard too; a young woman whose existence I had not even been aware of until a few hours ago. Holding the piece of paper on which she had written down her telephone number, I pondered her story as I entered her details into my mobile phone. I had sensed that Elise was on a desperate quest to find out who she actually was, after her life had been thrown into confusion. The revelation that the man who she had always thought of as her father, actually bore no blood ties after all, must have been difficult to come to terms with. In some ways, I felt that her story was concordant with mine and that we both had questions to which there might never be any answers. Elise had spoken to me, a total stranger, in such an imploring way simply because I had told her that I once knew her mother. This most tenuous of links between us appeared to be enough to encourage in her the faintest glimmer of hope that perhaps I might offer her the answers which she most desperately craved.

I looked over at the lads playing pool just as Baseball Cap playfully nudged his friend's cue as he lined up his shot, knocking the white ball off its intended course.

"Fuck off, you prick," barked Ponytail, turning to square up to his mate.

"Alright lads, calm it down," the landlord implored from his standpoint behind the bar.

"Oh, piss off, Ken. We're only having a laugh," replied Baseball Cap with a sneer of disrespect.

Ken said no more on the subject and returned to his tasks of drying the beer glasses and, of course, staring at me whilst I, in return, glared back. I should not have been surprised though, as Dartford had never been the friendliest of places. Back in the days when I was a snotty kid, we would slip into the town's shops on the route between school and the bus stop with the expressed intention of stealing sweets, porno books or packs of Top Trump playing cards. It was not because we either wanted or needed these, but it was a game to us. We considered it as payback to a local community who, more often than not, were hostile to us outsiders. Although we lived on an estate less than three miles from the town centre, it was still beyond the Dartford Heath boundary, and as such we were considered outsiders. Bexley, Swanley, India, they were all foreign countries as far as the locals were concerned.

I took another mouthful of beer and looked down at my phone on the table. Alex's offer of regular work and a fresh start in Prague was beginning to seem like it could be the most viable option to me. The places that I had once thought of as my home and the very roots of my existence were now totally alien to me. For so long I had dreamed of returning home after my release and picking up just where I left off, but in reality I was feeling that there was nothing here for me after all. I selected Alex's number on speed dial and after a few rings he answered. I wanted to keep the conversation short so as not to use up too much of my credit on an international call, and we spoke in his native tongue. I was interested in his offer; my work here was done and it was my intention to make arrangements to fly out to Prague as soon as possible.

"Oi, why don't you fuck off back to Poland," Baseball Cap sneered, loudly enough to ensure that I heard, obviously antagonised by hearing a foreign language being spoken in his local. The two lads looked at each other and laughed, considering their less than latent racism to be something of a victory for the sovereignty of their nation. Annoyed by such a rude and unnecessary interruption, I glared over at them and concluded my conversation with Alex before slipping the phone back into my pocket.

Happy that I had made a decision regarding the direction of my future, I finished my beer and prepared myself to leave the less than hospitable establishment. As I was in no particular rush to vacate the premises, I thought that I should take full advantage of the facilities before commencing my journey back to Dave's place. As I walked passed the pool table on my way to the toilets, I heard one of the lads mutter under his breath, "fucking Eastern European cunt."

The toilet stank with the pungent stench of stale piss and fetid shit. The door of one of the toilet stalls was open and, like passing the scene of a nasty road accident, I was unable to avert my gaze from the carnage within. Someone had obviously been extremely unwell and had barely made it to the safety of the porcelain before emptying their bowel. The resultant mess had then been left untouched and displayed for all to see. Disgusted, I stood at the urinal and relieved myself, passing the time by reading the graffiti written in marker pen on the white tiles.

I washed my hands and then discovered that the automatic drier did not work. A quick scan around did not reveal any paper with which to dry myself either. I shook off the excess water from my hands onto the floor and dabbed the remainder on my t-shirt. I walked out of that disgusting excuse for a toilet, relieved to fill my lungs with the less noxious air back in the bar area. As I past the pool table, a vicious sounding voice piped up beside me. "That's right, you cunt. Just keep walking, all the way back to fucking Poland, or wherever you're from."

"Pardon?" I asked in a polite tone, turning to face Baseball Cap, who had abandoned his game of pool in favour of squaring up to me instead.

"You fucking heard," he sneered, slamming his cue down on the green baize table. "I told you to keep walking all the way to fu…"

He had no chance to finish repeating his sentence. More out of instinct than any kind of premeditation, I picked up the beer bottle which had been placed on the edge of the table by its neck. Without a moment's thought there was a crack followed immediately by the tinkle of broken glass, and the flow of his oratory was checked by the broken bottle that slashed deep across his left cheek. He yelped in pain, shock and abject horror, raising his hands to his face in a vain attempt to stem the flow of blood. Without even so much as a second thought, I jabbed the broken bottle into the back of his left hand, causing him to cry out in pain as the remaining long shard sliced in between his fingers. He dropped to his knees, still clutching his face in both hands as the thick, sticky claret pumped relentlessly from his hidden wound, oozing its way between his fingers and running along his arms.

I dropped the broken bottle on the floor and turned to face his less talkative pony-tailed friend. Ponytail held his pool cue aloft in both hands, nervously dancing on the spot from one foot to the other, like a boxer waiting for his opponent to drop his guard. "You'll get one shot, and one shot only, so you better make it count, you little prick," I sneered, picking up the other cue from the table. He pointed the end of his pool cue at me and then jabbed it defensively in my direction. Like a golfer taking a shot off the first tee, I drew my weapon back and swung it with full force. As the cue caught him squarely across the neck it snapped, sending the broken piece clattering across the floor. I dropped the remainder of the wooden handle, grabbed the lad's ponytail tightly and hammered his head down face first against the angled edge of the pool table. Offering no resistance, he weakly and silently slipped onto the floor.

I stepped back to survey the damage that had been triggered by one single out of place remark. On one side of the pool table, Baseball Cap writhed on the floor, groaning and clutching his shredded face. His cap was inexplicably still on his head as if it was glued on in some way. It may even have been possible that he would have left the pub with one less eye than he had entered with. Feeling strangely offended by his cap's stubbornness and fuelled by adrenaline, I was unable to resist the urge to assert my dominance. As I kicked out, his head jolted sideways and the offending cap rolled across the floor. On the other side of the table, Ponytail lay silent and motionless, perhaps either unconscious or just not having the appetite to inflame the situation further. The scene had played out in slow motion, just like a motorcycle accident I had many years before. In reality, the whole thing had probably been over in less than thirty seconds.

I turned to look in the direction of Ken the landlord, who at this point appeared to be watching me cautiously while simultaneously dialling a number on his mobile phone. Whose number, I wondered, the police? After all my attempts to remain cautiously undetectable, there was no way I wanted to be apprehended for a stupid bar brawl. I had far too much to lose. I picked up my empty beer glass from the table which I had earlier vacated, and launched it in Ken's direction. He cowered, fumbled and then dropped his phone as the glass crashed into the optics behind him, sending shattered shards cascading and tinkling to the floor.

Swiftly, I threw back the hinged flap on the counter and walked behind the bar. The landlord's phone lay where it had fallen with a crack across its screen. I brought my heel down upon it hard twice to ensure that it was permanently disabled. Standing over the cowering wretch, I hissed, "after a bad day, I come in here for a quiet drink and this is what I get? You people need to learn some fucking manners, my friend." I grabbed him by the collar and hauled him to his feet. "One drink, one fucking drink was all I wanted, and what do you do?" I asked, before answering my rhetorical question. "You just stood there fucking eye balling me, you worthless piece of shit."

"Please, please don't hurt me. Take whatever you want," Ken gibbered imploringly as I dragged him out from behind the bar and past the two blood stained lads on the floor. I pushed him forcibly through the gentleman's toilet doorway, before hurling him into the disgusting toilet cubicle. Losing his balance and slipping on the piss-ridden floor, he fell, landing wedged between the stinking faeces smeared lavatory bowl and the cubicle partition.

"Now clean that up, Ken, you filthy bastard," I shouted from the cubicle doorway as he struggled to get to his knees, "and then get those two pricks to a hospital." I turned to leave, pausing momentarily as I held the door open, and called back to the landlord, "and make sure you're more hospitable next time I come in here." The slashed faced young man was still groaning and writhing on the floor as I stepped over his prostrate figure. "Thanks lads, it was nice meeting you," I muttered as I headed towards the exit.

With one hand I pulled up my hood as I hauled the door open with the other, exiting The Ship public house without looking back. It was raining heavily as I stepped out of the pub and onto the pavement. A young couple hurried past without paying any attention to me, appearing far more concerned about being caught in the deluge with inadequate clothing than anything I might have done. Outside it was like day had turned to night. The clouds were heavy, dark and foreboding and a million rain drops danced on impact, their relentless pattering creating a discordant cacophony. Cars splashed past in both directions with their headlamp beams reflected in the wet tarmac, soaked by the torrential downpour. A bus stopped to allow passengers to alight and despite their apprehension of leaving the dry confines of the vehicle, they scattered and scurried in each direction like rats. No one paid me any attention as, with head bowed and hood up, I made my way inconspicuously back towards the town.

Chapter 21

A Guilty Complex

It was gone six o'clock when I finally returned to Dave's and, after peeling off my saturated grey hoodie, I wearily sat down on his sofa with a huge sigh. Dave was watching television and catching up with the evening's local news. "How did you get on today, then?" he enquired, while maintaining a watchful eye on the screen. "Did you find her?" Just as I began to talk him through the day's events, or at least some of them, a news article came on which alerted both his attention and mine. A very smartly dressed young lady was reporting from outside a public house in Dartford which had apparently been the scene of a vicious and nasty incident earlier in the day. The young reporter related the story of how the landlord and two patrons had been viciously assaulted in an unprovoked attack.

"I am joined by the investigating officer, Detective Inspector Burton. What can you tell us about these attacks?" she began, holding her microphone in the direction of D.I. Burton.

"Our investigations are ongoing at this point," he commenced "but I can confirm that two victims have been taken to hospital, where one is said to be in a serious but stable condition." The young reporter probed for further enlightenment into what had happened. "We understand that the landlord was assaulted and locked in the lavatory and that two gentlemen were injured when they came to his aid," added D.I. Burton in a very matter of a fact manner, without giving too much away.

"Can you confirm eye witness reports that one of the victims has lost an eye in the attack?" questioned the reporter, only to receive a very non-committal response merely confirming his previous statement that two victims had been taken to hospital. "Have you made any arrests in relation to this crime?" probed the reporter once more.

"As I said, our investigations are ongoing," said the Detective Inspector bluntly. "We have a detailed description of one of the assailants, whom we believe to possibly be of Eastern European origin." The young reporter signed off from the scene and the cameras returned to the studio, where the programme drifted into an uplifting 'good news' story about an elderly gentleman who had been reunited with his war medals.

"Anything to do with you?" Dave asked, peering over his laptop.

"What? The war medals?" I replied flippantly.

"No, you fucking idiot," Dave quipped sneeringly. "I hope you haven't been upsetting Detective Inspector Burton today." I did my best to assure him that I had not, but Dave raised his eyebrows questioningly. "I wonder if he's related to that prick who used to be our local copper."

Now there was an individual who had not crossed my mind for many a year. Police Constable Leslie Burton had indeed been our local copper. A stocky fellow with a bushy ginger beard, PC Burton had been a nasty bastard who would cruise around our neighbourhood on his police issue Honda CB200 on the lookout for unsavoury characters like us. PC Burton was clearly a policeman who had watched far too many 1970s American cop shows and had a serious complex about being given a girls' name. Rumour had it that Leslie Burton had approached his superiors at Swanley nick and requested a larger motorcycle, as he was struggling to keep up with some of the local hoodlums who rode more powerful machines. Rumour also had it that his superiors had declined his request on the basis that they considered him to be as much of a dick as we did.

PC Burton had to contend with trundling around the streets on his 'hair dryer' while putting up with the local herberts calling out "alright, Leslie" whenever he rode past. In his bid to garner respect within the local community, he would randomly stop anyone under the age of twenty and make a note of their names and addresses in his legendary notebook. I could remember one occasion when he kept me standing in the pouring rain for twenty minutes while checking my details on his police radio. The fact that he was getting just as wet as I was mattered not to PC Burton, for he was a man hell bent on being an arsehole.

Dave and I joked about the time that Leslie had been forced to pursue two young lads on foot. Their crime had simply been to refuse to supply PC Burton with their names and addresses upon instruction, and instead they chose to sprint off up the alleyway. With his police issue motorcycle helmet still firmly in place, he had left his bike unattended by the side of the road and set off in hot pursuit. Paul Blackstock, affectionately known locally as Blacko, had taken this as an opportunity to wheel the bike around the corner and hide it behind the parade of shops. We observed from a safe distance as PC Burton returned breathless from his valiant but failed attempt to apprehend the young felons. He stood perplexed, first looking one way and then the other, unable to fathom where his police motorcycle had gone. We watched him radio the station, obviously trying to explain why he was currently marooned. We had all sniggered childishly as we watched him set off in the wrong direction in search of his motorcycle and, as soon as he was safely out of sight, Blacko had simply wheeled the bike back.

By the time that Police Constable Burton had returned to the scene of the apparent motorcycle disappearance, his superiors had arrived in a squad car and were waiting for him. In fact, they parked right next to the police issue motorbike parked neatly and conspicuously outside the shops, exactly where Burton had left it. We had all nonchalantly strolled past, sniggering to each other while PC Burton did his best to explain how this minor miracle had occurred. Overhearing the local Superintendent barking back, "you are an imbecile, Burton," was music to our ears and became the standard catcall that would serve to undermine the officer's authority thereafter. Dave and I both agreed that regardless of whether or not PC Leslie Burton and Detective Inspector Burton were related, they were probably both knobs.

"So, did you find her?" Dave enquired nonchalantly, pressing me for an answer to his original question and reminding me that I had changed the subject in the hope that he might forget. It was my own fault as I had decided to tell him of my intentions to search for Debbie, knowing full well that he would be interested in the outcome of my endeavours. The only information I had regarding her possible whereabouts had been gleaned from Gary, prior to his unfortunate gas leak accident. "The last I heard, she was in a nut house or somewhere, down near Dartford, I think." Those had been his words so far as I could remember, and I was pretty sure his information had at least narrowed my search options. Dave, in his measured wisdom, had not considered this a good idea. He reasoned that even if I found Debbie, an unannounced visit to see her in a psychiatric unit was fraught with innumerable possibilities, none of which were destined to end well. He considered that even if she decided to divulge her personal reasons for perjuring herself during my trial, neither she nor I were likely to benefit from the outcome if she chose to impart that knowledge. I understood his standpoint but the compulsion to find her was too overwhelming. My course over the past few days had reached a point where I was once again a passenger on a runaway train.

I had not mentioned to Dave that I had already hunted down both Peter and Gary, but had merely told him of my intention to look up some old friends. Although technically this was not a lie, I had neglected to mention certain aspects which were central to the facts. After all, I was grateful to him for putting me up and I was not there to complicate his life, nor did I want him to be implicated in any crime. He was a good man and a loyal and trustworthy friend, and I was enjoying his company and the opportunity to catch up. Besides, I did not think that he or his wife, regardless of her current absence, would be comfortable with knowingly harbouring a criminal.

"Yes, I found her," I finally replied, the tone of my voice denoting that the achievement had not exactly been a triumphant one.

"And?" Dave responded, sounding tentative and dubious, relieved that I had not returned to his house wielding a machete and covered in blood.

"And nothing," I had replied, prior to revealing both the ease with which I had found her and the condition I had subsequently found her in. "There was just nothing behind the eyes. Just blank," I explained. "I tried to talk to her but she just sat in a chair and stared out of the window. There wasn't even a flicker." I also told him about meeting the young woman who had turned out to be her daughter, imparting some of her life story just as she had told it to me.

"You're not thinking that she might be your kid, are you?" Dave asked in a tone which sounded like he was berating my thoughts, even before I had uttered a word on the subject.

"I don't know, mate," I replied, thoughtfully. I had really been trying hard to purge such considerations from my mind, but the fact that Dave had even deemed it significant enough to mention, just started the whole thought process churning once more.

"Talking about your past history," Dave said, changing the subject, "Did you hear about Beth?"

"Who, BJ?" I asked frivolously.

"Yeah, that's right. She died." The bluntness of Dave's delivery regarding such sad and shocking news instantly made me realise that the superficial and thoughtless nature of my initial response had been wholly inappropriate and downright disrespectful.

"How?" I enquired imploringly.

"It was breast cancer," Dave replied, solemnly. "Christmas Eve, eight years ago. She was only thirty-nine." Dave clearly sensed my shock. "She left four kids, all by different fathers, and a husband who'd lost a leg in a motorbike accident." I was reeling from the shock of this news, and fully aware that I should not take Dave's cynical choice of words in the context in which he had delivered them. I was sure that his words regarding the tragic passing of Beth had less to do with implied promiscuity, and more to do with the way that men seem unable to display sensitivity when discussing such difficult subjects in each other's company.

"My God," I eventually responded, hardly able to comprehend what he had told me, "I was only thinking of her the other day." I genuinely felt saddened to hear of her passing and although she had not been the girl for me, I had always thought of her fondly. I had wished her better fortune, certainly better than she had got. I sat for a moment, astonished, considering how all our lives might have differed had I not encountered Debbie in the pub all those years ago, or had I been enticed into her bed. Could I have done anything that might have changed that tragic outcome? A sudden tidal wave of guilt and melancholy had momentarily washed away all thoughts of Peter, Gary, Debbie and even Elise.

"Do you remember her brother, Adam?" Dave shook me back from the past and into the present. "Spider, we called him, the world's oldest paper boy." Although he had not crossed my mind in many years, indeed I did remember him. We had dubbed him the world's oldest paper boy because long after he had left school, a lack of employment opportunities had meant he was still doing a paper round in his late teens. He had long before been nicknamed Spider though, in reference to his slight build. As Beth's older brother, Adam had not taken kindly to our parting of the ways and had chosen to confront me, to fight for his sister's honour. At the time, I already felt guilty about causing Beth's emotional pain, and the last thing I wanted to do at that point was to inflict physical pain on her brother too. I had tried to walk away but he was hell bent on satisfaction. Our duel had been over as quickly as it had begun and, as I helped Spider back to his feet, I certainly gleaned no personal satisfaction from dumping him on his backside.

I sat and listened with interest as Dave related Adam's story as had been reported in the local press. Apparently, Spider had been employed as a lorry driver, transporting timber to the UK from mainland Europe and for some time, his return journeys had been scrutinised by the authorities. Following one trip, customs officials had stopped him at Dover Docks and, following a thorough search of his vehicle, they found a huge cache of class A drugs. Although Spider had vehemently denied any knowledge of the cache, he had been found guilty of drug trafficking and subsequently sentenced to twelve years in prison.

"You're shitting me," I exclaimed. "Spider? A twelve year stretch?" Surely Dave was joking. The Spider that I remembered was a clean cut and generally law abiding individual, who had never been on the wrong side of the law as a kid. I found it impossible to comprehend how he could have made such an enormous transition from paper boy to international drug smuggler; it was an implausible juxtaposition. Still, for a man who, over the same period, had made the transition from warehouse boy to murderer, via near drug induced annihilation, I was in no position to sit in self-righteous judgement over anyone.

"I shit you not," offered Dave stoically, before adding, "mind you, one of your other old flames did quite well for herself, I heard."

"Who was that then?" I asked.

"Lisa," replied Dave. "Apparently she's now a pretty successful barrister and married to a doctor too. They've got themselves a nice house out Chislehurst way, I believe. So in your legacy of death and madness you at least left one success story. I quite liked Lisa," Dave confessed. "She was a nice girl, too nice for you anyway."

As the evening rolled on, Dave and I enjoyed a bottle of wine and a few beers as we continued to reminisce about the old days, swapping tales of people we had once known. The television burbled away in the background, ignored and irrelevant and, as if it were a child desperate for attention, it eventually interrupted our nostalgia trip with the transmission of the late local news, and an update regarding the Dartford pub incident. According to the news anchorman, two men had been arrested in connection with the crime.

How typical of the local constabulary, I cynically thought to myself. They're still fitting poor bastards up even after all these years, eh? I nearly felt a compulsion to confess, but instead took the opportunity to inform Dave of my intention to relocate to Prague and take up Alex's suggestion of making a go of the club. "I'm sure you'd like Alex," I told him, almost imploring him to pack his bags and come with me. Dave merely wished me well as I made my preparations for life version two, and I was unsure whether he was sorry to see me go or relieved to see me leave. As far as I was concerned, the laughter and camaraderie which we had shared over those few days had been the highlight of my return to England. I felt great sadness at the prospect of leaving such a friendship behind, but I also knew that it was impossible for me to stay. I could only hope that rather than being the end of something, it would prove to be a new start.

As I lay awake in Dave's spare bedroom that night, my tormented mind swung like a pendulum as my thoughts deprived me of the respite of sleep. For the passing of Beth, I felt sadness and an inexplicable feeling of loss. For the passing of Gary and Peter, I felt nothing other than a feeling that a chapter had been closed. As for Debbie, well, I was content that her destiny would ultimately lie beyond my intervention. I had learned that I would have to find a way to come to terms with the guilt and regrets of my past, and build a better future in which I could take pride. Although I had the opportunity to build that future, as I lay restlessly in bed, I could not help but wonder if Elise and little Gracie might somehow play a part in it.

Somewhere in the darkness, my mobile phone buzzed to alert me of an incoming text message. I knew exactly who it would be, but ignored it and closed my eyes.

Chapter 22

Revelations

A friend once asked me if I was truly happy. A simple question one might think, and one with a simple answer; either yes or no. Without thought or hesitation I answered yes. I have since pondered that question and others many times. Heaven forbid you were to ever spend half of your life locked away and withdrawn from the world around you, but it does afford one the opportunity and time to think. Segregation from society, from friends, from family, leaves a huge empty space, a space in which self doubt and loathing replaces attachment, and belonging and personal identity slowly erodes. Over time it becomes easy to stand back and look at one's self and begin to see things from a different perspective. It becomes a way of escape. After all, shut away, often with only one's own mind for company, is not always the best place to be.

So, define happiness if you can. It's not as easy as it sounds after all. Happiness and misery, pleasure and pain, love and hate; they are all two sides of the same coin. I believe that misery may be the preset of the human condition and that feelings of happiness are solely dependent on others. Our friends and loved ones want us to be happy, not because it benefits us but because it benefits them. Spend an evening with a friend who is feeling down and you will undoubtedly do your best to cheer them up. Next time, ask yourself why you are doing it. Is it because you honestly want to see them merrily skipping home like a lamb, winning the lottery and living a carefree life of gay abandon, or is it because you cannot face the prospect of spending an evening in the presence of a miserable bastard? We all have our own shit to contend with and a friend in need is a pain in the arse.

Perhaps I have become far too cynical, but before you judge me, ask yourself to define love. Love is considered to be a beautiful, pure and wonderful emotion, but is it? Unconditional love between most parents and their children does not fall into the same category as love between partners in a relationship. Parental love is born out of a genetic bond that develops soon after conception. It is not just an emotion, it is selfless and something which is almost tangible. But can love between two partners in a relationship be defined in the same way? The answer is no. Whoever loved for the benefit of another? Surely that would amount to pity. We love others because it benefits ourselves. It is a selfish emotion that is born out of a desire to attach ourselves to another human being, in an attempt to complete something inside ourselves which we consider to be missing.

How many times have you heard couples describing their union as being like two pieces of a jigsaw puzzle completing a picture? At times I feel like all the love in the world would not complete my picture, and even if it did, it may not make pleasant scenery. I must contend that there are many people who are much better human beings than I, but I must also find consolation in the fact that I am sure that there are those who are much worse.

oooOOOooo

Patricia Fankham had grown up in post war Deeside, a tough, industrial conurbation close to the border with Wales. Times were hard for working class families and being the eldest in a trio of sisters, Patricia was tasked with caring for her siblings while their parents worked long hours for little reward. Eventually, to help balance the family's books, Patricia found herself packed off to a convent school in nearby Chester. After leaving school at fourteen years old, the independent young girl turned her back on her old life and headed for London. Although the streets she found there were not paved with gold, her education ensured that within a short time she had secured a position working in a bank. Patricia fought hard to conceal the truth of her working-class roots, and her elaborately woven tales of a fictionally affluent childhood in upmarket Chester would earn her the nickname, Posh Pat. Although she had little to spare from her wages after paying her weekly rent, Patricia could just about afford an occasional Saturday night at the dance hall with her friends. It was on one such evening that she was to meet Alan, the man who would eventually discourage her from such unladylike practices as dancing, working and having independence. Instead, she would bear his children and enter a life of marital servitude, tending to Alan's every whim and ensuring that he never needed to lift a finger in the home again.

By all accounts, Alan Fankham was not 'most parents'. He had been a sickly child, spending much of his early formative years in and out of sanatoriums as a result

276

of his poor health. While performing his military National Service following WWII, he had been part of the horrific excavation and clean-up work at the Bergen-Belsen concentration camp, the memories of which would trouble him thereafter. He grew into a man of rotund stature, and would never be someone whose health could ever be remotely described as even nearing a peak of physical fitness, but nevertheless he had somehow managed to father two children. Despite his often poor health, his seed had somehow dribbled from his shrivelled nether regions and limped its way along Patricia's fallopian tube, where it had clung to an egg more out of desperation than some inherent instinct for reproduction, just like it was a piece of passing driftwood. Not only had this minor miracle occurred once, but twice. Every parent dreams that their offspring will grow up to make them proud, but Alan and Patricia Fankham were never destined to be that lucky. Even to a man as unfortunate in his genetic make-up as Alan, his offspring had an uncanny knack of never failing to disappoint, but in death he would find a way to mock them both.

I had actually only met the man a few times myself, to be honest. In fact, he had not even attended his own daughter's wedding, but she did eventually get her own back by not being present at his funeral either. Following his stint of National Service, Alan had spent the majority of his working life employed as a civil servant for the Ministry of Defence until he had been medically retired on the grounds of his long standing ill health. He had garnered disdain from within his own family for his proud and open admissions relating to his long term memberships of two clubs. While most men of mature years would be satisfied with joining a golf club or perhaps a working men's' club, Alan Fankham found relaxation in the form of a naturist club, set in the heart of the Kent countryside, and he also frequented a fetish club in East London. Alan would never see how his predilection towards what some may have considered to be a perversion or, in the very least an unusual lifestyle choice, served to infect those closest to him, and in the long run it affected his own life too. To Alan, though, his sexual interests were of paramount importance

Even within the confines of the naturist fraternity, Alan was considered something of an oddball. He was known for offering to draw nude portraits of female members which would require him to ask if he could initially photograph them first. Unfortunately, Alan's artistic portraits could only be described at best as rudimentary, or what some people would more bluntly describe as utter shit. Eventually, some sections of the club membership began to question whether his interest was in the 'cave paintings' he would produce, or if it were just a ruse to photograph members' wives with their kit off. Perhaps his poor conduct within the 'club' was only surpassed by his poor choice of friendships, and his subsequent loyalty to those friends. I refer of course to dear old 'Uncle Henry'. When confronted by his daughter's accusations relating to Uncle Henry's advances, he chose to remain loyal to his friend while demanding his daughter's silence with regard to the matter. It was his poor judgement in this matter that would serve to form the cornerstone of his relationship with his daughter thereafter.

Alan also had a rather slovenly approach when it came to hiding his cache of adult literature and videos around the family home. Although there may be little doubt that his father's openness contributed to Peter's unhealthy preoccupation with matters of a sexual nature, I dare say that any bar-room psychologist worth his salt could well consider one particular event as being the pivotal and defining moment in planting the first seed of deviancy. Alan had originally been initiated into the nudist fraternity by a neighbour who worked for the British Leyland Motor Company. The two neighbours had seldom so much as nodded to each other, but on the Sunday morning that Alan saw Martin Simmons washing his brand new, bright red Austin Allegro 1300 on the driveway, the dynamic of their acquaintanceship changed, because that car was the exact model that Alan wanted. Some weeks before, Alan had visited a local car dealership in Sidcup and picked up some brochures, and he had been thumbing through their pages ever since.

Although Patricia was never encouraged to have opinions or interests far beyond the realms of kitchen utensils or cushion covers, even she was convinced by Alan's considered opinion that the new improved 1975 Allegro model would be the future of British family motoring. As they had sat together on the couch thumbing through the brochure's pages, Alan could imagine himself proudly driving to work in his red Austin Allegro, wearing a white shirt and matching red tie. Patricia thought how nice it would be to enjoy a family holiday, somewhere pretty where she could cook and wash up while looking out of a different window. With a basic model coming in at close to a whopping £1200 however, the only sticking point was the price.

When Alan first clapped eyes on his motoring dream parked on his neighbour's driveway, gleaming in the sunshine, he felt duty bound to initiate a meaningful conversation for the first time. It turned out that Martin Simmons was a union representative at British Leyland and, on the days when he was not out on strike, he would spend his time in the office negotiating good deals for colleagues, family, friends and of course himself too. Alan stood transfixed, watching his neighbour polishing the gleaming red paintwork of his new acquisition, seduced by the car's curves. What he wanted more than anything else in the world was a saloon model with 1300cc of power, four doors and bright red paintwork, brand new and parked proudly on his suburban driveway, serving as a symbol of his status as a somebody.

"Perhaps I could get you a discount on one just like mine," suggested Martin, buffing the car's bonnet to a shine which reflected his beard and bald head. Those were the magic words that Alan was hoping to hear, and within a few weeks he would have his own brand new Austin Allegro parked outside his house. On the day that the car was delivered, there was perhaps an initial element of disappointment on Alan's face. He had stood looking out of the living room window all morning, like a child at Christmas watching for Santa, as he anticipated the arrival of his new wheels. However, due to some mix up or another at the showroom, the car which arrived was an estate model with two doors, and it was also dark green. Following a quick phone call, during which it was explained to Alan that to change the vehicle might take a good few months and work out more expensive too, his disappointment subsided a little and he decided that the car would stay. Besides, Patricia liked the colour as it matched their new bathroom suite. Alan took the car keys, unlocked the driver's door and climbed inside the Fankham family's new car, so new in fact that it still had protective plastic covering the seats. He caressed its ultra modern square steering wheel, breathed in the fresh smell of its velour upholstery and stroked his hands along the dash. After turning the key in the ignition, the Allegro fired into life and Alan sat back in his seat to listen to the gentle purr and chatter of the engine.

"The Fankham family's first brand new car," Alan thought to himself, brimming with pride. He considered the moment to be an announcement to the world that Alan Fankham, husband, father and civil servant, was a man of means. The colour was actually starting to grow on him and as he reversed the car onto the drive for the first time, he considered that the estate model offered greater all round vision, that was until a sickening scraping sound indicated that he had caught the rear quarter panel on the garden wall. Alan jumped out of the car, inspected the damage, held his head in his hands and sobbed like a child. Thankfully, Martin Simmons was able to organise rapid repairs as well as discounts, and within weeks the car was as good as new and a friendship between the neighbours had been cemented.

Subsequently, Mr and Mrs Simmons would become regular visitors to the Fankham house. Martin was always a chatty and amiable fellow, especially after a few drinks, and perhaps his wife's quiet nature was in part due to the fact that she seldom got a word in edgeways, and so just gave up trying. Edna Simmons' stature could perhaps be most accurately described as short and dumpy. She wore a disproportionately large pair of heavy framed glasses which rendered her features almost amphibian like in appearance, and her permed hair made her look as if she was permanently wearing a hat.

It was during one such social evening that Martin first mentioned the naturist club which he and his wife frequented during their spare time. He described in depth their social events, friendships and sporting pastimes too, all conducted and enjoyed in complete nudity. Martin loved the sense of liberation and freedom that developed when such exploits were undertaken naked. Edna nodded in agreement with Martin's every word, and although Patricia was less than comfortable with the topic of conversation, Alan discretely held a cushion over his groin to hide his erection. The Summer of 1976 was long, stiflingly hot and a summer during which Alan and Patricia spent every weekend enjoying the company of their new friends at the Fun in The Sun Club.

By the time that the chilly winter weather had arrived, occasional evenings in the Fankham house saw the youngsters, Peter and Deborah, packed off to bed early pending the arrival of the Simmons couple. The Brandy and Advocaat would soon start to flow and Alan would put the Demis Roussos 'Big Tree' LP on the turntable, and by the time the album had clicked and crackled its way to the final track, 'Forever and Ever', the two couples were invariably naked and drunkenly giggling and cavorting together, with their clothing and underwear discarded randomly around the living room.

Young Peter would lie awake in his room, listening to the muffled laughter downstairs and wondering why his presence was not required. Usually when the Fankham's held a soiree for family or friends, his mother would invariably insist that her young son should entertain the gathering with his vocal rendition of 'Me and You and a Dog Named Boo'. Peter's tuneless squawking became an integral part of any such soiree, and would mean that he was allowed to stay up later than usual. He always loved the adulation, the applause and generally being the centre of attention, while his mother knocked back the sherry and cooed over her little soldier's talent. On one or two evenings when the laughter downstairs had kept him awake, Peter had secretly stood at the top of the stairs to listen more closely. He could hear the music and the laughter, and could just about make out what he thought to be his mother's voice, caterwauling along to the whining vocal of the rotund, warbling Greek, which emanated from the stereo speakers in the living room.

One evening when his inquisitive nature finally got the better of him, Peter had ventured down the stairs and stood in the hallway with one ear pressed against the living room door, listening to the sounds within. Suddenly the door had opened and Peter had come face to face with a horrified bespectacled lady with no clothes on, and then caught sight of his mother wrestling naked on the floor with Mr Simmons from number 22, his shocked father stood equally disrobed and was holding the cine camera which was usually only reserved for family holidays. Although that was the last time that the Fankhams would entertain the Simmons in their own home, the mental images of what he had seen that night had a profound impact on the eleven year old Peter. He soon became aware that his little chap, previously reserved only for peeing out of, would often take on a life of its own, and he also learned that stroking it could be a pleasurable experience. So began a relationship between Peter's hand and his penis, in which the two appendages were to become almost inseparable.

Patricia Fankham had never really been enamoured with stripping off in public or in front of the neighbours.

She had tried hard for her husband's sake to fit in with the other middle class wives at the club, but she had never felt either friendship or acceptance. She grew to dread passing through the huge electronic gates and along the wooded driveway to the club, but Alan loved it. He looked forward to going all week, and on a Friday evening he would be like an over-excited child. Patricia silently resented that she was always left marooned with the other wives while Alan went off to enjoy himself with his friends. She hated the fact that her husband would openly flirt with other women, and that he would belittle her in front of them. Although Alan considered himself to be the life and soul, Patricia grew embarrassed of her husband's antics after learning that many male members considered him to be a buffoon, while many of the female members thought that Alan was something of a pig.

Other than feeling like a spare part at the club, if it were not for her weekly shopping trip to Bexleyheath Broadway or fucking Mr Simmons from number 22, Patricia Fankham would not have had any social interaction at all. After years of playing the dutiful, if not downtrodden wife, Patricia shocked the family by running off with Jason McBride who was less than half her age, and tended the bar at the Fun in the Sun Club. Alan never considered that this betrayal and abandonment was in any way his fault, and although his visits became less frequent, he still continued to pay his annual club membership fees. While on his final holiday in Turkey, Alan Fankham was questioned by the police following a complaint that he had been taking photographs of topless women on a beach. After being allowed to return home, Alan suffered a heart attack and died. In his last will and testament, he left a few thousand pounds to his son, a few thousand pounds to his daughter and the rest of his estate was put into trust for his granddaughter, with the provision that she may not draw funds until her thirtieth birthday.

Chapter 23

A Testing Time

I confess that the chance encounter with Elise at the hospital had been playing heavily on my mind. The more I pondered her words that afternoon, the more I questioned whether or not there was a possibility that I could be her natural father. Maybe I had no right to interfere or, on the other hand, maybe I had a moral obligation. While I wrestled blindfold with my conscience, part of me had to concede that I could be putting two and two together and coming up with five. I had to ask myself who would benefit most from learning the answer; Elise or I. Nevertheless, the question troubled me greatly. I contested that Elise may well not welcome having her world turned upside down by a stranger who she had only met briefly, while on the other hand, surely she deserved to know the truth about her lineage, whether I held that key or not.

I would be the first to admit that I must surely top any list of undesirable fathers. Ex-convict, liar, murderer; none could be considered as qualities which would read well on my curriculum vitae. In my defence, the spiral into a sociopathic and emotionless chasm had not been my choice. I longed to feel something other than the hatred which had filled my every waking hour for longer than I cared to remember. I needed a focal point to lead me on a pathway somewhere warmer and brighter than this; something or someone who could plant a seed of purity and encourage me to be a better person than the one I had become. If I were not already destined to burn in the fires of Hell, then I needed a route to redemption. Once again I questioned who would benefit most from learning the answer; Elise or I. Surely, it would be Elise.

A cursory internet search revealed that DNA testing kits are now widely available and reasonably priced too. I gave Dave the money and asked him if he could order me one in his name, being mindful to ensure that Steven Caldwell left no physical foot print in the country of his birth. The kit was delivered the following day and I had been anxious and quick to follow the instructions closely. The pack which I received contained four sterile packed swabs and two envelopes, one marked 'Father' and one marked 'Child'. I broke open one pack and rubbed the cotton end of the swab along the inside of my cheek for the required ten seconds, ensuring that I rotated the swab just as suggested in the instruction leaflet.

After carefully placing the swab in the correct envelope, I broke open another swab packet and repeated the procedure inside the opposite cheek, before placing it carefully in the same envelope. The instructions recommended that I waited around seven or eight minutes before sealing the envelope, in order to allow the swabs to dry out a little. According to the enclosed literature, the DNA on the swabs would remain stable for up to sixty days. This I thought, would allow sufficient time for testing to be carried out, if of course Elise wanted the test to be carried out. Although it took time to choose the right words, I clumsily penned a short letter to accompany the DNA testing pack, as a way of explaining to Elise why I thought that the procedure might answer some questions for her.

I had already discussed my idea in depth with Dave, and initially he had not thought it a good idea. He questioned whether raking up the past and casting doubts on her identity would be such a good option, but I reasoned that he had not been the one who had spoken to her and sensed her desperation and longing. Finally, Dave had conceded that maybe there was a possibility that if Gary was not her biological father, then perhaps I could be. We both reasoned that it was also not implausible for Debbie to have lied about Gary not being Elise's biological father just to hurt both her former partner and her daughter. After all, Debbie did not have the best track record when it came to telling the truth, and when someone was as deeply troubled as she, then it would be impossible to second guess anything which went on inside her head. Either way, Dave finally conceded that Elise should at least be offered the opportunity to make her own decisions. If Elise chose not to proceed with the test, then it would ultimately be her choice, and it was not as if she would ever need to see me again unless she wanted to.

I had tried not to consider how the outcome might affect me personally, and after sealing £1000 as a gift inside an envelope, I wrote 'To Elise' on the front of it. I handed the envelope to Dave, along with the repackaged DNA testing kit, and asked him if he would kindly deliver it to her after I had gone. Dave was not exactly comfortable with doing it, but once he had agreed, I wrote down Elise's address for him.

"What's this?" asked Dave, with a look of bewilderment, when I handed him a second envelope with his name written on it. My mobile phone vibrated on the coffee table and then rang. I looked down at it, sure that it would be Pam even before I saw her name displayed on the screen. Even though it had been the fifth time she had tried to telephone me that day, I once again allowed the call to cut straight to voicemail. I knew that the two of us needed to talk, but I had other things on my mind too.

"It's just a little something to cover your trouble," I replied in answer to Dave's question about the envelope. I felt a need to make a contribution and show my gratitude to him, not just for his hospitality and the use of his car, but for his loyalty over the years. Perhaps it was little more than a token gesture, but I had stuffed £500 into his envelope.

For the remainder of the evening I had been in a rather pensive mood, pondering the possibility of Elise being my daughter, and wondering if I was getting carried away. I had liked Elise and had sensed a certain affinity which I could not explain. What if she was my daughter? I would then have to contend with suddenly becoming not only a father, but a grandfather too. If it turned out that she was not my daughter, then was I building myself up for nothing? And what if she decided that she did not want to go through with the test at all? After all, we had only met once and spoken for a short time, and I had not even revealed my true identity to her. I began to think that if I was in her situation, I would want neither Steven Caldwell nor John Turner to turn out to be my father. The more I thought about it, the more the situation became a complete 'head fuck'.

In some ways I felt like I wanted to stay there in England. Catching up with Dave had made me want to try and pick up my life where I had left off, and my feelings were exacerbated by a sense that there was still, and always would be, a piece of me there. In reality, I understood that I could never live out the rest of my life in anonymity, under a stolen identity, nor could I forget that I had been responsible for the deaths of two individuals. Although I doubted whether anyone would particularly mourn the loss of either Peter or Gary, I still had an inkling that a judge may not take too kindly if the police were to implicate me in either tragedy. There was also the little matter of the unfortunate and regrettable Dartford pub incident to take into consideration. It was becoming a growing concern that the incident had received so much media interest, and I was forced to concur that even though up until that point I had been very lucky, I also realised that luck is a precious commodity which has a tendency of running out.

Once I had fully considered all my options, I came to the conclusion that realistically I only had one. Alex's proposal that I relocate to Prague would afford me the opportunities which I needed to start my life afresh. I would be around people who I both knew and liked, and I had the prospect of a business opportunity to consider too. It might never be an opportunity to bring me riches beyond my wildest dreams, but I was sure that it would enable me to lead a life of relative contentment, in which I would not spend the rest of it looking over my shoulder.

By the following evening I would be in Prague.

Chapter 24

The Rocky Road to Reality

As the plane made its steep ascent on a grey and dreary evening, I looked down on the patchwork of fields below. The roads and motorways which criss-crossed a Surrey countryside dotted with farms, dwellings and golf courses diminished in size until the nose of the jet burst through the cloud cover until we emerged blinking in the brightness of the sunshine beyond. I sat back in my seat, closed my eyes and began to ponder the life that lay behind and the one which lay ahead. It seemed that for much of my early life, I had been content in my naivety, and happy in the benign nature of my erstwhile shallow existence. I suppose that Honesty and Reality had never really been countries in which I wanted to dwell too long, and in some surreal way it had taken Debbie, Gary and Peter to teach me a valuable lesson. For their part in my education, I hoped that they had in turn learned something too. I could only hope that, as I would be the last person they would ever lay their eyes upon, Gary and Peter had learned that a dog does not forget its tormentors and, given a chance, it will eventually bite back.

Perhaps unwittingly, in his cynical and blunt way, Dave had also played a major part in opening my eyes to aspects of my life which I had not previously seen, or wanted to see. Whatever he had lost over the years in terms of physicality and mobility, Dave had replaced with wisdom and insight. In some ways, I suppose that I had imagined a triumphant return to my homeland; a dark and dangerous avenging angel, swooping down from on high, black of heart and devoid of emotion, hell bent on purging the world of the evil forces which had caused me pain. In reality, I have to contend that I am no demigod after all, but I am simply a human being with the same, if not more, frailties, imperfections, hopes and fears as everyone else. In that respect, I therefore had to conclude that revenge had been something of an anti-climax. I had not uncovered all the missing jigsaw pieces, but if I threw in a few assumptions for good measure then I reckon that the picture had become clear enough.

Above the clouds the sky was clear and blue, and I put on my sunglasses to protect my eyes from the glare of the autumn evening sunshine. The thick white clouds below floated gently past us, creating a vision of serenity and tranquillity. To the eye, the sun conveyed an atmosphere of warmth while the clouds below conveyed an aura of comfort which almost seemed to entice me to venture beyond the confines of our Airbus A319. In reality, I understood that at 33,000 feet, with the air outside possibly being as low as -60 degrees centigrade, the oxygen level in my blood would rapidly drop to a point where I would lose consciousness. Severe hypothermia would set in and I would plummet to my death at 250 mph. In a world where confusion, lies and chaos reign supreme, nothing is ever as clear as it may initially appear.

While the cabin crew served us our cups of in flight coffee, the elderly lady who occupied the seat next to mine merrily informed me that she was flying out to the Czech Republic to visit her son and daughter-in-law. She was most excited by the prospect of seeing her beloved grandchildren too. "They're meeting me at the airport, you know." Her voice quavered in anticipation of a wonderful family reunion. "Are you visiting friends or family?" she asked.

"No," I replied in a cheery tone, removing my sunglasses and turning to face her, "I'm just returning from an educational trip."

"Really?" The elderly lady seemed intrigued. "And did you learn much?" she enquired.

"Yes," I replied with a smile, putting my sunglasses back on before turning to gaze out of the window once more, "I learned that I'm my own worst enemy." The old lady smiled a bewildered smile and opted not to venture any further with the conversation. While sipping the remainder of my coffee, I hoped that she enjoyed her family reunion and wished her a safe journey, before resting my head back against the seat and closing my eyes once more.

"We're on the same aeroplane, dear," she said, placing her frail hand reassuringly on mine, "so I hope it will be a safe journey, for both our sakes."

Chapter 25

Rebirth - Life V2

After getting to Gatwick Airport in plenty of time to catch my flight, I had grabbed a quick beer to steady my nerves, following the tension of ensuring my safe passage through security without having my forged documents scrutinised too closely. Clint Eastwood had obviously done a faultless job, I thought to myself. Another thing that had been playing heavily on my mind was that I could not continue to avoid Pam's phone calls and messages. So, as I relaxed in the departure lounge, I decided it was about time that I called her back.

I was not overly surprised when Pam did not sound particularly happy that I had taken so long to get in touch. "Where on earth have you been?" she had asked tersely. The truth of the matter was that Pam's knowledge and involvement concerned me greatly. Other than Dave, who I trusted implicitly, Pam was the only person who could attest to my whereabouts and who could also implicate me in any wrongdoing. Although I was certain that, if she were asked, she would know nothing about Gary's explosive demise, she did however know everything about why Peter was dangling on the end of a rope in his barn.

In the days before calling her, I had been mulling over how best to put my quandary into words which would not inflame her anger. I felt backed into a corner, put on the spot and devoid of a plan, so I came up with the best I could.

"I'm really sorry, Pam, but I've been away for a few days and I'd left my phone at Dave's," I lied. Yes, I admit that it was a shitty excuse but I somehow reasoned that it was not a complete untruth. It was not a lie that my phone had been at Dave's, but I just neglected to mention that I had been there with it.

Pam was also disappointed to learn that I was leaving the country without her, and she expressed her desire to get away too. Considering the circumstances, she felt that we were in it together and that I was wrong to run out on her. She did have a point, but I reasoned that under such circumstances, it would not be beneficial for partners in crime to travel anywhere together. I explained the decision to relocate to Prague and told her of my plan to stay with friends for a few weeks, just while I sorted out a place of my own. Sensing Pam's unease and mistrust, and in a desperate bid to placate her, I suggested that she could fly over when I was settled.

Pam sounded happy about my proposal and I promised to keep her updated. "Make sure you do," she said. Although I was not sure of what Pam's long term plans might involve, at least our conversation had bought me a little time to decide what my long term plans were. Boarding the plane that evening, I considered that even if Pam and I were not in the same boat, we were both adrift on the same ocean. Both she and I were looking for a fresh start and in many ways we were intrinsically linked.

Having not previously pondered the possibility of circumstances matching the two of us together, I swiftly convinced myself that getting to know her better and sharing her company might not be a bad thing. In fact, I actually began to relish the idea.

oooOOOooo

Alex and Kristina did all they could to make me feel at home during my first few weeks in Prague. They took me into their home while I hunted for an apartment of my own, and even if at times I felt like I was outstaying my welcome, they would hear nothing of it. Of course, no sooner had I arrived than Alex brought up the subject of the club. He sounded overjoyed when I told him that I was still interested and that I was now prepared to talk business.

"Have you taken care of your business in England?" Alex enquired knowingly. I assured him that indeed I had, and given the circumstances, he considered that it might be best for all concerned if we did not discuss the matter further. I agreed that he was probably right.

"So, when do I get to meet this mysterious owner of Heaven and Hell?" I asked him.

Alex grinned. He knew that I was intrigued and he was clearly taking pleasure from knowing something which I did not. "I shall call him and arrange for you to meet him," he replied.

Work at the club had progressed slowly since I had last been there, and when I did not have appointments to view prospective properties, I spent my days assisting with the renovation and refit of our venue. Each time I asked Alex about the owner who I was anxious to meet, all he would reply was "you'll have to wait and see." Finally, following a lengthy telephone conversation, Alex announced that the gentleman would be arriving the following day and that he was looking forward to discussing business with me.

Still having a few months left on my lease in Poznan, I had been fortunate to do a deal with the agent there. After giving up the apartment and offering to relinquish any balance that I might be due, the agent had agreed to forward my few possessions to Alex and Kristina's address. I had arrived in Prague with only a bag containing a few items of clothing, but Alex had been intrigued to learn what was contained in the large package which I had sent to his address from England, marked for my personal attention. "You'll have to wait and see" was all I kept telling him. On the way back to Dave's, following the explosive visit to see Gary, I had made a detour into Birmingham where I had bought a guitar hard case in which to carry the 1978 Les Paul Custom which Gary had so kindly looked after for me for so many years. I had asked the shop assistant if he would also be kind enough to let me have a cardboard box large enough to send the case abroad, which he did. After returning to the car, I took the guitar from the boot, placed it carefully in the case and had then taken it to a local post office.

Alex told me how he had been rehearsing with a drummer and a bassist and he was now itching to get Skazaniec up and running. "So, Steve, tell me," he began, "what's in that parcel?" Alex was clearly intrigued and so I considered this a good time to open the package and check on its precious contents. After sliding the case out of the box, I slowly unfastened all the clasps and lifted the lid to reveal the instrument contained inside. To be honest,

I did have concerns that the cargo may not have fared too well after its journey across Europe, not to mention the damage it may have sustained after it had crushed Gary's skull.

"Fucking hell," exclaimed Alex. "Where did you get this?"

I inspected the instrument, front and back, checking for signs of damage. Using the sleeve of my shirt, I attempted to wipe away a few previously unseen brown flecks from the guitar's white body, presumably the result of it crushing Gary's cranium. "It's mine," I finally replied proudly, passing it to Alex for his perusal. "The Spaceman had kindly looked after it for me for all these years."

"Really?" Alex responded quizzically, taking his time to feel the guitar's weight and look it over closely in a way that only a musician would. "That was very kind of him." After a few minutes of inspection, he added, "I'd clean the blood stains off, if I were you. Does she have a name?" he asked as he handed me back my long lost instrument.

"Murder One," I answered impassively as I carefully put the guitar back in its case. Alex looked at me knowingly. Without saying a word, his expression said it all.

oooOOOooo

The following morning afforded me a lucky break in my home hunting endeavours. The apartment which I had been booked to view was not only available for immediate lease, but it was also situated very close to Alex and Kristina's home too. A spacious two bedroom property, it was situated on the ground floor, merely a stone's throw from Vitkov Hill and within my anticipated budget. As I looked around the apartment, I began to ponder the possibilities of maybe getting myself a dog, and taking daily walks to the top of the hill to admire the view across the city. Of course I also thought about Pam too. I anticipated that the apartment would offer everything that I required to consider calling it my home, so without further hesitation the deal was done.

With a spring in my step and a sense of expectation, I made my way to Heaven and Hell for the arranged meeting with the mysterious owner. Upon my arrival at the club, Alex met me at the door and directed me into the office. Apparently the gentleman had arrived on a morning flight and had been waiting for me, so I pushed open the office door and walked inside. As I had not requested that my legal advisor also be present at the meeting, I was a little bemused.

"Hello Thurstan," I said, more than a little taken aback, "I did not expect you to be here today."

Thurstan reached forward to shake my hand. "Well then, who did you expect," he replied, "the Mafia?"

Looking around quizzically, half expecting to see a man in a suit and smoking a cigar, it took a few moments before the penny finally dropped. "You're... you're not the secretive owner are you?" I questioned tentatively, not wishing to appear foolish.

"Yes I am," Thurstan replied, looking a little concerned. "I hope you're not too disappointed." After assuring him that it was not the case, he explained how he initially bought into the project some twelve months earlier. At the time when he and Alex had been holding discussions about the disappearing witness, Alex had mentioned about the club and how work was going slowly. He feared that the current owner had lost interest and perhaps his heart was no longer in it. Thurstan, on one of his regular business visits to Prague, had met with the owner who indeed was looking to sell up. With the global financial crisis biting hard, the previous owner felt that the club was a risky proposition and that it was high time he realised some of his assets. As a result, Thurstan was able to take over the reins of a project which excited and interested him, and at a bargain price too. However, as his funds were limited, he had hoped that I might be interested in a partnership deal. He had considered that as I might be interested in investing in my own future, a partnership in Heaven and Hell could ultimately be beneficial to us both.

Without wishing to railroad or coerce me into anything, Thurstan had asked Alex to sound me out with regard to my possible interest. Fearing a possible conflict of interests, he had wanted to keep his involvement quiet so that I did not feel pressured into a decision that I was not 100% happy with. I thanked him for his consideration and informed him that I now felt in a position to make a commitment to a project which I was also enthusiastic about. Being both a lawyer and my financial advisor too, Thurstan was keen to make me aware of the implications involved in relation to his conflicting interests before we entered a business partnership. He suggested the offer of a 30% stake in the venture which, if I were agreeable, would give a cash injection that would ensure that the club could be open in time for Christmas. Thurstan surmised that if I deemed this to be an acceptable offer and were to work in the club too alongside Alex, then not only would I have a regular wage but also a 30% share of the profits too.

Despite not having any experience or business acumen, this proposal still sounded like it would suit me very well, and so my second deal of the day was done. Assured that Thurstan was someone who I could also trust implicitly, I agreed to leave the formalities in his capable hands. Alex was overjoyed to hear the news of our impending partnership and the three of us went to the bar across the road to have a celebration drink. In the absence of cherry vodka to accompany our beer, Alex joked that he was a little disappointed that the deal had to be sealed with a shot of Slivovica instead.

Later that evening, Alex introduced me to Marek, a Slovakian born bass player, and Tibor, a drummer who was Hungarian by birth. Ultimately, Alex explained, Marek would be responsible for providing the security at the club too, and he enthused that both he and Tibor fitted the pre-requisite criteria for our band. Despite my initial trepidation as to how the rusty nature of my playing might be viewed by three musicians who had been rehearsing diligently in recent weeks, I was looking forward to being artistically reunited with 'Murder One', and rehearsing with other musicians too. I listened to the others as they ran through a few numbers together while I tuned the guitar which I had not played for over twenty-six years. As a trio, they sounded raw but surprisingly tight. Alex appeared to sense my apprehension as I finally plugged my instrument into the spare amplifier with a buzz and a crackle. "Here's one for you," he announced, bursting into the intro of 'Borstal Breakout'. Marek and Tibor both joined in almost simultaneously. Alex's vocals rasped through the number with practically no hint of his accent and, by the time the song had reached the chorus, Murder One was sounding brutal and we were ripping through the chord changes like the thirty-seven year old guitar and I had never been apart. On our second run through of the song, Alex changed the lyrics to 'Warsaw breakout', spitting out the vocals with grit and venom. By the end of our first session as a four piece, Skazaniec were actually sounding like a decent band.

The day had started full of expectation, anticipation and apprehension, but by the end of it, I had a home, a business venture and a hard rock band. All in all it had been a good day, a very good day in fact. I was full of excitement and enthusiasm in the knowledge that life and the future had much to offer. Despite the lateness of the hour and the international time difference, I emailed Dave urging him to come and visit as soon as he could and I also sent Pam a text message to update her on the day's events. I re-read the words I had just keyed into the message, 'come to Prague, you'll love it'. My thumb hovered over the send key for an eternity. I did not want my words to sound too cool, but neither did I want them to sound like I was too keen either. Modern life was proving to be full of quandaries.

I pressed 'send' regardless.

Chapter 26

Making the Headlines

The local press in both Stroud and Nantwich had run stories on Peter and Gary respectively and had featured articles on their websites too. Gary's unfortunate demise had simply been reported under the headline 'Man Dies in Canal Boat Tragedy'. Ah, a tragedy indeed. The short article simply stated that a local man, Gary Spackman, had died as the result of an explosion which local fire investigators had suggested could have been the result of a poorly installed LPG oven, which might have leaked gas and in turn may possibly have been ignited by a burning cigarette. The article went on to mention that Mr Spackman had been seen drinking in a local pub and that a police spokesperson had said that they were not treating the incident as suspicious.

Peter's obituary had made for far more in-depth journalistic analysis, however. Under the headline 'Local Man in Horror Find', the article explained how Michael Sedgebury, a man living in the same village of Painswick, had gone to the property in search of Mr Fankham after his son had alleged that Peter had offered him drugs and alcohol and invited him to his home. The lad had not been enticed but had been too scared to tell his father. Eventually he confided in a school friend who in turn had told his parents, and the subsequent chain of events had led to Mr Sedgebury visiting Peter's home.

After receiving no answer at the door, Mr Sedgebury had decided to take a look around the property and had found Peter hanging in the barn. He had then telephoned the police to report the grisly find. The coroner had estimated that Mr Fankham must have taken his own life roughly two weeks previously. The news article also mentioned that a police search of the premises had uncovered a cannabis factory inside the property. The journalist who wrote the article must have done extensive investigation work and had delved deep into Peter's history. It was reported that Peter had previously served a prison sentence, after a police investigation had discovered indecent images on his computer and that upon his release, Peter had been placed on the Sex Offenders Register.

As word had circulated, local residents had been outraged that such a person could have been allowed to live amongst them without any prior warning. Subsequent interviews with village residents who had either been in contact with, or who had known Peter, resulted in descriptions such as 'weird', 'strange', 'creepy'. I read how local children had taunted Peter and called him 'Beast', and I thought back to the conversation I had with him about his broken window. Without offering any explanation he had merely hissed, "fucking kids, I hate 'em." How typical of Peter, I thought on reflection; it was always someone else who was in the wrong.

I did feel sorry for Michael Sedgebury for having to be the one who discovered Peter Fankham's mortal remains, but what would any angry parent have done in similar circumstances had he found Peter alive that day? I doubted that Mr Sedgebury had simply popped round for a chat. Maybe he would have beaten Peter to within an inch of his life; maybe he could have even killed him. Either way, I reasoned, Michael Sedgebury could have found himself on the wrong side of the law, and so maybe, just maybe, my intervention had preserved his liberty.

I cannot say that reading either article gave me any pleasure whatsoever. I did not read them and consider them to be akin to some kind of trophy, nor did I feel any sense of glory or revel in my revenge. Yes, of course I had wanted revenge, but I was not proud of what I had done. I had tried to forget those events, put them behind me and move on. Although I had reasoned that I had paid for my crimes in advance, I certainly had no intention of ever going back to prison.

As the weeks had passed, I had heard nothing. There was never the knock on the front door which I had so often half expected. I had striven to make my revenge look like accidents or suicide, and had gone to great lengths to disguise the fact that I had even been there. I had to know that I had successfully buried my past deep enough to ensure that it could never come back to haunt me. It had been with great trepidation that I finally plucked up the courage to put the names 'Peter Fankham' and 'Gary Spackman' into an Internet search engine to see if the results might implicate me or jeopardise my future in any way.

I had been harbouring concerns surrounding the wrongful arrests of the two men in relation to the Dartford pub incident too. After having watched the television news back at Dave's house, I wondered on what grounds or evidence they had been arrested, and ultimately what had been their fate. It had not taken me long to find the details of that incident on the internet either. The pair of unnamed men were described as being Latvians who resided locally and were employed by a construction company in Gravesend. According to the pub landlord's version of the story, he had unfortunately needed to bar the two men from his premises a few days before the incident, as they had allegedly been upsetting his regulars. Further police investigation had been based on an eyewitness account which had placed both men close to the scene at the time of the incident.

Despite their protestations of innocence, the two accused Latvians had been arrested on charges of malicious wounding, aggravated assault and vandalism. Following the intervention from the employer of the pair, who was willing to testify that his employees had actually been working on a house extension in Greenhithe at the time, the police were forced to investigate further. During the course of this further investigation, the owner of the property confirmed that both men had indeed been working at his home until around seven o'clock in the evening on that particular day. With great reluctance, the police had released both men.

In an interview with the local newspaper regarding their ordeal, the two men were quick to praise the diligence of the police force and to thank those who had supported them throughout. When asked about their take on the pub landlord's claim that they had upset his regulars, the men explained what occurred when they had gone into the pub for a drink one evening. The pair had been subjected to racist abuse from a few of the regulars and the landlord had refused to serve them. And therein lies another story.

I had read the articles about Gary and Peter devoid of pleasure but with an overwhelming sense of relief; relief that neither death was being investigated further. However, I had also been relieved to learn that the false arrest issue surrounding two innocent men had been brought to a fair and just conclusion. It was time to finally move on, safe in the knowledge that it is only God and I who will ever know the whole truth and it will only be God who can eventually judge me.

When my time comes and I finally stand before my maker, I can only hope that He will judge me kindly.

Chapter 27

Hell Hath No Fury

I will always remember my father, many years ago, telling me a story of how one of his work colleagues had been caught out cheating on his wife. Not content with just cutting up the man's clothing with a pair of scissors and smashing the windows of his car with his own golf club, the spurned wife had then grabbed a kitchen knife and stabbed him in the penis when he tried to calm her down. Although superficial, the wounds had still required hospital treatment and on his return to work, the hapless fellow had been forced to endure all manner of jibes. Luckily for him, the wounds to his pride were far greater than the wounds to his penis. Back then, in the days of my innocent youth, that tale had been the first time that I had heard how the fairer sex could react with such spite and venom. "Believe me son," my father had said, "Hell hath no fury like a woman scorned."

Although it might be open to conjecture that a woman scorned hath no fury like a man fucked over, nevertheless I was certainly not in any position to put that theory to the test. Within a week of moving into my new home, Pam had arrived and began to busy herself with giving the place a woman's touch. While I spent my days working hard to ensure that the club would be open on schedule, Pam spent her days buying furniture and furnishings. During her first few weeks in Prague, Pam proved to be a valuable asset and had a keen eye for a bargain. My little Volkswagen Polo, along with my meagre possessions, had arrived from Poznan courtesy of the Polish letting agent, and the car now allowed Pam the freedom to travel wherever she pleased. She proved to be a highly competent driver, unfazed by continental road layouts.

Pam and Kristina also hit it off immediately, even if Alex was astute enough to detect that I was a little reticent with regard to our relationship. It was not that I did not find Pam to be a wonderful woman to have around, in fact I found her laughter and keen sense of humour to be quite infectious, and it was not that I did not enjoy her company. She was a woman who had clearly been left scarred and wounded by her own personal experiences, and she was brimming with enthusiasm for a new life in a world without Peter. I knew that she deserved better than to be held at arms' length, and I also realised that the missing piece of the puzzle was something that I had lost from within me. My personal experiences had reduced me to a point where I had become little more than an emotional wasteland. Not only had I built walls, but my walls had a perimeter fence, topped by barbed wire and patrolled by ferocious guard dogs. None of this was Pam's fault though, but for the time being we both seemed to be content with tiptoeing around subjects like 'relationships' and 'commitment'. I could only hope that once the seeds of a better life were sown, then the missing pieces would grow and flourish.

Pam's daughter, Ruth, had thought that her mother must have suffered some sort of aberration when she had announced that she was heading to a foreign country to be with someone she had only just met. It had been an understandable reaction I suppose, given the circumstances, but even though her daughter had been overjoyed when her mother had mustered the fortitude to leave Ruth's evil step-father, she had no idea that her mother had been complicit in his death.

For my part, I had to admit that I enjoyed having Pam around. On occasions, it did seem as though she were trying a little too hard to prove herself to be indispensable, and although I would often urge her to relax and just enjoy herself, she appeared to have an innate desire to please. Within two weeks of her arrival, Pam had transformed the apartment from an empty shell into a home. There were times when I felt that perhaps her presence was almost smothering, but not to an extent that I felt compelled to express any desire to be given space. I reasoned that such feelings were the result of spending half of my life devoid of many important social interactions, and such issues were mine to overcome. When isolated from society for such a long period, time and space becomes the norm. Isolation is an integral part of the punishment, and institutionalisation is an unfortunate by-product which does not bode well with interactions in the outside world. I considered my desire to keep Pam at arms' length to be an unhealthy one, and as part of my transition, I would have to fight it. After all that Pam had been through herself, she deserved happiness.

I would work at the club during the day, putting in long hours to ensure that we remained on course for our scheduled opening, and Alex and I helped out wherever we could in a bid to ensure that the project remained within budget. My days were often tough, physical and stressful, but usually during our evenings together, I found Pam to be a very calming influence. In the seventeen months or so since my release from prison, I felt that I had come a long way, and life was beginning to feel normal, or at least how I perceived normal might be.

One evening at the beginning of December, following a day beset by problems, the forty minute walk home seemed longer than usual as I had much on my mind. A visit from the building inspector had not gone well and he was not willing to issue a pass certificate, on the grounds that he considered our level of sound insulation to be inadequate. Prague is a city which has rather strict regulations regarding noise levels in clubs, and although the recommendations which the inspector made did not spell out total disaster, we were looking at it costing us time and money, both of which were running out. While I had been trying to reach Thurstan on the phone, an argument had broken out between a plasterer and the electrician and as a result, the electrician had walked off the job. Walking back to the apartment in the cold and dark, I felt the chill of winter biting into my fingertips. The prospect of a hot shower and a strong cup of coffee upon my return was all that urged me onwards up the hill to the apartment, my legs were weary and heavy and my knees were stiffened by the cold.

"Good evening, Steve," Pam called out cheerfully from the living room as I walked in through the front door, "you have visitors."

Momentarily, my heart sank as I hung up my coat and struggled to bend down to remove my boots. Who on earth could it be? I wondered. What did they want? It had to be the electrician, I reasoned, and he had most likely come for his money which of course I did not have on me. Before entering the living room, I braced myself for diplomacy; a tall order at a time when I certainly did not feel in a very diplomatic frame of mind.

A young woman sat in the armchair with a small child on her lap. "Hello Dad," Elise greeted me with a faint tremor in her voice and a nervous smile. "Meet your granddaughter. This is Gracie," she said, gazing down at the small child on her knee. Her words reverberated inside my head as I stood in the doorway in a state of shock and utter perplexity.

"I'll leave you to it and go and prepare dinner," Pam said, flashing me a huge smile. "I take it you'll be staying for dinner, Elise."

"If that's alright with Dad," she replied.

I walked across the room without saying a word and knelt down in front of Elise, placing a trembling hand on her arm. "Hello sweetheart," I said softly, looking into the concerned eyes of the little girl and taking hold of her tiny hand. Gracie pulled her hand away and looked at her mother for reassurance.

"It's alright, Gracie," said Elise comfortingly, "this is your granddad."

The little girl looked back at me and briefly placed her hand on my cheek, before withdrawing it. Gracie wiped her little hand on her dress and looked back at her mother. "Why's he crying?" she asked innocently.

"He's just very happy to meet you, sweetheart," Elise quietly explained. Gracie looked back at me and after

312

processing this information for a few moments, she laughed. In all honesty I had not even realised that I was indeed crying; it was just raw and honest emotion, an outpouring of which I had not experienced for as long as I could remember. I knelt up and hugged them both, holding them close like I never wanted to let either of them go again. Since leaving England I had not allowed myself to ponder such possibilities and had immersed myself in work. The setting up of new projects and my flourishing relationship with Pam had all been welcome distractions, but no matter how hard I tried to fill the void inside me, there was always a nagging feeling that something fundamental was missing. Suddenly I knew exactly what that missing piece had been. Elise held onto me tightly too, and I could feel her tears trickling down her cheek and onto my neck.

After a few minutes, Gracie began to wriggle, growing uncomfortable within the constriction of our group hug. Elise and I composed ourselves, smiling as we both wiped away the moisture from our eyes. "I bet I look like a panda," Elise said, embarrassed.

"Of course not," I replied encouragingly, "you look beautiful. I'm just so happy that you are both here. I never dreamed that this could be possible." I took Gracie so that Elise could go to the bathroom and freshen up and I sat my granddaughter on my knee while she showed me her favourite book. Just to practice the word 'granddaughter' in my head filled me with an overwhelming joy. After we had eaten the meal that Pam had prepared for us, we sat around making small talk and entertaining Gracie until it was beyond her bedtime. Elise settled her young daughter down in the large bed in the spare room, read her a story and then returned to the living room.

Elise confessed that she had initially been shocked to find her Aunt Pam, who she had not seen for some years, to be the one who greeted them on the doorstep when she and Gracie had arrived. In turn, Pam had been equally taken aback when she had opened the door to find her niece holding a little girl who she had not previously met. However, both of them conceded that I too would be stunned to find them in my living room on my return from work. Elise and Pam had been afforded an opportunity to become reacquainted before my return from the club, and Elise was happy to find that Prague was not the city of complete strangers which she had anticipated. So, what had happened since Elise and I had met in the hospital some three months previous? I wondered. I did my best to explain to her how our initial encounter had played out in my mind constantly ever since. Much of what she had told me had been a source of torment which I felt unable to ignore, and I apologised if a DNA testing kit arriving on her doorstep had caused her to recoil in shock or horror.

Elise explained that although she had been astounded to receive such an unusual package, she had understood my reasons after reading the letter which I had included. She too admitted to having sensed a profound and inexplicable connection when the two of us had met that day, and considered that maybe it had been fate, for want of a better explanation. Elise confessed that initially she had felt confused, overwhelmed and had not known exactly what to do for the best. Her own family had left her ultimately abandoned and feeling bereft. Even her own mother had marooned her, estranged from every family tie that she had ever known. The man she had always considered to be her father turned out to not be a blood relation after all, and her mother's family rifts with her own father and brother had left Elise devoid of anyone in her life other than her own young daughter. Even her Aunt Pam, who she had always liked, became a distant memory. This issue, though, had been confronted by Elise and Pam before I had returned home, and it was a subject that they had put to bed after Pam had given her a little insight as to how things had been from her standpoint. Elise had always been wary and uncomfortable around her uncle Peter, so Pam's revelations had not come as too much of a shock.

Elise confessed that she had left the DNA kit to one side and took her time contemplating what she should do for the best. Aware that her need for attachment left her emotionally vulnerable, Elise had not wanted to pin her slender hopes on a faint possibility that her biological father might be alive and well after all. Her mother had told her in no uncertain terms that her real father had died many years before, so why would she give any credence to a stranger's notion? Elise also considered that as her mother had lied on so many previous occasions, there was always a possibility that she may have altered the facts this time too. Elise was nevertheless at pains to understand why she would have felt a compulsion to mislead her own daughter about something like this.

I glanced over at Pam who, in turn, glanced back at me knowingly. Although neither she nor I chose to voice our thoughts as to why Debbie might have had her reasons, it seemed pretty obvious. Had Elise ever known the truth, she may have developed a desire to learn more about me or my whereabouts, and that was a chance that Debbie could not take. She was a woman who had dug herself into a hole with one lie after another, and all she could do was just keep on digging.

Elise explained how many sleepless nights had followed. Aware that the DNA testing time was soon to expire, she had finally been driven by her need for answers and had followed the instructions as suggested in my letter. On the morning when the envelope containing the test results had been delivered, Elise had been too frightened to open it. For two days, the envelope had sat on her kitchen worktop, urging her to open it and reveal the answers contained inside. Finally, she had plucked up enough courage to tear open the envelope and read the results. Although she had not fully understood the implications which the letter suggested, a telephone call to the laboratory would later confirm that, without doubt, the test had concluded that I was indeed her biological father.

Elise had considered calling me there and then to tell me the news, but initially she needed to come to terms with this revelation herself. She also wondered how I might respond to the news, and how I might react to discovering that I had a long lost daughter and a granddaughter too. I had striven to keep such thoughts from my mind, but had Elise been aware that it was something for which I desperately hoped, it might have made her decision to call a much easier one. Amidst the confusion and her struggle to come to terms with this discovery, her anger towards her mother had intensified. A lifetime of lies and deception had reached a pinnacle at which point, Elise had no longer been aware of who she was.

Elise apologised for turning up at my door unannounced, but confessed that she had been desperate to escape and felt a need for her and Gracie to run away. The only person she could run to was the father she had never even known. She was grateful for the money that I had put in the envelope which Dave had given to her, and decided that she would use some of what remained to come and find me. Once Elise had made her decision, she contacted Dave and explained her situation as best she could. After seeking assurances that Elise would keep my whereabouts a closely guarded secret, he had given her my most recent address. Upon her arrival at the airport, she had given my address to a taxi driver who had delivered her and her daughter safely to my door.

Despite the fact that Elise had brought very few personal possessions with her, mainly essential items for Gracie, it was apparent that she was not planning on returning to England any time soon. After Elise had turned in for the night, Pam and I discussed the evening's events and we both agreed that the apartment afforded enough space for the four of us to live in relative comfort.

"She's your daughter," Pam exclaimed excitedly, "and you both need time to get to know each other. I just can't believe that neither of you have ever known." As the shock of the evening began to subside, I finally allowed myself to consider the implications that being a parent and a grandfather might entail. Excitedly, I had to conclude that I could not quite believe it all either. Life certainly has a distinct ability to confound when you least expect it, I thought to myself as I finally stepped into the shower at the end of a very long day. Despite the lateness of the hour, I found myself looking forward to the future even more than I had been previously. My mind raced while considering a fresh beginning with the family that, just like my freedom for twenty five years, I had so cruelly been deprived of.

oooOOOooo

Over the next few days we soon settled into a routine together, and Elise and Pam got on like they had never been distanced. They both understood that I wanted to spend more time with them and less time working, but they were also aware that time was running out and the club's opening deadline was drawing closer by the day. Alex and Thurstan also understood the delicacy of my personal situation, and both urged me to ensure that time was spent getting to know my daughter and granddaughter too. On a chilly morning, nearly a week after Elise and Gracie had arrived, we took the Metro to Holesovice followed by a short bus ride, and were soon at Prague Zoo. Despite the weather, we enjoyed a wonderful day getting to know each other. Gracie was captivated with watching a polar bear through the viewing windows of its enclosure as it swum underwater. She placed her tiny hands on the outside of the glass as the enormous beast turned, using its huge paws to push against the other side of the glass and propel itself majestically through the water. She watched in amazement as brightly coloured birds flew above our heads in the indoor rain forest biome, resting momentarily to refresh themselves at the edge of a pool which was fed from a cascading waterfall. Small monkeys chattered at us from the treetops above, while Gracie pointed them out and clapped her hands in delight.

I felt blessed to have been granted the opportunity of becoming both father and grandfather, and I was determined to take my responsibilities seriously. With the seasonal festivities looming fast, I wanted to ensure that Elise and Gracie would both have a magical Christmas to remember. With that in mind, Pam had been happy to look after Gracie while her mother and I went Christmas shopping. It would also afford us the opportunity to talk and get to know each other a little better. Having already explained to Elise why I had been away for so long and why I had initially lied about my real name, Elise wanted to know a little more about my time in prison. I had assured her that I had been convicted of a crime that I had not committed, and how the real culprits had literally got away with murder. However, Elise's enquiring mind wanted to know more, and so I gave her sketchy details of how I had been awoken one morning by policemen at my hotel door who had subsequently discovered the body of a dead woman in the bathroom.

"Did you know her?" Elise asked as our car pulled up at a set of red traffic lights.

"No, not really," I replied hesitantly. "I had met her briefly at a party the night before, but that was it, I assure you. Her name was Annika Radwanski," I added.

Out of the blue and just as the lights turned to green, Elise said, "It was Gary and Uncle Peter who killed that woman, wasn't it?" I looked at her dumbfounded.

"What makes you say that?" I asked in bemusement as the driver behind sounded his car horn to remind me that the lights had changed.

"Once when I was quite small, I overheard them talking," Elise calmly explained, "and I heard mum saying 'when he gets out he'll come looking for us for what we've done'. Uncle Peter had said that if it ever happened they would deal with it. I remember being frightened and I asked mum who was coming for us and she told me not to worry because I was safe. They were talking about you, weren't they? And that's why you killed Gary and Uncle

319

Peter, wasn't it?" she added straightforwardly. "I know their deaths looked like accidents, but it was you, wasn't it?"

I pulled into the car park, unable to choose the right words to say and unable to look her directly in the eye. My heart sank. I sat in silence and stared straight ahead, my vision not focused on anything in particular. "I don't blame you, Dad." Elise offered, placing her hand on my arm and gently patting it reassuringly. "Anyone would have done the same thing in your situation, I'm sure. And that's why you were at the hospital that day too, wasn't it?" she added, "but I don't understand why you didn't kill her too."

Eventually I turned and looked Elise in the eye. She had spent a lifetime being lied to by people who she trusted and I knew that she deserved to hear the truth, regardless of the possible consequences for me. "When I looked at her there in the hospital," I began, "she just looked so helpless. I had been angry with her for so long but in the end, I didn't feel that I had the right to take her life. I don't know why, but seeing her like that, I guess I just wasn't angry with her anymore." At that point I expected Elise to open the car door and walk out of my life forever.

"I had sat in that room with her so many times," said Elise quietly, "and thought about killing her myself. I was also angry with her for everything that she had done, and when those test results confirmed that my real father wasn't dead after all, I just couldn't believe it. I could have forgiven her for just about anything; for lying to me, for hitting me, but not telling me the truth about my father, well, that was the final straw." Elise sat in silence for a few moments. She looked out of the side window as the rain started to patter down and I sensed that she had more to say but was trying to choose the right words. I watched as Elise pressed her index finger against the window, following the course of a droplet of rainwater as it trickled down the outside of the glass. As her droplet's journey quickened and became indistinguishable from the all the others, she coolly and casually admitted, "And that's why I killed her."

I sat motionless, stunned and unable to offer any response whilst Elise coldly explained exactly what she had done. She had gone to visit her mother and seeing a syringe and hypodermic needle on a temporarily unguarded nurse's trolley, she had picked it up once she was sure that no one was watching. When safely in the confines of her mother's room, Elise had taken off one of her mother's slippers while she sat in her chair by the window. She drew up a syringe full of air and plunged the needle between her mother's toes, injecting the air to create an embolism that would eventually make its way to her mother's heart. She replaced the slipper, placed the syringe in her own pocket and then left the hospital. Later that day she received a telephone call from the hospital informing her that her mother had been found dead. Elise showed neither guilt nor remorse as she related her version of events, but I sensed that in telling me, a huge weight had been lifted off her mind. Her confession certainly explained why she had been so keen to get her and her daughter away from England.

"Does anyone else know about this?" I asked her.

"No," replied Elise, "just you and me."

"OK then," I said after moments' thought, "let's keep it that way, shall we." Elise looked at me and smiled a huge smile of relief. I leaned across and gave her a hug.

Elise clung to me, her arms wrapped tightly around my neck. "Thanks, Dad," she whispered.

'Thanks, Dad'. Those two words were affirmation of my status as parent, cementing a bond between father and daughter. "Right, are you ready to go Christmas shopping now?" I enquired, changing the subject.

"Yes," replied Elise, with a sniff and a smile, "I think I am."

We stepped out of the car and I held my daughter's hand as we walked across the car park in the pouring rain. We had both sold our souls for a handful of broken promises, but fate had played its own hand and eventually brought us together. I had not needed any DNA test after all, as clearly there was no doubt that Elise was indeed my daughter.

Chapter 28

Let the Good Times Roll

We had worked hard together as a team and pulled out all the stops to ensure that Heaven and Hell would be ready for opening night. The building work and refitting of the cellar bar had finally been completed by the second week in December, and Pam had proved herself to be quite adept at handling the publicity. We had booked two popular local bands who had both been keen to perform on the opening night of the newest rock club in the city, and Pam had designed the promotional flyers and organised the printing too. Skazaniec, of course, were billed as the opening act; our club, our party, our rules. Alex had been spreading the word of our upcoming debut performance amongst his friends and acquaintances, informing everyone that it would coincide with the inaugural club night. I had urged Dave to come over, but my pleas had been to no avail even though I had offered to pay his airfare, and promised to ensure he would be home in time for Christmas. We advertised the opening night as 23rd December and hoped to create a buzz of expectation

The intended opening date had looked precarious at times though, and the last few weeks had been beset by problems. However, as a team, we had pulled together, shown a dogged resilience and refused to be beaten. Eventually the club's level of soundproofing had been passed as adequate, and Thurstan had succeeded in convincing our electrician to stay on and finish the job. A portion of the money that I invested had been used to purchase a decent back line, which included a reasonable P.A. system, Marshall amplifiers, a Pearl drum kit and a decent sound desk. Our budget had been pushed so close to the limit that, despite being able to strike up a good deal with a local alcohol supplier, we had not enough in the business account to fully stock the bar. As a rather unorthodox Christmas present, Thurstan's father had kindly and generously given him a cash advance large enough to ensure that at least our initial few weeks should go without a hitch.

On the afternoon of Heaven and Hell's grand and auspicious opening, our band members had arranged to meet early and have one final run through of our pre-arranged forty minute set. After some discussion, we had narrowed our repertoire to ten songs including a couple of classic punk rock covers which all four of us loved, plus a few of Alex's old songs, such as 'Broken Promises' and 'Dog Eat Dog' along with a few numbers from the old L.I.A.R. set list, including 'Old Dog, New Tricks', and just for my benefit, we agreed to conclude with 'Time To Waste'. That number had been the last song that I had played with my former band, and Alex, Tibor and Marek all understood that for me, the song would be something of a personal catharsis.

Kristina's neighbour had kindly offered to look after Gracie for the evening so that both Elise and Pam would be able to attend the opening night too. We were all hugely anticipating enjoying the culmination of our joint efforts, hopefully unfolding to make a memorable night. I admit that I was excited about the opening of Heaven and Hell; after all, the club was destined to be my livelihood but in all honesty, I anticipated that playing in a band once more would be my personal highlight. I was relishing the opportunity of reliving my misspent youth and clawing back some of those wasted years. As our opening night was scheduled for the day before Christmas Eve, I was also excited at the prospect of sharing the festivities with friends and family too. Kristina and Alex had invited us all over for Christmas Eve, and Pam and Elise had been relishing assisting with the festive preparations.

Because Elise and I had always been denied knowledge of each other's existence, I began to resent the fact that I had been deprived of the opportunity of watching my own daughter growing up and sharing in her birthday and Christmas celebrations. My sense of indignation relating to everything that I had missed in Elise's life, made me determined that she and little Gracie would enjoy a magical and memorable Christmas. A few days previously, Pam, Elise, Gracie and I had braved the cold to enjoy the delights of the Prague Christmas Market. Together, we put aside all the stresses of recent weeks, forgot all our troubles and revelled in the festive atmosphere in the main square. Elise had been captivated by the thousands upon thousands of twinkling lights adorning huge Christmas trees, and was enthralled by the beautiful horse drawn carriages. We were all fascinated and amazed by the Astronomical Clock, a timepiece of such beauty and complexity that legend has it that its maker was blinded to ensure he would never build a better one. Together, we took a stroll through the winding and narrow streets to Charles Bridge and looked across the river to the brightly illuminated castle on the hillside opposite. By the time we returned to the warmth of the apartment, we were exhausted. My arms felt weary from carrying my granddaughter for much of the way, but it felt good. I could not envisage a time when life had not felt any better.

I arrived, with my guitar case, at the club on the afternoon of our grand opening just before 2pm, ahead of our pre-arranged meeting time. Alex was already there and as I made my way down the stairs and swung the door open, I could hear that he was prepared already. Alex announced that Marek had messaged to say that he was on his way and would arrive shortly, and true to his word, he turned up just a few minutes after me. Everything was in place to ensure that our opening night would be a success. The security for the evening was arranged to make sure that all those in attendance would be safe from trouble, and two of Kristina's friends had agreed to help out working the bar, at least until Alex and I were able to take over at the helm. Thurstan had hoped to arrive in time to catch us running through our set list and he was bringing the float money for the cash tills too. Surely nothing could go wrong.

With Alex, Marek and I all set to go, the only person missing was Tibor, and as time ticked away we began to grow more agitated. Alex had tried to call him but got no answer, and eventually just before 3pm, Marek received a message that Tibor was not coming.

"What do you mean, he's not fucking coming?" bellowed Alex, his anger and frustration clearly overflowing.

"He just says sorry, and that he is returning home to Hungary," replied Marek in shock and disappointment. At our last rehearsal, I had noticed that Tibor had appeared a little distant and that his drumming had lacked its usual enthusiasm, but none of us had considered for a moment that he would let us down right at the last moment. Alex tried to telephone Tibor again but his call was diverted straight to voicemail. By the time that Thurstan arrived, struggling through the door with a large cardboard box and his leather briefcase, he found the three of us sitting around a table, disconsolate, crestfallen and drinking beer.

"What's the matter?" he asked. "I expected you to be running through your final rehearsal."

We explained the situation and how Tibor had let us down, and we were all disappointed that it was obvious that Skazaniec would not be playing that evening after all. I anticipated that Thurstan would grab a beer too, slump down at the table with us, and then the four of us would get annihilated together as we watched our plans unravel as the whole thing fell apart at the seams. Surprisingly though, Thurstan seemed unperturbed. He merely asked us to give him a few minutes while he stocked the tills with the float money that he had brought with him. After putting the remainder in the safe, Thurstan returned through the door at the side of the stage, removed his tweed jacket and folded it neatly before draping it over Marek's bass amp. We watched as Thurstan set himself on the drum stool and loosened his tie. Following two kicks of the bass drum he picked up two sticks.

"What the fuck are you doing, Thurstan?" asked Alex, clearly not in the mood. "This is no time to piss about."

Undaunted by Alex's admonishment, Thurstan proceeded to belt out the drum intro to 'No Fun', before unleashing an impressive improvised drum solo. Alex, Marek and I looked at each other in amazement as Thurstan coolly climbed down from the stage, grabbed himself a beer and sat down with us. "I didn't know you were a drummer," I said in total astonishment.

"You never asked," replied Thurstan as he took a long mouthful of beer.

"No, no, no," exclaimed Alex, jumping up from his seat, animated and agitated. "It would never work. Don't even think it."

Not one to be dissuaded, Thurstan calmly inquired, "well, why not? I've watched you rehearse many times, I know the songs, I know the set list so what have you got to lose?" Eventually we all agreed that under the circumstances, Thurstan was right. What did we have to lose? Tibor, the man mountain who had been rehearsing with the band for months, was definitely not coming, that was for certain. So, with less than five hours to go before our debut, we found ourselves considering replacing a rock and roll monolith with a lawyer wearing a white shirt and tweed jacket. What on earth could possibly go wrong?

The four of us climbed onto the stage, picked up our instruments and took to our places. Amazingly, Thurstan never put a foot or a drumstick wrong during the entire set. Without ever saying a word, he had quietly set about taking care of the business, financial and legal side of the project, while all along harbouring a secret desire to be a drummer in a band. By the time we had completed our run through of the set, our disconsolation had been replaced by smiles and laughter, and Thurstan was clearly revelling in the back slapping and adulation which he received from Alex, Marek and I. Despite Tibor's bombshell exit, we were beginning to think that it might just work.

"OK, Thurstan," I said, "we'll give it our best shot. As you said, what have we got to lose?"

"Other than our pride and dignity," Alex interjected, laughing as he playfully slapped Thurstan on the back.

"But first you must get rid of that shirt. It's not exactly rock and roll, is it?" Marek chimed in.

"I may have just the thing," offered Thurstan, opening the lid of the cardboard box which he had earlier left on the bar. He pulled out a t-shirt and announced, "I had these made," he said, holding up a garment neatly emblazoned with the band's name. "I thought that there might be quite a market for these later. You can have any colour you want, as long as it's black." Thurstan joked, removing his now sweaty white shirt. We all stood in shock and awe as Thurstan disrobed at the bar, revealing previously hidden full sleeve tattoos and a large chest piece depicting skulls and roses, above which in bold but intricate script were the words 'Heaven and Hell'.

"Fucking hell," exclaimed Alex in total astonishment as Thurstan pulled on one of the t-shirts, "the lawyer's a fucking beast."

"What?" Thurstan responded coolly, "haven't you lot ever seen a tattoo before?"

oooOOOooo

By six o'clock the other two bands had arrived and were sound checking. Erik, a Swedish friend of Alex, had agreed to DJ and manage the sound desk for the evening. He already worked in a few local music venues but appeared keen to branch out. Our opening evening would provide him with an opportunity to audition and he promised that the music played in Heaven and Hell would sound great with him at the helm. As the other bands sound checked, we were convinced that Erik was right and we looked forward to the possibility of our club growing into a force to be reckoned with. Our official opening was advertised as 7pm and, although punters were not exactly queuing around the block, after Thurstan had opened the doors, we received a steady trickle of curious customers into our 480 capacity venue. By the time that Elise, Pam and Kristina arrived at 7:30, we had around two hundred and fifty people inside. Fifty people had been included on the guest list but some two hundred customers, each having paid the 100kr entrance fee - a little under three pounds in English money - were anticipating a good evening.

I stood at the bar with Elise and Pam, feeling a little nervous ahead of the band's debut. Thurstan's drumming prowess had been immense during our short rehearsal, but the fact that he confessed to having never played in public before made the rest of us feel uneasy. Besides, I had not played in public for over twenty-six years and I was hoping that I was not going to choke when we eventually took to the stage.

I felt a hand rest on my shoulder. "Hello you old bastard," came a familiar voice behind me which immediately made me turn on my heels.

"Dave," I shrieked in bewilderment, "what are you doing here?"

"That's a fine welcome. I travel half way around the world to find out what all this shit is about, and that's how you welcome me. I even had to pay at the fucking door because you didn't even put me on the guest list." Dave had never been one to understate anything and his powers of exaggeration were as legendary as was his ability to emotionally blackmail. I asked Kristina's friend who was working the bar, to reimburse Dave's 100kr entrance fee and asked her to ensure that for the rest of the evening, my oldest friend would want for nothing.

"I'd expect nothing less after coming all this way," said Dave with a smile as I passed him a free beer. He gave Elise a welcoming hug and then shook hands with Pam in a true gentlemanly manner, giving her a kiss on the cheek for good measure. "I Hope you're taking good care of these lovely ladies, Steve," he said.

"No wonder you've still got your coat on, Dave," I said, tugging playfully at his sleeve, "it must be very cold up there on the moral high ground."

Marek tapped his wrist, signalling to me that it was time for us to prepare backstage as we were due to start in around five minutes. Pam, Elise and Kristina were planning to watch our set from the side of the stage and, thinking of Dave's leg, I suggested to him that he might be better off standing with them, as the club appeared to be practically full. We all made our way to the backstage area just in time to find Alex giving Thurstan a few gentle slaps on the cheek.

"Don't let us down, man," Alex was urging him, his voice sounding concerned. It appeared that Thurstan, standing poised, already stripped to the waist with drum sticks in his hand, had been knocking back the hospitality and had turned from mild mannered legal professional into a rock and roll animal. If I was about to relive my youth, then Thurstan was preparing to live out his dream.

I politely introduced Dave to Kristina and the other band members too. "I've heard all about you, man," said Alex as he grabbed Dave's hand and shook it firmly. "I just hope I do your songs justice this evening. The pressure is on now," he exclaimed.

We heard Erik cue up 'Complete Control' and we took it as our pre-arranged cue to take to the stage. We picked up our instruments and made our entrance to the cheers of the awaiting audience, some of whom appeared to be already wearing our t-shirts even though we were yet to play a note in anger. Thurstan climbed awkwardly and uneasily onto his drum stool, taking a moment to adjust the height of his cymbals, while Alex adjusted the angle of his microphone stand before tapping the mic to ensure it was on. Marek and I, with our backs turned to the audience, studiously took a few moments to ensure that our instruments were in tune.

Already I could feel the sweat running down my forehead, stinging my eyes, and I knew that the stage lights were not to blame; I was nervous. As Erik drew his DJ set to a close, I could feel the tension rise. Alex stood at the front of the stage, his arms outstretched like some kind of skinhead messiah, his guitar hanging at his waist. He surveyed the audience, almost with a look of contempt, as I unleashed a thunderous 'A chord', allowing 'Murder One' to drift into feedback.

"Borstal Breakout. Let's have it." Alex screamed into his microphone as Thurstan clicked his drumsticks above his head three times, cueing us to tear into the song's intro. The audience in front of the stage, caught in the moment and fuelled by sheer volume, pogoed, jostled and fought each other. Alex, Marek, Thurstan and I fed off the intensity of the audience and as sheer adrenaline consumed my nerves, I thrashed through the chord changes with legs spread wide like Johnny Ramone. With fists raised in the air, many in the crowd joined in with the chorus with enthusiasm. By the end of the song, the sound of 'Murder One' rang in my ears like a buzzsaw cutting through a jet fighter. I was back.

A group of Alex's old compatriots raised their glasses in the air and made themselves heard as he introduced 'Broken Promises'. "This one is for politicians everywhere," he spat with venom. "Here's another old song, 'Dog Eat Dog'," he would later announce to more riotous applause from his compatriots. "While the rich are still getting richer, the poor still keep getting poorer. Nothing ever changes." While we tore through the old L.I.A.R. number, 'Old Dog, New Tricks', I turned and glanced towards Dave, standing stage side with his arms folded. He mouthed the words of the chorus and gave us a 'thumbs up' in approval of our updated version.

Our forty minute set seemed to draw to a close almost before it had started. There had been a few little mistakes along the way, but hardly a thing which anyone would even notice or even care about. Thurstan, despite having drunk more than he should have, showed himself to be an excellent replacement for Tibor. Not only had he proved himself to be a good lawyer and loyal friend, but his transformation into punk rock drummer was incredible. How long had the confines of his profession frustrated him I wondered, as I watched him wiping his sweat drenched face with a towel. Whether or not his father approved of his son's sideline could be open to conjecture I suppose, but the fact that Jacob had generously financed the stocking of the bar, showed that he supported and encouraged his son in his venture. Regardless of whether or not Thurstan would want the position of drummer in our band to be a permanent one, I could tell that he was living his own dream.

I walked to the side of the stage where Pam stood waiting for me with a beer and a towel. I wiped my face and then hugged her and Elise, overjoyed that they had witnessed me rolling back the years. I hoped that they had both enjoyed being a part of the evening as much as I felt pleased that they had been part of it.

"You always were a show off," Dave said, shaking my hand. "You've done well, mate. I'm glad I came."

The Skazaniec members took to the stage for our encore, and we played an extended intro to 'Time To Waste', palm muting the guitars while Alex introduced the band to rapturous applause. He thanked the audience for coming out to see us and joked that they were the best audience we had ever played to. He explained to the crowd how 'Time To Waste' was a song of great personal importance to me and that it had not been played in public for many years. "It's a L.I.A.R. number," he announced, "and I think that we may have a moment of history in the making, right here, on this stage, tonight." I for one was wondering where Alex was leading and the extended palm muting of the intro was beginning to make my hand sore. "Tonight," Alex continued, pointing towards the side of the stage, "we have a special guest. Would you please give a huge Heaven and Hell welcome to the man who co-wrote this song, all the way from England, Mr Dave Bradshaw."

Alex and I both beckoned to Dave, who appeared mortified and not unlike a rabbit caught in the headlights, but the roar of the crowd made it clear that Dave would have to make an appearance, whether he wanted to or not. He stepped out of the shadows and into the glare of the spotlights, raising his hand in appreciation of the raucous applause he was receiving.

Alex placed his arm around Dave's shoulder. "This is your song, my friend," he said reverently, passing Dave the mic stand, "you must be the one to sing it." Alex stepped away, leaving Dave at the front of the stage to face nearly five hundred cheering onlookers. Sensing his reluctance to perform after so many years, I moved alongside him, put one foot on the monitor and tore into the opening riffs, accompanied by the rest of the band. Taking his cue, Dave took the mic stand in both hands and launched into the opening verse, his trademark guttural vocal growled the lyrics just as I had remembered. When we reached the chorus, Dave held the mic so that we could share the vocal duties. In unison we sang our hearts out. "You're out of place, you're a disgrace, I ain't got time to waste on you." It was a more pulsating and electrifying moment than I could have ever envisaged possible.

The song drew to a close and audience members applauded, cheered and whistled their approval as we left the stage feeling as though we had thoroughly enjoyed ourselves. Dave roundly received the adulation of the rest of the band for his impromptu performance, as did Thurstan too, while I had an awaiting congratulatory embrace from both Elise and Pam. Our work for the night was done, and we left the stage for the remaining two bands to continue the evening's entertainment where we had left off. For us, an evening of reflection, alcohol, friendship and laughter awaited, as we retold stories of the old days and discussed our possible futures.

Perhaps in some ways I had fantasised that the evening may see me rise like a phoenix from the ashes, finally laying the old to rest and starting anew, surrounded by the people who I considered to be among the most important to me and my future. The night prior to my arrest in Krakow had been my personal pinnacle as a musician of limited ability, and I had wondered if my Skazaniec debut could even come close. As I relaxed with my beer, listening to the chatter and laughter of the rest of our crew, I concluded that this night had far exceeded anything that I could have possibly imagined.

Leaning forward, I whispered in Elise's ear, "I love you and I hope that you and Gracie will stay here with us."

Elise held me tightly. "I love you too, Dad. We're going nowhere," she said "this is our family, right here."

I hoped that there would be many evenings in the future as good as this one, but I also knew that there would be much hard work for each of us along the way. The future may be uncharted and unwritten, but I could at least be certain that it was going to be a very good Christmas.

Epilogue

I remember that as a child I once read a story known as The Parable of the Snake. It is a tale that has been told around the world in various guises since the days of Ancient Greece, and had even been adapted as one of Aesop's Fables. But, for now, let me relate the parable as best I remember.

Once upon a time there was a serpent that had been badly injured by another animal. Unable to slither away to safety, the snake would surely have died if a benevolent man had not witnessed its suffering by the side of the road. The kind man carefully wrapped the snake up and took it to his house where he bestowed the kindest and gentlest care on the stricken reptile until it was healed and could return to the wild. Just as the man was releasing the serpent back into the grass, the ungrateful reptile turned and bit him on the hand.

"What did you do that for?" cried the man, knowing that the venom of that particular snake was invariably fatal. "Did I not care for you when no one else would?"

The snake looked up at the benevolent but now doomed man and hissed, "What did you expect? You knew I was a snake when you found me."

oooOOOooo

We can spend our entire lives thinking back and asking the same question, 'What if?' Each decision with which we are faced is a potential junction on our road between birth and death, and it is a road on which there is no turning back. This is one of the few lessons that I have learned over the years. Is there a man or a woman alive who has never been envious of someone who, for instance, has won millions on the lottery? I doubt it. Personally speaking, and please forgive my cynicism, I believe that we are all dealt a hand of cards at birth and the only thing that will ever make any difference is how we play the hand we were given. Once fate has decreed our path, not even that elusive lottery win will change our ultimate direction.

Consider, for a moment, Gary Spackman. With envy, he had coveted what I had; he had wanted my wife and he had wanted my place in the band, yet what did he do with his prizes? Nothing; he wasted it all. Gary was a man who would always live in the shadow of his successful older brother. His brother worked hard, started from scratch and slowly built up a business. He had a family for whom he provided, and provided for well. Gary, on the other hand, only ever wanted to take the short cuts in life; he was a chancer, a vulture, poised and ready to pick over the carcass of other peoples' lives.

Peter and Debbie Fankham, brother and sister, were definitely two peas from the same pod. Neither of them ever seemed secure or comfortable in their own skins, and always did their best to assimilate themselves with those around them. It was a thin veil to disguise who they really were. Maybe it was only in the latter years that the poison which festered within them both would ooze to the surface like some fetid purulence, infecting those with whom they came into contact. Maybe in truth it was always apparent, but as they grew older perhaps they just wearied of hiding it.

Peter's life was mapped out for him from childhood. He was never the brightest pupil at school and no matter how hard he would ever try, he would never meet his father's expectations of what a son should be. He had grown up in an environment which most people would consider to be unusual at the very least. At an early age, he had secretly thumbed through his father's pornographic magazines and watched his father's pornographic videos. His obsession with such imagery was something that he would carry through life. It had long been considered that Peter was either gay or bisexual, but such practices would have been despised in the family home, and he always did his best to not displease his father. I am no psychologist, but I am sure that there was something in his upbringing that gave rise to Peter's lack of self-esteem, something that would ultimately develop him into a domineering bully with an unhealthy sexual interest in those much younger than he. Perhaps such an unhealthy interest stemmed in part from his inability to form any sort of meaningful relationships in his younger years. Despite his bravado, Peter's character literally fell apart if ever he were faced with someone psychologically stronger than he.

And so what about Deborah Fankham herself? Ultimately, what led her to the point of breakdown? What was it about her that made her so nihilistic and hell bent on destroying anything of any emotional value? Perhaps more to the point, what was it about her that got under my skin, causing pain, resentment and hatred to fester for so long?

One thing was for certain, the only person she ever really cared about was herself. Selfish and self-centred, she played a game and played it well for as long as she could. Perhaps it was the pressures of life, work and responsibility which had finally combined to take their toll, dragging her down into an abyss of depression and despair. Maybe it had been the years of taking drugs that had warped, twisted and corrupted her mind. Maybe her habitual penchant for smoking cannabis had finally caused cavernous cracks to appear in her already fragile psyche. I doubt that the career on which she embarked had helped much either. Surely the pain and distress of seeing many of her patients answering their final call must have been hard to bear. Rarely does death provide an uplifting ending.

Deborah Fankham definitely shared her brother's lack of self-esteem. Coincidence, or a product of the same vile upbringing? That lack of self-esteem could only ever be countered if she were the centre of attention. Whether it was in a sexual or social context, she always craved the validation that would only come from the attention and adoration of those who were in her company. It seems as though Debbie, as she in turn grew older and her own looks began to fade, even grew resentful of her own daughter's youth and beauty. She grew spiteful as her grip and control on those left around her began to slip. Debbie's life was a house of cards, built on one lie after another, and it was all poised to come tumbling down sooner or later. Each step she took was one more on the descent into her own self-made hell. Despite the outward vivacious nature of her personality, she lived her life proverbially with one foot in the gutter and the other poised to slip on a banana skin.

I have long come to the realisation that, to Debbie Fankham, I was merely a convenience; someone who served a purpose at the time. I was another stepping-stone on her chaotic journey, just as those who went before, and just as those who were destined to follow. One by one she had eventually isolated herself from friends and family until all she had left was a chair by a window and a void to stare into. She was a woman cursed with a reverse Midas touch and everything she touched turned to shit. In her relationships with family, friends and lovers, and in the opportunities which life had offered, her nihilistic approach and self-centred nature enabled her to ruin everything which she came into contact with. Eventually she would spiral into despair, breakdown and psychological oblivion.

My years of confinement had enabled deeply skewed resentments and cynicism to fester inside me, eating away at my very soul and spawning an overwhelming desire for revenge. Like an unsuspecting and naïve man being led down a dark alley to be mugged, I had unwittingly allowed Debbie, Peter and Gary to reduce me to a point bordering on inhumanity, and perhaps that says more about me than it does them.

I now realise that what I had once considered to be love, loyalty, friendship, respect and camaraderie, had merely been illusions created by our mutual drug habits. In the illusion we had enjoyed good times without conscience or fear of consequence, but in reality we were all lost souls. I now concede that lost souls, meandering aimlessly through life, will only ever cling to another lost soul and only for as long as they serve a purpose. If it were not for those years of confinement, one thousand miles from home, then maybe I would have figured out the truth about that unholiest of trinities sooner. Instead, it took me over a quarter of a century to realise that Debbie, Peter and Gary were merely empty shells of human beings, stumbling from one disaster to another; flotsam and jetsam floating on the periphery of humanity. The fact that they had such a bearing on the direction which my life had followed, once again, says more about me then it does them.

As I now ponder past events, I can conclude that, regardless of the trials and tribulations which I encountered along the way, I would not exchange my life for any of theirs. Step by step, inch by inch, I clawed my way back up from the very depths of my personal perdition to a point where I now have a family and a future to look forward to. Had events not taken the twists and turns which ultimately transpired, then I might have remained trapped in their vortex of decline, and so perhaps I should thank them.

Yes, there were many indicators and events which pointed to Debbie's own spiralling decline, and perhaps the most poignant indication was in the words she spoke when confiding in Dave. She had revealed the darkest secrets of her family history to him, reaching out in desperation and clutching at the very edge of her emotional precipice; maybe that was where it all started to fall apart, right there in the very fabric of her childhood. Her memories poisoned while being robbed of her innocence by those who she should have trusted the most. By the time I had met the girl with the reverse Midas touch, perhaps she was already emotionally dead, fated to spend a miserable life destroying anything of worth. Fatefully, I had fallen for her charade and the charms which she skilfully used to disguise a side of her that she was reluctant to show.

I consider myself to be the fortunate one, as now I have the opportunity to pick up life from the point where my liberty had been snatched away. Others in this saga have been less fortunate. Annika Radwanski was certainly less blessed than I, as her life came to an abrupt end barely before it had started. She had been a talented young musician with a bright future and would have undoubtedly grown up to make her family proud had it not been for that unfortunate twist of fate - wrong place, wrong time.

Without need for my intervention, Debbie was destined to spend her last few months gazing aimlessly though a window. I wonder what, if anything, went through her mind at the moment when her own daughter injected her with the minuscule time bomb which would ultimately kill her. Air; a commodity so vital for our survival, yet all it took was 5cc of it to end her life. It is easy to be philosophical, but I contend that revenge far outweighs philosophy, and I'm sure that Gary Spackman and Peter Fankham would both agree if they were able. Maybe Debbie had eventually found the guilt of her lifetime of lies and deception to be too much to bear, but who am I to defend the indefensible? For I was just one of many who was drawn to her like an insect gets drawn to a Venus Fly Trap. I doubt that in reality she ever gave a damn about my feelings nor those of others, and driven by her self-centred character, I suspect that the words empathy, love and loyalty were not to be found in her dictionary.

I harken back to my rudimentary Psychology studies while I was still in prison, and ponder the Nature or

Nurture debate which sits as the very cornerstone of that complex subject. The Nature argument suggests that aspects of the human condition are predetermined genetically, while the Nurture argument asserts that our pathway through life is influenced by external factors such as experiences or learning. Peeling away the veneer from my adversaries revealed a road map, the course of which they may have embarked upon following events in their childhood. Parents, after all, carry the greatest influence on their children and can either take the credit or shoulder the blame for the outcome.

And so, my friend, remember the Parable of the Snake. For if ever you suffer the misfortune of feeling its fangs buried deep in your flesh, feeling its poison coursing through your veins, do not blame the snake; blame yourself for getting too close. I can only hope that the shadow of my past has been buried deep enough that I may move on without fear of its torment or persecution. I too have secrets that I wish to lock away from the world for eternity.

I often feel like a spectator of my own life; disconnected, disembodied and watching from an intangible distance as someone who looks and sounds like me rakes over the embers of my existence. I am neither who I was, nor who I want to be. How long must I function as an entity marooned in this purgatory? Will I forever wander lost on the road between Hell and Redemption, or will my daughter and granddaughter take my hand and lead me safely to the place where I want to be? On those dark nights when my conscience plagues me and the respite of sleep proves elusive, my moral judgement battles to convince me that I paid for my crimes in advance, and so I owe nothing. While Pam sleeps soundly, I occasionally find myself gazing at her through the darkness and inexplicably resenting her presence. I respect her, but I do not love her. Her knowledge of who I am and what I've done binds me to her as her eternal hostage. Often she reassures me that with her I am safe, but can she be so certain that she is safe with me? For in reality, either I too have become the snake, or I am the one who was born bad.